# Praise for
# EVERYONE BRAV

## 'AN ADDICTIVE, PROPULSIVE READ

. . . Cleave writes with an engaging intensity, a determination
to tackle big moral issues, and a willingness to take risks.'

*The Sunday Times*

## 'A COMPELLING AND FINELY CRAFTED NOVEL

. . . The Second World War is dangerous territory for a contemporary novelist:
the enemies they face include familiarity, cliché, and the reader's knowledge that
any number of things happened then that were far stranger than fiction.
For a writer to succeed in setting a tale in a period of heightened emotions,
they need first to keep their own emotions under close control.

**Ian McEwan did this with *Atonement*, Sarah Waters
did it with *The Night Watch*, and Chris Cleave does
it too with *Everyone Brave Is Forgiven*.'**

*Financial Times*

'Loosely based on the author's
grandparents' stories, this is **a superb
novel that breathes fresh
life into an often brutal
scenario**. Particularly astute at
demonstrating how war seeps into
the psyche and changes it, this is
**beautifully written** . . .
**gut-wrenching** . . . 
**all, ho**

*Daily Mail*

'**Cleave cements his
reputation as a skilful
storyteller**, and a sensitive
chronicler of the interplay between the
political and the personal . . . intricately
researched and evocatively conveyed.'

*Observer*

**CKER'**

*Stylist*

'**BRILLIANT** [and] **FEARLESSLY WRITTEN**
. . . Thoroughly absorbing.'

*Metro*

'A **SPECIAL** book'

*Good Housekeeping*

'**TENDER** and **TOUCHING**.'

*Mail on Sunday*

'**I WAS BLOWN AWAY BY IT**.'

*Woman & Home*

'**Brings both the Blitz and the siege of Malta to unforgettable life.**'

*Irish Times*

'**IT'S A WAR NOVEL BUT NOT AS YOU KNOW IT**
. . . his best book to date.'

*Esquire*, Top 10 Best New Novels of 2016

'**MAGNIFICENT AND PROFOUNDLY MOVING**
. . . **This dazzling novel of World War II is full of unforgettable characters**
and the keen emotional insights that moved readers of
Chris Cleave's *The Other Hand*.'

*Shelf Awareness*

Chris Cleave's debut novel *Incendiary* was a prize-winner and international bestseller and his second novel, *The Other Hand,* found phenomenal success both in the UK and abroad, hitting number one on the *New York Times* bestseller list. His third book, *Gold,* confirmed his status as one of our most powerful, important and psychologically insightful novelists. Chris lives in London with his wife and three children.

chriscleave.com
Twitter and Instagram: @ChrisCleave

CHRIS CLEAVE

# EVERYONE BRAVE
is
FORGIVEN

SCEPTRE

First published in Great Britain in 2016 by Sceptre
An imprint of Hodder & Stoughton
An Hachette UK company

First published in paperback in 2016

1

A CIP catalogue record for this title is available from the British Library

B format paperback ISBN 978 1 473 61871 8
A format paperback ISBN 978 1 473 62686 7
eBook ISBN 978 1 473 61868 8

Typeset in Sabon MT by Hewer Text UK Ltd, Edinburgh

Printed and bound by Clays Ltd, St Ives plc

Hodder & Stoughton policy is to use papers that are natural, renewable
and recyclable products and made from wood grown in sustainable
forests. The logging and manufacturing processes are expected to
conform to the environmental regulations of the country of origin.

Hodder & Stoughton Ltd
Carmelite House
50 Victoria Embankment
London EC4Y 0DZ

www.sceptrebooks.co.uk

*For my grandparents – Mary & David, NJ & M*

# CONTENTS

# PART I

## *PRESERVATION*

War was declared at 11.15 and Mary North signed up at noon. She did it at lunch, before telegrams came, in case her mother said no. She left finishing school unfinished. Skiing down from Mont-Choisi, she ditched her equipment at the foot of the slope and telegraphed the War Office from Lausanne. Nineteen hours later she reached Victoria, in clouds of steam, still wearing her alpine sweater. The train's whistle screamed. London, then. It was a city in love with beginnings.

She went straight to the War Office. The ink still smelled of salt on the map they issued her. She rushed across town to her assignment, desperate not to miss a minute of the war but anxious she already had. As she ran through Trafalgar Square waving for a taxi, the pigeons flew up before her and their clacking wings were a thousand knives tapped against claret glasses, praying silence. Any moment now it would start – this dreaded and wonderful thing – and could never be won without her.

What was war, after all, but morale in helmets and trucks? And what was morale if not one hundred million little conversations, the sum of which might leave men brave enough to advance? The true heart of war was small talk, in which Mary was wonderfully expert. The morning matched her mood, without cloud or equivalence in memory. In London under lucent skies ten thousand young women were hurrying to their new positions, on orders from Whitehall, from chambers unknowable in the old marble heart of the beast. Mary joined gladly the great flow of the willing.

The War Office had given no further details, and this was a good sign. They would make her a liaison, or an attaché to a general's staff. All the speaking parts went to girls of good family. It was even rumoured that they needed spies, which appealed most of all since one might be oneself twice over.

Mary flagged down a cab and showed her map to the driver. He held it at arm's length, squinting at the scrawled red cross that marked where she was to report. She found him unbearably slow.

'This big building, in Hawley Street?'

'Yes,' said Mary. 'As quick as you like.'

'It's Hawley Street School, isn't it?'

'I shouldn't think so. I'm to report for war work, you see.'

'Oh. Only I don't know what else it could be around there but the school. The rest of that street is just houses.'

Mary opened her mouth to argue, then stopped and tugged at her gloves. Because of course they didn't have a glittering tower, just off Horse Guards, labelled 'Ministry of Wild Intrigue'. Naturally they would have her report somewhere innocuous.

'Right then,' she said. 'I expect I am to be made a schoolmistress.'

The man nodded. 'Makes sense, doesn't it? Half the school-masters in London must be joining up for the war.'

'Then let's hope the cane proves effective against the enemy's tanks.'

The man drove them to Hawley Street with no more haste than the delivery of one more schoolmistress would merit. Mary was careful to adopt the expression an ordinary young woman might wear – a girl for whom the taxi ride would be an unaccus-tomed extravagance, and for whom the prospect of work as a schoolteacher would seem a thrill. She made her face suggest the kind of sincere immersion in the present moment that she imagined dairy animals must also enjoy, or geese.

Arriving at the school, she felt observed. In character, she tipped the taxi driver a quarter of what she normally would have given him. This was her first test, after all. She put on the apologetic walk of an ordinary girl presenting for interview. As if the air resented being parted. As if the ground shrieked from the wound of each step.

She found the headmistress's office and introduced herself. Miss Vine nodded but wouldn't look up from her desk. Avian and cardiganed, spectacles on a bath-plug chain.

'North,' said Mary again, investing the name with its significance.

'Yes, I heard you quite well. You are to take Kestrels Class. Begin with the register. Learn their names as smartly as you can.'

'Very good,' said Mary.

'Have you taught before?'

'No,' said Mary, 'but I can't imagine there's much to it.'

The headmistress fixed her with two wintry pools. 'Your imagination is not on the syllabus.'

'Forgive me. No, I have never taught before.'

'Very well. Be firm, give no liberties, and do not underestimate the importance of the child forming his letters properly. As the hand, the mind.'

Mary felt that the 'headmistress' was overdoing it, rather. She might mention it to the woman's superior, once she discovered what outfit she was really joining. Although in mitigation, the woman's attention to detail was impressive. Here were pots of sharpened pencils; tins of drawing pins. Here was a tidy stack of hymn books, each one covered in a different wallpaper, just as children really would have done the job if one had tasked them with it in the first week of the new school year.

The headmistress glanced up. 'I can't imagine what you are smirking at.'

'Sorry,' said Mary, unable to keep the glint of communication from her eyes, and slightly flustered when it wasn't returned.

'Kestrels,' said the headmistress. 'Along the corridor, third on the left.'

When Mary entered the classroom thirty-one children fell silent at their hinge-top desks. They watched her, owl-eyed, heads pivoting. They might be eight or ten years old, she supposed – although of course children suffered dreadfully from invisibility and required a conscious adjustment of the eye in order to be focused on at all.

'Good morning, class. My name is Mary North.'

'*Good morning Miss North.*'

The children chanted it in the ageless tone exactly between deference and mockery, so perfectly that Mary's stomach lurched. It was all just too realistic.

She taught them mathematics before lunch and composition after, hoping that a curtain would finally be whisked away; that her audition would give way to her recruitment. When the bell rang for the end of the day she ran to the nearest post office and dashed off an indignant telegram to the War Office, wondering if there'd been some mistake.

There was no mistake, of course. For every reproach that would be laid at London's door in the great disjunction to come – for all the convoys missing their escorts in fog, for all the breeches shipped with mismatched barrels, for all the lovers supplied with hearts of the wrong calibre – it was never once alleged that the grand old capital did not excel at letting one know, precisely, where one's fight was to begin.

# SEPTEMBER, 1939

**M**ary almost wept when she learned that her first duty as a schoolmistress would be to evacuate her class to the countryside. And when she discovered that London had evacuated its zoo animals days before its children, she was furious. If one must be exiled, then at least the capital ought to value its children more highly than macaws and musk oxen.

She checked her lipstick in a pocket mirror, then raised her hand.

'Yes, Miss North?'

'Isn't it a shame to evacuate the animals first?'

She said it in full hearing of all the children, who were lined up at their muster point outside the empty London Zoo, waiting to be evacuated. They gave a timid cheer. The headmistress eyed Mary coolly, which made her doubt herself. But surely it was wrong to throw the beasts the first lifeline? Wasn't that the weary old man's choice Noah had made: filling the ark with dumb livestock instead of lively children who might answer back? This was how the best roots of humanity had drowned. This was why men were the violent inbreds of Ham and Shem and Japheth, capable of declaring for war a season that Mary had earmarked for worsted.

The headmistress only sighed. So: the delay was simply because one did not need to write a marmoset's name on a luggage tag, accompany it in a second-class train compartment and billet it with a suitable host family in the Cotswolds. The lower primates only wanted a lorry for the trip and a good feed at the other end, while the higher Hominidae, with names like Henry and Sarah, had a multiplicity of needs which a diligent bureaucracy had not only to anticipate but also to meet, and furthermore to document, on forms that must first come back from the printers.

'I see,' said Mary. 'Thank you.'

Of course it was that. She hated being eighteen. The insights and indignations burned through one's good sense like hot coals through oven gloves. So, this was why London still teemed with children while London Zoo stood vacant, with three hundred ha'penny portions of monkey nuts in their little twists of newspaper waiting unsold and forlorn in the kiosk.

She raised her hand again, then let it drop.

'Yes?' said Miss Vine. 'Was there something else?'

'Sorry,' said Mary. 'It was nothing.'

'Oh good.'

The headmistress took her eye off the ranks of the children for a moment. She fixed Mary with a look rich in charity.

'Remember you're on our side now. You know: the grown-ups.'

Mary could almost feel her bones cracking with resentment. 'Thank you, Miss Vine.'

This was when the school's only coloured child, sensing an opening, slipped away from the muster and scaled the padlocked main gate of the zoo. The headmistress spun round.

'Zachary Lee! Come back here immediately!'

'Or what? You'll send me to the countryside?'

The whole school gasped. Ten years old, invincible, the negro boy saluted. He scissored his skinny brown legs over the top of the gate, using the penultimate and the ultimate wrought-iron Os of LONDON ZOO as the hoops of a pommel horse, and was immediately lost to sight.

Miss Vine turned to Mary. 'You had better bring the nigger back, don't you think?'

It was her first rescue work of the war. Coppery, coltish Mary North searched the abandoned zoo using paths that were still well tended. On her own, she felt better. She sneaked a cigarette. With the other hand she massaged her brow, confident that frustration could be persuaded not to settle there. All downers could be dispatched, as one might flick ash off one's sleeve, or pilot a wayward bee back out through an open window.

She had already checked the giraffes' paddock and the big cats' dens. Now, hearing a cough, she tiptoed into the great apes' enclosure through a gate that swung unlatched. She kicked through the straw, raising a scent of urine and musk that made her heart rattle with fright. But she hoped it was not easily done, for a zookeeper to miss a whole gorilla when he was counting them into the evacuation lorry.

'Come on out, Zachary Lee, I know you're in here.'

It was eerie to be in the gorilla house, looking out through the smeared glass. 'Oh do come on, Zachary darling. You'll get us both in trouble.'

A second cough, and a rustle under the straw. Then, with his soft American accent, 'I'm not coming out.'

'Fine then,' said Mary. 'The two of us shall rot here until the war is over, and nobody will ever know what talent we might have shown in its prosecution.'

She sat down beside the boy, first laying her red jacket on the straw to sit on, with the rosy silk lining downwards. It was hard to stay glum. One could say what one liked about the war but it had got her out of Mont-Choisi ahead of an afternoon of double French, and might yet have more mercies in store. She lit another cigarette and blew smoke through a shaft of sunlight.

9

'May I have one?' said the small voice.

'Beautifully asked,' said Mary. 'And no. Not until you are eleven.'

From the muster point came the sound of a tin whistle. It could mean that heavy bombers were converging on London, or it could mean that the children had been organised into two roughly matched teams to begin a game of rounders.

Zachary poked his head up through the straw. It still amazed Mary to see his brown skin, his chestnut eyes. The first time he had smiled, the flash of his pink tongue had delighted her. She had imagined it would be – well, not brown also, but certainly as antithetical to pink as brown skin was to white. A bluish tongue, perhaps, like a skink's. It would not have surprised her to learn that his blood came out black and his faeces a pale ivory. He was the first negro she had seen up close – if one didn't count the posters advertising minstrelsy and coon shows – and she still struggled not to gawk.

The straw clung to his hair. 'Miss?' he said, 'Why did they take the animals away?'

'Different reasons in each case,' said Mary, counting them off on her fingers. 'The hippopotami because they are such frightful cowards, the wolves since one can never be entirely sure whose side they are on, and the lions because they are to be parachuted directly into Berlin Zoo to take on Herr Hitler's big cats.'

'So the animals are at war too?'

'Well of course they are. Wouldn't it be absurd if it were just us?'

The boy's expression suggested that he had not previously taken the matter under consideration.

'What are two sevens?' asked Mary, taking advantage.

The boy began his reckoning, in the deliberate and dutiful manner of a child who intended to persevere at least until he ran out of fingers. Not for the first time that week, Mary suppressed both a smile and a delightful suspicion that teaching might not be the worst way to spend the idle hours between breakfast and society.

On Tuesday morning, after taking the register, Mary had written the names of her thirty-one children on brown luggage labels and looped them through the top buttonholes of their overcoats. Of course the children had exchanged labels with one another the second her back was turned. They were only human, even if they hadn't yet made the effort to become tall.

And of course she had insisted on calling them by their exchanged names – even for boys named Elaine and girls named Peter – while maintaining an entirely straight face. It delighted her that they laughed so easily. It turned out that the only difference between children and adults was that children were prepared to put twice the energy into the project of not being sad.

'Is it twelve?' said Zachary.

'Is what twelve?'

'Two *sevens*,' he reminded her, in the exasperated tone reserved for adults who asked questions with no thought to the expenditure of emotion that went into answering.

Mary nodded her apology. 'Twelve is jolly close.'

The tin whistle, sounding again. Above the enclosures, seagulls wheeled in hope. The memory of feeding time persisted. Mary felt an ache. All the world's timetables fluttered through blue sky now, vagrant on the winds.

'Thirteen?'

Mary smiled. 'Would you like me to show you? You're a bright boy but you're ten years old and you are miles behind with your numbers. I don't believe anyone can have taken the trouble to teach you.'

She knelt in the straw, took his hands – it still amazed her that they were no hotter than white hands – and showed him how to count forwards seven more, starting from seven. 'Do you see now? Seven, plus seven more, is fourteen. It is simply about not stopping.'

'Oh.'

The surprised and disappointed air boys had when magic yielded so bloodlessly to reason.

'So what would be three sevens, Zachary, now you have two of them already?'

He examined his outstretched fingers, then looked up at her.

'How long?' he said.

'How long what?'

'How long are they sending us away for?'

'Until London is safe again. It shouldn't be too long.'

'I'm scared to go to the country. I wish my father could come.'

'None of the parents can come with us. Their work is vital for the war.'

'Do you believe that?'

Mary shook her head briskly. 'Of course not. Most people's work is nonsense at the best of times, don't you think? Actuaries and loss adjusters and professors of Eggy-Peggy. Most of them would be more useful reciting limericks and stuffing their socks with glitter.'

'My father plays in the minstrel show at the Lyceum. Is that useful?'

'For morale, certainly. If minstrels weren't needed I daresay they'd have been evacuated days ago. On a gospel train, don't you think?'

The boy refused to smile. 'They won't want me in the countryside.'

'Why on earth wouldn't they?'

The pained expression children had, when one was irredeemably obtuse.

'Oh, I see. Well, I daresay they will just be awfully curious. I suppose you can expect to be poked and prodded at first, but once they understand that it won't wash off I'm sure they won't hold it against you. People are jolly fair, you know.'

The boy seemed lost in thought.

'Anyway,' said Mary, 'I'm coming to wherever-it-is we're going. I promise I shan't leave you.'

'They'll hate me.'

'Nonsense. Was it minstrels who invaded Poland? Was it a troupe of theatre negroes who occupied the Sudetenland?'

He gave her a patient look.

'See?' said Mary. 'The countryside will prefer you to the Germans.'

'I still don't want to go.'

'Oh, but that's the fun of it, don't you see? It's a simply enormous game of go-where-you're-jolly-well-told. Everyone who's anyone is playing.'

She was surprised to realise that she didn't mind it at all, being sent away. It really was a giant roulette – this was how one ought to see it. The children would get a taste of country air, and she . . . well, what was the countryside if not numberless Heathcliffs, loosely tethered?

*Let us imagine*, she thought, *that this war will surprise us all.* Let us suppose that the evacuation train will take us somewhere wild, far from these decorous streets where every third person has an anecdote about my mother, or votes in my father's constituency.

She imagined herself in the country, in a pretty village of vivid young people thrown into a new pattern by the war. It would be like the turning of a kaleidoscope, only with gramophones and dancing. Just to show her friend Hilda, she would fall in love with the first man who was even slightly interesting.

She squeezed the coloured boy's hand, delighted by his smile as her bright mood made the junction. 'Come on,' she said. 'Shall we get back to the others before they have all the fun?'

They stood up from the straw and she brushed the child down. He was a bony, startle-eyed thing – giving the impression of being thoroughly X-rayed – with an insubordinate crackle of black hair. She shook her head, laughing.

'What?'

'Zachary Lee, I honestly don't know why we bother evacuating you. You look as if you've been bombed already.'

He scowled. 'Well, you smoke like this.'

He gave his impression of Mary smoking like Bette Davis, as if the burning Craven "A" generated a terrific amount of lift. The cigarette, straining to rise, straightened the wrist nicely and lifted the first and second fingers into the gesture of a bored saint offering benediction.

'Yes, that's it!' said Mary. 'But do show me how you would do it.'

Slick as a magician palming a penny, Zachary flipped the imaginary cigarette round so that the cherry smouldered under the cup of his hand. He cut wary eyes left and right, drew deeply and then, averting his face, opened a small gap in the corner of his mouth to jet smoke down at the straw. The exhalation was almost invisibly quick, a sparrow shitting from a branch.

'Good lord,' said Mary, 'you smoke as if the world might tell you not to.'

'I smoke like a man,' said the child, affecting weariness.

'Well then. Unless one counts the three Rs, I don't suppose I have anything to teach you.'

She took his arm and they walked together – he wondering whether the lions would be dropped on Berlin by day or by night and she replying that she supposed by night since the creatures were mostly nocturnal, although in wartime, who knew?

They rotated through the exit turnstile. Mary made the boy go first, since it would be too funny if he were to abscond again, with her already through to the wrong side of the one-way ratchet. If their roles had been reversed then she would certainly have found the possibility too cheerful to resist.

On the grass they found the school drawn up into ranks, three by three. She kept Zachary's arm companionably until the headmistress shot her a look. Mary adjusted her grip to one more suggestive of restraint.

'I shall deal with you later, Zachary,' said Miss Vine. 'As soon as I am issued with a building in which to detain you, expect to get detention.'

Zachary smiled infuriatingly. Mary hurried him along the ranks until they came to her own class. There she took plain, sensible Fay George from her row and had her form a new one with the recaptured escapee, instructing her to hold his hand good and firmly. This Fay did, first taking her gloves from the pocket of her coat and putting them on. Zachary accepted this without comment, looking directly ahead.

The headmistress came to where Mary stood, twitched her nose at the smell of cigarette smoke, and glanced pointedly heavenwards. As if there might be a roaring squadron of bombers up there that Mary had somehow missed. Miss Vine took Zachary by the shoulders. She shook him, absent-mindedly and not without affection. It was as if to ask: Oh, and what are we to do with you?

She said, 'You young ones have no idea of the difficulties.'

Mary supposed that she was the one being admonished, although it could equally have been the child or – since her headmistress was still looking skywards – it might have been the youthful pilots of the Luftwaffe, or the insouciant cherubim.

Mary bit her cheek to keep from smiling. She liked Miss Vine – the woman was not entirely made of vipers and crinoline. And yet she was so boringly wary, as if life couldn't be trusted.

'I am sorry, Miss Vine.'

'Miss North, have you spent much time in the country?'

'Oh yes. We have weekends in my father's constituency.'

It was exactly the sort of thing she tried not to say.

Miss Vine let go of Zachary's shoulders. 'May I borrow you for a moment, Miss North?'

'Please,' said Mary.

They took themselves off a little way.

'What inspired you to volunteer as a schoolmistress, Mary?'

Pride would not let her reply that she hadn't volunteered for anything in particular – that she had simply volunteered, assuming the issue would be decided favourably, as it always had been until now, by influences unseen.

'I thought I might be good at teaching,' she said.

'I am sorry. It is just that young women of your background usually wouldn't consider the profession.'

'Oh, I shouldn't necessarily see it like that. Surely if one had to pick a fault with women of my background, it might be that they don't consider work very much at all.'

'And, dear, why did you?'

'I hoped it might be less exhausting than the constant rest.'

'But is there no war work which seems to you more glamorous?'

'You do not have much faith in me, Miss Vine.'

'But you are impossible, don't you see? My other teachers are dazzled by you, or disheartened. And you are overconfident. You befriend the children, when it is not a friend that they need.'

'I suppose I just like children.'

The headmistress gave her a look of undisguised pity. 'You cannot be a friend to thirty-one children, all with needs greater than you imagine.'

'I think I understand what is needed.'

'You have been doing the job for four days, and you think you understand. The error is a common one, and harder to correct in young women who have no urgent use for the two pounds and seventeen shillings per week.'

Mary bristled, and with an effort said nothing.

'All the trouble this week has come from your class, Mary. The tantrums, the mishaps, the abscondments. The children feel they can take liberties with you.'

'But I feel for them, Miss Vine. Saying goodbye to their parents, for who knows how long? The state they are in, I thought perhaps a little licence—'

'Could kill them. I have no idea what these next few weeks or months will bring, but I am certain that if there is violence then we shall need to have every child accounted for at all times, ready to be taken to shelter at a moment's notice. They mustn't be who-knows-where.'

'I am sorry. I will improve.'

'I fear I cannot risk giving you the time.'

'Excuse me?'

'At noon, Mary, we are to proceed on foot to Marylebone, to board a train at one. They have not given me the destination, although I imagine it must be Oxfordshire or the Midlands.'

'Well, then . . .'

'Well, I am afraid I shan't be taking you along.'

'But Miss Vine!'

The headmistress put a hand on her arm. 'I like you, Mary. Enough to tell you that you will never be any good as a teacher. Find something more suited to your many gifts.'

'But my class . . .'

'I will take them myself. Oh, don't look so sick. I have done a little teaching in my time.'

*But their names*, thought Mary. *I have learned every one of their names.*

She stood for a moment, concentrating – as her mother had taught her – on keeping her face unmoved. 'Very well.'

'You are a credit to your family.'

'Not at all,' said Mary, since that was what one said.

Noon came too quickly. She retrieved her suitcase from the trolley where the rest of the staff had theirs, and watched the school evacuate in rows of three down the Outer Circle road. Kestrels went last: her thirty-one children with their names inscribed on brown baggage tags. Enid Platt, Edna Glover and Margaret Eccleston made up the front row, always together, always whispering. For four days now their gossip had seemed so thrilling that Mary had never known whether to shush them or beg to be included.

Margaret Lambie, Audrey Shepherd and Nellie Gould made up the next row: Audrey with her gas-mask box decorated with poster paint, Nellie with her doll who was called Pinkie, and Margaret who spoke a little French.

Mary was left behind. The green sward of grass beside the abandoned zoo became quiet and still. George Woodall, Jack Taylor and Graham Brown marched with high-swinging arms in the infantry style. John Cumberland, Harry Rogers and Carl Richardson mocked them with chimpanzee grunts from the row behind. Henriette Wisby, Elaine Newland and Beryl Waldorf, the beauties of the class, sashayed with their arms linked, frowning at the rowdy boys. Then Eileen Robbins, Norma Reeve and Rose Montiel, pale with apprehension.

Next went Patricia Fawcett, Margaret Taylor and June Knight, whose mothers knew one another socially and whose own eventual daughters and granddaughters seemed sure to prolong the acquaintance for so long as the wars of men permitted society to convene over sponge cake and tea. Then Patrick Joseph, Gordon Abbott and James Wright, giggling and with backward glances at Peter Carter, Peter Hall and John Clark, who were up to some mischief that Mary felt sure would involve either a fainting episode, or ink.

Finally came kind Rita Glenister supporting tiny, tearful James Roffey, and then, in the last row of all, Fay George and Zachary. The coloured boy dismissed her by taking one last puff of his imaginary cigarette and flicking away the butt. He turned his back and walked away with all the others, singing, towards a place that did not yet have a name. Mary watched him go. It was the first time she had broken a promise.

At dinner, at her parents' house in Pimlico, Mary sat across from her friend Hilda while her mother served slices of cold meatloaf from a salver that she had fetched from the kitchen herself. With Mary's father off at the House and no callers expected, her mother had given everyone but Cook the night off.

'So when are you to be evacuated?' said her mother. 'I thought you'd be gone by now.'

'Oh,' said Mary, 'I'm to follow presently. They wanted one good teacher to help with any stragglers.'

'Extraordinary. We didn't think you'd be good, did we, Hilda?'

Hilda looked up. She had been cutting her slice of meatloaf into thirds, sidelining one third according to the slimming plan she was following. 'Two Thirds Curves' had been recommended in that month's *Silver Screen*. It was how Ann Sheridan had found her figure for *Angels With Dirty Faces*.

'I'm sorry, Mrs North?'

'We didn't suppose Mary would be any use at teaching, did we, dear?'

Hilda favoured Mary with an innocent look. 'And she was so stoical about the assignment.'

Hilda knew perfectly well that she had neither accepted the role particularly graciously nor survived in it for a week. Mary managed a smile that she judged to have the right inflection of modesty. 'Teaching helps the war effort by freeing up able men to serve.'

'I had you down for freeing up some admiral.'

'Hilda! Any more talk like that and your severed head on the gate will serve as a warning to others.'

'I'm sorry, Mrs North. But a pretty thing like Mary is hardly cut out for something so plain as teaching, is she?'

Hilda knew perfectly well that Mary was already suspected by her mother of dalliances. This was typical her – baiting the most exquisite trap and then springing it, while seeming to have most of her mind on her meatloaf.

'I'm just jolly impressed that she's sticking with it,' said Hilda. 'I can't even stick to a diet.'

With unbearable ponderousness, Hilda was using her knife and fork to reduce the length of each of the runner beans on her plate by one third. With diligence she lined up each short length beside the surplus meatloaf.

Mary rose to it. 'Why on earth are you cutting them all like that?'

Hilda's round face was guileless. 'Are my thirds not right?'

'Just put aside one bean in three, for heaven's sake. It's dieting, not dissection.'

Hilda slumped. 'I'm not as bright as you.'

Mary threw her a furious look. Hilda's dark eyes glittered.

'We have different gifts,' said Mary's mother. 'You are faithful and kind.'

'But I think Mary is so brave to be a teacher, don't you? While the rest of us only careen from parlour to salon.'

Mary's mother patted her hand. 'We also serve who live with grace.'

'But to do something for the war,' said Hilda. 'To really *do* something.'

'I suppose I am proud of my daughter. And only this summer we were worried she might be a socialist.'

And finally all three of them laughed. Because really.

After dinner, on the roof terrace that topped the six storeys of creamy stucco, Hilda was weak with laughter while Mary seethed. Their white dresses flamed red as the sun set over Pimlico.

'You perfect wasp's udder,' said Mary, lighting a cigarette. 'Now I shall have to pretend forever that I haven't been sacked. Was all that about Geoffrey St John?'

'Why would you imagine it was about Geoffrey St John?'

'Well, I admit I might have slightly . . .'

'Go on. Have slightly what?'

'Have slightly kissed him.'

'At the . . .?'

'At the Queen Charlotte's Ball.'

'Where he was there as . . .'

'As your escort for the night. Fine.'

'Interesting.'

'Isn't it?' said Mary. 'Because apparently you are still jolly furious.'

'So it would seem.'

Mary leaned her elbows on the balcony rail and gave London a weary look. 'It's because you're not relaxed about these things.'

'I am very traditional,' said Hilda. 'Still, look on the bright side. Now you have a full-time teaching job.'

'You played Mother like a cheap pianola.'

'And now you will have to get your job back, or at least pretend. Either way you'll be out of my hair for the Michaelmas Ball.'

'The ball, you genius, is to be held after school hours.'

'But you will have to be in the countryside, won't you? Even your mother will realise that there's nobody here to teach.'

Mary considered it. 'I will get you back for this.'

'Eventually I shall forgive you, of course. I might even let you come to my wedding to Geoffrey St John. You can be a bridesmaid.'

They leaned shoulders and watched the darkening city.

'What was it like?' said Hilda finally.

Mary sighed. 'The worst thing is that I loved it.'

'But I did see him first, you know,' said Hilda.

'Oh, I don't mean kissing Geoffrey. I mean I loved the teaching.'

'What are you cooking up now?'

'No, really! I had thirty-one children, bright as the devil's cufflinks. Now they're gone, it feels rather dull.'

The blacked-out city lay inverted. Until now it had answered the evening stars with a million points of light.

'Why not the kiss?' said Hilda after a while. 'What was wrong with Geoffrey's kiss anyway?'

# OCTOBER, 1939

When war was declared, Tom Shaw decided to give it a miss. It wouldn't last in any case – the belligerents on both sides would pull back from the brink, as children did when encircled in the playground by a mob calling for a fight.

It took skill, at twenty-three, to be sad. The trouble was, he noticed things that made one melancholy. He noticed the way the West End players didn't bother to remove their stage paint if the matinée was close to the evening show – so that when one went out in Soho one might see Rosencrantz drinking a half-pint, in a corner, in the indifferent afternoon light. He noticed the neat cropped circle achieved in grass whenever a horse was tethered on common land by a fixed length of chain – the circle being of invariant geometrical perfection notwithstanding the temperament of the beast: whether skittish or placid, obstinate or obliging.

His colleagues at the Education Authority had all left to join the Army, and his supervisor had ascended to the Ministry to help coordinate the evacuation. Tom seemed to be the only man in London who did not think the war an unmissable parade lap, and so he'd been given a school district to run instead. A man might celebrate the promotion if he didn't have the gift for noticing that the schools were empty.

He took a walk at dawn. High up on Parliament Hill the blackberries were in season, bursting with the bright sweetness they only gave in the best years. In any other October, children would have got to these bushes first. Tom took off his hat and filled it.

He looked down on his new district as it awoke: the scholastic subdivision of Kentish Town and Chalk Farm. Marking his fiefdom's northerly limit was the railway, steam rising even now as the day's first batch of evacuees went west. The Regent's Canal was his southern border, busy with barges lugging goods from the docks. Within these bounds no child would learn its letters, no teacher would receive her wages in a manila envelope with its tie closure sealed in red wax, no chalk would be brought forth from its Cretaceous slumber to be milled into rods and applied to blackboards, unless he himself ordained it. Glancing left and right to make sure he was alone, he raised an imperious arm.

'Learn, little people! I command it!'

His mouth was full of blackberries, the effect rather undermined. He let his arm drop and wondered what he ought to do with the day. The only school-age children who remained were the frankly unappealing – the crippled and the congenitally strange, those the country folk wouldn't accommodate. The negro children too, of course – only a few had been evacuated and those were already starting to trickle back. The evacuation was a beauty contest in which the little ones were lined up in church halls and the yokels allowed to pick the blonds.

Tom was left with twenty mothballed schools and a light scattering of the children who were either too complicated to educate, or too simple. To cheer himself up he practised the trick of flipping a blackberry from his hand to strike his elbow and bounce into his mouth. He was no good at it at all – he didn't get it once in six attempts – but he was sure he would improve with time. It was the great folly of war that it measured nations against each other without reckoning talents like these.

He lifted his eyes. Beyond his zone, London sprawled away to the rank marshes in the east and the white marble walls of the west. Along the line of the Thames they were testing a flock of miniature zeppelins. Tethered on cables, these were supposed to offer a variety of protection – albeit of a vague and unspecified stripe. The balloons' snub noses swung left and right in the fickle breeze, giving them the anxious air of compasses abandoned by north.

Tom took his hatful of blackberries with him down the hill, back into the furious city with its mushrooming recruitment posts. Strangers met his eye, anxious to nod the new solidarity. *YOUR* COURAGE, *YOUR* CHEERFULNESS, *YOUR* RESOLUTION read the billboards that used to hawk soap.

It was still only eight – too early for the office – so he went back to his garret. Home was a sitting room with two bedrooms attached, in a townhouse off the Prince of Wales Road. The attic had been converted – as his flatmate Alistair Heath put it – in the same way the Christians had converted the Moors. It seemed to have been done at the point of a sword, leaving the continual threat of reversion. Winter brought leaks and bitter draughts, summer a canicular heat from which slight relief could be obtained by running one's head under the tap of the little corner kitchen.

Tom found Alistair sitting on the bare floorboards in his pyjama bottoms, smoking his pipe and stuffing shredded newspaper into the pelt of a ginger cat. The head and shoulders were done, the empty eye sockets bulging with newsprint.

'My god,' said Tom, 'is that Julius Caesar?'

Alistair did not look up from his work. 'Grim times, old man. The taxidermist sent him back unfinished. Tea's in the pot, if you're interested.'

'Why didn't they finish him?'

'Perhaps he was incurable.'

25

'Insatiable, more like. Remember how he used to strut back in here after a big night out?'

Alistair grinned around his pipe stem. 'I miss the randy old bugger. Came in the first post – landlady brought him up just now. Tanned and neatly folded and wrapped in brown paper. Not his usual entrance.'

'Feeling a little flat.'

'I'm stuffing him with editorials. He'll be full of himself.'

Tom offered his hatful of blackberries. 'Going to make jam. Try one?'

Alistair did. 'Good god, forget jam. You could make claret.'

Tom tipped the blackberries into a pan, stooped to retrieve the ones that had missed, and ran in a cupful of water.

'Was there a note with Caesar?'

'An apology. Shop closing down, regrets etcetera, we herewith return all materials. I can't imagine there'll be much call for taxidermy until the war is over.'

'They should just call it off,' said Tom.

He set the pan to simmer, and turned to watch Alistair sewing up the cat's belly. He was handy at it, putting in a row of small, neat stitches that would disappear when the fur was brushed over them. Tom had always admired Alistair's hands, strong and unfairly capable. Alistair could mend their gramophone, play piano – do all of the things that made Tom feel like a Chubb key in a Yale lock – and he did them without seeming to worry, as if the hands contained their own grace. Alistair rather overshadowed him, though Tom supposed his friend didn't notice. Blond and robust, Alistair had the stoic's gift for shrugging off war and broken plumbing with the same easy smile, as if these things were to be expected. He was good-looking not by being ostentatiously handsome but rather by accepting the gaze affably, meeting the eye. It was Tom's experience of Alistair that women sometimes had to look twice, but that something drew the second look.

Alistair tapped out his pipe. 'I shan't be home tonight. I'm taking Lizzie Siddal to the countryside.'

'Oh? Which painting?'

'The "kiss me, I can't swim" one.'

'*Ophelia*?' Tom mimed the gaze and the pious hands.

'We've built a box for her and we're driving her to Wales in an unmarked lorry.'

'I didn't know there was such a thing as a marked lorry, in this situation. Is there actually a fleet of government lorries labelled PRICELESS ART TREASURE?'

'Do leave it out,' said Alistair. 'You take all the romance out of mundane logistical operations.'

'Anyway, if it's so secret, should you even be telling me?'

'Why? You won't tell Hitler, will you?'

'Not unless they give me back my secret radio transmitter.'

'It is all rather evil and sad,' said Alistair. 'I spent five months restoring the frame on *Ophelia* – just the frame – and now we're boxing her up and burying her in some old mine shaft for who knows how long.'

Tom poured the whole of their tea sugar from its Kilner jar into the pan, brown lumps included.

'I wouldn't mind,' said Alistair, 'only I hate to think of it down there in the dark. It makes one think: what if we lose the war?'

Tom stirred the sugar into the fruit. 'There won't be a real war.'

'What if all of us are swept away and no one remembers Ophelia, and she remains there for all eternity, in the dark, under a mountain?'

'They'll always have Caesar. They can reconstruct our aesthetics from that. Even if you have overstuffed him.'

Alistair eyed the cat critically. 'Have I? No. The old man always had to be careful about his weight. This is him in one of his especially sleek periods.'

'It's not an entirely terrible fist you're making of it. You really might consider being a conservator or something of that ilk.'

'You should see the Tate now,' said Alistair. 'The light is boarded out, the great gallery echoes and the paintings are all dispersed.'

'Well, sign it and call it Modern. Anyway, damn you. I have a dinner date this evening. Marriage is a certainty and you should prepare a best man's speech forthwith.'

Alistair lifted the half-stuffed cat to his ear and listened to what it whispered. 'Caesar decrees that you tell all, without leaving anything out.'

'Well, she's called Mary North and—'

'God in heaven, Tom Shaw, are you actually blushing?'

'It's this jam. It's the heat of the pan.'

Alistair stuffed paper into the cat's hindquarters. 'Caesar assumes she is beautiful, brighter than you, and unable to cook?'

'Caesar knows my type.'

'Then you'll pardon me if I don't wear down my quill with a wedding speech right at this minute. This one will end where all of your romances do, Tommy: with you gazing wistfully at the receding figure of a nice girl who has grown fond of you but who has reluctantly concluded that you are neither wealthy nor gifted at dancing.'

Tom turned up the heat under the pan. 'It's different this time. I've already talked with Mary quite a bit. We've things in common.'

'Such as?'

'Such as our attitude to children, for example.'

'The two of you have discussed it already? I don't believe I've even told you where babies come from.'

'Not having them, you fool. Educating them.'

'You haven't been talking shop at her?'

'She came to talk to me, if you must know. I couldn't get a word in.'

'And what was the gist?'

'That teaching has to change. That the teacher must be an ally of the pupil, and not just a disciplinarian.'

Alistair yawned. 'Caesar proclaims that Mary gives him a headache.'

'Caesar pronounces before learning that Mary is jolly attractive.'

'Then why is she interested in you? I'm surprised you show up on her retina.'

'She came to the office, to ask me for a job. Apparently the War Office assigned her to teaching and we found her a post at Hawley Street School, but she got the boot for being incorrigible. She wants a new class to teach.'

'I didn't think you had any classes left?'

'That's what I told her, and yet she insisted. I said, "I'm sorry, but we've already evacuated everything with two legs and one head," and she said, "Well I'm afraid that's just not good enough." Hands on her hips, and deliciously pink. So naturally I asked her what she damned well expected me to do about it, and she said: "I think you should damned well take me to dinner."'

Alistair stared at him.

'What?' said Tom.

'Where to start? As I perceive it, you have three immediate problems. The first is one of professional impropriety. The second, personal ugliness.'

Tom raised two fingers. 'And the third?'

'Is that your jam is looking punchy, old boy.'

'Damn it!'

The pan was at a murderous boil, spitting hot lava in all directions. Tom advanced on it, using the pan lid as a shield, spoon extended to the limit of his reach to turn off the heat. The boil faded to an aggrieved hiss and then to an occasional vindictive pop as a captured pocket of air escaped.

'Think you caught it in time?'

Tom gave it a prod. 'It will set, I can promise you that. It could be jam, or it could be brittle.'

'We all know a girl like that.'

Tom ignored him. 'Meeting Mary is the first thing to make me feel that this war might not be completely awful.'

'Oh, Tommy, just because the grown-ups have left you alone in the nursery for a little while, it doesn't mean you can draw on the wallpaper.'

'Oh, come on. This isn't kids' stuff. I'm taking her to Spencer's.'

He'd tried for a worldly tone, but it came out sounding shaky. Maybe Alistair had a point. *And*, he thought – *my god – she is only eighteen*. The worst thing was that he knew her age only because he had gone straight from his office to the personnel department and pulled her file from the records.

'Sorry,' said Alistair. 'Don't mean to be discouraging. I suppose I'm just envious of your dinner.'

'No, that's quite all right. I mean, now that I come to think, I can't be sure what she meant by it. Maybe she does just want to talk about a job.'

Alistair raised an eyebrow and returned to his taxidermy.

'What?' said Tom.

'Nothing.'

'No, what?'

Alistair snapped a length of cotton with his teeth and threaded his needle again. 'Only you could fret about what "dinner" meant.'

'Yes, but what *does* it mean, in this context? Is she implying that she sees me as more than a job opportunity? Or is she demonstrating that I am so evidently just that, that she can safely invite herself to dinner with no possible danger of misconstrual?'

Alistair stared into space for a moment. 'No, I'm afraid you've lost me. Could you do me a diagram, with different coloured pencils?'

'Or even,' said Tom, 'could she be ambivalent about her feelings with regard to me, or unsure about my intentions with regard to her, and therefore, since she is very bright, could she have been making the suggestion in a deliberately obtuse fashion in order to observe the sense in which I construed it? You know, to see how I would react?'

'And how did you react?'

'I might have become slightly tongue-tied.'

'Oh, perfect. Fortunately she is unlikely to eat you for breakfast, since dinner will be the occasion.'

'Go to hell. But seriously. What do you think? You're an experienced man.'

'I'm an experienced man who is currently stitching a dead emperor's arsehole shut.'

'Yes, but even so.'

Alistair let his needle and cotton drop and looked up in exasperation. 'There are two kinds of dinner and two kinds of women. There is only one combination out of four where both will be rotten.'

'But how awful if that was the case!'

Alistair said nothing. He finished stitching, snapped the thread and set the cat up on its paws. The balance was off at first, and he splayed the limbs until the creature held more steady. 'There,' he said. 'Caesar bows to no man.'

He filled his pipe, lit it, and sat cross-legged on the floor, looking at the cat. There was something awry in his own posture, in his stiff back, and it saddened Tom. Sometimes it was no longer altogether funny, this double act they played in which he was the boy to Alistair's man of the world. They had fallen into the roles in some primordial conversation in their friendship – something that must have raised a laugh at the time – and the joke had been good enough to bear a few cycles of elaboration and eventually to become a habit between them. And now here they were, two finches evolved to feed on a fruit that was probably becoming extinct.

Tom lit a cigarette and tried to make himself enjoy it. He took the empty Kilner jar, chipped out the last brown encrustations of tea-soaked sugar, rinsed it, and set it to boil in a pan of water. While the jar sterilised he took a spoonful of the jam and blew to make it cooler.

In the bright morning wash from the garret's single skylight, the jam glowed in the metal spoon. Its centre, where it was deepest, was indigo. At its shallow edges the colour thinned to a limpid carmine. He closed his eyes and tasted it. By luck he had arrested it on the verge of caramelisation, between honeyed and bitter. The sweetness of the blackberries revealed itself incompletely, changing and deepening until it dissolved from the back of the tongue with the maddening hint of a greater remainder. He was left with a question he couldn't phrase, and a galaxy of tiny seeds that tantalised the tongue.

He stood with his eyes closed for a full minute before he took another spoonful. He was absolutely uncertain. Perhaps it was the most exquisite thing that had ever been cooked, or perhaps it was perfectly ordinary blackberry jam, on an averagely bright October morning, in an unexceptional attic in which two typical young bachelors were putting off the real duties of the day in pursuits at which they did not excel. Perhaps it was only average jam and perhaps Caesar, corpulent and lumpy and with his empty eye sockets spewing shreds of newspaper, was only a poor stuffed cat.

Tom poured the jam into the hot boiled jar, snapped the lid

shut and ran the glass under the cold tap to let the vacuum make the seal. He dried the outside of the jar, licked a bookplate label to activate the gum, stuck it onto the flat roundel on the jar and wrote: 'London, 1939'.

'Well?' he said. 'And so what if she does only want a job? Teaching is important work, and I think she might be good at it.'

'You've lost me again. Did you want to marry her, or hire her?'

'I haven't the budget for either. I was just grateful for a civilised conversation. Honestly, she might be the only person in this city apart from you and me who understands that there are many ways to serve. That one isn't being unpatriotic by declining to rush off like a schoolboy to fire popguns at the Germans.'

'The Germans did rather start it.'

'Yes, but you know what I mean.'

Alistair tried to smile.

'What is it?' said Tom.

'I suppose all of us have to look at our job and ask how it now serves the cause. I suppose one is lucky if a simple answer presents itself.'

'But it's hardly us, is it?' said Tom. 'Me with my district, and you dashing all over these isles stashing our heirlooms into caves. The question would be more pointed if one was . . . I don't know . . . a speculator, or a thief.'

Alistair tweaked the cat's tail, pointing the end skyward the way Caesar had worn it in life.

'I walk past a recruitment post every morning, on Regent Street. You overhear the damnedest conversations in the queue. I think the fear of going to war is less than the shame of admitting that your country can get along quite well without whatever-it-is that you've been up to. In the end, of course, the conclusion of the man is the same as that of the military – that getting killed is the least one can do in the circumstances – except that the two parties reach the same conclusion by different routes.'

'You've thought about it, haven't you?'

'I've had nothing better to do. The Turners went weeks ago. We have a few Romantics left to move out of the side galleries, then half a dozen Surrealists. Soon we'll be down to the paintings I could have done myself.'

'But you've said it often: we can't let them make us into barbarians. Someone must stay behind who understands how to put it all back together.'

Alistair looked at his hands. 'Well, the thing is, that someone shan't be me.'

Tom felt the shock of the words before he understood their meaning. A constriction in the veins, a sense of imminence, time clenching like a sphincter. A half-second's diminution of the hearing, so that he felt his ears roar for one heartbeat.

'God, you haven't . . .'

Alistair looked up. 'I'm sorry. I did it yesterday.'

Tom stood with the jam jar still gripped in his hand.

'It's all right,' he said. 'It's all right. There's bound to be something we can do. There will be a procedure, for people who have signed up by mistake. It must happen fifty times a day. There will be some kind of system for it.'

'The whole point of the system is that one cannot go back, surely. I signed a solemn contract. In any case, it was the right thing to do. I'm going, Tom.'

'When?'

'They didn't say. They gave me three days' pay and told me to await instructions. There will be recruit training and an officer cadet course, then I suppose I go wherever I'm needed.'

'This isn't some horrible joke?'

'I'm afraid not.'

Tom sat down on the floor beside his friend and stared around

34

at the place. The garret changed as he looked. Its devil-may-care medley of bric-a-brac was transformed now into banal juvenilia. As he watched, each carefully cultivated eccentricity – from the unswept floor to the scattered library books – shrugged off its enchantment until all that was left was an attic flat in an unexceptional borough of London. The flat would revert to the landlady, their life to the world.

*Oh* – thought Tom – *so it finishes as quickly as this. All the things we make exceptional are merely borrowed from the mundane and must without warning be surrendered to it.*

'I'm sorry for what I said, about running off like schoolboys.'

'That's all right. A lot of them practically are. You should have seen the recruiting line. I'm twenty-four and I felt like the old man.'

Tom swallowed. 'Do you think I should volunteer too?'

'Good god. Why?'

'Well, I mean I honestly hadn't thought about it until now.'

Alistair threw a balled-up sheet of newspaper. 'You're made to be an educator, you old fool. Find a way to do your job again, and then do it. If one could stash schoolchildren down a disused mine in Wales then I'd insist you enlisted with me, but until then I'd say that war isn't on your curriculum.'

Tom was silent for a minute. 'Thank you.'

'I thought you might take it harder.'

'I will miss you.'

'You certainly will. You'll have no one to tell you to cheer up. That's why I'm giving you Gaius Julius Caesar. Every time you look at him, I want you to imagine him saying: "Tom, for god's sake cheer up!"'

Alistair whipped the cat around when he said this, so that it addressed Tom directly. He had sewn two large coat buttons over the sockets for eyes and they were pearlescent and exuberantly mismatched, so that the effect was of a startling and demented supervision.

'Well, I want you to have this,' said Tom, giving Alistair the jar of jam.

Alistair peered at the label. 'A crude etiquette but a famous vintage, the '39. I believe I shall lay it down. We shall open it together at war's end, yes?'

Tom looked at him. 'Will you be all right?'

'How should I know?'

'Sorry.'

'Christ,' said Alistair. 'I'm sorry.'

He lay on his back on the floor, holding the jam up to the skylight.

'Tea?' said Tom after a while.

'If you're making.'

'There's no more sugar, I'm afraid.'

Alistair said nothing. Tom watched the scarlet and the purple light shift across his friend's steady face.

# OCTOBER, 1939

Since Mary must neither bump into her mother nor anyone who conceivably might, she had a day to fill on her own. Autumn had come, with squalls of rain that doused the hot mood of the war. She walked along the Embankment while the southwesterly blew through the railings where children used to rattle their sticks. In the playground at Kensington Gardens the wind scoured the kiteless sky and set the empty swings rocking to their own orphaned frequency.

How bereft London was, how drably biddable, without its infuriating children. Here and there Mary spotted a rare one that the evacuation had left marooned. The strays kicked along on their own through the leaves, seal-eyed and forlorn. When she gave an encouraging smile they only stared back. Mary supposed she could not blame them. How else would one treat the race that had abducted one's playmates?

The wind that buffeted her had already blown through half of London, accruing to itself the pewtery, mouldering scent of all missing things. Mary drew her raincoat tight and kept walking. In Regent's Park the wind wrenched the wet yellow leaves from the trees. Horse chestnuts lay in their cases, grave with mildew. She supposed that nature had no provision for conkers beyond the earnest expectation that boys in knee shorts would always come, world without end, to take them home and to dangle them on shoelaces and to invest each one with brash and improbable hope.

Mary found a café where she was not known and sat at the back of it, away from the steamed-up window. Over stewed tea she took paper and pen from her bag to write to Zachary.

Just writing the address made her fret. It was one of those villages in the faraway England that London never called to mind unless some ominous thing happened – a landslip, or the birth of a two-headed foal – that brought its name into the newspaper. She did not know how parents could bear to ink such addresses onto letters for their children. Corfe Mullen, Cleobury Mortimer, Abinger Hammer: these, surely, were places of obfuscating mist and sudden disaster, from whence one knew nobody, and of which one knew nothing. Places full of country folk: eerie and bulb-nosed, smeared with chicken blood on full-moon nights.

*Dear Zachary,*
   *I feel dreadful that I was not able to keep my promise to come with you, but I hope that you do understand the need for the evacuation.*

She gnawed at the top of her pencil. Now that great solid London was blacked out and dug in, here was this awful silence that the wet wind couldn't disguise. Autumn had come but the Germans hadn't, after all.

*I trust you have found a good family to take care of you.*

The wind rattled the café's windows, and in the absence of shrill voices she could hear the cutlery scrape as the couple in the corner chased peas around their plates. They were parents, of course they were: there was no other way to collect such intricate worry lines. *Are we quite sure we have done the right thing?*

On every corner Mary had passed that day there had been posters explaining that the children should remain evacuated

– that the greatest Christmas gift to Herr Hitler would be to bring them home into harm's way.

*I am sure you are being jolly fearless.*

Mary frowned and rubbed this out. The authorities imagined that the individual was a glove, requiring only the animating hand of a slogan. She could almost see her father, in some windowless room of the House, penning the script in committee. All morning the damp southwesterly had caught at the corners of the new slogans and sent them flapping against the billboards, exposing the fossil seams of earlier exhortations in their sediment of paste.

*Even though I was your teacher for only a week, I should like you to know that you are a blazing creature despite being an absolute knave, and that I slightly miss teaching you. I trust things are going well for you, but just in case they are not – and if you can bear to hold your nose and make a promise to a silly woman who has already broken hers to you – then please guarantee me that you will write to let me know.*

She signed the letter 'Miss North', tucked it into its envelope, and went out into the rain for a post box.

She was home at five, as dusk fell. The front door swung open when her foot fell on the first of the steps that rose to it.

'Thank you, Palmer,' she said, giving him her raincoat to hang.

'How was teaching?' called her mother from the drawing room.

'Well,' said Mary, 'you know children.'

'I only know you, darling, and I daresay they aren't all so maddening.'

39

Mary popped her head through the drawing-room door. 'I am fond of you too, Mother.'

'Fortunately I had Nanny whenever it got too realistic.'

'Where's Hilda? I saw her coat in the hall.'

'I made her go through to the scullery. I don't care how much good these cigarettes do your chests, they are ruinous for the curtains.'

'They are slimming.'

Her mother lowered her voice. 'They are slimming you, darling. They must do the opposite to Hilda.'

'Perhaps she lights the wrong end.'

'Her life is a carousel of torpid men and toffee éclairs. I tell her she should volunteer for war work, like you, or at least find a man who will.'

'She is fond of Geoffrey St John.'

'As tripe is fond of onions, darling, but what a fright they look together in the pan.'

'Don't be mean about Geoffrey, Mother – he kisses rather well.'

Her mother treated her to a knowing expression that Mary felt sure was pure bluff. It was how mothers carried on, after all, with a glint in the eye that implied a sure clairvoyance and also that it was your turn to talk. This was the velvet rope mothers offered: enough silence to make a noose with.

Mary breezed from the drawing room, blowing a kiss on the way out.

In the hallway the familiar air of the house closed around her – the beeswax on the banisters and the Brasso that burnished the stair rods. A hint of laundry on the boil. Somewhere far within, crockery clacked as a maid addressed the detritus of afternoon tea. Coal rumbled as it was decanted from scuttle to purdonium. That evening, it seemed, the fires would be lit for the first time since March.

In the scullery Hilda was smoking by the small window.

'And what of wild intrigue?'

Mary grinned. 'I'm working on Tom. I shall telephone him again today. I'm sure he'll find me a post. I keep reminding him there are scads of children who haven't been evacuated.'

Hilda mimed a hunchback with the twisted face of a lunatic.

'Oh, stop it,' said Mary. 'I see no reason why they shouldn't all be given a chance to learn. I just need to persuade Tom.'

'He seems a drip, if you ask me. You go for dinners, you practically beg him to kiss you, yet he offers you neither his lips nor his patronage. I should move on.'

'Yes, but he is a man, though, don't you see? You could knit one quicker than you can make one fit off-the-shelf.'

'Move on, darling, before the drip-drip leaves you soaked.'

'All it is, is that Tom is rather shy. When I'm with him . . . well, it's nice.'

Hilda offered an eyebrow.

'No, really! Tom is lovely.'

'What's he like?'

'Thoughtful. Interesting. Compassionate.'

'These are English words for ugly.'

'Not at all. He's tall with soft brown eyes. He's quite gorgeous and I don't think he has any idea, which is sweet.'

'Don't forget you only care because he can offer you a job.'

'Which I need, thanks to you dropping me in it.'

'Well it's your own fault if you won't tell the truth to your mother.'

'Oh, but who does? You punish me too hard over one little kiss.'

Hilda affected puzzlement. 'Kiss?'

'No! Oh, Hilda, don't say you are over it already. I just spent the whole beastly day in the rain doing my penance for the Geoffrey Indiscretion.'

Hilda yawned. 'Have Geoffrey, if you wish. He still flatly refuses to volunteer for the war.'

'As do you.'

'Which is why I need a man I can nobly support.'

'In absentia, though.'

'Oh, in furs.'

'Tom won't sign up and I admire it. He . . . well, it's just not him.'

Hilda widened her eyes. 'Mary North!'

Mary smiled. 'Well, and so what?'

'You are actually soft on the man!'

'No, no, but he has – oh, you know, *eyes*, and he is tall, and . . . well, I think it's lovely that he thinks teaching is important, because I think so too.'

'Since when?' said Hilda.

'Since the moment they said I couldn't. Why must we do what we're told?'

'To keep life pleasant and convivial?'

'Says the girl smoking in the scullery! Why not say to Mother: "I *shall* smoke in your drawing room, and if you must replace those curtains then do let me pick you out a pattern that is not so exquisitely vile." She'd respect you for it.'

'She'd never let me visit again.'

'Which might force you to widen your circle of friends.'

Hilda blinked.

'Oh,' said Mary, 'I didn't mean it like that. It's just that you're the way you are, and I'm the way I am.'

'And you are determined to fall in love with Tom, apparently, just because it goes against all available grains.'

'One dinner, one lunch and three telephone calls. I hardly call it love.'

'What do you call it? Do you want him to give you the teaching job, or do you want, you know, him?'

Mary bit her lip. 'Is both allowed?'

'If I said no, wouldn't you only go and do it?'

Mary took her arm. 'And we need to find you a nice soldier, do we?'

'An airman would do at a pinch. I draw the line at navy blue.'

'Nice girls do. I shall keep a lookout for you. Of course it is quite ridiculous in any case. There is no actual fighting, is there?'

'God no,' said Hilda. 'They're nice in uniform, not battle dress.'

# NOVEMBER, 1939

An artillery shell rose over Salisbury Plain and slowed in the rain at the zenith of its arc. Beneath it the wide grasslands moved in a green blur that resolved, as the projectile slowed, into sedges and mosses heavy with rain. With the scream of a fresh start the shell dropped from the sky and buried itself in the ooze.

There was a deficiency in the impact fuse, and the shell did not explode. It lay in its pocket of black mud in the bed of a shallow ravine. Its mechanism trembled. The thing could barely contain itself.

Three miles distant, Alistair Heath stood in driving rain while a sergeant major screamed at him.

'WHAT MAKES MY GRASS GROW?'

'*Blood, blood, blood!*' the men replied.

'WHOSE BLOOD?'

'*The enemy's!*'

'WHOSE ENEMY?'

'*The King's enemy!*'

Alistair joined in the bayonet drill without enthusiasm. He had heard the shell falling – a stray from the gunnery range. The first problem of war was that no one was any good at it yet.

He could not help thinking of shells as things he had always collected, with his sisters, on the beaches at Lulworth and

Bracklesham. When the instructors spoke of firing them, he could not help seeing the dumpy 3.7-inch howitzers projecting cockles and scallops in looping trajectories over a blue horizon. Invariably the scallops, when he visualised them, were the jaunty little things from Botticelli's *The Birth of Venus*.

'HEATH!'

'Yes?'

'PERHAPS YOU BELIEVE YOURSELF TO BE ABOVE ALL THIS? ARE YOU GIVING THIS VITAL DRILL, MISTER HEATH, ONE HUNDRED PER CENT OF YOUR GRACIOUS CONCENTRATION?'

'Oh yes, absolutely.'

'OH YES ABSOLUTELY WHAT?'

Alistair could not think what the man was driving at.

'Yes, I am giving it my full attention.'

'YES I AM GIVING IT MY FULL ATTENTION WHAT?'

The man was retarded. The wind blew over the wide miles of Salisbury Plain – hateful and blasted, pocked with the charred metal twisted in the violent shapes it had cooled to. It was a southwesterly wind, wet with brine from the Channel, sharp from the numb Purbeck Hills. It had passed through no city and picked up nothing of the scent of men and their consolations. It slowed Alistair's brain and took the feeling from his fingers. And here the sergeant major stood infrangible in the wind and the rain – as he had stood the whole fortnight now – with his chest puffed out and his stomach sucked in and his face vermilion with fury. Now he was staring at Alistair and still waiting, apparently, for him to say something.

'Oh!' said Alistair. 'I mean, *sir*.'

The other men laughed. After a month, one shouldn't forget the word.

'WHAT, SIR?'

'I'm sorry?'

'WHAT IS THE MESSAGE THAT YOU ARE COMMUNI-
CATING TO SIR, SIR?'

'Oh I see,' said Alistair. 'Sorry. I am giving this exercise one
hundred per cent of my attention, sir.'

'THAT IS BETTER,' said the sergeant major.

Alistair was glad the man felt that way. The bayonet drill
resumed.

'WHAT MAKES MY GRASS GROW?'

*'Blood, blood, blood!'*

'I CAN'T HEAR YOU, LADIES! WHOSE BLOODY
BLOOD?'

*'The enemy's blood!'*

'WHOSE ORRIBLE NARZI ENEMY?'

'The King's horrible Nazi enemy!'

'THEN KILL THE ENEMY! WHAT DO YOU SUPPOSE
THE POINTY END IS FOR? DO IT TO HIM BEFORE HE
DOES IT TO YOU!'

The men roared and the sand oozed in clotted clumps from
the bags they stuck with their bayonets. Every wound Alistair
drove into the wet sacking opened a corresponding rent in his
morale. How he hated this – the indefatigable tyranny of the
sergeant major, and the insidious Salisbury chill that grew inside
one like an infection after two weeks camped out under dripping
canvas. Most of all, he hated the flicker of warmth that hatred
gave you. You imagined the sergeant major on the point of your
blade, and felt a horrid little twitch at the thought of driving it
home.

He executed the bayoneting to the minimum standard that left
the King's enemy eviscerated, and when it was over and the
sergeant major blew the whistle, he took his rifle and walked off
a little way. He unstrapped his helmet and let the rain wash the
sand off his face. He threw his pack down on a tussock to keep it
off the sodden ground, and ducked into its lee to light his pipe.

The damp tobacco shivered in the bowl. The matches failed one by one. In bleak exhaustion, Alistair watched the last one stutter.

'Nuh . . . need a light, Huh . . . Heath?'

It was Duggan, the only man on the course from that indeterminate age the other side of thirty. He was the one who used the standard-issue folding knife and fork to skin and bone the sardines from their ration tins, as if he were taking tea at Fortnum's. He held his rifle slightly away from his body when they marched, the way one might carry a child that had wet itself.

'Thanks,' said Alistair.

With Duggan's cigarette lighter it was easier. His pipe caught and the mild blue smoke was a comfort. It blew, he supposed, towards London.

'In the muh in the muh in the mood for company?' said Duggan.

Alistair eyed his pipe bowl. 'I'm stuck for conversation, after that drill.'

Duggan sat on his own upturned pack. 'If the wuh . . . wisdom of age may guide you, I pretend that the suh . . . sandbag is just a suh . . . sandbag.'

Alistair looked up. 'It bothers you too?'

'The way I see it, all the bloodthirsty sh . . . shouting is more for the benefit of the muh . . . men. You'll be an officer, I take it?'

'I hope so. I'm to begin a conversion course, assuming I get through this one without bayoneting the sergeant major.'

Duggan got a cigarette lit. 'I shouldn't think they'd necessarily muh . . . mark one down for that. Anyway, I daresay officer training will be a more suh . . . civilised business.'

Alistair nodded. 'They'll assemble us around a cheese board. The CO will ask, "What do we serve with this?" and as one we shall reply . . .'

'*Port! Port! Port!*'

'Whose port?'

'*The King's port!*'

Alistair grinned. 'We are officer material.'

Duggan gave a wire-thin smile and used the hot end of his cigarette to trace the undulations of the plain. 'Don't you luh . . . loathe this vile place?'

Alistair puffed at his pipe. 'It was a paradise before the Army took it over. Full of little hamlets bursting with cheerful cottages, every one of them with a roaring hot fire and a unicorn tethered outside.'

'Suh . . . sounds like Peckham.'

'Is that where you're from?'

Duggan shivered. 'In the suh . . . sense in which the human suh . . . soul is eternal, no one is actually *from* Peckham. Some of us are living there pro tempore, suh . . . so help us.'

'I'm north of the river. Camden.'

'Oh the guh . . . glamour. And what did you do up there, before you began doing whu . . . whatever the Army tells you?'

'I was a very junior conservator at the Tate. I made tea and reminded the night cleaners not to use Vim on the actual canvases.'

'One wonders how the nation will muh . . . manage without you.'

'Oh, and I suppose you were the Archbishop of Canterbury?'

'I'm an actor. Oh, the stuh . . . stammer disappears on the stuh . . . stage.'

'And you signed up for this?'

'I was suh . . . sick of being Second muh . . . Murderer. And so here I am. Rehearsing to be the fuh . . . first.'

'And how are you finding it?'

'Costumes are rather drab but there aren't many luh . . . lines to learn.'

'It's the one show you hope will never make it to the West End.'

'Amen.'

Alistair tapped out his pipe on the side of his boot. 'Miss London?'

Duggan shook his head. 'I duh . . . didn't get through the bathing-suit round.'

Alistair smiled. 'I miss being allowed to mind my own business.'

'I muh . . . miss it too.'

'Are you married?'

Duggan held up his cigarette and let the wind whip the ash away. 'You ruh . . . really are young, aren't you?'

In the southwest the horizon was gone now, lost in a flat zinc mist. Above them the base of the cloud was dropping, black cords of rain dragging it down. As the weather closed, the men occupied a shrinking remainder of the plain between the grass and the falling sky. The company exchanged the blackly comic looks of men about to be engulfed by worse of the same.

The sergeant major blew his tin whistle. 'MIST COMING IN! TAKE NOTE, YOU HOPELESS BASTARDS! TAKE NOTE!'

Duggan frowned. 'Take note of whu . . . what exactly? Will that awful man never tire of being unhelpful?'

Alistair blew on his hands to warm them. 'What do you suppose he thinks we should be doing?'

'About the mist? Well we can hardly shh . . . shoot it, can we? And yet they have issued us with th . . . these.' Duggan flicked the barrel of his rifle with a fingernail, making the dead note of a stopped bicycle bell.

'Do you suppose he means we should put on more clothes?'

'I'm wuh . . . wearing everything they gave us. Aren't you?'

'Well should we eat something, then? To keep our energy up?'

'Did the suh . . . sergeant major order us to eat anything? I don't think I could bear being bawled at again.'

'We could use our initiative.'

'Did he spuh . . . specifically order us to use our initiative?'

'I have some jam in my pack.'

Duggan threw him a look. 'You've been lugging jam around? Isn't the stuh . . . standard-issue suffering heavy enough for you?'

Alistair opened his pack and fished out Tom's jar. 'Blackberry. Been carrying it to remind me of home. I was saving it for the end of the war, but that's no use if one dies of misery in the meantime. Got a spoon or something we can eat it with?'

Duggan looked around. 'You won't luh . . . laugh? I've some biscuits my duh . . . dear mother baked.'

Somewhere close, the sergeant major was yelling again, the words snatched and broken in the wind. Duggan took the biscuits from his pack. They were wrapped in a blue linen tea towel and tied with parcel string.

Now with a silent rush the mist washed over the company and the plain vanished entirely. Nothing was visible outside the tight globe each man crouched in. They sprawled on their packs, smoking and talking in low tired voices, answering the encircling greyness with the blank orbs of their eyes.

Alistair's thoughts stalled. After a fortnight of this sour cold and this enervating wind and this incessant sergeant major, his fatigue ran so deep that only the sight of the wide plain had convinced him of his own residual magnitude. Now he felt snuffed and extinguished. He blew on his hands and waited for the whistle to sound and an order to be given that would invest him once more with purpose.

Duggan was working at the knot that tied the biscuits in their blue cloth. His fingers stopped as the light gained a darker inflection. Two boots sank into the mud between Alistair and Duggan. The two men looked up.

'OH, WELL ISN'T THIS DELIGHTFUL! THESE TWO LONDON GENTLEMEN HAVE COME TO THE COUNTRYSIDE FOR A PICNIC!'

Grey forms converged in the mist. They turned into men that

Alistair recognised, their faces variously animated by apologetic solidarity or leering glee. He stood. Duggan drew himself up more slowly, first placing his parcel carefully on top of his pack.

'SATISFIED, DUGGAN?'

Duggan nodded. 'Yes, Suh . . . Sergeant Major.'

'THAT PARCEL POSITIONED ENTIRELY TO YOUR LIKING, IS IT?'

'Quh . . . quite, thank you, Sergeant Major.'

Without breaking eye contact with Duggan, the sergeant major nudged the package off its perch and smashed it into the ground with his boot. He ground it under his heel until it was half submerged in the mud.

'AND NOW?'

Duggan looked down at the muddy tea towel and the shattered biscuits dissolving in the rain. He raised his eyes to the sergeant major's.

'Now your wuh . . . wife will have to bake me some muh . . . more buh . . . biscuits, Sergeant Major. I can pick them up next time I'm wuh . . . with her.'

The company sucked in its breath. The sergeant major rocked back on his heels and smiled, slowly, in a leer that exposed the teeth to their roots. The wind whipped at the men's rain jackets.

'Very good, Duggan,' said the sergeant major finally. It was the first time any of the company had heard him use a normal speaking voice. He retreated and crouched beside his own pack, downwind, to communicate with parties unknown over the field radio.

Now the company clustered around. Once they were sure the episode was over and the sergeant major's attention otherwise engaged, a few of them shook Duggan's hand. A cigarette was offered, and lit for him when it was clear that his own hands were shaking too badly to do it.

Alistair watched how the men acted with Duggan: chummily,

though ready to disperse if the sergeant major should return in wrath. They did not yet know the ways of the Army – whether a besting once acknowledged was forgotten, or whether grudges were held over things like this. There were nervous laughs. No one attempted a re-enactment of the incident. They waited nervously in the fog: a chance agglomeration of greengrocers and machinists and accounting clerks, rifles slung.

From a little way off, Alistair watched them with a tired apprehension. His pipe was far beyond relighting now, his fingers stiff and unfeeling. He retrieved Tom's jam from the mud, wiped the jar off and replaced it in his pack. (He should be at the garret now, eating the damned jam with a spoon.) It was a struggle, with one's body shivering right down into the deep muscle, to concentrate on staying as dry as one could and not simply bursting into tears.

Dusk came, and with it the rumble of an engine. A canvas-backed lorry, its slotted lights throwing a demure downward glance in the mist. It drew up, engine running. An orange glow from the cab, the driver smoking. The sergeant major jumped up on the bonnet to address them.

'RIGHT, YOU LUCKY LADS! THIS WEATHER ISN'T LOOKING TOO CLEVER AND SINCE I AM A BENEVOLENT GOD, I AM TREATING YOU ALL TO A NICE WARM NIGHT IN BARRACKS! PACKS ON, HOP IN NOW, AND DON'T SAY DADDY ISN'T GOOD TO YOU!'

The men cheered. Alistair wrestled his stiff limbs over the tailgate and collapsed into the laughing crush of men on the benches in the back of the lorry. The man to his left slapped him on the back and offered him a dry cigarette. Alistair smoked it wolfishly. With an ache so terrible that it was funny, the feeling returned to his hands and feet.

All around him now the company bent to the task of complaining. Their faces lit erratically in the drawing glow of cigarettes, the men named the plain an evil place and enumerated the bodily modifications and inventive sodomies they would vest upon the person of Adolf Hitler, at war's end, for causing them to have spent winter weeks on Salisbury, when after all they were handsome young men with important peace-time work to do, such as drinking and philandering and sleeping both of those things off.

They called the Army an arse hat and its brass hats brass arse-holes. They denounced the ice wind blowing through the canvas canopy, and they cursed the hardness of the lorry's metal benches. They articulated the opinion that the optimal stowage location for those benches would be up the arse of the lorry driver, to whom it was pointed out that the small effort of bringing seat cushions with him from barracks might have been a nice touch.

Next they insulted the boot-makers who had made the boots they all wore, which were constructed entirely of hate and which kept the freezing water in but not out. These boots were to be shoved up the boot-makers' arses.

Now the men expressed the hope that the presumed designers of the Lee-Enfield MkIII rifle might experience, when urinating, defecating or ejaculating, a blockage of the same unshiftable cussedness that the men had experienced when prone in the frozen mud of the firing range and trying with numb fingers to persuade the magazine to surrender a bullet to the breech. It was decided that all of the boot-makers (with the boots already in situ up their arses), should be put up Lee and Enfield's arses: the left-boot-makers up Mr Lee's and the right-boot-makers up Mr Enfield's. Finally Lee and Enfield should be inserted headfirst up each other's arses, since they were so very keen on breech loading.

There was nothing the military had that the men did not believe would be more properly stowed within the concavities of other personages, animals or objects. There in the budding warmth in the back of the lorry, while their wet clothes steamed and a canteen of spirits was passed from hand to hand, the men squared the whole Army away, calibrating every one of its tyrannies and stowing it like a Russian doll up the arse of the next-smallest tyranny, until the whole great apparatus of war seemed certain to find its inevitable resting place, deep within the German Führer's fundament.

In short, the men were happy. From the litany of their grievances only the sergeant major was absent, since it was his intervention that had gifted this sudden warmth and this freeing of tongues. Alistair had to hand it to the magnificent bastard: he was not without genius. Over two frightful weeks he had driven the company to the brink and then, sensing desertion or mutiny, he had sidestepped like a matador. Now, as the wind outside rose to gale force, the sergeant major sat aloof in the cab with the driver, letting the company vent, his power over them doubled by his act of magnanimity.

Alistair made himself comfortable on the bench and drank from the canteen when it was passed to him. The men were all right. They had been pushed to their limit, and if there had been nothing particularly exalting about how they had reacted, then his own behaviour had been unexceptional too. They passed him the drink with no distinction. Maybe this was more than he had a right to expect.

As the warmth spread through him and they all waited for the lorry to drive off, Alistair let himself relax. Now that the need for alertness was gone, he was drowsy. He hadn't realised, until now, quite how exhausted he had become. His eyes closed. The cheerful complaining voices lost their distinctness. They merged with the idling note of the engine and the roar of the wind without.

He snapped awake when the tailgate of the lorry banged open. From the startled expletives of the company, he understood that some of them had drifted off too. A cold blast blew in as a flap of canvas was drawn back. The sergeant major shone a torch. The men winced and screwed up their eyes as the beam danced over them and came to rest on Duggan.

'Out you hop, Duggan, there's a good chap,' said the sergeant major.

'Excuh . . . cuse me?' said Duggan.

The only sound was the soft chugging of the lorry's engine.

'HARD OF HEARING? I SAY AGAIN, MISTER DUGGAN: PAUSING ONLY TO GATHER UP THE KIT WITH WHICH HIS MAJESTY THE KING IN HIS GENEROSITY HAS SEEN FIT TO ISSUE YOU, MAKE LIKE A BUNNY RABBIT AND HOP HOP HOP OUT OF THIS LOVELY TRUCK!'

'Wuh . . . what?'

'YOU WILL MAKE YOUR WAY TO BARRACKS ON FOOT DUGGAN! NIGHT NAVIGATION EXERCISE, YOU LUCKY MAN! PULLED YOUR NAME OUT OF THE HAT AT RANDOM SO HELP ME GOD!'

Duggan did not move.

'WELL COME ON, DUGGAN! WHAT ARE YOU WAITING FOR? EVERY MINUTE YOU SIT THERE ON YOUR ARSE IS A MINUTE YOU ARE KEEPING THESE SOLDIERS FROM THEIR STEAK-AND-ALE PIES AND THEIR HOT BATHS AND THEIR BEDS!'

'Buh . . . but I don't know how to get to buh . . . barracks.'

'BARRACKS IS IN WARMINSTER, DUGGAN, EXACTLY WHERE WE LEFT IT!'

'I know where buh . . . barracks is. I don't know whu . . . where we are.'

The sergeant major leered. The loose flap of canvas set up a volley of sudden claps as a gust caught the lorry, rocking it on its springs.

'DO YOU OR DO YOU NOT MISTER DUGGAN HAVE IN YOUR POSSESSION ONE BRACKETS ONE COPY OF THE

MAP WITH WHICH YOU WERE ALL ISSUED MISTER DUGGAN HIS MAJESTY'S ORDNANCE SURVEY SIX INCH TO ONE MILE ENGLAND DASH WILTSHIRE COLON ZERO FIVE TWO?'

'Yes buh . . . but I don't know whu . . . where we are on it.'

'DID YOU OR DID YOU NOT MISTER DUGGAN WHEN I WARNED YOU THAT THE MIST WAS CLOSING IN USE THE LAST VISIBILITY TO TAKE BEARINGS WITH YOUR MARK TWO HAND-BEARING COMPASS AND LANYARD THEN TRANSFER THOSE BEARINGS ONTO THE AFOREMENTIONED MAP AS PER YOUR TRAINING MISTER DUGGAN IN ORDER TO TRIANGULATE YOUR POSITION?'

'Nuh . . . no, Sergeant Major.'

'Oh,' said the sergeant major reflectively. 'Could be a long night for you then. Never mind, lesson learned. Come along now, out you hop.'

Duggan's face blanched in the hard disc of torchlight the sergeant major kept him pinned in. His eyes were red. 'You can't duh . . . do this.'

The sergeant major said nothing and kept the torch trained. Duggan appealed to the company.

'He can't duh . . . do this. He can't suh . . . single me out!'

Alistair could not watch Duggan's face, urgent with expectation, falling when nothing came back from the other men. There was only a soft scraping of boots on the wooden floor of the lorry as positions were adjusted.

'Duggan,' said the sergeant major, 'I can understand that you may not wish to do this alone, so let me give you a choice. If you are not out of this vehicle in thirty seconds, then everyone will get out and the whole company will march back to barracks with you. Is that what you want, Mister Duggan?'

Duggan was dazzled by the beam. 'I . . . I . . .'

There was silence for five seconds, then ten. In the dark a man coughed, and stretched it into a muttering. The hard guttural of the cough disguised the initial consonant: *et out!

A pause, then more coughing from the men in their darkness. *et out! *et the hell out of here! *et the bloody hell out Duggan you useless *astard! The men coughed their judgement, each damnation blent with a paroxysm of the diaphragm so that the men spoke not only with their tongues but also with their tired bodies that were scourged and sleepy and did not want to go back out into the storm.

Alistair did not join in, but though he wished they would stop he did nothing. Duggan turned to him – or almost to him. Blinded in his small circle of light, he addressed a place slightly to Alistair's right. In a small voice on the edge of cracking he said, 'Huh . . . Heath?' And then, when no answer came, 'Alistair?'

Alistair clutched his arms tight around himself. He heard the roaring of the gale and felt the fragile warmth within him. He would be so quickly struck back to numbness if he went out into it all again.

He made himself look at Duggan. The man had a strangely flat face, almost concave. It was a weak face – Alistair saw this now, and wondered why he hadn't noticed before. It would not be a difficult one to take aversion to. *If I had a face like that*, Alistair thought, *I should probably have learned by his age to be more careful who I was rude to.*

Alistair looked at the weak, beseeching face and felt a surge of anger. This was a man he had spoken with for only a few minutes, and who therefore had no claim to fraternity. They had exchanged a few witticisms, that was all. They had sat out of the wind for a moment, enjoying a solidarity which, now he came to think of it, had been rather smug and based on the understanding that they were cut from finer cloth than the other men. And now here he was, warmed by those other men's whisky.

'Alistair?'

The wind whipped at the canvas. The men waited on his word. But Alistair did not want to go back out into the storm, and so in the darkness he said nothing.

In the spotlight of the torch, Duggan's pleading look softened into misery and then dissolved entirely. Finally, as he took his pack and rifle and clambered towards the tailgate, Duggan, the actor, was expressionless.

The lorry lifted on its springs and settled again as his weight dropped over the back. The sergeant major extinguished his torch and slammed the tailgate shut. Alistair felt the lorry rock again as the sergeant major climbed into the cab, then the door slammed and the lorry lurched as the driver set it in motion over the tussocks of grass. In the back, all of them sat in silence as the lorry picked up a lurching, jolting speed over the trackless plain.

No one joked now, or swore, or passed whisky. Now each man alone in his sodden clothes weighed the warmth of the things he had gained against the cost of them, and since the price had been paid by all of them acting together, it was best now if they all sat alone. Rain roared against the canvas and entered in chill streams wherever it found ingress. The wind blew knives.

'Damn it,' said Alistair.

He took up his rifle and pack, gripped the steel hoops of the canvas top to keep his balance, and stumbled over the legs and packs of the men to reach the back of the lorry bed. He braced, then launched himself over the tailgate.

The fall winded him. He lost his equipment. He rolled over in the sodden grass, coming to rest jack-knifed and gasping. Twenty minutes of warmth had been enough to make him forget the nature of cold completely. Straight away, he doubted whether he could survive. He picked himself up and stumbled in a half-crouch with his back to the gale as he retrieved first his pack and then his gun. The rain beat on his bare head – his helmet was gone. His rifle was slick with rain. He shouldered the awful thing.

The lorry did not slow or change its note, and he did not expect it to. In the back they would all be feeling the lifting of a burden now. The remaining men would be talking again, and promising to stand pints for the man that had gone over. They would not all be certain of his name.

Alistair watched the slit beams of the tail lights disappear, and set his back to their direction. He retraced the track they had driven, estimating the distance and the time. As he went, leaning into the gale, he shouted for Duggan. The stars were nowhere. The night was furiously dark.

Three miles to the west, the unexploded shell trembled at the approach of the lorry. Through the soil, beneath the roar of the wind, the vibrations came softly at first. As the sound drew closer it resolved into the groaning of leaf springs and the grinding of the overwrought transmission. Closer still, the bass rumble of the lorry was louder than the moaning of the gale. The impact fuse almost triggered. In the back of the lorry the soldiers were singing an Al Bowlly number.

> Life is just a bowl of cherries,
> Don't be so serious, life's so mysterious

The soldiers' voices lurched as the lorry swayed. There was the thin metal sound of a harmonica, setting up an answering oscillation in the cold brass jacket of the artillery shell. Men were beating time with their boots on the floor of the lorry. The reverberations filled the soil as the rumble approached, almost over the top of the shell now.

*You work, you save, you worry so,*
*But you can't take your dough when you go, go, go*

The lorry was ten yards away from the shell. Down in the wet earth the points of the impact fuse buzzed and rattled and came in contact with each other and exerted a pressure that was almost enough. The lorry came closer. Nearly underneath it now, the shell vibrated with every nuance: the secondary rhythm that the sergeant major tapped out on the dashboard, slightly out of time, his cheerful swaying now that the men could not see him, the pop of the small chained cork as he shared his hip flask with the driver, the asymmetry of the load where the men huddled in the back on the less draughty side, the squeal as the wet fan belt slipped, the flatulence of the soldiers as it was transmitted through the long hard benches and broadcast through the treaded rubber tyres and into the saturated earth.

The men sang and the lorry drove directly over the top of the shell, the wheels passing to each side and missing it completely. It settled a little deeper in the cold mud as the vibrations diminished again. The men drove on to barracks, unaware that everything was new. It was not as if the Army issued them each with a stopwatch that started again from zero each time they were spared. (Even if the Army did, the watch would not have operated reliably, and the men would have earmarked an arsehole to stow it in.)

Three miles to the east the ground surprised Alistair by falling away, so that he had to accelerate to keep his footing. In the dark he ran blindly down the slope and found Duggan by tripping over him, bringing a yell of shock. He stopped and leaned on his rifle, panting.

'Duggan?'

'Huh . . . who is it?'

'It's me. Heath.'

'Alistair?'

He crouched, using his hands to establish the orientation of Duggan's body. He was on his back, just off perpendicular to the slope, with his head uphill. Alistair's best guess at the terrain was that they were close to the base of a shallow draw. Water ran noisily in what must be its base.

'Are you hurt?'

'I don't know. I fuh . . . fell.'

Alistair felt down Duggan's sides. 'Your legs are in the water.'

'Are they? I can't fuh . . . feel them.'

'Come on, let's get you out of there.'

He unstrapped his pack, settled it on the slope, then took Duggan under the arms and heaved him clear of the water.

'There,' he said. 'Are you all right?'

'As an actor? I'm truh . . . tremendous.'

'Where's your pack?'

'I don't know.'

'Where's your gun?'

'It's called a ruh . . . rifle, Heath. You should know better.'

'Where the hell is it?'

The gale moaned above the lip of the draw.

'I duh . . . I don't know. I'm suh . . . suh . . . sorry, Alistair.'

'Don't be, you fool.' He put himself between Duggan and the wind.

'The suh . . . sergeant major kicked you out too, I suppose?'

'Something like that.'

'He really is an abysmal buh . . . bastard. I could have him buh . . . barred from every club in Soho.'

Alistair helped Duggan to a sitting position. 'Can you stand?'

'I can tuh . . . try.'

Alistair held him until the feeling came back into the man's legs and he could stay up on his own.

'Sh . . . shall we go?'

'If you think you can walk?'

'It muh . . . might not exactly be what you would call muh . . . marching.'

'You must just do your best. Here, hold my arm.'

They struggled to the lip of the draw. The wind rediscovered them and sent them staggering until they found their balance and leaned into it.

'Don't get separated!' shouted Alistair. 'I'll never find you again!'

'Have you your cuh . . . compass? I've luh . . . lost everything.'

Alistair felt for it on the lanyard around his neck, and brought it before his face. 'I can't see it.'

'Then how do we nuh . . . know the way?' shouted Duggan. 'It's dark as muh . . . miners' lungs.'

Alistair yelled into his ear. 'This wind is southwest. Barracks are more or less west, I think. If we keep the wind on our left, between our nose and our shoulder, I think we can get ourselves there.'

They struggled forward, with the gale contesting every step. Their saturated clothes clung to their skin, making another resistance to be fought against. The sodden ground sucked each footfall down and hated to let it rise. They persevered for an hour, then two, with Duggan's hand growing heavier all the time on Alistair's shoulder. Alistair took the windward side and sheltered the man all he could, but Duggan began to fall silent.

Alistair was weakening too. From the darkness before them came strange coloured flashes, which might have been real or might not. Fragments of songs and advertising slogans played in his ears, so clear that it was hard to believe he was not hearing them. *Brylcreem your hair – she likes it that way*. He shook his head to clear it. *Lovely day for a Guinness*. He forced himself back into the reality of it: wind on his left cheek, guiding Duggan over the worst of the uneven ground. For a while it worked. He raised one boot, then the other, then one boot, then the other, then *They're jolly well taking daily Bovril.*

A gust caught him in the face and snapped him awake. He found himself motionless, with Duggan leaning against him. He didn't know for how long the two of them had been standing like that, asleep on their feet. He shook Duggan alert and called a rest, and the two of them ducked into the poor shelter of a hillock that they sensed rather than saw. They put their backs to the slight slope and drew up their knees. Now that they had stopped, the cold was frightening.

'Duggan?'

There was no answer.

Alistair shook him. 'Duggan! We can't sleep. We'll fall unconscious.'

A short pause. 'Well that would nuh . . . never do. What would the suh . . . sergeant major do without us?'

'He'd probably be court-martialled for leaving us out here.'

'Then I'm tempted to die just to spuh . . . spite him.'

'That's the spirit that will win us the war.'

'How fuh . . . far now, do you think?'

Alistair thought about it. His best guess was that the company had been six or seven miles east of barracks when the lorry had come. He was reasonably sure that the two of them had walked in the right direction, but it was impossible to know at what rate. At times they had hardly made progress at all. They had travelled perhaps two or three miles in as many hours, and that they had between three and five more miles still to go.

'Not long at all now,' he said. 'Another hour should do it.'

'Juh . . . jolly good,' said Duggan. 'I have more of those buh . . . biscuits back at buh . . . barracks, you know.'

'Fine,' said Alistair. 'That will be just the ticket.'

'Stuh . . . steady on, old boy. I never suh . . . said I would share them.'

Alistair grinned, feeling the stretch in his numb cheeks for the first time in hours. He stood with difficulty, shouldered his pack and rifle, then felt for Duggan's hand to pull him up to his feet.

'Come on, you old dog, let's get you back to your kennel.'

They set out into the gale again, struggling forward with heavy boots.

Now, at last, came the longed-for hint of dawn. It came slowly, this restitution of shape to the world. With the cloud so thick and the sun still below the horizon it did not seem that the light came from any one origin but rather that the near tussocks and the distant berms and their own outstretched hands all glowed, each with their own pale effusion. It seemed like something holy. Even the wind relented and began to drop with the dawn. The rain slowed to a drizzle and the venom went out of it.

In the feeble light they came across parallel tracks with freshly cut tyre marks in the wet sedge. Now they had only to follow the lorry home. Both men understood then that they were saved. They looked at each other and smiled shyly, knowing that they would make it now, and that their friendship formed in the darkness would carry on into the light.

Duggan found his strength again. He no longer needed to hang on to Alistair's shoulder, and they walked side by side and made quicker progress into the west. The rain stopped entirely and the wind dropped. The base of the cloud began to rise. From beneath the earth the sun came up, red and ancient, contracting and brightening as it rose at their backs. Their long shadows preceded them across the plain.

'My buh . . . boots are killing me,' said Duggan with a grin. 'I miss cuh . . . comfy shoes. Are you for Chelseas or pumps?'

'I'm a loafer who favours a brogue.'

'I like a guh . . . good heel on a shoe and I don't care for those fuh . . . fussy leathers like pigskin or cuh . . . calfskin. Just give me something that can tuh . . . take a decent shine. I don't mind as far as the cuh . . . colour goes. Black is all right, I suppose, but tan is fine tuh . . . too and even a beige or—' He stepped on the unexploded artillery shell, and it tore him apart.

# NOVEMBER, 1939

At barracks Alistair kept returning to awareness to find himself engaged in some activity: showering, or shaving, or eating green soup and white rolls in the NAAFI. Men of all ranks came and talked at him soundlessly, and from their demeanour he tried to gauge which were offering consolation and which were giving orders. Officers seemed to be waiting for him to say something. He tried 'sir', but it did not make them leave him alone.

The explosion had deafened him. At dinner a single drop of blood splashed down beside his bowl and he stared until he understood that it had come from him. He traced its point of origin to his ear. Embarrassed, he left the table with his food untouched.

Alone in the dormitory, with his hearing beginning to return, he opened his locker. There was to be a kit inspection at dawn – there always was – and his equipment was a state. He balled up newspaper, stuffed it into his boots and stood them on the paraffin heater. It was against regulations, and Alistair knew that if the sergeant major saw it then he would say: 'THE REGULATIONS ARE THERE FOR A REASON. WHAT IF EVERYONE PUT THEIR BOOTS TO DRY ON TOP OF THIS PARAFFIN HEATER?' And Alistair, along with the other men present, would be required to suppress the answering voice that said: *Everyone would have dry boots.*

Alistair folded his two dress shirts into regulation rectangles and squared them away in the top left position in the locker, with the collar side at the back and the forward edge parallel to the edge of the metal shelf and one exact quarter-inch back from it. Some fellow sufferer in history had scored a line into the metal shelf of the locker, to facilitate the alignment. This was the only humanising decoration that Alistair had found in the barracks. In the caves of Lascaux he had seen aurochs and megaloceros daubed in mineral paint. In the restoration rooms of the Tate he had held his breath over Turner's brushwork.

He took off his trousers to fold them, and found an envelope in a pocket. The post had come during the day, clearly, and he must have lined up with the other men to receive it. There had been so many lines that day. Armoury, brigadier's office, laundry, infirmary. He had handed in his rifle, his report, his clothes, his body, until there was nothing left to surrender and he had been dismissed to light duties.

He opened the letter.

*Dear Alistair,*

*I, Caesar, have been keeping an eye on Tom for you – or rather, I have been keeping a rather fetching mother-of-pearl coat button on him, since that was what you saw fit to equip me with. I have much to report, so pin back your ears. (After all, you did pin back mine.)*

*Since you left for pastures more exciting, your flatmate has seen his own existence considerably enlivened. You know that I disapprove of humans and their laughable choices of mate, but in this case even I must admit that your friend Tom has picked a corker. Mary North is the loveliest thing I have ever seen, despite her damnable lack of tail and whiskers, and her strange habit of walking on her hind legs.*

Alistair put down the letter and went over to the paraffin stove. His boots steamed. He turned them to let the heel sides dry, and pulled out the tongues. He eyed the boots critically. It would be important to take them off the stove before they were absolutely crisp, or else the leather would ossify. Then he would get blisters on the next march – and the company didn't slow for blisters. You marched until they burst, and then until the flesh rubbed raw. Blisters were the true reason the men hated the enemy. The invasion of Poland was terrible, of course, but at least it was an event that had taken place outside of everyone's boots.

He returned to his cot and tried to make sense of the letter. He hadn't slept since reaching the barracks at seven that morning and collapsing at the gate. The high whining sound was still in his ears. He read the first paragraph again. Dimly he understood that his friend, Tom, was writing to him from the point of view of their stuffed cat. Caesar he could call to mind easily, fluid and feline as he stalked the old garret. He found it harder to recall Tom's face, and when he did so it was confounded with elements of Duggan's. The man had been so pale, prone on the red grass in the red bloom of the sunrise. His lips had seemed dark as cocoa, although of course they must have been blue. The red light had been blind to the colour. The dark lips had moved for a while – Duggan had said something – but Alistair's ears were blown. The lips, excused from their colour, had formed words relieved of their sound.

He noticed his hands holding the thin blue paper of the letter. Despite the shower he had taken, there was a black residue under his fingernails and in the creases of his knuckles. He had tried to hold Duggan's head up – he remembered it now. As if we hadn't all to drown.

*Last night Tom took Mary to see a show at the Hammersmith. I wasn't invited, I must disgustedly*

*observe, but from what ensued upon their return I must*
*conclude that the evening went well. Ah, Alistair, I always*
*said that you were astute, for a human! You noticed*
*straight away, of course, that I wrote 'upon their return',*
*and yes, it is quite true. Abandoning propriety, Tom*
*invited Mary to inspect the old garret, and inspect it she*
*did! You should have seen the scorn with which she*
*surveyed the living arrangements – I am quite sure that she*
*was one of your regimental sergeant majors in a past life.*
*And then, before Tom walked her home, the two of them*
*danced to the gramophone and – oh, I tell you what, I*
*can't be bothered to be the cat any more. Mary's a knock-*
*out, Alistair, that's what I'm trying to tell you, and I'm*
*grateful to you for making me go through with that first*
*dinner.*

The residue on his fingers troubled him now. He put the letter
down and ran hot water into a washbasin in the row at the end
of the dormitory. He dipped his hands and let them soak. The
blood dissolved from his fingers. It leached in tiny red clouds,
escaping from each fold of skin and diffusing until the water in
the white basin turned a pale orange. He dried his hands on his
vest.

*The thing is, Alistair, I am keener on her than she is on*
*me. I know she wants me to give her a job, and I fear that*
*as soon as she realises I have no job to give her then she*
*will be off. And then of course there is the issue of her*
*social standing—*

Alistair closed his eyes, thinking of their gramophone – the
Columbia portable with its shabby leatherette case. When one
opened it up there was unannounced wonder: the burnished

Plano-Reflecto tone arm, the plush red platter that the discs spun upon, glossy debs on a velveteen settee. It was perfectly built for peacetime: the balance of the tone arm assuming a stable foundation, the calm government of its rotation implying an excess of time.

*—since she is of an entirely different social class, and I cannot help but think that her interest in me might have more to do with what her family will think than with what she feels. But perhaps I am underestimating her. Perhaps you are thinking that I simply ought to take my courage in both hands and—*

Alistair let the letter fall. He wondered what they had danced to. Al Bowlly was the thing that season. 'Hold My Hand', if Tom had dared. Lying on his cot, Alistair heard the music quite clearly in his mind. *Hold my hand, No matter what the weather, Just you hold my hand, We'll walk through life together . . .* He thought of Tom dancing with the girl, and he was happy. Sleep came, finally, with the music swelling into the vacuum in his mind where there had only been that high, thin whining. The gramophone spun and he slept, with the letter still in his hand. He had kissed Duggan as he was dying. It had seemed the only thing to do.

The company stood around Alistair's cot now. No one spoke. One man brought a blanket and laid it over him. Another took Alistair's boots from the paraffin heater before they desiccated, and rubbed black polish into them and buffed them up and aligned them carefully on his locker. There was always an inspection at dawn.

# MARCH, 1940

At breakfast Palmer brought the post on a pewter tray. The silver was used only when Mary's father was in residence – this being one of a hundred idiosyncrasies that might have originated in some long-forgotten instruction from the family, or arisen spontaneously from the coppery circuitry in Palmer's internal machinery that gauged what was fitting. If Palmer were lost to them, along with the stock of method and lore of which he alone was the repository, then Mary felt sure the family would be obliged to disband. They would screech apart from one another as atoms released from their bond. Palmer, then: with the morning post, on the pewter tray that lent the white envelopes an oysterish hue.

'Oh!' said Mary. 'Here's another one from Zachary.'

'But look here,' said Hilda, 'you are hardly the nigger's mother.'

'No, I daresay I would have noticed.'

Hilda, who hadn't Mary's facility for overlooking Palmer's hovering presence, coloured slightly. Mary took Zachary's letter from the envelope.

'I hope you don't encourage him by replying?' said Hilda.

'Darling, I wrote to him first. Anyway, must you call him "nigger"? It doesn't seem entirely big-hearted.'

Hilda yawned. 'I'll say ten Hail Marys.'

'The negroes are no viler than we, you know. In faculty, fitness and faith they are our perfect equal.'

'Hardly!' said Hilda. 'But I've nothing against them. I might even prefer them to other foreigners – since at least one knows where one stands.'

'Does one?'

'Well, one really oughtn't to write to one.'

'Stop it,' said Mary. 'Anyway, this won't be writing so much as marking the child's work. Honestly, look at this!'

*Deere Miss Northe, I doe note licke the villije the uthae chilrene are verie meene. I doe note licke the howse waire I am staeine the woemane is verie verie meene.*

Hilda squinted at the pencil work. 'How old do you say the child is?'

'He is ten.'

'And is this him writing with his fingers, or his toes? Only I've heard they have equal facility with both.'

'Oh, tosh. His fingers are used for the extraction of nasal mucus, or for counting when under duress. His feet are reserved for football. He is no different from any other boy, you see, except that his spelling is quite original. He is a perfect spark, only no one bothers to teach the negroes properly.'

Hilda sniffed. 'He spells as if he has picked up a job lot of letter "e"s on the cheap, and now is anxious to offload them.'

'But wouldn't you? If I had never been taught to spell, I daresay I might chuck in an "e" whenever reasonable doubt arose.'

'You're saying you can't blame him?'

Mary gave an approving look. 'Now you're getting it.'

*The uthere childrene chaese me and whene theye catche me theye tacke offe my claothes and theye hurte me wythe styckes ore nyves plese helpe me.*

Mary's smile froze.

'Yes,' said Hilda, reading over her shoulder, 'but children exaggerate, don't they?'

*And I am soe colde it is soe colde hiere plese helpe.*

Mary put the letter down on the pewter tray.

'I'm quite sure it can't be so bad as all that,' said Hilda. 'With my nephews, one simply has to remind them to jolly well wear a jumper.'

'Perhaps I ought to go to him.'

'Yes, and perhaps you should knit him balaclavas, and bake him flapjacks iced with your tears, and send him woollen socks.'

'Oh, do put a woollen sock in it.'

'But he is in the Cotswolds, darling, not the Crimea.'

Mary ignored her. 'I will go to see the child's father.'

Hilda snorted.

'No, really. I will talk to him, and express my concerns.'

'But what good will that do?'

'He probably doesn't understand our system. He most likely does not realise that he has a perfect right to bring his son back home.'

'Sorry to nit-pick,' said Hilda, 'but you see, there's a war.'

'Yes, but do you really think there'll be bombing? This beastly thing has droned on for how long now?'

'Six months.'

'And the only pasting we've had is with posters urging valour.'

'Even so, you're hardly going to tell the father to bring the boy home.'

'Surely it is my duty to tell him that he *could*. This is the thing, you see: unless one more or less lives with the authorities, as I do, one probably doesn't understand that one can simply say "no thank you".'

'So you are planning to walk into a negro family's house—'

'I was planning to knock.'

'—and tell them what they should do with their child.'

'What they could usefully do, yes.'

'Notwithstanding your belief that they are just as intelligent as us.'

Mary frowned. 'You are a mousetrap of a friend, all soft cheese and hard springs.'

'I use you for practice. One day I'll have a husband.'

Mary took a second envelope from the tray. 'God help the poor man.'

'God will take my side,' said Hilda. 'He is only human, after all.'

'Oh!' said Mary, blushing slightly. 'This one's from Tom.'

'Come on, read it out.'

Mary drew Tom's letter closer. 'I think I might rather—'

'Oh go on! Don't be such a prude!'

'It's just that I'd—'

A cough came from the end of the breakfast room, by the double doors, which had swung open soundlessly. Palmer's cough had the twin qualities of apology and watershed. Mary thought him the very best.

'Miss Hilda?' he said.

'Yes?'

'I have taken the opportunity to stop a cab for you.'

Hilda blinked. 'Oh. Yes. Well, thank you, Palmer.'

The imperceptible nod. The dispassionate eyes, already fading from memory. Palmer's face had the property of oneness with the crockery and the dado rails, while his structuring of the day had the feature of seeming contiguous with one's own desires – so that Hilda, even as she stood, must already be convinced that she had somehow wanted the taxi. Mary supposed that an asset like Palmer would be a supreme unguent

74

in these times of heightened stress at the ministries. She felt a twinge of apprehension at the thought that he might be requisitioned.

She kissed Hilda on both cheeks, waved her off down the steps into the drizzling morning, and opened Tom's letter in the hallway.

*Dear Miss North,*

So: Tom was 'Miss North'ing her, on headed notepaper from the Education Authority. Mary thought she might fall down. She leaned against the hall stand with its cut-glass jar of peonies. She hadn't thrown wine over Tom at their last dinner. Nor had she gone the other way, undressing over dessert. All she had done – and this hardly seemed to merit the official stationery treatment – was to have drunk slightly too much and to have asked him, quite politely, if he wouldn't mind kissing her.

*Dear Miss North,*
*From the records of this office I see that following your*
*release from your posting to Hawley Street School you*
*have no current role with the Authority.*

Mary felt that she might cry. It wasn't as if she had hidden it.

*I note also your several requests to this office to be*
*allowed to resume your war service in teaching.*

Oh – perhaps she had slightly nagged him. But she had been quite fun about the whole thing – or at least she had tried to be – and the awkward truth of it was that she really did want to teach, and she really did like him. Perhaps she had been clumsy in asking to have both. She read Tom's next line through splayed fingers, in case it was too awful for words.

*I am therefore pleased to inform you of your selection by this office for a new position that has been created at Hawley Street School. You are to report to—*

Mary read no further until she was already in a cab.

*You are to report to these offices to collect keys and then make the building ready. You are to select one classroom of robust construction with access to basement or cellar in case of air raid. You are to make arrangements in anticipation of a class of mixed ages and abilities.*

If Tom's intention had been to avoid any appearance of impropriety by keeping the communication official, then she rather subverted it by rushing to his office, dragging him out to the café over the road, and drinking only three sips of tea before kissing him on the cheek. He touched his face as if her lips might have left a tangible remainder: a smoking impact crater, or an epistolary X with the ink still wet below the signature.

Later, when she was alone in the raw wet wind, strangers smiled at her in the street. It was eerie. The raindrops were champagne bubbles bursting on her skin. The iridescent spills of fuel oil on the wet tarmac of the road were tiny proofs of the covenant.

She supposed she must be in love. That Tom was slightly infuriating, and that she didn't mind in the slightest, might be proof of it. And of course it would be nice if he were more daring about the whole thing, but she could be patient. Soon Tom would realise that there was nothing more important than Mary North – that it was only her sorcery causing the planets to stay aligned and preventing the milk from curdling.

Almost as strange as being in love was being in it with someone she liked: someone her mother would not countenance nor Hilda even consider. Without the war, how would one ever meet an ordinary man like Tom?

And here was what she wanted to know (now that she had left the café, and London closed around her with its smell of coal smoke and lorry exhaust and Tube ventings and railway grease and frying and horse droppings and wet masonry and exhaled cigarettes and damp worsted overcoats and quick brown water coursing in the gutters and slow brown water infusing with disintegrating newsprint in the puddles, along with the flotilla of butts already smoked) – here was what she wanted to know (as the clouds made the day dark and she pulled her mackintosh tight and crossed Chalk Farm Road between the cars with their slotted headlights that made them look as if they had just arisen after a heavy night and were fumbling for the tin of aspirin) – here was what she wanted to know: was one meant to feel certain, about love?

She carried on down Chalk Farm Road, lighting a cigarette and exhaling a little of her buoyancy. Her feet seemed to touch the pavement again, and it was wet, and she noticed the water stains on the mid-tan leather of her Oxfords.

After their last dinner – the slightly-too-much-wine dinner – they had gone for a walk on Hampstead Heath, in a mist so thick as to have been almost a paste. You could have lost your gloves in the fog and found them half an hour later, still suspended in the air at wrist height. She had tried to get them lost in the vapours but he, misreading the situation entirely, had piloted them back to safe streets with a quiet and unerring skill. If it had rather irked her that she must contrive to produce in Tom the behaviours her mother insisted held primacy in all men, then she had forgiven him on the spot when he gave her a shy, proud smile. Her heart had lifted in her chest, as the magazines insisted it must.

She remembered him like that now: transported from cares, his cheeks damp from the mist and flushed for once with something other than embarrassment. Was it love that she felt? Or did she just find him sweet for not allowing them to become lost on Hampstead Heath and only discovered years later, with her mackintosh in tatters and his beard down to his knees?

Mary hurried on and tried to pick out the landmarks. The worst of it was that people were still high on the intrigue of the war, and prone to suspicion if you asked them for directions. Such people, and they were not always joking, would ask you who was the Prime Minister – as if no enemy spy could possibly speak the name without combusting.

How much better it would be to ask her: If you are one of us then how – hypothetically – would you know if the trembling physical feeling you had for a man, say, five years your senior, handsome without being a knockout, and from a slightly inferior social background to your own but not in such a way that it was necessarily a problem provided that you remembered to show him the right way to hold a sherry glass before he met your father – how would you know if that feeling was love?

The worst thing would be to decide that it was love, and then discover – after one was taken – that it hadn't been. No: the worst thing would be to decide that it wasn't love, and then to discover years later – old and unconsoled – that it had been. No: the worst thing – the worst, worst thing – was this having to decide.

She sighed, and turned left into Hawley Street. She hadn't had a moment to really look at the school until now. It was a grimly masculine building, red bricks set off in three frugal bands by courses of hard London yellows. The windows rose from wide sills to gothic arches; the gables were decked out with barge boards and topped with lanceolate finials. Mary thought these the most fun bits of the building: these spikes aimed skywards, impalers of trespassing angels.

She stepped from the gloom of the street into the dark of the school and used her cigarette lighter to find the switch. The bulbs came on down the corridor. Mary wrinkled her nose. There was a lot of dust, thin in the centre of the corridor and deeper at the skirting boards where the draught had piled it into drifts. There were the tracks of gnawing creatures, the serpentine lines swept by their naked tails and a crusting and crumbing of the dust where their urine had soaked and dried. All this dust, and the shuttered school smell of inkwells and spit balls and apple cores gone rotten in desks. What could she do about it all, alone, even with soap flakes and an optimistic outlook and three days to go until Monday morning?

The quiet, too, was unsettling. Into this air multiplication tables had been recited, the changeless alphabet chanted, the four house songs sung in quadratic symmetry. The Lord's Prayer had been intoned by impish voices with every imaginable variation and subversion. And now the unceasing hymn was struck dumb. If the war so far was a phoney one, this silence was real.

She went from classroom to classroom, switching on the lights. She tried to brush off the solemn mood that was settling on her. Of course a school made one feel rather alone. The rows of desks in each room, the stacks of identical hymnals, the massed coat hooks lining the wall: the multiplicity of everything was bound to single one out.

She went first to the classroom – Kestrels class – that had been hers in September. She realised it wouldn't be suitable. It was robust enough – all the classrooms were built from spine and vim in the good Victorian manner – but it wasn't close enough to a basement. She walked the corridors, opening doors until she found one that led down wooden stairs.

Below ground, the smell was older. She found superannuated atlases in tumbling piles, with the earth's poles marked by whirlpools. There were the musty props of ancient school plays

– Tuck's staff, Banquo's shroud, Peter Pan's cap. A maypole lay askew, bound in its own ribbons. In the glow of her lighter's flame the hoard stretched away into blackness. Fifty children could shelter down here if needs must.

Mary knelt to sift the treasures. Here were cross-stitched samplers, and mouldering report cards with examination results for needlework and recitation. Here were handwriting exercises with passages dutifully copied: *At the door on summer evenings sat the little Hiawatha / Heard the whispering of the pine trees, Heard the lapping of the water.*

She felt five years old, and five hundred. Here was the remainder of ten thousand educations, the bones drifted down to this depth. It was the fossil of one's country. She ached, because the war had cut the thin cord that bound each child to its ancestors with links made from cross-stitch and calligraphy. She walked up into the corridor. The school was absolutely silent. How violent it was, this peace where children's voices should be. The ache in her chest hardened to anger, until she shook with it.

Sparrows classroom was closest to the cellar. She gauged what needed to be done. The boards would have to come off the tall windows, for a start. If a raid came – well, that was what the cellar was for, but until then her classroom would be a place of light. And the dust would have to be swept, and the mustiness purged with vigorous airing. If a ladder and paint could be found then she would get the children to restore these walls to white.

This parquet floor would scrub up, these chairs would rediscover their élan after a once-around with screwdriver and sponge, and as for the desks with their intricate chronicle of graffiti, either they could be sanded bare, or the opinions of generations of pupils could be allowed to stand. Mary found that she didn't much mind either way. Beyond the superficial errors of spelling there was little that she felt justified in correcting, after all, when she read the collective wisdom concerning Miss Vine.

At the front of the classroom the mice had got onto the teaching desk and eaten the carton away from the chalk, so that it lay splayed. They had eaten the bitter leather from the corners of the gym mats piled in the corner. They had taken the barren seeds from the beanbags that were used for throw-and-catch. They took what the war could give them.

Mary gathered the chalk and found a pot for it. She wrote her name on the blackboard: 'Mary North'. Then, to see how it might look, she rubbed out 'North' and wrote Tom's surname, forming the letters slowly and carefully in the exemplary hand required for blackboard work. When her fingers gripped the chalk, the pink blood shrank from the knuckles so that something of chalk's nature seemed to seep into her.

*Mary Shaw.*

To see how it might sound, as she turned from the board she said brightly to the room: 'Hello, class. My name is Mrs Shaw.'

She lifted her hands to her mouth. Tom was standing in the doorway of the classroom. His efforts to disappear were to his credit, but unsupported by a pitiless physics that refused to let him vanish. He squirmed and tried to shrink behind the door, and gave up on that and instead pretended to have been whistling a tune. He gave up on that too, since if he really hadn't heard what she had said, then here it was, inscribed on the blackboard in the Marion Richardson script that was favoured for the modern and unambiguous manner in which the letters were made.

*You silly girl*, she thought. *If he has any sense he will never speak to you again.* And the worst thing about it, as she watched his resigned smile, was that she really did like him a lot. His awkwardness was gone, in this moment when it finally couldn't matter any more. There was something honest in his surrender to the situation. It was only now that she understood how difficult it must have been for him, to like her and to be petitioned by

her at the same time. All he had needed was for her to understand that things should be taken carefully and slowly. She
dropped her hands and mirrored his sad smile.

'Sorry,' she said.

He watched her in the half-light of the electric bulbs.

'No,' he said. 'It's I who should apologise, Mrs Shaw – it seems
that I am late to this class. Have you already taken the register?'

She hesitated, then beamed. 'Oh! I mean . . . well, as it
happens, you're in time. I was just about to do it.'

He gestured at the rows of desks. 'Oh, so may I . . .?'

'Yes . . . oh yes, sit anywhere. No, actually – sit down here at
the front where I can keep an eye on you.'

She invested her face with the appropriate severity. He took a
desk in the front row. His knees came halfway to his chin when
he sat in the tiny chair. He laughed. She frowned.

'Settle down.'

From the drawer of the teacher's desk she took a pencil and
the register book, blew off the dust and opened it to the first
fresh sheet. At the top she wrote: *Sparrows Class, Spring Term,
1940*. She wrote Tom's name on the first ruled line.

'Tom Shaw?'

'Present.'

'Splendid,' she said, looking at his name on the clean page.
'Well, you are my first.'

# APRIL, 1940

'I'm quite sure you're doing it wrong,' said Hilda, wincing as Mary dug the comb into her scalp.

'This preposterous hairdo is wrong. I'm following the instructions exactly.'

'Oh do give it here,' said Hilda, snatching American *Vogue* and jabbing at the illustration of Step 3. 'See? It says to tease. And you are back-combing.'

'I am teasing.'

'You aren't,' said Hilda. 'And I should know.'

'Oh do it yourself then, if you're so good.'

Mary threw the comb onto Hilda's dressing table, where it clattered against the china pigs she kept there. She lit a cigarette and flopped on the end of Hilda's bed.

'All right,' said Hilda. 'I'm sorry. Perhaps it just wants more sugar water.'

'Are you sure? When it dries you'll look like an iced bun.'

'You're jealous I thought of it first.'

'Hardly, Hilda. What we see laid out in these instructions is not a hairdo. It is a folly.'

'Then it is a folly everyone's wearing this season.'

'And therefore you suppose that officers will be attracted to it.'

'With any luck they'll lick it. Keep going with the sugar, won't you?'

Mary raised an eyebrow. 'You're sweet enough.'

Hilda made a pleading face in the dressing-table mirror. 'Don't leave me half done like this. I look like Frankenstein's mistress.'

'It's an improvement.'

'Charming. Is this how you are with the children in your class?'

'Oh no, as Miss North I am sweetness and light. That's why I have all this frustration to take out on you.'

'Have you any more pupils yet?'

'Still only four. One mongol, one cripple and two that barely speak.'

'He has done you proud, that man of yours.'

Mary stubbed out her cigarette. 'It will take time. More will come once the parents realise that there isn't to be any bombing.'

'Still, if it were me I shouldn't bother. It seems an awful lot of trouble to go to, opening a school for the sake of four no-hopers.'

'That's the difference between us. I want a better world, you want better hair.'

'Hardly as an end in itself. I want the hairdo so I can get a man in uniform.'

Mary sighed, stood, and picked up the comb again. Hilda smiled at her in the mirror, and Mary returned the favour.

'Your face is not entirely dreadful to behold, you know,' said Mary, angling Hilda's head. 'You might almost pull off this look, in conditions of very low light.'

'Sadly your flaws as a friend would be visible in pitch dark.'

'You are indolent and asinine,' said Mary.

'You are obstinate and self-satisfied,' said Hilda.

Mary worked as well as she could, segmenting the hair on the top of Hilda's head into bands, front to back, and pushing each band in turn down to its roots with the comb until it developed sufficient body to bolster itself. It was rewarding work, what with gravity being such a bully and hair so plainly the underdog. Hilda's scalp was warm and the air in her room was pleasantly muggy with breath and cigarette smoke, while a fresh rain lashed the window and ran down the pane and caused Pimlico to warp and swim.

'And your mother?' said Hilda, after a while.

'Barely seen her in days. I had hoped to show her the school, now I'm no longer pretending, but she is too busy whoring for Father. He is set on becoming a cabinet minister, and of course there are luncheons and functions.'

'I'd murder to have your mother. If mine has ambition then it is somewhere at the back of a drawer.'

'Yes but here is the war – don't you see? – shaking everything up. Father's world seems so small now. All those closed committees of men who were at school together. All the beaming wives competing. All of us daughters racing for husbands when the trap opens. Glossy fillies that we are, keeping dutifully in our lanes.'

'Just so long as you stay out of mine.'

'Careful, Hilda – remember who has the hair pins.'

'Well don't come crying when you grow out of your little pauper.'

'Tom is hardly poor.'

'He lives in an attic, for pity's sake. You told me so yourself.'

'Yes, but—'

'An *attic*, Mary. I'm sure you don't love him at all. You only love the idea of your mother's face when she meets him.'

Mary ignored her. She layered the bands of aerated hair, starting at the back and working towards the forehead to make a gratifying mound.

'It's the same reason you write to that negro,' said Hilda. 'It's to say to your mother, *Look at me!* If I were you I would simply go to her lunches and dinners. Smash the teacups if you must.

Kiss the Minister of Aircraft Production. But at least do it when your mother is jolly well watching.'

Mary fixed her with a pitying look. 'I write to Zachary because he is a human being.'

'Is that what you told his father? He must have been impressed.'

Mary turned Hilda's head left and right in the mirror, a little more sharply than was absolutely necessary. 'I told him that he might consider bringing his child home. And that I could assure him of a school place, with a shelter in the event of any raid.'

'Did he look at you like this?' said Hilda, making a rubbery grimace and widening her eyes to make saucers of incomprehension.

'He wore a coat and tie like any man, and received me very civilly.'

'Did you make him presents of coloured glass beads?'

'He told me about his life in America.'

'And counted the spoons when you left.'

Mary smiled. 'Your attitude is just like society's.'

'Oh good,' said Hilda.

Mary lifted the hand mirror so Hilda could see herself from the back.

'Interesting,' said Hilda.

'What is?' said Mary.

'Nothing,' said Hilda, supposing that it would have to do until she could get to the salon.

# MAY, 1940

In the garret Tom lay back against the bolster and drew on the cigarette Mary put to his lips. The cigarette's pull lit them up, flaring and fading again.

Outside, wardens policed the blackout. Light, which had always united the city in a universal glow, had shrunk back into points. It was its old self again: a privateer, a dweller in nooks. People sheltered flames from draughts. Shadows grew by accretion, thickening nightly, as if the day wouldn't rinse off the dark.

Tom blew smoke at the ceiling. Mary curled her foot around his. He held back a laugh.

'What?' said Mary.

'Nothing.'

'Tell or be sorry.' She plucked at the hairs on his chest.

'Ow! I was just thinking how different it feels.'

She looked wistful as she tapped ash from her cigarette. 'You won't love me any more, now that we've done it.'

'It isn't that.'

'What, then?'

'Actually,' he said, 'I was thinking how much more I love you.'

In truth this is what he had been thinking: that from now on – at work, on the bus, in the park – he would have more fellow feeling with dogs who were sexually experienced than with men who were still virgins.

'And what are you thinking?' he said.

Mary was thinking how much she was enjoying the war. The passions, which had been confused against the general glare, could flicker in the blackout. With love, one could glow. One did not need the intense flame after all. Now she could feel as she did – happy – as the ancients evidently had and her mother probably hadn't. The capital's heart had moved from Pimlico to Piccadilly, where the loud circus of electric bulbs was silenced and Eros, unsighted and teetering on his pedestal, now loosed his arrows into the dark. London lit her up from the inside. The great diurnal city learned the language of the night.

She said, 'I was thinking I love you.'

'I love you too.'

'But you are a man. You will move on, to plunder the next settlement.'

He nodded. 'Primrose Hill.'

'Or Hampstead.'

'Can't I plunder you a bit more first?'

She inspected her nails. 'From time to time, I daresay. If I have nothing on.'

'I like you best when you've nothing on.'

She flicked his thigh. 'Dirty old man.'

'I'm twenty-four.'

'Yes. It's indecent.'

He worried that it was. 'I do love you, you know.'

'But do you really?'

'Yes.'

'But do you *really*, Tom?'

'Absolutely. I'd show you the readings on my dials, but we would have to open the inspection hatch in my chest.'

'Could we? I should like to be sure.'

'I didn't bring the right tools.'

She rolled onto her back and blew smoke in a slow blue jet. 'I hate you.'

He frowned. 'You can't prove it.'

'I haven't got dressed for you. I won't even get out of bed for you.'

'Not even if I do . . . this?'

'Especially not if you do that.'

She put the cigarette to his lips again and he drew on it. The flare lit up two pale discs in the darkness of the garret: Caesar's button eyes, watching from the top of the piano. *For god's sake cheer up*, Tom told himself involuntarily. His muscles tensed.

'What's wrong, darling?'

'Nothing,' he said, but the moment was broken. She rolled onto her stomach to stub out the cigarette.

Tom realised, with a guilty ache, that he hadn't thought about Alistair for days. Lately his friend's letters made him miserable. Of a long march with heavy packs Alistair had offered: *The trick is to wear two pairs of socks, one thin and one thick.* Of life in barracks he had written: *It is gayer if one takes the view that it is Butlin's with guns.* There was no substance. His last really personal letter had come months ago, in December, when Alistair had written rather rawly about a soldier who had been blown up in training. Since then, the distance between them had started to show in the letters.

Tom tried to put Alistair out of his mind. It was four o'clock on Saturday morning. The wine was nearly finished. They had another hour of darkness before the daylight came. Mary rolled onto her back and lit up again, and he put his hand between her thighs.

She blew a smoke ring. 'This war is amazing. Is that terrible to say?'

'Well I shouldn't go writing it on the blackboard.'

'I am nineteen and I have a school of my own. I can teach the children however I like, and I can hug them when they graze their knees.'

Tom thought it was lovely that she was so happy, but it was a shame that she was still talking, given that his hand was where it was.

He said, 'You'd have found something terrific, even without the war.'

'You and I wouldn't have been thrown together. Thinking about it makes my head spin. Imagine how many there are like us, at this moment, lying in bed because the war has brought them close. In Cairo. In Paris.'

'Yes.' He moved his hand between her legs.

She said, 'In Germany, too, I suppose.'

This caused his hand to stop. The continuation should have been natural. There should have been bliss, and instead here were the Germans.

'Steady on,' he said. 'The Hun do not go to bed with one another.'

'Well then, and how do they make little Hun?'

'In factories on the Ruhr. According to detailed blueprints. I don't know.'

He wished she would leave it. Beyond the four corners of the bed, the world could go to hell and seemed determined to exercise that privilege. To speak of it was to bring it under the covers with them, into the warmth and the darkness. And now he couldn't stop thinking of it. Far out there in the night somewhere, his best friend was shivering in a bunk, with bromide in his tea and postcards of Betty Grable. He felt guilty again, and sighed.

'What's wrong?' Mary said.

'It's just that I feel such a shit.'

'Whatever for?'

'For not joining up. For being here when the world is there.'

Mary stubbed out her cigarette. The movement set the bedsprings quivering. His hand, between her legs, could neither

sensibly advance nor retreat now but simply cupped her, fool-
ishly, with its own instinctive tenderness.

She said, 'You aren't meant to be a soldier.'

'Why not? I could fight.'

'You couldn't shoot someone.'

She stroked his face. It seemed to him that her touch traced his
limits.

'I could kill if I had to.' Immediately he felt the absurdity of it
as a boast.

She smiled. He flushed. 'Well perhaps you don't believe it, but
I could.'

He took his hand from between her legs, propping himself on
one elbow in the dark. She flicked on her cigarette lighter. In the
provisional light it made between them, she looked at him so
calmly that he was ashamed.

'God,' he said. 'I'm sorry.'

'Don't be.'

She snapped the lighter shut, and in the quick darkness he saw
the bright negative of the flame. She rolled onto her side and
took his hand and put it back between her legs. 'If they call you
up for the war, go. Until then, don't spoil it.'

'Mary, I . . .'

'Shh, darling. Let's not let the war win.'

He moved his face close to hers. 'When I said *I love you*,
before?'

'Yes?'

'I didn't mean it. But now I think that I do.'

'Oh yes. Oh, me too.'

Tom understood why the good actors in the movies never said
it with a smile. To be in love was to understand how alone one
had been before. It was to know that if one were ever alone again,
there would be no exemption from the agony of it. It wasn't the
happiest feeling.

Afterwards, she laid her head on his chest and yawned. Her copper hair spilled over him. They shared a cigarette and her face, with its sheen of perspiration, reflected the orange glow.

He said, 'Do you want to sleep?'

She considered the question as if the idea were new, then shook her head. It was raining and a grey light loomed in the garret, threatening to return all things to their quotidian form. Tom felt the grip of an unnameable fear but Mary lit another cigarette and smiled at him so impishly that it restored his faith. The bright sexual smell of her, her slightly comical frown of concentration, her breasts quivering as she worked the wheel of the lighter. Her slim belly as she sat up in bed to find the ashtray. The rain came in squalls, hard as handfuls of rice against the window.

He made them both tea, in the jam jars they used for cups, and climbed back into bed. They sat against the headboard and leaned shoulders. They were tired, their eyes cast inward. They forgot to sip the pale tea. The steam condensed on the inner rims of the jars.

He said, 'Have you ever been . . . you know. In bed with anyone before?'

She blinked. 'Oh yes.'

As if it were nothing. Tom's fear returned. He supposed he had been perfectly prepared for her answer to be yes or no, but this third possibility had not even slightly occurred to him: that perhaps it really *was* nothing. It had seemed the most important thing that had ever happened to him. But of course he had been a fool. He felt as if he could easily cry.

He wouldn't let himself, of course. He would set his face just like this: in this worldly grin. And when their conversation naturally picked up again he would engage in the new topic with all levity. As if yes, this were nothing, and that therefore this feeling he had – that he had been struck through like the clumsy first draft of a letter – were nothing, too. And still . . . and still.

He realised he didn't mind if she had slept with five men, or even a dozen: he just wanted Mary – who had trembled in his arms and crushed her face into his neck – he just wanted Mary to speak about what had happened as if it were *something*. Tears threatened again and he stopped them.

She was digging him in the ribs.

'Darling?' he said, keeping his tone light.

She prodded him again and he turned to look. She was watching him strangely and he didn't understand. There was so much, he now realised, that he did not understand. He had lost his virginity – sailed to a place where land had been marked on the chart – and yet here was just more open sea.

He could not decipher her eyes. An anxiety came over him that she wanted them to make love again. He didn't know if he could. Then he worried that perhaps making love was not what she wanted at all, and that maybe this strange and terrible look she was giving him was something else, a prelude to the sort of conversation where she would be serious and kind. She would speak softly, noticing the lateness of the hour, and saying that perhaps they should sleep after all. And then, as soon as the time was decent for young women to take to the streets, she would excuse herself and leave.

He stroked her cheek. How pathetic he was. She had seen his reaction, and she must think him ridiculous. Now that she was certain to leave, he understood that he did not even care if she felt nothing for him, or for any of the men she had slept with. What he could not bear was to be without her. How dreadful the days would be from now on. How empty.

She smiled.

'What is it?' he said.

'I haven't slept with anyone else.'

'So why . . .?'

She took his hand. 'I wanted to see if it counted for you.'

Above them the dawn sounded with engines. Tom drew the blanket around them. He held Mary close in the improvised darkness. How bedclothes would protect them, he didn't know. The engine noise drew nearer and increased in volume until it was directly overhead, rattling the windows. Then it faded away to the east. Aircraft were being delivered, or pilots trained – that was all – and afterwards they laughed at their own fear.

At sunrise, with the rain blown over and the wet pavements gleaming, they went for a walk. They wore the clothes they had worn to the dance the night before, since Mary had no others and Tom saw no need to let her be the only one. They strolled easily together, holding hands and swinging their arms and making no strenuous effort to avoid the puddles, being both of them protected by love against discomforts of any kind.

The streets were still nearly empty – London was theirs alone – and if from time to time it pleased the lovers that a bread van should drive past on its rounds, or a policeman walk by on his beat, or the last fox of the night nose for scraps in an alley, then they caused it to be so. They strolled until the pavements grew busy around them and the traffic began to clot in the streets. They walked and they did not need anything at all, until very suddenly they needed everything. They understood that they were famished and so they ran into a café and ate like wolves. They drank dark stewed tea that made their teeth buzz in their sockets. Afterwards he decided that he must absolutely buy her a book, and she decided that she must absolutely buy him a paper knife, and they went in and out of shops until these things were done, and then they were calm again.

They sat together on a bench in Trafalgar Square, holding the new things in their hands and being delighted with them, while Tom also felt solemn in a way that had no limiting degree. They watched the grubby pigeons flock.

She yawned and laid her head on his shoulder.

'Are you tired?' he said. 'Shall we go back to the flat and sleep?'

'I ought to get home. Palmer will fret.'

'Your dog?'

'Yes,' she said, and wondered why she had. The distance between them was nothing – and simultaneously it was so huge that, in the moment, she had not found the heart to speak of it. She felt a heavy sadness.

'What are you thinking?' he said.

'How glad I am. What are you thinking?'

He was considering the idea of her having a home, a pet, two parents. He had not given any thought at all to the concept that she hadn't simply materialised in the world, at eighteen, in perfect crimson lipstick, laughing, at the exact spatial coordinates and the exact time at which he had first met her. She was so perfectly unique that the idea of her being made ordinary by friends – oh, and worse, by family – made his chest sink unbearably.

He said, 'The same. So glad.'

She kissed him. 'I should go.'

'Oh . . . yes. Yes, of course.' He gave her an anxious look. 'What do you suppose you should tell your family?'

She stroked his cheek. 'I shall tell Father I stayed overnight with my friend Hilda. I shall tell Mother you are lovely.'

'You will tell her?'

'Women share everything. It's the blessing we received when we turned down muscles and moustaches.'

He squeezed her hand. 'I'll walk you to the Tube.'

She didn't tell him that she never caught the Tube. (She wondered if one bought a ticket beforehand, or whether there was an inspector who came through the carriage.) They got up from the bench and walked back across Trafalgar Square, breaking into a run to scare the pigeons. They ran, breathless and laughing and desperately sad, with their hands clasped tight and the birds clattering up before them. They flocked and swirled and ascended through the city's blanketing cloud, emerging into the sky. A life unmoored from the embattled earth, a thing begun again, looping and wheeling in the pacific air.

Mary held tight to Tom's hand and thought it heartless that the two of them had to stay below, in London.

She said, 'I'll be fine from here.'

'I wish you hadn't to go.'

'Just until Monday. Come and pick me up after work.'

'But will you be all right?'

She said, 'Why would I not be all right?'

He thought about her question. In fact there were so many reasons. Of course there was the war, which he increasingly believed might bring death from the sky at any time despite his own insistence that the thing would fizzle out. Then there were orders which could come quite arbitrarily, posting either of them to another city, or another country, where distance would begin to work its curse of transforming a lover's hand into handwriting.

There were mechanical accidents: machinery was well known to be full of spite for slim bodies such as the one he now clung to. Bearings lived to seize, axles to shear, cables to snap. Accidents of the heart were a worry, too. She was beautiful: other men could see this as well as he. She was bright and unconventional and her faithfulness could not be assumed. There would come suitors who were taller, or richer, or – most dreadful of all – who could make her laugh. How he feared men who could make her laugh.

Next there was disease: less of a threat than good humour but still not to be entirely discounted. Influenza came once in each generation and was overdue in theirs. Cancer or consumption might take her. A scratch on her finger might fester, a cold sore give ingress to a greater chill. There was a whole category of mishaps inseparable from physics – the tumble, the slip and the choke; collision, combustion and shock. And of course he could not even begin to quantify the risks posed by third parties. Friends might queer her affections. Fiends in alleyways might murder her or worse. Her parents, picking from a list of his faults, might seize on his pacifism or his poverty. They might set about dissuading their daughter, using all the tricks of their art. It was not a level playing field where parents were concerned: they had known her in every year of her life, he not yet in every season of the year.

Finally there were the imponderables of memory and the psyche. She could wake up tomorrow with no recollection that she had ever known him. Or she could walk past a café and stop dead in her tracks, overcome by desire for the waiter. And worse than all of these things, because so much more likely, were the mundane human dissatisfactions that absence would allow to incubate. What if he had said something to unsettle her – a single word could be enough – and she, brooding on it, came to decide that he did not truly love her? Or what if he had been unsatisfactory in bed? The more he thought about it now, the more he worried that there was something he should have done but had not – or, worse, something he had done too much of. At times they had moaned like animals. Surely this was monstrous? Surely in solitude she would now reflect with shame, and not wish to see him again?

These were only the first thoughts that came. The more he considered it – oh god, her lovely face with that mocking little grin – the more causes there were for anxiety. Separation was air in the lungs of fate, and so when it was time for them to part after their first night together and he asked her, 'Will you be all right?' and she replied, 'Why would I not be all right?', in fact so many reasons presented themselves that it immediately began to seem fantastically improbable, if he let go of her warm hand now and allowed her to walk away into this grey morning that smelled of spring, that they would ever see each other again.

It seemed so much safer to stay close and to let the great disintegrating power of the world do its work on other lovers instead. But since he did not know how to put all of this in a way that would not seem pathetic, he simply said: 'All right, I shall see you on Monday.'

It was not the same as charging down a machine-gun nest armed only with a Bowie knife, or strapping in to the tail-gunner seat of a four-engined heavy bomber. And no one else would ever know, of course – since one did not get a medal for letting go of a woman's hand on a grey Saturday morning in the middle of a European war. But to have faith – that a lover would be constant and life clement – this did require courage in a city more disposed to beginnings than safe continuations.

As she walked away from him he turned his back, to show that he could.

For her part, Mary did not find it at all difficult to walk away from Tom. She simply walked for a while, wearing yesterday's clothes. Yes, the war was a blind roulette. Yes, the city was full of beautiful women who might tempt him: some of them more thrilling than she was, a few already wearing summer dresses. It all weighed less heavily on her, since weightlessness was in her nature and because in any case one simply had to live. Oh, and yet—

'Darling?' she called, spinning round.

The crowd had taken him, though. She had imagined that he would still be standing there, watching her. And now she felt a dreadful uncertainty about love.

# JUNE, 1940

Vapour trails twisted high above Alistair's train from Dover. He angled his head out of the window, into the warm slipstream bitter with coal smoke. He knew the RAF was milling rings with the enemy up there, but from where he watched, the aeroplanes were invisibly small and it seemed as if the steam from his own locomotive rose up into those thin and tortured contrails. As if nature had congealed, and gases no longer dispersed but only bifurcated and twisted around themselves: as if there were no more forgetting.

The train's whistle screamed. London was close now, with an ominous gravity that clutched at his cells. He had meant to visit Tom straight away – that was the point of coming to town – but now that it was so near, he felt he ought to settle himself first. He would fire Tom a quick note for the afternoon delivery, use the day for some errands, and see his friend in the evening.

*Dear Tom,*
*They have given the regiment leave, which we have surely earned with our magnificent display of backwards marching all the way through northern France.*

He put the pen down for a moment, reaching for the right tone. The enemy had run them ragged, from the first failure in the Ardennes to the final evacuation at Dunkirk. The Germans had had more concentration, more conviction, more force. When one thought of the enemy it was with a queer mix of fear and admiration. It was absurd that one could not simply hold up one's hand and say: 'Look here, well done, I think that will do for now.'

*I am slightly injured in the arm, but still surely a better batsman than you. Also they have made me Captain. You are to think of me as a blazing comet, inbound, in an officer's uniform with a wound medal.*

Splinters of glass were still working themselves out of him – he had got the arm up just in time to shield his face when a window had blown out in Mont-de-Piété. It was nothing. More than pain, it produced an unwelcome feeling of separation from the people around him. He supposed he ought not to be surprised. The product of war was solitude, after all – the lover bereaved, the conversation truncated – so it was hardly amazing if a near miss left one feeling a little disconnected.

*As for you, I trust that Caesar is a vigilant chaperone and*

In a group of poor positions dug into the beach at Dunkirk, less than a week ago, Alistair had huddled with his men. Shells had screamed down and exploded on the beach at unpredictable intervals. Smoke blinded everyone: a sharp amalgam of black soot from ships that were stricken, and white chemical smoke that the British destroyers were laying in a screen. It made a lachrymose fog that reddened the men's eyes and left their throats raw.

Alistair stood above the lip of his dugout. 'How do you like this weather?' he called to his senior sergeant, Blake.

'Very seasonal, sir,' the man shouted from the next dugout. 'With your permission I might take a few of the men along the beach for ice creams.'

'Very good,' called Alistair. 'See if you can pick up some deck-chairs while you are at it. We could rent them out here quite tidily.'

'Captive audience, isn't it, sir?'

Alistair nodded. 'Get HQ on the radio and have them send us a Punch and Judy booth. If you behave, I shall let you be Judy.'

He waited for Blake's comeback, but Blake collected shrapnel to his body and crumpled sideways without fuss. Alistair tensed his muscles and readied himself to jump out of his dugout and help Blake. But here he was, sitting in a train carriage, writing a letter to Tom. He rubbed his temples, coaxing himself back into the present.

*. . . that Caesar is a vigilant chaperone and that*

Alistair's men had been on the beach for two days. Mingled with the smoke was the stink of faeces and urine. There was no possibility of establishing proper latrines, and so they used their own dugouts. Bombs hit the beach fifty to the hour, whistling down through the haze from bombers unseen. At longer intervals the yellow-nosed Messerschmidts burst over the coastal dunes with no warning – so low that one could make out the rivets – and tore up the beach with their cannon. Sand lifted in gouts, to fall again in an endless fine rain. Men died with their gaze open to heaven and sand accruing on their eyes.

*. . . is a vigilant chaperone and that your dancing is improving.*

He leaned his forehead against the train window, breathing hard. He watched the green fields rush by. Only this was real, he told himself: this ripening wheat, that flint-walled barn, those ewes. What he had not understood, before battle, was that time could become a ribbon to be looped and pinned back to its centre, the petals of a black rosette.

*I won't cramp your style with that girl of yours, so I shan't stay at the garret. I shall stay at Robertson's – that little hotel on Shooters Hill Road. Call for me there when you get this.*

The train hissed into Charing Cross. Alistair folded the note for Tom into its envelope, took his duffel bag from the rack, and stepped down onto the platform.

It was hot in London. He walked north from the station – at noon by his watch – but no clocks struck. The bells were blanketed in their belfries, to be rung only if the enemy invaded. Such plans were a comfort to civilians, he supposed, although having met the Germans in their present humour Alistair felt it unlikely that bells would make much difference – whether silenced, rung or melted down and made into metal plates for tap shoes.

He found a post box, hesitated, and put the note for Tom back into his pocket. Perhaps he should make sure of a room at Robertson's before he told Tom to meet him there. They usually did have rooms, but with the war, one never knew.

With his handkerchief he wiped away the sweat and the train soot. In the Strand, bodies careened off him. Everyone jostled and bumped. There was a new way of moving that he could not seem to weave himself into. The city was in a gasping hurry but it wasn't the old surge of rush hour, where the great press of bodies used to flow together like a tide. Now everyone seemed to be moving at cross purposes.

Alistair fought a rising perplexity. He couldn't thread himself through the new crowds. There were so many people, all out of phase. It seemed to him that the un-rung hours had lost their habit of strict separation and begun to overlap, to slide over each other like the scales of something serpentine and recursive. Day shifts and night shifts and swing shifts jostled and perplexed him, and as he ran his errands across the capital it seemed that whatever bus he caught was full of wan girls in overalls. They were as likely to be coming from work as going to it. He tried to talk with them, but apparently the language had changed. The English he spoke seemed to amuse them, or to irk them. It was as if he had learned it abroad.

'Have you come far?' he asked a young man in a tin hat and tweed.

'What?' said the man, eyeing him warily.

Alistair was used to the battle-shocked look in his men. His own commanding officer had been killed at Saint-Quentin, when the enemy had found their range with mortars. Keen to move out and getting no answer on the field telephone, Alistair had jogged half a mile to ask for orders in the stone barn where their command position had been established. When he arrived, the place stank of meat and there was no one alive in it. A mortar round had gone through the roof and the stone walls had contained the blast. The air was still hot. All his senior officers lay rent and scorched. The colonel sat upright at a camp table, blood-less and grey, the line of his moustache expressing indignation, the handset of the field telephone still clasped in his hand. *This is a dreadful hotel and I wish to complain about the incessant noise.*

He jogged back to his position, assembled everyone who was still alive in the company, and led them to the coast. All the way he hoped to meet a senior officer with a better plan. He only stopped, after ten days, when he reached the main force at Dunkirk. Two of his sergeants were gone, along with five of the corporals. Most of the men were injured, and six would need to be carried to the boats. Alistair oversaw the construction of stretchers.

It relaxed him, working with the men on these practical and necessary tasks. It was only in such matters that he felt useful. He was good at restoration. If the task had been, say, to rebuild Europe rather than to blast it to pieces, Alistair might have worn his rank with more pleasure and felt less bashful about asking the men to follow him.

As it was, though, they seemed happy enough to take his lead. They marched when he asked them to march. They continued to fire their rifles at the enemy rather than at each other, even after a month with little sleep. They drank sandy tea, flinched at the worst bangs, and wrote letters to their girlfriends at home. When he made his rounds they called him sir, offered him brews and biscuits, and were glad when he dropped in to their dugouts. That his presence seemed to help them was reason enough to keep going. For their sake he hoped he would not be killed – the issue had ceased to interest him personally. He tried to do his best for them, and to soothe them when they looked back at him with this wide-eyed stare.

The young man before him was alarmed. Alistair took the man's arm, thinking to reassure him, but the fellow pushed him away and hurried off along the length of the bus. Alistair blinked. Of course: a bus. London.

He got off as soon as the bus slowed. In the street, nothing was right. The cigarettes smelled of burning farms. Passers-by perplexed him with musk and naphtha. The bakeries, which had always operated at dawn, now seemed to be baking again in the late afternoon. He supposed all the new night workers must need feeding. The smell of warm bread filled Piccadilly as he walked to his bank. It was comforting and unsettling, both at once. The bakers on their shop-window slates chalked the batch up as Resurrection Bread and when Alistair asked one of them why, the man told him: *Lo, it has risen again.*

Even at the Ritz the dining times had been doubled up to accommodate the new martial schedules. Alistair looked in through the tall windows and saw ladies laughing around cake stands and samovars, beside tables of men who were still finishing lunch. When port and macaroons were simultaneously visible in W1 then something dreadful was coming down the line, surely. Why did people seem so unconcerned?

Alistair loosened his tie in the heat and walked down to the Embankment, taking the side streets to avoid the bedevilling crowds. Now that his small tasks were done, he felt surplus and foolish. He sat on a bench and frowned at the Thames. An oily tide was coming in from the estuary, setting up a confused chop against the river's flow. The white gulls lurched about on it, looking seasick and hot.

He had imagined it would take all afternoon to meet with his bank manager, his tailor and the family's lawyer, but in the event he had only been a few minutes with each before he had been on his way again. They had all received him cordially, but with glances at the clock. He had the impression of being closely followed around town by some more important and indefinable presence that had made a proper appointment. Perhaps the war was good for business. Perhaps it would be even better if it weren't for all these soldiers in the way.

Alistair watched the queasy gulls squabble and bob. In the hot afternoon he lurched in and out of time. He had telephoned and got a room at Robertson's but he still held off posting his note to Tom, deciding to wait until he felt steadier. He didn't much fancy seeing his old colleagues at the Tate, either. The only thing worse than finding the place depressing and empty would be to discover that they had brought the pictures back after all. He didn't feel like seeing anyone he knew. The city had him on the back foot.

He watched the brown water swirl. On the way back from Dunkirk, crossing the Channel in a wet mist lit with flashes of white and red, they had picked up a downed RAF man in a tiny yellow rubber dinghy, waving. Alistair had helped him to climb up the netting into their little boat. Shivering, still in his parachute harness and Mae West, the man's face and arms were black with oil. He gave a salute, which Alistair returned. Alistair found the man some blankets and a tarpaulin to keep the wind off. It turned out that between them they had the makings of a smoke – the airman's pipe was undamaged and Alistair's tobacco dry. They shared the pipe at the foot of the mast, without speaking.

After a while Alistair said, 'How was the water?'

'Brisk,' said the RAF man. 'How was France?'

'Crowded.'

Alistair got up from the bench, which he told himself was real, and walked to Soho. He had hours to kill before he could reasonably go to his hotel. Like the ball in a bagatelle he bounced from café to cabaret, while London continued to look him straight in the eye. As if it had battled the tanks itself, in its spiv hat and spats.

There was cold iron armour massing, just a few miles away across the Channel. Any other city would be chewing its knuckles and digging a hole to hide in. Alistair wanted to yell at people: *The bullets actually work, you know!* What they did not understand was that the city could be extinguished. That every eligible person could die with the same baffled expression that he had seen on the first dead of the war, in those earliest shocking days before the men had learned to expect it. *I'm so sorry – I think I am actually hit.*

Night came, and it was still hot. In the blacked-out streets Alistair mingled with the uniformed men. They sought each other out for the comfort of it but they did not speak. Some men, like him, walked aimlessly, while others prowled the midnight dances for the pale excitable girls who were out before their shift, or after it – the latter being considered the more waltzable proposition. With Mars and Saturn in the same heaven, the young women air-raid volunteers wore silk beneath their tunics. The uniformed girls winked at Alistair. Sick of himself, he found that all he could do was salute them.

He supposed he should go and see a show. But all the cinemas were showing patriotic movies and all the theatres were full of dislocated men like him, stretched too thin across time. There were musicals with Broadway stars and dancing troupes, set in Monte Carlo, Ceylon, and Siam. London was perfectly prepared to give him a night out anywhere on earth, and yet all he asked was to come home.

At midnight, in the dark, in the silence that ought to have been filled with churches striking the hour, Alistair carried his duffel bag to Waterloo. He waited overnight on the platform and at dawn he caught the first train out to his parents' place. It would be quiet out there. He would go for long walks. In the country-side, surrounded by the oaks and the marsh harriers and all the other singular things, he was sure he would feel himself again.

# JUNE, 1940

At the first evacuation school things went bad, and they sent him to another village on his own. The new headmaster stood Zachary up in assembly and said there would be no detention for being a nigger but there would be a detention for bullying one.

It was a limestone village in a limestone valley, the people having travelled no further than the stones of the houses they lived in. Beyond the last building but before the first quarry, the Back Acre buzzed with summer flies. Zachary was nervous because the field was overlooked from everywhere. There was a tractor, rusted down to engine block and axles. There were clumps of red valerian and tangles of rambling rose, but nothing you could really hide behind. It was the worst place for Simone Block to say she would meet him, but that wasn't her fault. She didn't know people.

Simone had said to meet her at eight and he had been waiting since eight in the morning, in case that was what she meant. It had seemed like the sort of thing he ought to understand, and he hadn't wanted her to think him any more stupid than she already did. He had waited all day and now the sun was sinking over the western rim of the valley. Zachary narrowed his eyes. The slope was a wave and the yellow stone buildings of the village were fishing boats steaming up it, trawling with long black shadows. In the evening mist the church tower was a lighthouse, glowing red on its western parapet, guarding the fleet with its light. Everyone would be saved. He was a coastguard, looking out over a wild sea, and—

He made himself stop. This was how he always tripped up, seeing what wasn't there and not what was: the foot outstretched to trip him, the spit ball aimed at his head. Across the Back Acre the bees buzzed from bloom to bloom, smart in their striped jackets, heads in the game. The more he ought to concentrate, the more his thoughts wandered.

'What time does this say?' his class teacher would ask, pointing at the clock face on the blackboard. And Zachary would stare at the hands, trying to remember which way they spun, while tears began. And outside there would be a bull getting walked down the lane with its bell ringing, and Zachary would hear the brass edge of its chime softening as it dissolved in the summer air and made its tumbling ascent. The edge of the sound continually tucked under itself as it rose, a slow brass thunderhead, and he noticed it and noticed it and noticed it, and then suddenly everyone was staring at him, and the question was still: 'Zachary, what time does this clock say?', and he had no idea – no idea at all – and the whole class was jeering him and he hung his head.

He had been alone since September, until a week ago when Simone had brushed past him. He braced himself for the scratch or the slap, but instead she had turned and given him a quick half-smile – right there in the classroom, where anyone might notice.

The next day she had touched his hand at morning break.

'Zachary? Don't be sad.'

He was surprised three ways. One, to realise he was sad. Two, that someone had noticed it before he did. And three, that someone had talked to him. He had stood there, perfectly still, watching her walk away.

He thought about her now: her dirty brown hair and chipped teeth. Her skin, lighter than the other children's. The villagers freckled and bronzed in the summer but she stayed white. The girls in the class left her out of skipping. He let his thoughts go away with it for a while: imagining being so white that people teased you.

She was from far away, like him. He worried he should know. For others, probably, as simple as looking at the hands of a clock and saying, 'Five to nine' would be to look at Simone Block and say, 'She is from France', or 'She is from Holland'. He didn't even know what he was supposed to know.

She was late. He worried she wouldn't arrive. Also, he worried she would. He hid at the edge of the field, where foxgloves and wood anemones gave cover. The country children's eyes were always ranging, spectacular with sight. In the schoolyard he had seen a boy stoop during football, pick up a stone and throw it into a hedge where Zachary had only seen shadows. A thickening of the silence, a closing in of children: a stunned and bloodied rabbit dragged out by the tail to have its neck cracked. Before the creature's legs had finished twitching, the game had restarted from a throw-in.

Though the evening was warm, Zachary was cold from hunger. His host family gave him nothing, and it was hard to go around the farms looking for windfalls without bringing sight on himself. Better to be hungry and hidden. He watched where the rabbits and the deer went. He saw with the eyes of a prey animal, looking for gaps to slip through. He was better at it than the village children were. He had kept himself to himself until, in the schoolyard, Simone had let a scrap of paper fall beside him. He had put a foot over it until it was safe to pick up. He'd unrolled it, read it and eaten it in one smooth motion. *I like you*, the note had said. She didn't know what they could do.

From his pocket he pulled stalks of green wheat and rolled onto his front to eat the soft parts at the base of the stems. The mist was thickening with the sunset. He rolled a rotten stump, caught woodlice as they fled, and ate them. They balled themselves up at the end – the fools, the half-men, the easily scattered tribes from the books near the start of the Bible – and you could crunch them like silvery pills. He ate an octave of them, humming. They tasted of summer rain.

He had wanted to write a note back to Simone but he had been ashamed. He didn't know whether he likked, likede or lyked her, to, too or two. Instead he had slowed by her desk, just for a moment, when he came into class the next day. He had dared a glance at her, and she had responded with a smile so warm that he had almost forgotten himself and grinned back.

The light reddened. A lacewing touched down on his arm and he pinched its head and ate it. When he looked up, Simone was pushing her way through the long grass towards the centre of the field. In her white shirt and black pinafore she strode between the thistles, making no effort at all to hide. His heart jumped. He hesitated for a moment, then rose above the foxgloves just high enough to catch her eye and beckon her over.

When she was safely in the cover of the field border he brushed a place clean for her on the dry moss.

'Show me behind your ears,' she said straight away.

He angled his head for her and she folded each ear forward to look behind it. 'It's not done by the sun, then. Or else you'd be paler here.'

'It's the same all over.'

'Did you start off normal and go that colour?'

'No. I was like this since I was born.'

She gave a sympathetic nod. 'Then it's your parents' fault.'

'I don't think—'

'Shh. Does it hurt?'

'Does what hurt?'

'Your skin.'

'No, it doesn't hurt.'

'It doesn't feel burned at all?'

'No.'

'I don't mean like agony, like *arrrrrgh!* I mean like when you get too close to the fire and your hairs curl up and it's sore.'

'It's not sore.'

'And it's your father who's a cannibal?'

'He's a musician.'

'Then it's your mother?'

'She's dead, but she was a singer.'

Simone folded her arms. 'It has to be either the mother or the father.'

'Who what?'

'Who eats people. Otherwise the baby comes out white.'

He couldn't think what to say. 'We came from America.'

Simone looked sceptical. 'And are all the others ignorant like you?'

'All the other what?'

'All the other coloureds.'

He shook his head. 'I've always just been stupid.'

'I didn't say stupid, I said ignorant.'

'Same thing.'

'Stupid is you can't learn, ignorant is you haven't learned yet.'

'Well I'm stupid. You've seen when it's my turn to read in class.'

'Why don't you just sound out the letters?'

'They won't stop for me. I don't know how you make the letters still.'

'They just *are* still, stupid.'

'Not for me.'

She took his hand. 'You're shaking.'

'I am not.'

'Why are you shaking?'

'I'm scared. Aren't you?'

She brought his hand back and looked at him so tenderly that his heart caught. 'Why did they send you here on your own?'

He looked away. 'It doesn't matter.'

'Why don't you go back to London?'

'When I write to my father he says I have to be patient.'

'So, you need to write a better letter.'

'Writing moves worse than reading. Like the words hate the pen.'

'I'll write it down for you. Would you like me to do that?'

Zachary let his eyes drift out over the Back Acre. The sun had sunk below the rim of the valley now, and the shadow line was racing up its eastern slope. He watched the blazing oaks cut down by the edge of darkness. He knew every animal on the hillside and how it moved: he learned fast, by careful sight. He knew the farmers' bounds and the villagers' feuds, constantly shifting. He stayed ahead of them, failing only when thought had to be halted and put into words, and the words immobilised on the page. He was incapable of understanding how things always moving were stilled: he was stupid.

Simone was tugging at his hand. 'What would you say, if I could write it down for your father?'

'I'd say you were right. That I'm sad.'

She blinked. 'Just that?'

He gave a worried look, anxious he'd said the wrong thing. She pulled his hand closer. 'I like you. The others can say what they want.'

He dared a quick smile. She said, 'Should I kiss you?'

He pulled his hand away. 'No.'

'But why?'

'You don't know what they'd do, the others.'

'I don't care.'

He turned from her for a moment, his thoughts fluid, ranging across the darkening country. Every sound was enfolded in awareness, the running of the river, the cooing of the wood pigeons at roost, the crackling of sticks in the undergrowth nearby that must be a fox or a stoat beginning its evening round. He looked at Simone again, and in her face there was no anxiety, and it seemed to him that he should try to do what she asked.

He closed his eyes and moved his lips close to hers, and for a moment as she kissed him there was a stillness in his thoughts, and only the river ran, and only the sticks in the undergrowth cracked, louder now, rising almost into awareness but not wholly, because the kiss was his first and it was warm, and for a moment the sadness lifted and there was a stillness in him. Everything was still. And then a heavy flint caught him on the side of the head and he was stunned, and when he could see again there were more stones coming in through the dusk.

Simone was hit. Her tooth was knocked out and her eye was split wide and there was so much blood, and he wrapped his arms around her head to protect her but that only made the village children more furious. They were silent – and this was a terrible thing – they didn't jeer or laugh, only sent stone after stone whipping in. The air hissed with riverbed flints. Simone began to scream.

Zachary's eyes came wide open as he struggled up from sleep with his father's hand on his arm.

'You all right, Zachary?'

He blinked. It was full daylight, with fields rushing past. A third-class compartment with four seats taken. Himself, his father, a woman writing a letter, a man reading the newspaper. On the back of the newspaper, on the funny page, Hitler in his boxer shorts: *Let's catch him with his Panzers down.*

'Yes, I'm all right, I'm fine.'

'You were dreaming. It didn't look like the best fun.'

Zachary blinked. Through the window, below a stand of beech on the top of a green hill, a doe crept out into barley.

'I'm fine.'

His father had a right eye that strayed while the left fixed you. When Zachary was little and asked why, his father used to say he was keeping one eye out for trouble. Their joke was to guess which one.

Now his father said, 'I'm sorry I didn't come for you sooner.'

'That's all right.'

'They told us not to. They said to keep all the children where they were.'

'It's fine.'

His father laced his fingers on top of Zachary's head and stroked two thumbs along the lines of his eyebrows. It was something he'd always done, and for a moment Zachary felt that nothing had happened in between times. His mother hadn't been lost, they'd never crossed the ocean, they'd never been pulled apart.

His father said, 'Your old teacher warned me to fetch you home. I should have listened to her.'

'Miss North?'

'She said she was opening up that school again, and they couldn't stop us bringing you home. But I thought she was trouble. And you know trouble is one thing for her, and another thing for us.'

'I understand.'

'But look at you. Your poor face.'

Zachary shrugged. 'It doesn't hurt. It looks worse.'

'I raised a liar. Are you hurt anywhere else?'

Zachary looked up at him. 'When we get back to London can we go to the school, please?'

'I'm not sure it's the best thing.'

'Please?'

His father sighed. 'Well how can I say no to you now?'

Zachary looked back to the window. He wore the grey knee shorts and the grey coat in which he had been evacuated from London, and he had nothing with him but his gas mask in its box. Two things you could do with the gas mask: you could put it on so your breathing made a nice pop-pop, the valves clicking on the inhale and the exhale so your breathing had an off-beat. Or you could run a stick across the ribbing of the pipe that led from the filter to the mask, and the zip-zip reverberated through the rubber straps and sounded like a washboard.

'What can I do for you?' said his father. 'Need more cream on those cuts?'

'I wish it could go back to before.'

His father smiled. 'Before what? You start wishing it back, at your age, soon you're back in diapers.'

'You know what I mean.'

'I won't let them split us up again.'

It was better, from there. Low hills whistled by, woodland verse and field chorus, the rails in rattling tempo. His father fell asleep. London came closer. The other passengers divided their time between staring at the negroes and pretending they hadn't been. When they weren't looking, Zachary licked his fingertips and ate crumbs from the gaps between the seat cushions. The woman in the seat beside him was writing a letter, pressing on the cover of a book to do it. She paused to think, looking out of the window. Finally she fell asleep with the letter loose on her lap, and Zachary ate it. It was one page, written on one and a half sides, and the blue ink tasted of Simone's note. When the woman woke she looked at her lap and then around the floor of the compartment. Then she looked at him.

'Have you seen a letter I was writing?'

'Why are you asking me?' said Zachary. 'Why not ask one of the others?'

His lips and tongue were blue. The woman looked at him thoughtfully, then blinked and began writing all over again. At Reading, where she was alighting, she gave him a Mint Imperial.

At Marylebone the locomotive pulled up and vented steam as if the stuff had been hurting its belly. Zachary and his father stepped down from the carriage. On the station concourse the crowd seethed, harried here and there by its own urgent need. London absorbed them entirely.

Zachary leaned against an iron column. He was weak with hunger, though he wasn't about to make his father feel worse by admitting it. The blood drained from his head and he had to wait until the colour came back into the world and the ringing in his ears stopped. Dying might be like this, an infinite losing of balance.

They left the station to walk home. There were no smouldering craters. He had been evacuated for nine months, and the Germans hadn't attacked at all. It made no sense to him but he didn't even know how to begin asking his father why. It must be obvious. If there wasn't something wrong with him, he would be able to see some particular meaning in London's undamaged streets and say: 'Ah, so that's why they had to send us away.'

His mind drifted again. If there were bomb craters, you could see whatever was underneath London. You could climb down into the holes and come back up with your pockets full of it. Fossils, gold, instructions.

'You really want to go straight to the school?' said his father. 'You don't want to get cleaned up first?'

'I want to go.'

'But why? Haven't those people done enough to you?'

He didn't know how to explain it, how he was so weary of never understanding, so worn down and sad from it, and how a part of him dared to hope that Miss North might know the trick of making him less stupid.

'I just want to see,' he said.

'All right. But if you get a hard time, I'll get you out. From now on they don't split us.'

They walked through Regent's Park, past the boating lake where soldiers in khaki were rowing women in dresses. The men rowed badly, the women laughed and splashed water. Zachary's father pulled him up with a hand on his shoulder. 'You see them in their boats? You know what's crazy?'

Zachary looked, wondering what his father might mean, but he could see nothing. He had to assign it to that great category of words and clocks, of mysteries. 'I'm sorry,' he said. 'I don't know.'

His father laid a hand on the nape of his neck. 'It's the water. It's only a copule of feet deep. We could walk right across that lake if we wanted to. Take off our shoes and hang them round our necks.'

Zachary gave a small laugh, since this seemed to be what was wanted.

'But see,' said his father, 'they don't know they could just get out and walk. Like I didn't know I could just come and fetch you home.'

'It's fine,' said Zachary. 'It's not your fault.'

'It's no one else's. I'm happy for you, wanting that schooling. Maybe you won't finish dumb like me.'

Zachary looked out over the little lake. 'You're not dumb,' he said. It looked deep.

He held his father's hand and they took the canal towpath out of the park and on towards Hawley Street.

The heavy door of the school porch stood open. Singing came from inside. Had the rest of them all come back? He wouldn't be surprised by anything. It must have been written somewhere, and he had just sat there and blinked at it. He could hardly think at all now, he was so hungry. He looked around at the orderly, clean street. He looked down at his ripped shorts and his muddy legs and shoes. He did not completely understand the trick that had been played on him, but he was ashamed.

Inside the school, they were singing 'When a Knight Won His Spurs'. He hung on to the railings, feeling faint.

His father held him up. 'Still want to go in?'

Zachary nodded. The corridor was dark. He looked through the doors of the first classrooms. They were empty and dark too. All the windows were boarded up. They followed the sounds of the voices along the corridor, past more empty classrooms.

*No charger have I, and no sword by my side, Yet still to adventure and battle I ride.* Somewhere, in the heart of the school, one class was singing. They found the classroom and stood outside. Zachary eased the door open and blinked in the sudden light.

*Though back into storyland giants have fled ...* The singing tailed off as the children noticed Zachary standing there. There were only seven of them, not a whole class, and they were not all the same age. He recognised only two of them: most were not children he had been evacuated with. The older ones stopped singing first, and soon the little ones fell silent too. Last to stop was the teacher, who stood conducting the children with her back to the door. She carried on singing as she swept out the time in the air.

'... *And the knights are no more and the dragons are* ... oh do come along, children, what on earth is the matter, why don't you sing?'

She spun around and Zachary flinched. Then her face softened. She nodded to his father, took a step towards Zachary and folded him into her arms. He collapsed against her, too weak to talk.

'Zachary Lee,' said Mary. 'You are frightfully late, as usual.'

# JULY, 1940

**P**aris had fallen, the grandfathers manning the pissoirs as Hitler in his Mercedes cabriolet rutted the lawns of the Champ de Mars. The invaders marched behind his car with polished boots while the old men with their brandy headaches pissed venom against the zinc. The thing was to resist. It did not matter that it splashed back on their shoes.

In her classroom in Hawley Street, Mary chalked an outline of Europe on the blackboard and marked Paris with an Eiffel Tower. She topped off the tower with a beret and tucked a little baguette under its arm, since that was the only way the thing ought to be drawn.

'Who can tell me who built the Eiffel Tower? Yes?'

'Was it Napoleon?' said Maud Babington.

Mary smiled. 'Nearly.'

Betty Oates was waving her hand in anguish, as if the answer's continuing presence within her body was causing unbearable pain.

'Yes, Betty?'

'Gustave Eiffel!'

'Very good. The Eiffel Tower is made of ferrous metal and it has a magnetic field that generates romance within a mile of it.'

George Hampton, who was simple, became flustered at the word 'romance'. He was fifteen and handsome. Young women dropped their purses in front of him to start a conversation, until they realised what was the matter. Now he pressed both palms to his temples and made the noise of a door hinge wanting oil.

Betty, ever diligent, was writing in her exercise book: *Eiffel Tower. Magnetic field. Romance ≤ 1 mile.* George was still agitated. Poppy Brown, the mongol, climbed down from her desk and shuffled over to his place. She took his hands by the wrists and clapped them together until George forgot what had upset him. He wiggled his fingers, which to his great delight responded with pleasing undulant motions. *Pop-Pop-Pop*, he said, forming an accidental spit bubble with every bilabial. Poppy, who was five, clambered back up to her seat and stared at the blackboard with her slanted brown eyes that squinted outwards, her bottom teeth protuberant over the upper lip.

Mary said, 'Thank you, Poppy.'

Poppy pointed at the blackboard – her hand had a thumb and five fingers – and she said, 'That?'

'Is the Eiffel Tower, darling.'

Poppy made the shape of it with two steepled index fingers, then stuck one up each nostril.

'Don't do that, please.'

Poppy withdrew her fingers and inspected a strand of mucus that had followed them out, pea green and fabulous. She ate it.

'Ewww!' said Kenneth Cox. 'That! Is! Dis! Gusting!'

'Nevertheless,' said Mary, 'it is not yet rationed, and I don't suppose we must blame Poppy for making the most of it.'

The class settled. 'All right, children. Some of you have heard the news about Paris, and I daresay you are worried.'

Zachary said, 'What's happened in Paris?'

'The Germans have arrived there.' She made her tone disapproving, as if the Germans had arrived at an inconvenient moment, or with too much luggage.

She was glad Zachary had spoken up. Naturally he was timid, after everything that had happened. If she could get him to put up his hand for one question a day, it was a small victory.

She drew a swastika on the blackboard beside her Eiffel Tower. 'Who can tell me what this nasty symbol is?'

Thomas Essom, the cripple, gripped the push rims of his wheelchair. 'Swastika,' he whispered.

'It's all right, you know. You won't drop dead just from saying the word.'

Thomas tried again. 'Swastika,' he said, hardly louder.

He had been sent with another London school on a train to the West Country. They had wheeled him into the village hall where the evacuees were being chosen. He had waited all night. No one had wanted a polio boy, twelve years old and pimpled. They had not wanted him in the next village either, and finally his mother had gone out to bring him home.

It had been this way for half her class: the countryside had not wanted them. The others had been brought back to London simply because their parents missed them, and this too was an affliction – an oedema of sentiment or a hypertrophy of the heart – unpatriotic in a way that could not be formally censured. This was the situation of Maud, Betty and Kenneth. Only Beryl Waldorf, the beauty, fell outside the pattern. She had returned a month ago and not spoken since. She stared out of the window and hugged her arms tight around her. Something had been off – the parents had sensed it in her letters. The countryside had liked her too much.

These eight, then, were Mary's class so far. They were London's remainder, the residual air in its lungs.

She said, 'Well done, Thomas.' His lip trembled and he looked down at his desk. Children blamed themselves for what had happened to them. This was why she took pains, in this lesson every Friday, to give them the news of the war. At least she could set out before them, with chalk and modest redaction, the great currents that had washed them up here.

On the blackboard she marked the countries that, for now, belonged to the enemy. She was careful to make the swastikas small in relation to the other things she drew: a skier with a flowing scarf in Norway, a windmill in Holland. She loathed the way the newspapers printed maps with the stark Nazi symbol on a field of plain white, as if Hitler had sent armies of erasers. Better to crowd the swastikas in, to have them jostle for space. She drew them deliberately crooked. Her swastikas were degenerates that leaned at sickly angles and resembled one another vaguely, the offspring of first cousins who had married against the family's advice.

Finally she drew Britain, being generous with the width of the English Channel and giving the British Isles three times the area on the blackboard that they merited. She thought it unfair to expect children to understand that it was possible to resist, from an island the size of her hand, a tyranny that stretched the whole width of the blackboard from Brest to Bialystok.

'And so you see, the enemy has moved into France, but that, you may be perfectly sure, is as far as he will come. Who can tell me why that is?'

Betty had her hand up again, but Mary wasn't buying. 'What do you think, Zachary?'

His eyes came back into focus. 'I don't know. I'm sorry.'

'You mustn't be.'

He sighed. 'Sorry.'

She knelt by his desk. 'Anything in the Germans' way? Any water?'

His eyes brightened. 'Oh, the sea. The Channel.'

She smiled. 'You see? It's fine to raise your hand and say these things.'

'I thought it was something difficult.'

'You can trust a dunce like me, you know. If it was hard I wouldn't know the answer myself, and I shouldn't ask in case you showed me up.'

He held her eyes, his chin up for once. She hoped it was not too much to ask, that he should trust her. But then again it was not she who had been starved and stoned out of her evacuation village. It was not she who had needed a week in the Royal Free Hospital, with bed rest and vitamin shots, to recover from a trip to the countryside.

She stood to address the class again. 'And if they do somehow cross the Channel, we'll put up a ferocious resistance and they'll never get inland.'

The inscrutable looks children gave when they understood everything or nothing. In all likelihood they were simply tired. Mary decided to call it a day. She wound the Columbia gramophone that Tom had loaned her, and put Thomas in charge of choosing the discs. It was not officially recommended, an afternoon of light jazz and dance tunes – but neither was it explicitly stated that one ought to bore one's class to death on a Friday afternoon.

Thomas had turned out to be a handy gramophone operator. He had brought some recordings from home – Maurice Chevalier and Cole Porter – and since the children had been good all week she allowed those whom the mood took to dance. While the music played she opened the heavy hymnal in which the class had pressed summer flowers. The children who wanted to do collage came and took some. The others danced to the gramophone or went out to the corridor for hopscotch, which was another thing Mary permitted on a Friday afternoon to any child who could prove beyond reasonable doubt that the war had not been their idea.

Only Zachary sat alone at his desk, eating the paste he should have been sticking flowers with.

'Zachary, is there nothing you won't eat?'

His thoughtful chewing suggested he had taken her question under advisement.

'How are things at home?'

He grinned pastily. 'My father says I can go to the shop. He's giving me a ha'penny and I already have a ha'penny, so I can get eight pear drops at eight for a penny, or four barley sweets at four a penny, I haven't decided.'

It was a solemn choice. Mary nodded. 'Supposing you bought two barley sweets, how many pear drops could you still buy?'

'Four,' said Zachary.

'And what is one, minus two quarters, times eight?'

He eyed her as if astonished by the cruelty. 'Don't.'

'But it is the exact same question, don't you see? Mathematics is only life with the word "sweets" removed.'

He shrugged. 'Can I have a cigarette now?'

'Not until you are twelve.'

'But you said I could have one when I was eleven.'

'That was when you were ten. The rule is: no cigarettes until cigarettes are shorter than your fingers.'

He scowled. 'I hope the Germans invade and shoot you.'

'Then your new German teacher would be even stricter. They are famous for it, I'm afraid.'

'Will they come?' he said, with such unheralded anxiety that it caught her off guard. The music had stopped – Thomas was changing the disc.

Since all the children were listening, Mary laughed. 'Of course not!'

But of course the Germans would come. The reality was there on the blackboard and in the ache of her forearm. It was all very well listening to patriotic speeches on the wireless. It wasn't until one had used the whole board to map the great sweep of the Blitzkrieg that one realised how little extra chalk would extend the onslaught to London.

126

'What if they come at night?' said Zachary. 'When nobody's expecting?'

She shook her head. 'We have whole ministries full of people whose only job is to expect. They have plans for if the moon goes square and plans for if the sun loses his trilby. Trust me, children, we will be ready.'

Zachary tried a smile. But of course the Gestapo would murder him, after the Germans won. London would hold, and fight – it wouldn't be like Paris. There would be a siege, with horrifying hunger. The pigeons would be eaten, and then the rats, using trapping techniques that would be disseminated in illustrated pamphlets, and finally when the pigeons and the rats and the family pets were gone, the dead would be cannibalised in a systematic, orderly and documented fashion according to a protocol that doubtless already existed in the contingency files of one of the more tight-lipped ministries. Those left alive would be grateful for death by the time the city fell.

'So everything will be fine?' said Thomas.

'Yes, children, everything will be fine.'

Mary smiled for her class. But only the previous afternoon, over ice creams in Hyde Park, she and Hilda had discussed what they would do if the enemy came. The problem with an education was that one knew perfectly well what soldiers did when they sacked a refractory city – it was all there in Virgil and Gibbon.

'I should think the soldiers will ravish us until they are weary from it, don't you?' said Hilda, yawning.

Mary licked her ice cream. 'It might not be awfully fun.'

'Selfish, I know, but we probably ought to kill ourselves first.'

Mary said, 'Is your ice cream melting too?'

'Your problem is that you don't eat it fast enough.'

'Because vanilla goes straight to the hips. It is well known.'

'Give me yours as well, then. I intend to become as fat as a bus – then the Germans will jolly well rape you first.'

'But I thought you wanted us to do away with ourselves.'

Hilda gave a worried look. 'I might not manage it.'

'I can shoot you with my father's gun if you like. You know, the pretty one with the geese on the stock.'

'I'd hate for you to go to any trouble.'

'Oh no, really. It would be my absolute pleasure.'

'And you? I'd hate for you to be left out.'

'I can have Palmer shoot me. I'm sure he'll have a way of doing it discreetly, so that one hardly notices.'

'Oh good – let's have Palmer shoot both of us, shall we? I trust he has a Sunday firearm that he favours if your father is in residence, and a workaday gun if not?'

'I should be disappointed to find it were otherwise.'

'Have him shoot me in the heart, will you? This hair took all morning.'

'Consider him advised. But what shall we really do, if they come?'

Hilda dabbed at her ice cream. 'It would have to be the river. Weigh ourselves down with stones and wade in.'

'Very well,' said Mary. 'But nowhere downstream of Westminster.'

'Good god, no! One hopes for death, not mortification.'

Mary realised her class was looking up at her. She clapped her hands and smiled. 'Come along, then! Shall we have another disc?'

Thomas started up the gramophone with a Charleston from the Piccadilly Players. It was Tom's – one of the first discs he'd played her. Zachary went to the piano and played along. He found the key first time, showering playful notes on the off-beat. So long as a thing was not perfectly simple to learn, the boy was good at it. Searching for the key to him she had read his reports from the three years of schooling he'd had since he arrived from America. In every one of them his teachers had written: 'Must try harder'.

'Miss?' said Zachary, looking up from the keyboard. 'Are you all right?'

'I'm sorry,' she said. 'For what happened to you.'

'You didn't do it.'

'Yes, but . . . *we* did it.'

A shrug, a few chords. Then: 'Miss, would you like to dance?' He grinned, fingers spritzing the keyboard.

She laughed. 'Oh good lord, stop it!'

He held out his left hand while his right still played along. 'Well?'

On the disc the band sang 'Sunny Skies'. She said, 'I shouldn't.'

'Why?'

'I mean, I don't know if . . . we . . . should.'

He gave a quick smile and looked back down at the keyboard. 'All right.'

Mary's chest ached – which was unfair of it, since of course she was only being sensible. One oughtn't to dance with the children – of any stripe – and especially not a coloured one. Word would reach all of the parents by sundown, and there would be no end of unpleasantness.

But the ache deepened as she watched him play. And she thought: *but so what?* There might be a sniffy letter, even an official reprimand. Perhaps one ought to set one's own transgressions against the enemy's, these days. When one considered that the Germans would establish air superiority before bringing in a spearhead of tanks backed up by infantry in phased echelons, and follow up with collective reprisals against civilian elements that continued to resist, to dance seemed quite inoffensive.

'On second thoughts, thank you,' she said. 'I'd love to dance.'

She took his hands. The gramophone spun. And there, at the

point marked on the map in her original orders, in the small space of parquet floor she had scrubbed clean herself between the front row of desks and the blackboard, Mary danced the Charleston with Zachary and it seemed to her that both of them were rather good at it.

# AUGUST, 1940

Tom said, 'I had a letter from Alistair. His mob is due to ship out again and they're getting leave beforehand.'

Mary propped herself on the pillow and lit a cigarette. 'He's your friend, you should get him up to town.'

'You know I've tried. I wonder if we might go to see him instead.'

'To the provinces? Hay wains and bigotry? I can't say I'm tempted.'

'You know it isn't like that.'

'Unless one is coloured or otherwise vulnerable, darling.'

'And since we are neither of those things?'

'Then of course the provincials would doff their caps to us, the lambs.'

'Remind me never to get on the wrong side of you.'

'You see?' said Mary, tapping ash. 'You are brighter than you look.'

'I do miss Alistair, though. I worry something's happened to his head.'

'Shellshock, do you mean?'

'Oh god,' said Tom, 'not as bad as that. His letters are perfectly fine. For a start, they are letters. They're not – oh, you know – poetry.'

'At least there is that.'

'I can see it might feel queer, though, coming back to town after battle.'

Mary frowned. 'Is Alistair good-looking?'

'How should I know?'

'Well, is he tall?'

'I suppose so. Six-one, six-two?'

'Good. And his eyes?'

'I can't say I've ever noticed them.'

'I despair. But he is a full captain? Own teeth, no visible Nazi insignia?'

'Confirmed on all counts.'

'Then he'll do for my friend Hilda. Invite him for a double date. Tell him Hilda is pretty, and comfortably off, and disinclined to chastity. If that doesn't prise the poor man out of the countryside then perhaps it's best if he stays.'

'You really won't come to visit him there?'

Mary stubbed out her cigarette. 'Not till perdition congeals.'

'You shouldn't damn the whole of England, you know, over what happened to one boy.'

'I shall damn as I please. What is the use of coming from a good family, if one cannot damn as the need arises?'

'It's just that you seem rather soft on Zachary.'

'No softer than on any of my other children.'

'But last month – don't you see? Don't you think one crosses a line, slightly, when one actually dances with a nigger?'

'Must you bring it up again? And don't use that word. It's cheap.'

'Well it's only an endearment, isn't it? Like "Taffy" or "Jock". If the child were Welsh and I called him "Taffy", you wouldn't blink.'

'But the child is American. His father moved them here ages ago. Call him a Yank if you must.'

'And that would be better because?'

'Because "Yank" is a proper noun and it takes a capital and America has a capital too, whereas "nigger" has neither. The day we allow the child his own country and lodge our ambassador in its principal city is the day I shall let you call him "Nigger", and even then I shall jolly well expect to hear the capital N when you enunciate.'

Tom held up his hands. 'I didn't know he was American.'

'Half the black entertainers are. Where did you think they were from?'

'I assumed they were supplied by some ministry, in support of morale.'

Mary softened. 'You see! My Tom *is* still in there somewhere.'

'I suppose I'm just jealous.'

She kissed his cheek. 'He's eleven years old, darling.'

'Just . . . you know. Try not to dance with him again.'

She drew away under the covers. 'I shall dance as it pleases me.'

He grinned. 'But you don't want to make waves, do you?'

'We make pressed flowers. We make decorations with poster paint and glue. Waves don't come into it.'

'But you must see what I'm telling you.'

'I'm not entirely sure I do.'

'Please, Mary. Must we talk about work?'

'Oh, are we talking about work?'

'Well I suppose we are, now.'

'Fine, then I suppose I shall get out of your bed, now.'

She stalked across the garret, put on his discarded dressing gown, sat at the piano and struck an ironic discord.

He groaned. 'I'm sorry.'

'Oh, please, never apologise for being professional.'

He said nothing.

Finally, Mary sighed. 'What?'

'Well, you don't seem to see the trouble you could make.'

'For my teaching career? It could hardly get worse. I am on half-pay and I have half a class of retards, cripples and pariahs. If I were to be sacked I might consider it a promotion.'

'You wanted that job.'

'So what would you have me do? Bow to you in gratitude?'

'Look, you know I'm in a spot. I want the schools open as much as you do, and yet the policy is to maintain the evacuation. I have a little leeway but I'm walking a tightrope. You do understand the delicacy?'

'No, Tom, it never once occurred to me. I suppose it is because you are a man with weighty responsibilities and I am just a foolish young girl.'

Tom held his head and was silent for a minute. 'All right. Fine. Please may I have Mary back now?'

She went to ruffle his hair. 'Not until you've apologised to Miss North.'

Tom took her hand and kissed it. 'I'm sorry. I am. It's just that keeping the school open is harder than you know, and it's only really doable at all so long as no one, you know . . . notices.'

'Do give me some credit. I'm running a school, not a jive club. The children worked all week and this was half an hour on a Friday afternoon.'

'Friday, Saturday or Judgement Day. You dance with a n . . . with a negro boy, and people will talk.'

Mary pulled her hand away. 'Don't you suppose they have bigger things to listen to? You know, what with the Germans being so vocal?'

'But you know how people gossip. It's a comfort, isn't it, to fall back on the old prejudices when everything else is in flux.'

'Are we talking about other people's prejudices, darling, or yours?'

'I'm sorry?'

'It's just that no one else has complained, have they? I might have expected a note from a parent, or some busybody. But hardly from you.'

'Mary, please.'

'Don't *Mary* me.'

'Sorry. But it isn't for us to change how things are. I'm just an administrator. You're just a teacher.'

'Oh, I hope I don't teach. Because look what we did: we saved the zoo animals and the nice children, and we damned the afflicted and the blacks. You know what I do every day in that classroom? I do everything in my power to make sure those poor souls won't learn the obvious lesson.'

Oh but the peevish expression he gave her! She lit a cigarette. She was angry, she supposed, at more than just him. Even as she railed, a hollow feeling grew – that perhaps life would turn out to be like this. Not, after all, the effortful ascent to grace that she had imagined, but rather a gradual accretion of weight and complexity – and not in one great mass that could be shouldered as Atlas had, but in many mundane and antiheroic fragments with a collective tendency to drag one down to the mean. Perhaps life just turned a person who tried harder into a person who felt they must write it on someone else's report.

'If I were you,' said Tom, 'I should stick to reading, writing and arithmetic.'

'But what good is it to teach a child to count, if you don't show him that he counts for something?'

Tom held up his hands. 'I'm sorry, you're losing me.'

Mary exhaled smoke. 'Possibly I am.'

# SEPTEMBER, 1940

The packed eight o'clock brought Alistair's regiment to Waterloo from their Hampshire barracks. Into the sky the train disgorged vapours; into the capital, sixty officers and three hundred men. They had twenty-four hours' leave, orders to rest and recuperate and a tendency to do neither.

In his new uniform of a captain in the Royal Artillery, Alistair stood on the platform to wish his men the best. Wills would be drawn up, he supposed, and mothers reassured of sons' immortality, and fathers slipped letters to be opened in case of contradictory news. Blushing sisters would be introduced to suitable fellow officers, younger brothers issued with gobstoppers and wooden rifles. The enamoured would be betrothed, the betrothed espoused. Entire human lives would be conceived, in unorthodox locations, by hurrying bodies cheerful with wine and still mostly clothed, at two thirty in the afternoon. The Savoy's best spoons would be pocketed, things that were not cricket cricketed. He didn't even like to think.

A pair of brother officers invited him to breakfast but he declined. He invented some quick excuse – an aunt, or an aneurism – which he forgot as soon as he had uttered it but which the others seemed to find sufficient. In any case they left without taking offence. Alistair was so adept at this now – at keeping to himself – that he did it without conscious effort. He might have bowed out of this leave entirely if Tom hadn't insisted he come.

He watched his battery disperse. Each group of six or a dozen men ringed itself off from the others with laughter of its own particular key. Alistair knew the men well but he did not know how they formed their clans to go drinking in. He had ministered to them all under fire, without making any more distinction than the bullets and the shells had done. By what unobservable law did they now divide themselves into these friendship groups that cut across the lines of their official units?

Of course the men were not cattle, and yet he did not understand how fierce could be the loyalty to this or that faction, while another merited only disdain. And yet that was men for you: there was always this counter current, this Escheresque sleight that they performed without ever seeming to defy their orders. The Army made them into a flock of birds while the men made themselves into shoals of fishes, swimming in the contrary direction.

His men headed for the pubs in the back streets behind the station, where the licensing hours had been quietly surrendered. The soldiers would drink ale until dusk and then switch to whisky and fists. They would fight the Navy if available, other regiments if not, and the RAF as a last resort since it was not considered form to bother the afflicted. They would fight for the simple joy of doing so without 7.2-inch howitzers. Then they would return at dawn and call him 'sir', with their heels the regulation width apart.

Alistair knocked out his pipe on the heel of his shoe. If there was one thing the war had done, it was to change his mind about the class of people who never came into the Tate. Men and good paintings had a genius for escape from the frame.

He took a cab to Belgravia, where he had an appointment with the regimental physician. The fare was two shillings ha'penny and he handed over a half crown and told the driver to keep the change. The man blessed him, so Alistair tipped him another shilling. He thought: *This might be the last bright blue morning, the last London taxi in its livery, the last quiet shilling with its lion and its crown.* It occurred to him that no one who hadn't been in battle could know what things were worth.

At the doctor's offices they kept him waiting in a pink-carpeted anteroom with six Windsor chairs and a large framed print of the King. Looking up at him, Alistair began to feel that the King was an old chum. The King sat alone and rigorously upright in full ceremonial dress with what looked like ten pounds of medals and braid hanging off it. He rested one gloved hand on the pommel of a ceremonial sword. His expression suggested that he would not hesitate to use the sword on himself or others, should the portraitist require him to maintain the pose for one more damnable minute. Alistair's knees jiggled up and down as he sat.

This was what he had not understood, until the war: that all men were of one blood, embedded from king to serf in a perfectly rigid formalism and all quietly abstracting themselves from it. The men did it with fighting and cheap women, the officers with theatre and costly ones. Alone in his mind each man knew himself free as a king, while the King alone knew himself enslaved. Alistair felt euphoric. This was the great joke, and until the war he hadn't got it.

These insights were coming to him continuously, and with terrific effervescence, after yesterday's godawful low. He laughed at himself. There was no reason to fret about it: why should one expect to feel the same every day, in a world that was rearranging itself by the hour? He was pleased with this formulation, and said so to himself. He was pleased with . . . in fact no, it was gone – his thoughts were coming so quickly – but no matter. He was pleased with . . . well, he was just pleased.

The doctor called him in after ten minutes. He was a portly man with side whiskers, in a white cotton jacket with gold insignia – the effect, to Alistair's eye, falling somewhere between avuncular surgeon and cruise ship maître d'. The man remained seated behind his desk, not looking up when Alistair came in.

'Heath?' he said.

'Doctor.'

'Be seated. Nothing the matter, I hope?'

'Nothing,' said Alistair.

'No aches, pains, unscheduled loss of limbs?'

'I find I don't much care for seafood.'

'Good man,' said the doctor, inking his rubber stamp.

Holding it poised over Alistair's paper, he looked up for the first time. 'And how's morale?'

'Mine, or the men's?'

'Isn't it the same thing?'

'Morale is fine,' said Alistair.

'France, wasn't it, and then back across from Dunkirk?'

'Awful little town. Not one fish-and-chip shop.'

'No inflections of mood, no irritability, no anxiety?'

'No.'

'Any shellshock, jellification of the spine, malingering hottentottery?'

'Hardly.'

The doctor thumped down his stamp and slid the paper over. 'First class. Give this to the CO when you get back to barracks. I daresay you'll be posted soon?'

'Looks that way.'

'Good luck. Take quinine if it's Cairo, take salt if it's the desert, take precautions if it's a local girl. Avoid gin unless good tonic is available, smoke no more than one pack, and keep anything made of metal on the outside of your skin. Dismiss.'

'Thank you,' said Alistair, standing.

'Very good.'

Alistair hesitated in the doorway. 'There is one thing.'

'Yes?' The doctor was fanning the papers on his desk, looking for the next fellow's.

'A few of the chaps I was friendly with . . . well, they didn't make it back from France. And now . . . well, I do seem to keep myself to myself, rather.'

'Quite right,' said the doctor. 'Take it steady until you feel brighter.'

But Alistair still hesitated, wondering if there was a better way to put it. The men were good at calling the war a bastard and laughing at the mess it made of one's nerves. But it didn't do to be familiar with the men, and with his brother officers he could not trust himself to keep within bounds. He would find himself coming to, as if from a trance, to hear himself saying something like, '. . . and I didn't see him after that.' Which imposed on the others the burden of restoring the talk to a more pleasant level. People were good-humoured and patient but of course one hated to be a weight, and so he tended to take himself away.

But now he was making a fuss. It was hardly a medical condition, was it? One could live with a little loneliness. Men lived with ruptured gonads, with missing limbs. Men lived with their mothers-in-law, for pity's sake. He laughed, which was better.

The doctor glanced up at him and sighed. 'Look, old man, it's war. There isn't a pill. Find a sweet girl and forget it.'

'Thanks,' said Alistair, and went down into the street rather pleased with his prescription. He really ought to pay more attention to the whole business of courting. Even in war you were still more likely to be struck by a woman than by a bullet.

It was noon, which meant he was already late to meet Tom for lunch. He headed for Hyde Park and found that he was hurrying, which was surely a good sign. He hoped he would seem his old self to Tom – that they could simply pick it up where they had left off. And he was intrigued to finally meet Mary, and this friend Hilda with whom he was to be set up.

Entering Hyde Park, he entertained himself by forming a mental picture of Mary. It was rather sweet that Tom had got himself a girl. She must be steady enough for both of them, and probably thoroughly sensible. Not a head girl type, though – he couldn't see a woman setting her sights on Tom if she were popular enough in that way. Tom was a fine catch, of course, but perhaps for a nice girl who was herself sometimes overlooked.

No, Mary would be a practical girl with the motivation to wage what must have been a patient campaign against Tom's tendency to over-think. She would be pretty when she smiled, although perhaps less of a looker than his besotted friend painted her in his letters. She would be round-faced with round glasses, a little solid of leg, perhaps, and with a propensity for woollens and earnestness. Mary would be a terrific girl: game, good company, the daughter of a mother who also taught and a father who worked thirty minutes a day longer than his terms of employment strictly required. She would be as poor as Tom was, and all four of them would have a jolly lunch at the modest eatery Tom had proposed in his letter. 'Putting off the Ritz', was how Tom had phrased it.

After lunch they would all go their separate ways: Tom and Mary to an eventual marriage, Hilda to her own future, and Alistair to a rendezvous with the massed armour of the Wehrmacht.

Thinking about his imminent deployment, everything about London now moved him as never before. These mannered planes of grass in the park, those calm stone façades that rose above the bordering oaks, the ironed creases in the uniform trousers of the policeman who stood at Hyde Park Corner directing the traffic with his immaculate white armbands. All these timeless things could be seen more clearly when one had so little time oneself. In twenty-two hours he would board the train and be gone.

Back at barracks he would oversee the packing of his regiment. Every item would be documented and boxed and catalogued by the quartermaster, from the greatest artillery piece to the smallest dress-shirt stud. Then there would be the troopship: Biscay and Gibraltar, deck quoits for the officers and physical jerks for the men. Then it would all begin again: the war, with its fantastic shocks that knocked London out of a man and left him as he found himself now, with no immunity to the wonder of it.

He realised that he was standing quite still, eyes moist, halfway across Hyde Park. His pipe had gone out. He was standing by a tree. No, apparently he had taken cover by its trunk. He sweated cold. Dear god: without any fuss, and by some instinct he had picked up in France, he had found a concealed position. While his mind strayed, his body – unpiloted – had taken cover on a Saturday afternoon, as the bells of ice cream carts sounded. Pigeons paired. Squirrels did their mummery for sandwich crumbs and nuts. The Serpentine quivered as couples in rudderless love cooled their awkward oars in it. Alistair collected himself and walked on.

A crowd was out in the park. Men in uniform nodded to him in nonchalant fraternity. Pretty things swished by in dresses, giving him warm looks from under the brims of their hats. A girl smiled at him, a knockout girl in a WAAF uniform, and it was such a companionable smile that he grinned back, and just as he was thinking of some nice way to introduce himself, her skin took on the uneasy suggestion of bubbling and scorching and her hand – reaching up to touch her hair – seemed for a moment to be splintered bones that made jagged egress through the white cotton fingers of her gloves.

'I'm sorry,' he mumbled, and hurried on.

'I'm sorry,' he said again, long after she was too far away to hear.

It happened from time to time. It was just a maddening tic, like getting a popular jingle stuck in one's head. How one wished that all the gore had never got in there. Still, in this as in all other things, he felt certain that he would recover. The psyche, after all, could catch its breath again, as one recovered on the landing before tackling the next flight of stairs. In the meantime one could cheer oneself up, as he did now, by shooting one's cuffs and whistling 'Sleepy Lagoon'. He was still sweating cold, though, and the feeling took several minutes to pass and wasn't entirely gone even at lunch.

The place Tom had booked was at Lancaster Gate, and it was busy. Waiters addressed corks in a good-humoured frenzy and banged down the dish of the day with no more ceremony than it merited: it smelled brown, looked brown, cost one and six with a choice of dessert, and wasn't on the ration.

Tom rose and waved from a spot by the back wall. Alistair waved back and got so involved with piloting himself and his duffel bag through the tight press of diners that he didn't notice his friend's companions until he reached the table. Alistair smiled his introduction to them, then nodded politely at his friend.

'Excuse me, chum,' he said. 'You wouldn't have seen a bright-looking chap, about your height, only with a sorry excuse for a beard?'

Tom stroked his jaw. 'It has grown in rather obligingly, don't you think? And look at you! You look . . .'

'I know!' said Alistair. 'At least twenty years younger. It's the fresh air.'

They shook hands, and Alistair snatched another look at the women while he hung his jacket on the back of his seat. He had been right about Mary: she was a little slimmer than he had guessed, but there were the glasses – round, just as he had pictured them – and here was the button nose in the pretty round face that smiled at him now, under nice black hair in a modish pompadour that was fun if perhaps a little transatlantic. She seemed a charming girl, and he was delighted for Tom.

The other woman was a knockout, a redhead with peppy green eyes and a reckless, puckish stamp. Her hands fussed with her napkin. This must be Hilda. She smiled at him gaily, and he realised with a kick of nerves that he didn't entirely mind it. He saw now how it would all happen: after lunch someone would casually suggest the theatre, and naturally he and she would be seated together, and then afterwards they would all go to the dances.

She held his eye, nicely and without flirtation, and yet he felt that an acknowledgement was passing between them.

But now his stomach fell. He could not explain to himself the awful ache of melancholy that her simple, chummy smile provoked in him. A man ought to be glad. But her freckled face burned to bones before his eyes. Even when he blinked and her beauty was restored, his morale was left in ashes. Tomorrow he would be gone, and he guessed now – by the leaden sadness her beauty provoked – that he would never return. He broke off the glance, steadied himself, and looked to Tom.

'I'd like you to meet Mary,' Tom said, putting his arm around the woman Alistair had just been felled by.

Alistair smiled gamely while the universe splintered and re-formed itself into this different configuration with a concussion that none of the other diners seemed to feel.

'How do you do?' said Mary.

'How do you do?' said Alistair, since that was what one said.

'And this is Hilda,' said Tom, nodding to the girl with the pompadour.

'Delighted,' said Alistair.

'I hope you don't mind a gate-crasher,' said Hilda, managing to smile effervescently and look perfectly worried both at once.

It was a feat which in another time he knew he would have found endearing.

'Tell me if a gate-crasher turns up, and I'll tell you if I mind.'

Hilda laughed, and they shook hands. 'Tom said you were funny.'

'Did he also mention that I was rich and a world-renowned dancer?'

'Behave!' said Tom, and Alistair clicked heels and gave him a deferential salute that set both women giggling.

White wine came, and Tom filled their glasses. 'This stuff is actually champagne,' he said, 'only the bubbles have been requisitioned to give buoyancy to our submarine fleet. You will see that there have been a lot of changes while you've been away playing soldiers.'

'Apparently the girls have become lovelier,' said Alistair, flashing a grin at the women and intending to grace them both equally. His eyes snagged on Mary's, though, and in his embarrassment he almost blushed. She handled it calmly.

'Hilda is my loveliest friend,' she said. 'We were at school together.'

'I was the frumpy one,' said Hilda.

'Not at all,' said Alistair, coming gratefully back to her eyes.

A waiter put down four dishes of the day, in such a manner that nearly all the gravy stayed on the plates. 'Lamb,' he claimed, and took himself off.

Mary prodded at hers with a fork. 'Whatever it may have been, its suffering is over now.'

Tom raised his glass. 'Well, here's to us all. May we be as tough as the lamb, and luckier.'

'And here's to you two,' said Alistair, sweeping his glass in an arc that encompassed Tom and Mary. It gave both toast and fealty, and he marvelled that his arm had come up with the perfect movement all on its own.

'Yes,' said Hilda, 'aren't they sweet together?'

She smiled at him, he smiled back, and although he did not want it at all he saw now how the long day would be – how it must be – with the intimacies between himself and this perfectly nice girl serving as a proof that he was not fascinated by Mary. There was no use making a fuss about it.

'So, Hilda,' he said, 'tell me about yourself.'

She did.

After dessert the women went together to the women's room, and Alistair lit his pipe. Tom's cheeks were flushed with wine – they had taken a second bottle – and he drew fiercely on one of Mary's Craven "A"s.

'Isn't Mary something?' he said.

'Tom, she is one in a million. One in a thousand million.'

'Isn't she? Actually' – he leaned in and dropped his voice – 'it hasn't been plain sailing.'

'No?'

'Plus, I have to fight with this voice that insists she's too good for me.'

'That voice speaks the truth. If it gives you any racing tips, be sure to let me know immediately.'

'Do you suppose I should call the whole thing off?'

'Oh, Tom, I understand that your brain is large and perpetually at war with itself, but I hope it's not unkind to enquire why you don't simply ask her to marry you and let her decide if you're good enough?'

'Well . . .'

'Look, do you believe in the institution of marriage?'

'Of course.'

'And you accept that such beautiful lightning cannot strike you twice?'

'Well yes, I suppose—'

'Then shouldn't you get a ring on her as soon as possible?'

'It's just that I want to pick a moment when everything is going well.'

'Tom, there's a Blitzkrieg on. Women's hearts are being captured at astonishing speed. You can't just let a girl like that walk around in the wild.'

Tom slumped. 'As clear cut as that, you think?'

Alistair slapped his old friend on the shoulder. The wine made him warm and loose, and there was comfort in falling into their old roles of the sophisticate and the tenderfoot. Drink made everything better. The eye no longer saw what bodies became: the snapped bones and those poor, weeping veins missing their familiar connections. Drink was the warm resin that enveloped living bodies, fixing them in the amber of the present.

'I'm happy for you,' Alistair said, and he meant it. 'I don't know how you've done it, but I can only humbly marvel.'

Tom sucked on his cigarette. The women came back to the table: Mary first, with fresh crimson lips and a faint air of soap; Hilda following, sharp with *Vol de Nuit*, her hairdo reinvigorated.

'This dive still won't get a gramophone,' Hilda said, tapping out a menthol cigarette. Alistair lit it for her. She cupped her hands around the lighter, holding his for a moment. It was not an unpleasant feeling. He watched her face as she drew against the flame. She was a warm, likeable, undramatic girl. He had twenty-one hours left in the world.

'What kind of music do you like?' said Hilda, exhaling.

'Tell us about the war,' said Mary in the same moment, and then, 'Oh, I'm sorry.'

'No, I'm sorry,' said Hilda.

Alistair smiled from one to the other with modest neutrality. 'I'm ashamed to admit I'm no expert on either. I'm afraid you'll think me rather a bore.'

'Not at all,' said Hilda.

'Yes, rather,' said Mary at the same time.

She fixed Alistair with a look that was, he felt, principally comic. If there was a certain sharpness to it, the wine took the edge off. He took another sip.

'I like the big bands,' he said, struggling to name one. 'Something with a bit of zip.'

'Oh, I *adore* the big bands,' said Hilda. 'Bert Ambrose! Harry Roy!'

'Harry Roy,' said Alistair. 'Now there's a man who knows music.'

He hoped Harry Roy was a band leader and not a monkey mascot or a new kind of dance. Hilda seemed delighted, so it was probably all right. Her dimples were nice. He understood that he was seducing her, which it seemed would be achieved simply by remaining in the uniform of a captain in the Royal Artillery until such a time as it became appropriate to remove it.

'We only know what we read in the papers,' said Mary, lighting a cigarette.

Alistair's nerves sparked when he looked at her. He hoped the jolt wasn't visible in his eyes. How ordinary Hilda was, beside Mary – and how shabby his own need for warmth.

He took some more wine. 'You probably all know more than I do, about the overall situation. I'm afraid they only tell us chaps what we need to know: come here, look lively, bunk up, dig in.'

'Tom tells me you fought the Germans in France,' said Mary.

He looked down at his glass. 'Briefly, yes.'

'What was it like?'

In her face there was a simple anxiety that he could hardly bear. It made her so tender. He found he couldn't speak.

'Darling . . .' said Tom, putting a hand on her arm.

'Oh, I'm sorry,' she said.

'Oh no, that's quite all right,' Alistair said quickly.

She blushed, and he realised that perhaps she was a little drunk too. He was a swine for making the moment awkward. He wondered what he could say: to show by a temperate reply that her question had not been out of place, and also to answer her honestly.

But what ought he to tell her? None of it was suitable to relate. The Germans had swooped on them in stiff airframes with bull whistles screaming. Under the hardened sky they had squared off the undulant plain with grey armour. They took the direct line, scorning roads that had wound for millennia. People and animals were spooked – the land had no natural resistance to the pure black method.

How could one speak of it over lunch? After the hard planes and the hard tanks had come hard men in hard formations, banging their boots in adamant time. A terrible hardness was how it had seemed to Alistair: a preternatural hardness that ordinary men had fled from and exceptional men had dashed themselves against and been ground into the soft French mud, the perfectly regular imprint of the tank tracks making no distinction between corpse and clay. He saw his friends' faces crushed and flattened. He saw Tom's, and Hilda's, and Mary's faces crushed and flattened. Good god – he was gripping his wine glass. Good god.

'The Germans were just well organised,' he said. 'The next time we tangle with them, we'll be organised too.'

Mary said, 'You're just like my father.'

Alistair was relieved to move on. 'And what does your father do?'

'He's a politician,' said Mary, stubbing out her cigarette and holding his eye with an irony that she might be inviting him to share – he couldn't tell.

'He's MP for the Wensum Valley,' said Tom.

'Well then,' said Alistair, 'I'm sure you know more than I do about the war picture.'

Mary inspected her nails. 'I'm afraid they only tell us girls what we need to know: come here, look lively, bunk up, dig in.'

Alistair laughed, and Mary flashed him a prankish grin. How quickly she could turn in conversation.

Hilda, who seemed slightly at sevens with the whole exchange, shook their third wine bottle and proclaimed it empty. She stood, slightly unsteadily and with a clattering of cutlery to the floor.

'Oh come on, you lot, let's jilt this dump and go somewhere with music.'

Alistair took care of the bill – it was true what they said: you couldn't take it with you – and then they were out in the hot blue Saturday afternoon, in Hyde Park, Mary and Tom up ahead, arm in arm, and he bringing up the rear with Hilda, who shrugged her cardigan down off her shoulders and smiled up at the sun with half-closed eyes.

'Isn't this grand?' she said, taking his arm. 'It was stuffy in there.'

'Yes,' he said. 'Grand.'

'Don't you love the feeling you get when the sun comes out in London?'

'Are all the questions this easy?'

She laughed and leaned her head on his shoulder as they walked. The feeling of her at his side was pleasant, and now that they were outside and the first overpowering blush of her perfume had mellowed, she smelled warm and rather nice. Up ahead, Mary in her summer dress and white straw hat threw her head back and laughed at something Tom had said. Alistair felt unbearable anguish.

They bought ices from a kiosk and ate them as they walked. Mary slipped along with the carefree, long-limbed swing of someone on whom the present hour was neither too tight nor too loose.

Hilda was saying, 'Can't you just tell straight away, sometimes, when a person is all right?'

'You're doing it again,' he said.

'And you're noticing again, so we're even.'

'Isn't it fun to keep score?'

She poked him in the ribs. 'See? Now you're getting it.'

Over the streets, the barrage balloons bobbed nicely against a few small cotton-puff clouds. Hilda chatted happily. Wherever they were headed, Alistair guessed, it was likely to have wine.

The four of them wondered what they might do, since it was too early for dancing and too hot to keep strolling in the sun. A show would be the thing, but in theatreland nothing seemed to be beginning – it was four in the afternoon – and they bumped from place to place until Mary said they should go to the Lyceum. The minstrel troupe was playing there, as it had since forever, and she had a pupil, Zachary, whose father was a performer.

The hoardings had men in frock coats and hats, in blackface, cakewalking across the theatre's façade in their white spats and sticks. A fat white man in cork paint was calling the crowd in: *Come in dere, fine masters, you never seen such a show in all your life, you never heard such a fine music.*

'Must we?' said Tom. 'The whole coons-with-canes thing?'

'Oh, but it's done in a knowing way,' said Mary. 'It's a *clin d'oeil.*'

Tom looked to Alistair. 'What do you say? It's your leave, after all.'

Alistair, who had hardly been concentrating, understood that they were waiting on him. The caller, noticing the party's hesitation, stepped up to them with an encircling, ushering gesture that made it seem rudeness not to let him escort them to the box office. His cork paint was unconvincing, a line of sunburned pink skin glistening between the blacking and his collar.

'Forget your cares for an hour,' he said, 'as we transports you back through de magic of music an' laughter to de peaceful world of de plantation, where dat good old darkie humour lifted spirits an' lightened hearts.'

'Must you do that voice?' said Mary.

'Do let's go in,' said Hilda. 'It'll be just like on the wireless.'

'Indeed it will be finer,' said the caller. 'The BBC's troupe ain't got nothin' on ours. Here you will hear ballads too bawdy for broadcast, airs too 'airy for the airwaves, an' of course all of dis comes' – he addressed himself to the gentlemen of the party, and dropped the accent – 'with your first drink on the house, from a selection of beers, wines and spirits that are not commonly available under the present circumstances.'

'Oh what the hell,' said Alistair.

'Oooh!' said Hilda, clapping her hands.

Tom gave them both a sardonic look.

'Oh Tom,' said Mary. 'Must you spoil today?'

There was an edge in her voice that made Alistair look. He hadn't noticed Tom spoiling anything, but perhaps he had lost the skill of noticing when days were spoiled by anything subtler than shrapnel. He wondered if another drink might help.

The theatre was set out with tables in the stalls, and they took one close to the stage. It was agreeable down there, in front of the red velvet curtain, with the gilded columns of the proscenium catching warm glints from the curtain lights. Laughter from a dozen other tables rattled around, and above them conversation buzzed in the high circle.

Wine arrived just in time to stop everyone turning to gore. Another bottle followed, and the four of them relaxed in the soft pink glow of the table lamp. Alistair understood that his chair and Hilda's must converge a little with every glass, as Tom's and Mary's were doing on the other side of the table, until without any particular moment having been marked they found themselves arranged as two couples. Hilda's hand migrated to his knee, Alistair's arm curled around her waist, and there was something sweet and attentive in the way they carefully ignored each other while their bodies achieved all of this on their own.

Instead they laughed especially hard at a joke Mary made, and brought fascinated interest to bear on a long anecdote that poor Tom was struggling to make go nowhere, until finally, as the house lights dimmed and all eyes turned to the stage, Hilda's body was nestled against Alistair's. This thrilled and dismayed him, both at once. Through his uniform jacket he could feel her quick heart. Its fluttering made him sad: such a tiny pump, the heart, and such an endless flood, life.

The audience fell silent and the curtain came up on darkness. Behind the stage a red spotlight made a thin sliver of light that rose until it became the uppermost part of a disc, and then a half-circle, and then a whole circle rising over the stage. This was the sun, and as it rose it brightened from red to orange to white. The stage lights came up with it and illuminated the backdrop: a view out over London from the top of a hill, with spires gleaming and barrage balloons tethered above the sweep of the familiar city.

There was the Tower with its medieval walls, there St Paul's aping Rome, and there St Martin-in-the-Fields, the sober Greek temple impaled from beneath by that hysterical Georgian spire. Alistair brimmed with pleasure to see it spread out in the warm glow of the stage lights. Dear old London – the conflator of all centuries, the pigeon-feeding tramp wearing all of her clothes at once.

As the sun rose over the painted city, a chorus of blackface minstrels processed from the wings. A dozen came in from each side and arranged themselves in a semicircle open to the audience. In a whisper at first, rising in volume as the sun rose, they sang.

> *Bless this house, O Lord we pray,*
> *Make it safe by night and day.*

Whether it was the wine, or the city he had missed, or the seventeen hours he had left, Alistair found himself overcome as the voices swelled.

> *Bless these walls so firm and stout,*
> *Keeping want and trouble out.*

After the hymn, a negro made up as a white man took to the stage in top hat and tails and introduced himself as Mister Interlocutor.

'That's him!' whispered Mary. 'That's Zachary's father.'

The Interlocutor leaned in to the microphone. 'In these times of threat and anxiety, when our enemy besets us and we are weighted down with cares, it does the heart good to remember old times, when life – though it was hard – was familiar, and the negroes gathering together would lighten their heavy labours with song and with levity.'

One of the chorus men stepped forward, large crimson lips painted over his black face. 'Well Mistah Interloculator, I wouldn't be knowin' about no leviditty, excuse my ignorimiddy.'

The audience laughed and applauded, and Alistair laughed with them. It was a kick, after the poignancy of the hymn.

'Ah, Mister Bones,' said the Interlocutor with affection. 'I might have known it would be you.'

'Allus does seems to be me, Mistah Intercalculator, every time I check. Try as I might I can't seems to wake up lookin' like you.'

Everyone roared. Alistair lit Hilda's cigarette and she snuggled a little closer.

'And tell me, Bones, what have you been up to lately?'

'Well Mistah Innoculator, I have been out and about in de night.'

'In the night, Bones? Out?'

'Yes sir, why else do you suppose dey call it a blackout?'

Thump of a drum, crash of a cymbal. The audience cheered, the Interlocutor waved his cane like a baton and the whole chorus came forward to launch into an upbeat swing of 'Joshua Fit the Battle of Jericho'.

'Aren't they marvellous?' said Hilda, close to Alistair's ear.

'Tremendous,' said Alistair.

'How many of them do you suppose are actually coloured?'

'Well I daresay that fellow Bones is, and at least half of the chaps in the chorus line. Hard to tell, under all that war paint.'

'Aren't they marvellous?' said Hilda again, across the table.

'Terrific,' said Tom.

'Terrible,' said Mary, laughing. 'I mean, don't you think?'

'But it's only a *clin d'oeil*,' said Tom. 'Or at least that's what you said.'

'I know, but the *lips*, darling. The . . .' She popped her eyes wide.

'Oh, come on,' said Tom. 'Actually it's funnier than I thought.'

'But so humiliating! I'm sorry I dragged you all to see this.'

Tom yawned. 'I'd be surprised if they weren't all earning more than me.'

'Yes, well, maybe I should marry one of them,' said Mary, knocking back the last of her glass.

Alistair winked at Tom. It was rather fun to see his old friend in hot water. Mary caught Alistair at it, and gave him a look that seemed to be amused – though whether at him or with him, he couldn't tell. He signalled to the busboy for another bottle of white. By now, no one was counting.

As the spiritual ended and the applause faded away, the Interlocutor clapped his hands and a new backdrop fell. Now they were in Berlin, before a Reichstag with wonky columns and flags with a reversed swastika. Roman standards carried the Reich's eagle with pendulous breasts and a harlot's stockings and suspenders. As the audience laughed and booed, a performer detached himself from the semicircle and dragged a soapbox to centre stage where a microphone was standing ready. A single spotlight shone on him.

The man was white, and a little rectangular patch had been omitted from his blackface to give him the infamous toothbrush moustache in negative. He climbed up on the soapbox, knocked himself off again with an overzealous Nazi salute, then climbed back on again to laughter.

The audience settled. From offstage came the sound effect of a wireless being tuned. The performer leaned in to the microphone and spread his arms dramatically.

'Dis is Jaaarmany callin' . . . dis is Jaaaaarmany callin'.'

The audience howled.

'In August alone, de German navy did sink de followin' British ships: De HMS *Pinafore*. De *African Queen*. De Good Ship Lollipop.'

'My dear fellow,' the Interlocutor said. 'What nonsense!'

'Oh, you don't believe me? Den tell me, did you see any dem ships come into port recently?'

'Well, no . . . but—'

'Well den! Never doubt what de German wireless be tellin' you!'

He wagged his finger at the audience, who catcalled and jeered.

'We ended resistance in all de followin' countries: Xanadu. El Dorado. Atlantis. Although I think dere was something fishy 'bout dat last one.'

'Come on,' said Mary, 'let's get out of this dive.'

'Oh please,' said Hilda, 'let's give it five more minutes.'

Mary made a deferential bow. Up on stage, the Broadcaster was working himself into a frenzy.

'You British have no chance! We knows all your secrets! We knows everything 'bout your country!'

'Oh yes?' said the Interlocutor. 'Such as?'

'Such as the intentions of your leader, dat Mistah Winsome Chivalry.'

'Ah, you mean Mister Winston Churchill.'

The audience applauded his name, and the Broadcaster leered. 'Dat's right, de skinny guy. We know de man has no fight in 'im. He'll never attack.'

From the audience: 'Oh yes he will!' And the Broadcaster: 'Oh no he won't.'

As they went back and forth in raucous escalation, the semi-circle of singers set up a low, wailing, rising and falling note, quiet at first and then louder until the Broadcaster, finally appearing to notice it, broke off from haranguing the crowd and cupped a hand to listen.

'Oh lordy! De air-raid warnin'! Surely not here in Berlin!'

As the Broadcaster cowered in fear, the audience cheered with delight. The spotlight snapped off, the stage lights fell, and the chorus carried on their wailing, the note rising and falling in the dark. A silver moon rose over the backdrop, which had changed to a blacked-out London by night. The chorus steadied their wailing at its highest pitch and held it in a clear hum that sounded over the moonlit city. The note sounded long and sweet and finally rose into 'I Vow to Thee, My Country'. Hilda wept. Tom appeared to have something in his eye, and it seemed to Alistair that even Mary was pacified.

The curtain fell for the interval. The house lights came up. The Interlocutor came out from backstage and sat at a baby grand, front of house. He rolled up the sleeves of his tailcoat, propped up the piano lid, cocked his top hat back and began an incidental.

'Why don't you go over and say hello?' said Tom.

'Oh stop it. I'm ashamed.'

'But what did you expect?' said Hilda.

'I didn't realise the joke would be quite so much on *them*.'

The Interlocutor's right hand rippled up and down the high notes and his left pressed out the big chords, perfectly steady and regular, a steam hammer cutting out shapes. As he played he cast his eyes over the tables, smiling at the audience, giving a wink here and mouthing a 'thank you' there, while his hands played automatically. His face was calm under the thick white mask of greasepaint. He smiled at the table where the four of them sat, favouring them no more or less than the rest, and then his gaze moved on.

'Doesn't he recognise you?' said Hilda.

'Can't you see he is being discreet?' said Mary.

'We all look alike to them, is what it is.'

'Go *on*!' said Tom, squeezing Mary's arm. 'Go and say hello.'

Alistair saw Mary's discomfort. He said, 'I'll bet you can't be quite sure it's him.'

Mary threw him a grateful look. 'I'm not at all sure.'

Alistair said, 'He might be the Queen of Sheba under all that paint.'

Mary nodded quickly. 'I . . . um . . .'

'I move we get more wine,' Alistair said. 'What does the panel think?'

'Oh, wine!' said Hilda, clapping her hands as if it were a clever new invention.

Alistair signalled and a bottle arrived almost before his arm was fully extended. He filled all four glasses, displacing whatever volume of awkwardness had accumulated. It was obvious that the entire war could be solved in this way. The trick would be to reach for a corkscrew instead, every time some brass hat ordered artillery.

The interval ended, the stage lights came up and the Interlocutor climbed up into the beam of a spotlight. He waited for the crowd to settle.

'Ladies and gentlemen. Though these times are dramatic, the greatest drama of our lives still plays in the theatre of the heart, which is why our next number is a love song. But before we sing slow for you, let's all take a moment to think of our true loves. It could be you're lucky enough to be sitting next to them right now. Or maybe they're far away, posted overseas. Maybe the two of you haven't even met yet, and you're holding the idea of each other.'

As he spoke, the sound of the air-raid sirens came again. This time it was not the choir singing it – the effect came from offstage, as the wireless effects had done – and it seemed to come from all quarters at once.

'So our next song,' said the Interlocutor, 'our slow number dedicated to those who could not be with us tonight, is a particular favourite of—'

The sirens swelled, cutting him off.

'Isn't it clever?' whispered Hilda. 'I wonder how they do it.'

But Alistair saw the Interlocutor's expression. By the instinct his body had picked up in France, his hand swept the floor at his side and located his uniform cap. His foot reached under the table and drew his duffel bag towards him. As he took hold of it he felt the hard shape of the jar of Tom's blackberry jam. He had meant for them all to share it at lunch – perhaps with scones if the restaurant had been able to rustle some up – but now of course it would have to wait. That was this war all over: just when you got comfortable, they dropped the fire curtain.

He kissed Hilda on the forehead, told her she was adorable, and took a long, cold drink of the wine.

It was ugly when the house lights went up. The stage manager made an announcement no one could hear. People were making a racket asking what was going on, and soon the theatre was a confusion of people heading for contrary exits – not in panic but without decorum either, and not minding if they trod on a few feet. Everyone was in everyone else's way. No one seemed to know if there was a shelter in the theatre or whether they were supposed to try their luck in the public ones outside, and as a result the whole thing was snarled up and nervous.

'What should we do?' said Mary to Tom.

Tom looked to Alistair. 'What do you think?'

Alistair thought it strange that they deferred to him. His khaki was hardly native to these gilded columns and these pink velvet seats. Civilians must surely outrank him in this theatre. He laughed, then realised by their expressions how inappropriate it was. He held tight to the table. Now that he was standing, he understood that he was drunker than strictly necessary.

He looked around at the chaos of the theatre, the stalls in packed disarray and the great circle jammed with people trying to circulate in opposite directions. He hadn't a clue what to suggest.

'Miss North?' said a voice from behind them.

The Interlocutor had come down to their table. Alistair watched Mary compose herself and smile.

'You need to work on Zachary's writing,' she said, offering her hand.

'Yes?' said the Interlocutor as he shook it.

'He uses punctuation as if it were rationed and vowels as if he had hit the mother lode.'

From above came anxious voices as the upper circle pushed downstairs.

'Might the rest wait until parents' evening?' said the Interlocutor. 'Only I came to invite you people to share our basement shelter.'

'If you're sure it's no trouble,' said Mary.

'Why, what are you going to do? Heckle us?'

The Interlocutor led them backstage and down into the theatre's basement. It was arched and vaulted, twenty feet from floor to ceiling at the apex of each vault and never lower than fifteen feet at the pillars. The basement was as long and broad below ground as the theatre was above. It was lit by a hundred bulbs swinging on cloth-braided wire.

The Interlocutor ushered them along a narrow passage that had been cleared between the rolled backdrops and wooden façades and pantomime horses, to an area against one wall where the players and crew members were grumbling as they took their seats on wooden benches. Their voices echoed and boomed through the sound-box of the basement. The mood was of annoyance – the performance had been hotting up nicely, and here was another false alarm.

'Make yourselves easy,' said the Interlocutor, and they all sat.

'Isn't it a bore?' said Hilda. 'There should be a law that they can't do these drills at the weekend.'

The Interlocutor put two fingers in his mouth to give a whistle, and Zachary appeared from behind a rack of drapes.

'Fetch me the basin?' said the Interlocutor.

Zachary disappeared and came back with a cloth and a bowl of water, which he set before his father. The Interlocutor patted the bench beside him and Zachary sat down and grinned. 'Good afternoon, Miss North.'

'Mary, please. You needn't "Miss North" me out of school.'

'Fine, then you needn't call me Zachary.'

'Oh? What am I to call you?'

'"Mr Lee" will do just fine.'

Mary smiled. 'Very well then, Mr Lee. I should like you to meet my friends Mr Tom Shaw, Miss Hilda Appleby and Mr Alistair Heath.'

'Good afternoon,' said Zachary, more shyly.

'Don't say you live down here?' said Hilda, rather loud from the wine.

The Interlocutor looked up from scrubbing off his stage paint. 'We rent a room above a cobbler's. Which is fine except for the hammering. You might say the sole inconvenience is the sole inconvenience.'

Tom gave Zachary an avuncular smile. 'And you come along to watch?'

Zachary looked down at his hands. 'I help out.'

'Excuse the boy,' said his father. 'He's quiet around people.'

Tom ruffled Zachary's hair. 'No need to be shy, is there? We won't bite.'

Alistair watched Tom in the lurching light of the bulbs, and wondered if his old friend had always seemed such an ass. Perhaps it was only the wine wearing off, making Tom clumsy and Alistair unkind. He wished he'd thought to bring the bottle down with them.

'And how do you help out with the show?' Hilda was saying.

Zachary shrugged. 'This and that.'

'He's here to remind himself what not to do,' said his father. 'Boy's going to be a lawyer, or a physician.'

Mary smiled at Zachary. 'That's what you want, is it?'

'Sure.'

His father said, 'That's why it lifts me when he tells me how well he's doing in class.'

Zachary looked to Mary, widening his eyes in appeal. She hesitated, then smiled. 'He tries splendidly hard. And anyway, I don't see what's so wrong with what you do. You're marvellously good.'

Zachary's father wrung out the face cloth. The milky water ran into the bowl. 'It's a living, I suppose. And we don't bother anyone.'

'I have to ask,' said Mary. 'How do you find it? The show, I mean?'

He gave her a steady look. 'How do I find it, Miss North? I walk up the Strand and make a left onto Wellington Street.'

'But since you say that you want more for Zachary, I'm wondering if you mean . . . in some aspects . . . oh, it goes without saying that the performance is fabulous . . . but don't you sometimes find it just a tiny bit . . .'

'Sure,' said Zachary's father. 'You'd want more for your child.'

'But since you are . . . oh, you know, *in it*, aren't you ever tempted – forgive me – to challenge the attitudes?'

Zachary's father grinned. 'You're the ones fighting evil. We're just the help.'

'Oh stop it!' said Mary.

'It's you I feel for. We only do the act twice a day, but you people are on the whole time.'

Mary laughed. Hilda sniffed, doing her lips in a tortoiseshell compact. 'Shouldn't we have the all-clear by now? How long will they keep us down here?'

'Just till they've rattled their clipboards,' said Alistair. 'These drills don't mark themselves, you know.'

Hilda smiled. Alistair smiled back. It was nice that everyone smiled. Although something in her face was awry. Probably this, too, was just the wine wearing off. It was the least pleasant accident of consciousness, and poor Hilda could hardly be blamed for it. Ten minutes ago he'd been perfectly content with the press of her body. Whenever one thought about happiness, it was because it was wearing off.

Tom said, 'I hate to be a bore, but I'm not wonderful with underground spaces. I'm starting to feel queer, truth be told.'

'Hear, hear,' said Hilda. 'I don't see why we should stay put, just for the form. Why don't we go to Brown's and have a cocktail? We could all—'

The first bomb hit London with unimagined force. The concussion was unambiguous. First it came to them through the ground. The benches jumped beneath them, and everyone yelped.

Then the sound came, a deep bass shock, the echoes rolling in the basement's stone vaults.

'Oh Christ . . .' said Tom. 'This is it.'

Zachary buried his head in his father's chest. His father held him close, resting his chin on the top of the boy's head, his eyes wide. Three more detonations came, even louder.

Hilda grabbed at Alistair. 'Oh god . . .' Her breath came in quick gasps.

Alistair patted her hand. 'Try to breathe. We're safe down here.'

Zachary's father had his mouth close to the boy's ear. 'The sun shall not smite thee by day, nor the moon by night . . .'

Mary stood abruptly and smoothed her dress. 'I must go to the school.'

'What?' said Tom.

Mary picked up her handbag. 'Will you come?'

'But why . . .?'

'I have to make sure it's safe. I didn't bar the shutters, or anything.'

Tom was pale. 'But we can't go out there. It's . . .'

Mary hesitated. Alistair stood and guided her back to the bench.

'It's just a building,' he said. 'The doctors can save them every time.'

Hilda gasped. 'My parents!'

'They'll be fine too,' said Alistair. 'They'll have taken shelter as we have.'

A string of sharper impacts came, much louder and nearer. Hilda shrieked, and shouts came from the players.

'It's all right!' Alistair called back. 'That's ours. It's anti-aircraft.'

The detonations sent dust pouring from the ceiling. Alistair went around to settle people. He got the players to have

164

cigarettes, and one by one they lit up with shaking hands. This was what he always had his men do when they were rattled: smoke or brew tea, or write letters, or polish boots – anything to get back in character.

Alistair sat back down beside Hilda. Now the rumbling of the bombs was further off. It boomed through the cellar and set up a discordant vibration in the untuned strings of an old piano.

'Which of you requested this?' said Alistair. 'Worst tune I ever heard.'

Mary frowned. 'Philistine. You soldiers want everything in a major key.'

'Quite right too. And in four/four time so we can march to it.'

Tom said, 'I wish you two would stop pretending this is funny.'

Alistair nodded his apology. 'I know this isn't much fun.'

Tom pursed his lips. 'No, I'm sorry. I can't . . . it's just that . . .'

'It's all right,' said Alistair. 'I was exactly the same, my first time. Here, I know what'll cheer us up. Remember that jam you made?'

He was rummaging for it in his duffel bag when the array of electric bulbs flickered and went out. The players murmured in alarm. Beside Alistair, Hilda was tight as a board, the hysteria hardening beneath her skin. He was sobering up with every bang, and with each nervous twitch of Hilda's body he felt less inclined to soothe and more disposed to snap at her.

He sparked his lighter so at least they could all see. 'Does anyone have a piece of string I could hang this with?'

'I have some sewing cotton,' said Mary.

'Fine.'

'Does it matter what colour? I have pink, red and white.'

Alistair understood that she was being less than serious. His irritation vanished. With her cotton he fixed the lighter to a bulb flex. His fingers did the work with their old skill. The shifting flame tossed their shadows back and forth, as if they were not fixtures in society but only tricks of the light.

'It was good of you to invite us down here,' said Mary.

Zachary's father smiled. 'It was nice of you to come and see our show.'

'You must come and see ours. We'll have a nativity near Christmas.'

'Do you have enough children for all the parts?'

'I think so. One really only needs a holy couple, an angel and a narrator. Some wise men would be nice, but then isn't that just like life?'

Alistair winked at Tom. 'You're not going to let that stand?'

But Tom only gripped the bench and flinched at the bangs. In the guttering light Alistair saw the slow look Mary gave him.

'You're good with this,' said Hilda, her head back on Alistair's shoulder.

'Well I grew up in a mine, you see.'

She snuggled closer. 'I don't suppose you'd mind putting your arm around me?'

Soon the lighter flame burned out and all of them waited in the dark. More bombs fell, and with each one Hilda pressed closer. Once or twice at a particularly loud explosion she gave a shriek. When she was halfway into his lap, Alistair eased her off and stood up.

'Would you all excuse me? I ought to contact my regiment.'

'Will you come back?' said Hilda.

'Don't worry,' said Alistair.

'Oh, I wish you wouldn't go.'

Her voice was such a porridge of fright that it made him glad to leave.

Here and there the basement was lit by the glow of cigarettes, and a little further along someone had set up a candle. Alistair made his way to the staircase and up to the theatre.

Once upstairs, the sound of the anti-aircraft guns was loud and close. The backstage area was lit up by flashes entering through an open stage door. Alistair made for that, tripping over props and drapes, and then he was outside in the narrow alley beside the theatre.

It was half dark, and the hot air was sharp with smoke. Alistair scanned the sky, listening to the bombers and the anti-aircraft guns. Searchlights cut the crimson base of what might have been smoke or might have been cloud. From the noise and the angle of the beams, the main body of the attack was a fair way off: a mile, maybe two. Underground, with that awful resonance, it had seemed closer.

He went back into the theatre and nosed around by the light of the flashes until he found wine on one of the tables. He leaned back into the scoop of the baby grand, took a long drink and stared up at the theatre. The gun flashes glinted on the gold columns and the high proscenium arch.

'I'm to tell you to come back down immediately.'

He turned. Mary had come from the basement and now stood watching him. The occulting light lit her up, her cigarette smoke flashing silver.

'You probably ought to go back down yourself,' he said.

She said nothing, only stood with her arms crossed.

'Did the others send you to fetch me?'

'Hilda is a wonderful girl. We've been friends since we were six. She is mischievous and loyal, and very funny until a man walks into the room, when upon her IQ immediately halves. But it is only shyness, you see. I'm sure the phenomenon would vanish as you got to know her.'

He filled his pipe in the stuttering light. 'Would you like some wine? I'm afraid I was drinking from the bottle.'

'Ugh. You see, this is why I prefer civilians.'

'Do you have a lighter?'

She came to the other side of the baby grand and slid him the lighter while he slid her the bottle. She took a short drink. Outside, the anti-aircraft guns let off a salvo, making them both flinch.

'You really should go back down,' he said.

'I shall be glad to. Right behind you.'

'Look, Hilda is lovely. It's me. I'm really not myself at the moment.'

'Oh for pity's sake, who is? You're an army officer. I'm a schoolteacher. The whole world is in fancy dress.'

'I just need a bit of time.'

'Fine,' said Mary, 'I shall wait here with you.'

'I meant . . . oh, never mind.'

'I know what you meant,' said Mary. 'But Hilda is a hoot. She likes parties, and big bands, and subterfuge. You shan't tell me you don't like such things? She plays tricks on me, and runs rings around my mother, and she once set fire to a baronet's motor car because he lent it to Oswald Mosley.'

'Forget romance. We ought to parachute her behind enemy lines.'

Mary sighed. 'I wish you would kiss her, first.'

Alistair drank some wine. The flashes through the open stage door left green afterimages of the bottle glass. He said, 'Tom is a good man, you know.'

'Oh, I know. I hope you didn't read too much into . . .'

'It's just that the two of you seemed a little . . .'

'Well, it's the war, isn't it? It's one thing for you, being out there in the action. Cooped up in town, we get snippy.'

'Tom really believes in teaching, that's the thing. I suppose he can't bear to have it all interrupted.'

'I liked it about him straight away. Men usually bleat about one's looks, but Tom had to know exactly what I thought about the new Education Act.'

Alistair smiled. 'And he is a useful cook, of course. He can take thoroughly demoralised ingredients and give them back their will to live.'

'And he has taken great risks for me. It does his career no good to let me have my school.'

'But that is just like Tom, isn't it? Thoroughly unselfish.'

'Yes, thoroughly.'

'I rather resent having to surrender him to you.'

'Blame Hitler,' said Mary.

'Oh, I do. I will seduce his flatmate the moment we capture Berlin.'

'I hope you and Hitler's flatmate will be jolly happy together.'

'Well I'm glad that you and Tom are.'

'Oh, we are.'

'Well, that's fine,' said Alistair.

'And look, Hilda is terrific. You shouldn't judge her just because she—'

'Oh, of course not. Nobody is brave, the first time in an air raid.'

Mary took a longer drink of the wine. 'It's much better up here, isn't it? The bombs aren't nearly so close as one imagines when one is down below.'

'I expect they're attacking the docks.'

Mary slid the bottle back to him. 'Should we go and look? I mean, there mightn't be another air raid. I'd hate to think I missed the one chance.'

Alistair said nothing.

'What?' said Mary.

'You make it sound like the jubilee fireworks.'

'Are you scared?'

'Yes, and so should you be.'

'I'm a grown-up.'

'Still, I wouldn't want you to get hurt.'

'Let's not get hurt then. Let's just go a little way.'

He hesitated. 'All right.'

'As close as we can, just to see what it looks like.'

Outside, the sky was lurid. The sound of the bombs seemed distant, and it was hard to make out the direction while the echoes rolled up the white marble canyon of the Strand. Light came in all colours and from all directions. Smoke, or cloud, hung at a few thousand feet, looming blue-white when search-lights cut in on it from below, flashing yellow when exploding anti-aircraft shells lit it from above. It was seven thirty in the evening and the sun seemed to be setting in the west and the east simultaneously. Alistair stood a yard from Mary and they looked from one sunset to the other.

'What is that in the east?'

'I don't know,' said Alistair. 'Some new kind of searchlight.'

'So red?'

'Could it be lithium? I didn't know we had anything that bright.'

'I wish we could see over those buildings.'

'Come on,' said Alistair. 'We should go back.'

Mary craned her neck. 'But we haven't seen anything. Let's at least go as far as the river.'

'The wardens won't like it.'

'So? They can give us a good telling-off. You won't cry, will you?'

He grinned. 'All right. Just as far as the river, and then we'll go back.'

They reached the Thames and ducked under a barrier to get onto the half-built Waterloo Bridge. The pontoons were connected with a scaffold that sufficed if one didn't look down. Near the centre of the span, while the sun set over the water behind them, they had a clear view to the east. They stopped. Where the bombing was concentrated, flames rose hundreds of feet into the air. From time to time high above, the pale under-side of an aircraft would glow for a moment as it twisted through the light. The whole scene was inverted in the river, bent and shattered in the oily wavelets. As they watched the fires reaching down into the black depths, they felt the breeze on their backs as the distant flames drew air in. They stood with their hands gripping the scaffold, an arm's length apart. They listened to the roaring of the distant fires.

'Good god,' said Alistair at last.

Mary said nothing, only stared at the conflagration.

'Mary, are you all right?'

He moved a foot closer and then stopped, dropping the hand he had been about to put on her arm.

She looked up at him, took half a step forward, then hesitated. 'We shouldn't go any further.'

He smiled. 'No. This mightn't take two people's weight.'

She gave him a grateful look. 'We ought to go back. To be safe.'

'Yes. We really should.'

They stood at the centre of the almost-bridge and she said, 'I'm glad we went as far as we could.'

They walked back. The lacerated sky faded in the west and brightened in the east. When they reached the Lyceum they stopped at the stage door.

Mary said, 'You aren't coming in, are you?'

'I should find my regiment. The men get in a state without orders.'

She looked away. 'You must do the right thing, of course.'

'Would you say something to Hilda from me? And to Tom?'

'If you like. I'm sure they'll understand.'

'You're a rock.'

She looked up at him sharply. 'Alistair, are we cowards?'

Their faces flashed in the frank light of the guns, and he was silent.

\*　　\*　　\*

Back down in the basement someone had lit more candles.

Tom rose when Mary returned. 'Are you all right? What happened?'

'He had to go to his regiment. He said to let you know how sorry he is.'

Hilda slumped. 'But what took so long?'

'He couldn't leave until there was a gap in the bombing.'

'He's mad,' said Tom.

'It isn't as close as it seems down here. They're bombing the docks.'

'Perhaps we should all go up,' said Hilda. 'One would hate to miss out on the action.'

Mary said nothing.

'I was worried sick,' said Tom. 'I'm sorry. I know it's silly.'

Mary sat down with him. 'I was only upstairs.'

'I should have come up, I know. I was just—'

Mary took his hand to show that it didn't matter. Now that she was back in the basement she began to shake. They waited, down in the dark.

After an hour Mary said, 'I don't suppose there's any chance of a song?'

Zachary's father cupped his hands. 'Any of my boys awake over there?'

Some answering calls came.

'Well how about a tune?' he asked them.

There was nothing for a moment, while the sound of explosions rumbled on. Then a lone, low voice came.

> *The Lord He thought He'd make a man*
> *These bones going to rise again*

More voices joined.

> *Made him from mud and grains of sand*
> *These bones going to rise again*

Zachary's father joined in, with his eyes closed, and now Zachary too.

> *The Lord He spoke with monstrous voice*
> *These bones going to rise again*
> *Shook the world down to its joists*
> *These bones going to rise again*

The voices rang in the basement. On the bench beside Alistair's empty place, Hilda glowered at Mary. The city shook. Mary held Tom close and ran her fingers through his hair.

'It will be all right,' she said. 'You and I, we will be fine.'

'Yes,' he said.

'And tomorrow we'll all fix the mess, and on Monday everyone will go to work as usual.'

'I suppose so,' he said.

'What's the first thing you'll do on Monday morning?'

'I don't know,' said Tom. 'Inspect all the schools. Check for damage.'

She squeezed his hand. 'Good.'

'Then I suppose I will organise repairs as necessary, and check again that the open schools have adequate provision of shelters.'

'That's good, darling.'

> *Eve took the needle, Adam took the plow*
> *These bones going to rise again*
> *That's how we're all working now*
> *These bones going to rise again*

'And what will you do on Monday morning?' said Tom.

'I shall stand in front of my class and tell them none of this palaver is an excuse for not having done one's homework.'

'You could tell that to Zachary now. He might use this time.'

She lowered her voice. 'I go easier on him than the others. I think he might have something wrong with him, you know.'

'Besides being the wrong colour, you mean?'

She stared until she was sure he was only teasing her, and when he grinned she jabbed him in the ribs. 'You dog!'

'So what do you suppose is wrong with him?'

'You'll scoff, but I've researched it and I think he has word blindness.'

Tom groaned. 'No such thing.'

'But really. I've read papers on it.'

'By crackpots, I'm afraid. Oh, I know you mean well – but just think about it. How can one be blind to something that is right there on the page?'

She sighed. 'I don't know, darling.'

'Right there in front of one,' he said, picking up her hands and opening her palms like a book. 'No further away than this.'

'They say the eye sees, but there's a blind place in the mind.'

'And I say it is lack of effort. You must hold him to the same standard as everyone else. Because where should it stop, this fashionable clemency, once we allow that there are things we can see and yet be blind to?'

The singing voices swelled in the cellar and the bombs gave the percussion, and the great injured city went further into night.

'Oh, I don't know, darling. I don't know where it will stop.'

Alistair woke in the grey hours. The all-clear was sounding a huge C-sharp across the city. His body found coffee on its own. London created itself in concentric ripples widening from the cup.

Around him were some men of his regiment. Most were in

174

uniform; all were filthy and drawn. A brownish little café. A defeated sort of smell, of wet charcoal and bonfire smoke. No biscuits or buns available. Everyone's eyes downcast, faces blackened with soot. His watch was in his pocket, inexplicably. Seven in the morning. He put it back on his wrist. His wallet was gone. He thought: *They've stolen my leave.*

He had found his men and stood them drinks in the bars behind Waterloo. Then bombs had fallen near the station and he had organised the men into teams to help the rescue crews. They had used their hands on the piles of brick and timber, digging out civilians and parts of civilians. There had been some competition to see which teams could clear houses the quickest. There had been a grown hand holding an infant hand, with neither attached to anything. There had been an accordion with the Bakelite case blistered and charred. It had helped to be drunk.

Now he made his way to Waterloo Station, where the stationmaster gave him more coffee and let him scrub in the staff washroom. Alistair stripped to the waist and ran a slow trickle of brown water into the basin. The mains pipes were cracked, or the fire pumps were taking all the pressure. He cleaned up as well as he could, combed his hair with his fingers, and accepted a clean shirt that the stationmaster offered. He needed the man's help to do up the buttons – his fingers were blistered and cut.

He closed his mind to all thoughts of the previous night. This was what he had learned in France: that one could continue to operate quite adequately, so long as one stayed in the hour.

At eight thirty his men began to arrive back at the station, singly and in lurching groups. Alistair slapped each man on the back and got him roughly corralled at one end of the concourse. It was a relief to be back in charge of something simpler than himself. Though his head was hammering with the hangover, it amused him to discover that the men were worse off. After the rescue work was done it seemed that the majority had simply returned to the public houses, where normal service had continued in the cellars below the bars. It was impressive to see what the regiment had done to itself in twenty-four hours, with only indirect help from the enemy.

'Big night?' he said to a man who was bleeding from a cut above the eye.

'Yes, but we'll give it back to them double, won't we, sir?'

'The Germans?'

'Well the Navy was fortunate, sir, that the Germans interrupted.'

Alistair docked him two shillings of pay for fighting, wrote him a personal IOU for two shillings, and carried on.

A private was complaining, 'If the Luftwaffe had let me have one more hour, I'd have got her in the sack.'

'Look on the bright side,' said Alistair. 'If you'd had one more minute after that, you'd have got her in the family way.'

The man turned and saw him. 'Sorry, sir, didn't know it was you.'

'I hardly know myself. Never mix wine and whisky, that's an order.'

'Not unless you're buying again, sir.'

Alistair moved from man to man, keeping it light. Under the chatter the men shook with anger. When it was time to face the Germans again, the grudge would be particular.

His fellow officers were returning, looking rather better off than he, and they all set to work to reform the pacified and compliant men into the sterner geometries of war. On the station concourse the men lined up quite docilely in their ranks while the officers puffed on pipes and took the roll call and made sardonic enquiries concerning the men who were still AWOL. At nine, with the half-past raising steam at the platform and the men lining up to board, Alistair felt the universe returning to a bearable configuration.

He looked up from the company list and saw Mary arriving on the concourse in the dress she had worn the day before, conspicuous amid the uniforms. She carried his duffel bag, which he had left at the Lyceum.

His body's first instinct was to take cover. She hadn't seen him yet. He could easily just board the train, and he knew he ought to. Instead he waited and smoked his pipe. He could not stop watching her. He was a little sick at himself for it, but he was too tired now to be a saint.

As the men headed for the platform and their ranks thinned, Mary spotted him, broke into a smile and waved. He caught himself waving back, his chest tightening, immediately guilty now that the choice could not be unmade. She hurried over and then her face fell and she stopped a yard short.

She said, 'I was worried something might have happened to you.'

'It did. I popped into town and collected this hangover.'

'It suits you.'

'It's a little tight around the temples. The others are all right, I hope?'

'I told them I was going home to check up on Mother and Father.'

'Well, now you can.'

She looked down. 'You wish I hadn't come, don't you?'

He tapped out his pipe. 'It might have been better.'

She looked up with a spark of anger. 'I am in love with Tom, you know.'

'That's good.'

'He is the gentlest man.'

'Well, you know, I like him myself.'

'I'm sure we shall be married.'

'And I'm sure I'll be delighted for you. Let me know if you need a bridesmaid.'

They stood without speaking, while the last of the soldiers lugged bags towards the train and steam began to hiss from the locomotive.

Mary set down his duffel bag on the platform between them.

'Thanks,' said Alistair.

'Hilda was furious.'

'That's what you came to tell me?'

She closed her eyes. 'I came to make sure you were all right.'

'Well, now you can tell Hilda I'm all right.'

'Must you be so . . .?'

'I'm sorry,' said Alistair.

'No, I am. I'm just very tired.'

'We'll both feel better after a night's sleep.'

She managed a smile. 'Yes, I'm sure we shall.'

The locomotive's boiler hissed louder. Alistair watched the last of the men boarding. He nodded to the officers who stood on the platform, watching this presumed lovers' parting with theatrical amusement.

He turned back to Mary. 'Look, yesterday was . . .'

'Wasn't it? Maybe I was wrong to bring Hilda. I hope you didn't feel too set up?'

'It was sweet of you and Tom to do the up-setting.'

'I just didn't think you'd be so . . .'

Alistair waved it away. 'Hilda is lovely. I'm sure if there'd been more than twenty-four hours . . .'

'If there had been more time, or less, it would all have been easier. If it's an hour, one can say what one likes. If it's a year, one can be what one is like. A day is exactly the wrong length of time to be oneself in, don't you think?'

She looked at him desperately. He took a step towards her but the locomotive blew its whistle.

She said, 'You should go.'

He held her eyes. 'Goodbye.'

'Yes, goodbye.'

He picked up his duffel bag and turned to go.

Mary said, 'I hope you'll be all right.'

Alistair turned back. 'You'll be very happy. Tom is the best man I know.'

She hesitated. 'Tom always told me you were funny. I hadn't for a minute imagined you would be so terribly sad.'

Alistair set down his bag, put his hands in his pockets, and stared at his shoes for a moment.

'I'm hopeful,' he said. 'Aren't you?'

'Hopeful that what?'

'That this war does as much good as harm.'

'You sound like the government posters.'

He smiled. 'After the war there'll be less distance between us all.'

'Is that your theory?'

'I can prove it. Last night the men and I were in the back streets, to see if we could make ourselves useful. There was an old man we helped, in the wreck of his house in a bathtub he'd been sheltering in. It was half full of water from the hoses and when we got to the man, he scrubbed his back with a loofah to make us laugh. The whole street torn to shreds, and all of us in stitches. Don't you see? It makes me think there's hope.'

'Promise me you'll hold on to that.'

'Oh good lord, yes. Rather that than a loofah.'

She laughed then, brightly and without complication, and he laughed too, and for a moment the war with its lachrymose smoke was blown away on a bright, clean wind. Alistair marvelled that she could do such a thing with the tiniest inflection of her mouth and the lightest look in her eye: even exhausted, in yesterday's dress with her hair dishevelled, she could make the distance between them disappear.

The whistle screamed again, and an officer yelled from the platform for Alistair to board.

'Well, goodbye,' said Mary. 'Don't let the Germans take all the best seats.'

'Goodbye, Mary. Good luck.'

He shouldered his duffel bag and walked away down the platform. This was the end of it, he knew – they could give each other nothing more. There was a perfect sadness to it, but as the train took him back to the war and its hard hours issued singly, it wouldn't do to think of her. He left Mary to the hour in which she stood, beneath the hot black smoke that rose a mile above the wounded city.

# PART II
## *ATTRITION*

# SEPTEMBER, 1940

Hilda picked her up at noon and they took a cab east to look at the damage. Hilda wore black: melodramatic, Mary thought. With a handkerchief to press to her face in case of smoke and dust. And knee-high lace-up boots, since one couldn't anticipate the conditions underfoot. It seemed to Mary that Hilda was dressed for something between a funeral and Passchendaele. Mary had opted for pumps and a light blue day dress.

When they got to Bow she saw that Hilda had been right. Every window was out. In the bright sun, glass lay everywhere – so that if one half closed one's eyes the streets were bejewelled. Pavements were undulant, walls bowed, street lamps wilted by heat. The city's perpendiculars were defeated: it was as if the bombs had reserved a particular spite for right angles. The pipes were cracked too, and marshy water pooled in every new depression. Children splashed. The pigeons spritzed their wings in it.

Their road was blocked by rubble, and the driver pulled up. Hilda opened the door and hot air rolled in, heavy with soot and sewage. Everything smoked or steamed, as if one had crossed into a tropic of disaster. From the gaping fronts of bombed-out houses, the dazed locals stared. Mary stepped out of the cab into a puddle that leached foul-smelling mud through her shoe and into her stocking.

'Don't you think we should go straight back?' she said.

'Don't be wet,' said Hilda. 'These poor people have been through hell.'

'But I feel such a ghoul for gawping.'

'We're observing. And I'm damned if we'll be the only ones who haven't. It's all anyone will be talking about.'

Mary gave in. They linked arms, going around gas flares that rose from cracked mains. They gave a wide berth to sewage bubbling up.

'You see?' said Hilda. 'This is why I prefer the West End.'

'This isn't funny at all.'

Hilda looked as if she might cry. 'Did you kiss him?'

'I'm sorry?'

'Did you and Alistair kiss?'

Mary hesitated. 'Shall we talk about it at home?'

'There's no privacy there. If Palmer isn't hovering then your mother is materialising over one's shoulder. It isn't a home, it's a haunting.'

'At your flat, then.'

'But it's never the right moment, with you. You think you can do what you like, and we never mention it. But what about Tom? What about me?'

'I didn't kiss Alistair, if you must know.'

'I don't believe you for a moment.'

Mary shrugged. 'Fine.'

Hilda's hands shook. 'You can tell me. I won't say anything to Tom.'

'Gosh. Well. That's big of you.'

'Please don't be cross,' said Hilda, chewing her lip. 'I saw how you looked at Alistair.'

Mary softened. 'Well one does look, doesn't one? The eye may be an obligate scout but the heart is not an incurable follower. Anyway, I saw how you looked at Alistair too.'

'But I was there to look, and you weren't. We feign dispassion, don't we? It is called manners.'

'Have it your way. But I didn't kiss him.'

'Then what were you doing all that time?'

'We were talking. You should try it. It's hardly my fault if you pack your wits into a hat box whenever a gentleman calls.'

'But you've no right always to poach the man I like, just since you can.'

'I didn't poach. I took him his bag. I told you to do it but you wouldn't.'

'But I was furious with him, don't you see? For going off without saying goodbye. I could hardly show it by running after him with his luggage.'

'Well, you must tell me how fury is turning out for you.'

Hilda scowled at the ground. 'You'd be the same, if it happened to you.'

'You should have followed him out of the basement. You didn't have to send me.'

'But I was scared!'

'And you suppose I wasn't?'

Hilda only raised her hands and let them fall to her sides.

Mary closed her eyes for a moment. 'I promise I didn't do anything with Alistair. I'm in love with Tom and I try extremely hard to show it.'

Hilda gave her a bitter look. 'And did trying work, last night?'

'Yes. All that happened was that Alistair went away on a train, with his bag, to who-knows-where he's to be deployed. So if you've anything to say to him I suggest you jolly well write. I shan't think of him again. I have a man I love, and a class to teach, and for me the matter is closed.'

'And yet you are always, incorrigibly, you.'

'All I can tell you is how you seem to me now. This rubble was people's homes only yesterday. And here's you, standing on it and bleating. Sometimes, Hilda, though I try not to, I think you impossibly spoiled.'

The colour bled from Hilda's face.

'Oh no,' said Mary, reaching out. 'I'm sorry. I shouldn't have said that.'

Hilda pushed her arm away. 'I'm glad you did. Because although I've tried for years not to, I think you impossibly selfish. I know you kissed Alistair. I'm exhausted from always forgiving you, and I simply won't do so any more.'

'Please . . .' said Mary.

'No. Goodbye. I'll go home on my own.'

Glass cracked under her boots as she went. Mary slumped against a steaming wall and looked up at the sky. The blue was stained by updraughts of smoke as the air drifted towards the fires in the docks. How sad one could feel. She wondered how it had happened that Tom was so distant, and Hilda so bitter, and the world so thoroughly shattered.

She supposed she ought to go home. At least as one went west the streets would become clean and undamaged. One could always imagine that one's life, though smouldering in parts, might be undamaged in the west.

She took the long way home along the Embankment. The Thames was black with oil. Sickly foam gushed up wherever the deep current of the river was forced to the surface by obstructions: crashed bombers, buses blown off bridges – who knew what was down there now? The old and changeless river was suddenly uncharted. She stared down into the black water, scorched in patches by little pools of burning oil that whirled and eddied in the current. Flaming barges, their mooring ropes burned through, were drifting upstream on the flood tide. She wondered how far upriver the barges would get. If they kept on burning then it would be a furious light they cast on Pimlico, where Palmer, even now, must be readying tea to serve at four.

# DECEMBER, 1940

Snow was falling outside the window of Tom's office at the Education Authority. A secretary brought him a manila envelope containing a letter from the Royal Air Force. He gave a silent prayer of thanks. He had volunteered after that terrible night in the basement of the Lyceum, and held his breath ever since. Now he stubbed out his cigarette in the blue glass ashtray on his desk, took a deep breath and tore the letter open.

These were the facts: he had achieved an excellent pass on one hundred verbal and spatial exercises to be completed in ninety minutes. He had seen the numbers nine and four in a field of dots that would have seemed numberless to men who could not perceive colour. He had surrendered into glass vials 1 (one) fluid ounce of urine and 1 (one) of venous blood, and both had been assayed and found to be as suitable as such fluids could be.

Under the supervision of a moustachioed man from Bristol he had stripped to his smalls and completed fifteen press-ups and eight pull-ups, then climbed a rope eighteen feet in height and two inches in diameter. Using the checkboxes provided he had affirmed that he was neither an atheist nor a conscientious objector, and that his allergies were nil. A nurse had cupped his scrotum while he coughed, though the letter did not mention this.

It went on to confirm that he had performed well at interview. The recruiting officer had liked Tom's use of the RAF's published battle losses. Twenty men per day were being killed: Tom had framed it as one good man each hour. When viewed in that way, he had told the interviewer, one understood a life's value concretely. One saw the hours as a chain joining peacetime to peacetime, with oneself as a willing link. The recruiting officer had found his answer very satisfactory.

Tom couldn't wait to show Mary the letter. There had been such a distance between them since the raids began. Nothing was said but he missed the way they used to walk – as they had after their first night together – through a world made anew. He missed the way they had made rain hilarious, and passers-by mysterious, and bridges cross more than the river.

Of course there was the bombing, which kept them apart every night, she in the Anderson at her parents' home and he in the public shelter on Prince of Wales Road. But even alone together at the weekend in the garret, there was a certain hesitation. Their lovemaking felt like politeness.

But now here was the letter, to remake him in Mary's eyes and his own. Life had finally arrived and been released from its manila envelope.

In the final paragraph the recruiting officer regretted to inform him that his application had been vetoed by the War Office, who considered his current role essential. He read the thing through again, and there was no ambiguity. It was a feature of the authorities that they could exempt one's profession from service without sparing one's feelings. Tom sat in his empty office, laid his head on the desk and closed his eyes.

When he could no longer stand it he crossed the road to the public house and drank three doubles in a row. He went out into the snow, walked for a while without purpose and then headed for Mary's school. When he got there he knocked the snow from his shoes and coat, sat on a tiny chair at the back of her classroom and watched her taking the children through the dress rehearsal for their nativity play.

A saviour was born for all mankind: this seemed to be the gist of it. Everyone would be excused, for everything they'd done. It sounded neat. His hands still shook from the cold, so he clasped them to his knees.

Mary mouthed to him: 'Are you all right?' He smiled back at her across the children's heads while every one of his nerves vibrated with the high note of a cable approaching its maximum tension.

The little ones were in costume. Mary sat at the piano, producing a rather chirpy version of 'It Came Upon the Midnight Clear'. She even managed to swing the tune a little, giving the distinct impression that whatever had come on that clear midnight had come via the drinks cabinet. He ached for her. There was nothing she couldn't transform. It was unbearable.

She had cast a nice, sensible girl as the narrator. Betty came forward as the last chord faded. 'Long ago in the city of Nazareth, an angel came to Joseph and Mary. And the angel said . . .'

There was a long silence during which everyone looked at the angel.

From the piano, Mary whispered, 'Behold . . .'

Kenneth remembered his line. 'Behold! A! Virgin! Shall! Be! With! Child! And! Shall! Bring! Forth! A! Son! And! They! Shall! Call! His! Name! Emmanuel!'

'Speak up,' said Mary. 'There are a few Chinese who mightn't have heard you.'

'Emmanuel,' whispered Kenneth.

His wings, which were of papier mâché, slipped down to his waist. Poppy, who was dressed as a lamb, went behind him to hold the wings up to his shoulders. Together, they made a hybrid creature that had not been needed in any of the myths. Tom laughed, but tears prickled at the same time.

He supposed he was only exhausted. The bombing kept everyone awake. At the office one had become accustomed to colleagues making a sudden break for the lavatory. Everyone knew it was only to weep, and yet it would seem to outsiders as if the city were in the grip not of war but of some great bellicose incontinence.

He tried to concentrate on the play. Thomas, dressed in a toga and with a laurel crown on his head, propelled himself to centre stage in his wheelchair, which had been clad with gold boards to make it into a Roman chariot.

Betty said, 'And it came to pass in those days, that there went out a decree from Caesar Augustus.'

Thomas said, 'All the world shall be taxed!'

Maud came to the front with Zachary, both in robes and tea towels, with halos wobbling. Maud was a timid girl, rather a good casting for the virgin mother. Tom felt that Zachary was an inspired choice for Joseph, and he wondered if Mary had meant it as a joke. It would be easy to verify the divine provenance, the deity being white and the husband as dark as Herod's heart.

Now he worried that he didn't know whether she had meant it to be funny. He knew her less than he had at the start. The enemy dropped payloads of doubt.

He wished he had Alistair for advice. *Alistair, old man,* he might say. *I am beside myself. I am spent.* But Alistair was in Malta now, and his letters came infrequently. When they did, they had no substance. Everything operational was omitted, anything sentimental avoided, until only their old jokes remained. Perhaps the friendship was over. Perhaps it was not possible, after all, for a man who had gone to war to abide a man who had stayed.

He gripped his tiny chair and ground his teeth in misery.

Betty said, 'But in Bethlehem, there was no room for them anywhere.'

The children lined up to sing. They stood in order of diminishing glory, angels to lambs. Beside Poppy there were two more lambs in white jumpers with cotton-wool twists. There was little Beryl, the beauty with her fixed smile and disconcerting stillness, and there was the idiot George, whose size was alarming amid the diminutive cast but who followed Poppy with great docility. The lambs lined up beside Caesar, the holy spouses, the angel and the narrator. As Mary struck up the tune on the piano, they sang.

> No *beautiful chamber, no soft cradle bed,*
> No *place but a manger, nowhere for His head;*
> No *praises of gladness, no thought of their sin,*
> No *glory but sadness, no room in the inn.*

Tom lurched from anguish to a desperate urge to laugh again. How perfect that a saviour had come to a earth who could heal and forgive, but that what everyone sang about was the local guest house being full. It was a perfectly English take on a divine visitation – the kind of thing old colonels wrote indignant letters to the *Daily Telegraph* about.

*Sir –*

But there was a comfort, after all, in the old unchanging story. Perhaps the distance would close again between him and Mary. Perhaps it wasn't just him – maybe everyone felt unsure. From the crushing fatigue and the fear, the constant mental strain of saying to others, 'We shall prevail', and to oneself, 'I am defeated'.

Now, hearing the children sing, Tom felt a glow of hope. Perhaps the war would be won after all. Mary would laugh in his arms again, and the great moaning sirens would stop.

When the children came to the end of the song, Mary kept the music going softly while the holy couple laid a doll in a straw-lined milk crate.

Betty said, 'And she brought forth her firstborn son, and wrapped him in swaddling clothes, and laid him in a manger. And the shepherds came from the fields and asked Joseph the newborn's name. And Joseph said . . .'

A long pause. 'And Joseph said . . .'

Zachary was frozen, eyes wide.

'Come on, darling,' prompted Mary. 'Joseph said . . .'

Zachary burst into tears and bolted, slamming the classroom door behind him. The children began to laugh and murmur until Mary silenced them with two claps of her hands. 'Children! Please! We'll practise the hymn again. Mr Shaw, would you please go and see to Zachary?'

Tom found himself making the foolish gesture of *Who, me?* and almost died under Mary's patient look.

He found the boy in front of the school, kicking furiously at the snow.

'It's stupid!' Zachary shouted when he saw Tom. 'It's a stupid play and I don't even want to remember my stupid lines!'

Tom almost argued, then gave up and leaned against the porch.

Zachary scowled at him. 'You don't care?'

'It isn't *Hamlet*.'

'You're drunk.'

Tom lit a cigarette. 'Tell me, why do you come to school?'

'Get my education.'

'And what will you do with it?'

'Get a job. I'm not going in the minstrel show.'

'Why not?'

'You saw it. Would you be in it?'

'I can't imagine the equivalent. There's no such thing as a white minstrel show, is there? Unless one does count *Hamlet*.'

'I don't care about that.'

'You don't care about much.'

'You don't know.'

'But you keep running away. Miss North showed me your reports.'

'So?'

'So, I'm just saying. If you want to come to school, why do you run off?'

Zachary looked down. 'Are you going to give me detention?'

Tom couldn't help laughing.

'What?' said Zachary.

'Detention? No. Not unless you kick any more of that snow my way.'

Zachary stopped. 'It's too much, if you want to know.'

'What's too much?'

'Writing. Maths. All of them staring at me in class. My head goes *I can't do this, I can't be here*, louder and louder till I run. I want to stay but I can't.'

Tom turned up his collar against the cold.

'Well?' said Zachary.

'Well, what? I've no idea what's wrong with you.'

Zachary hesitated. 'But you think there's something?'

'Miss North thinks you have word blindness. She hasn't reached a diagnosis for me.'

'Why, what is it with you?'

Tom shrugged. 'With a name it might be excusable.'

The wind got up, whipping snow at their faces.

'How long do you want to stay out here?' said Tom.

Zachary dug his hands in his pockets and said nothing.

'It's harder to go back, isn't it?' said Tom. 'Why don't you let me drag you?'

Zachary showed no expression. 'Go in, if you're cold. I'll follow if I like.'

Tom weighed it for a moment, then said, 'Fine,' and went in. Halfway down the corridor, in case the boy was following, he said over his shoulder: 'The newborn's name is Jesus, by the way. In case the shepherds ask again.'

A pause, a scuffing of shoes behind him. Then, 'I'm not retarded.'

Tom grinned.

In the classroom Betty Oates was saying, 'An angel told the shepherds to come from the fields and look, and the shepherds came and they were amazed.'

George and Poppy had been giggling together, and now their laughter became hysterical. Mary frowned over the top of the piano. 'When your parents are here tomorrow for the real thing, neither I nor the angels shall expect to hear any silliness, is that understood? Now carry on, please.'

The children sang 'Silent Night'. They changed back into their uniforms and tidied the manger. They hung halos up on pegs and went home early, to be well ahead of the evening's raid when it came.

Mary sat down with Tom in the back of the empty classroom.

'You did well to bring Zachary back.'

'Oh, I didn't do anything. You were right about the boy. He's okay.'

She stroked his cheek. 'You're okay.'

'Ah, but you're something else.'

'That's what my father says, although I'm not sure he means it as kindly as you do. Walk me home?'

'I'm not sure . . .'

'Oh, you mustn't mind my father. He's almost never at home and if he is then he'll make you drink a glass of his Christmas wine, that's all. Palmer makes it from cloves and church bells and Dickens. Practise your face for me.'

Tom licked his lips. 'That is superb.'

Mary looked worried. 'Too much.'

Tom tried again. 'What an interesting flavour.'

She nodded approval. 'You oughtn't to overdo it, or Father will make you drink a second glass. It has happened before.'

'Did the victim survive?'

'The dog found the vat one year. We buried him under the japonica.'

They went outside. The snow fell in graceless clumps. It turned to a greasy slush on the pavement, and soon they were both cold and wet.

'Isn't it good?' Mary said. 'If this holds up there won't be a raid tonight.'

Tom eyed the sky. 'I really hate them, you know. I never thought I had it in me. But they really are the most hateful bastards.'

'That's why we call them the enemy. See how it works now, darling?'

He smiled. 'I don't know what I should do without you.'

'You'd live your life in terrible confusion,' she said gaily, taking his arm.

He slowed to a stop under the scant shelter of a grocer's awning. The shop window was cross-hatched with tape, and behind it the bacon slicer and the cheese wire and the black iron scales stood on the empty shelves, the vocabulary of a language with no remaining speakers.

'Tom? Darling?'

He realised he was still staring into the hungry shop.

'I think you should leave me,' he said.

The wind whipped wet snow at their legs. Engines raced as motor cars' tyres spun in the slush.

Mary said, 'Shall we go somewhere warm?'

They found a café, two tables wide, with empty sugar shakers and a bare Jacob's biscuit display case on the counter. They were the only customers. They took off their gloves but kept their coats and hats on.

'I don't suppose you've anything to eat?' said Mary to the waitress.

'There's only tea.'

It came in a brown glazed teapot. Looking into it as it was stirred, one could cultivate the hope that the tea was strong. One hoped, as one had hoped all through these gradually diluted months, until finally one poured it out over the quarter-inch of thin white milk and saw that it was practically clear. The leaves were used to exhaustion.

Tom rattled a teaspoon round his cup. 'I tried to join the Air Force.'

She put her hand on his. 'No . . .'

'I thought I might have it in me to shoot at the Germans' bloody aeroplanes, now that it's self-defence. But the War Office won't let me.'

'Oh, Tom . . .'

'I thought you might be proud of me in uniform.'

She took his face and angled it up to look at her. 'Do you really think so little of me?'

'You are a sweet, loyal girl. But we both know it isn't how it was.'

'Of course it isn't, you silly man. We're a thousand years older.'

'I sometimes imagine what it would be like for you if you were with a man like Alistair. Someone fighting the real war.'

They stirred the pale tea. The wet snow blinded the window.

'I don't imagine it,' she said.

'But you've thought about it.'

He waited. Her teaspoon clinked against the cup.

'I don't suppose I was meant to love a man like that, his heart made so heavy by war.'

'But he has had to become like that.'

'Well, we don't have to.'

'Don't we, though? I feel worse every day I stay behind. One knows one won't be killed, but that's hardly the same as living.'

'Please . . .'

He held his head in his hands. 'I'm no use, you see.'

'Don't,' said Mary. 'We'll get you back on your feet. A glass of my father's Christmas wine will do the trick. It's so ghastly, I promise it will make you forget these blues and pray for simple death.'

It made it all the more awful that she was so indestructible. 'Please,' he said. 'You'd be so much happier without me.'

'But it wouldn't be my life, don't you see? You are the one I've chosen, and I love you even more for being good enough to ask me *not* to choose you.'

A ghost of a smile rose in him. 'You are quite mad, I think.'

'Mother just calls me stubborn.'

Tom felt utterly spent, as weak as the tea. It was terrifying, how close one came to cracking up. 'God, I'm sorry.'

She shook her head. 'We must take turns, don't you think? Every time one of us is buried like this, we shall dig the other out.'

They sat for a few minutes in the empty café, finishing the tea while there was still warmth in it. Another couple came in and stamped the slush off their shoes, she in a long hooded cape and he in the uniform of a naval officer. The waitress served them biscuits from under the counter.

Mary laughed and took Tom's hand. 'Come on, let's get out of here.'

Out in the snow they drew their coats tight at the throat and walked hand in hand. Although the winter storm was bitter there was comfort in it, since it meant there would be no raid that night. Later they would sleep together – this was understood – and if there was less heat in it than there had been at the start, then perhaps there might be more warmth.

As the dark afternoon sank into night they made their way in silence through the blind city. Their footsteps were softened by the snow. The incalculable damage was hidden, the mounds of rubble turned by the drifts into the shapes of clouds or waves – forms that might naturally be expected to blow through when kinder weather came.

As the light and the sound faded to nothing, all that was left was the two of them. Underneath everything lay the colossal buried city – the patched-up pipes and the improvised lines of communication and the subterranean refuges from the great disincorporating influence of bombs. With the snow it was possible to forget it.

Perhaps, thought Mary, they really would rescue each other in turn. Perhaps the city would stand. For now, though, she could only hold Tom's hand. The snow settled. One settled.

The searchlight beams rose from their rooftop installations, up through the swirling snow, and played in blue-white circles on the base of the clouds. One could follow the elegant line of a beam up into the whiteness of the storm that spanned all of Europe in its vortex. One could take in the vast sweep of the winter and follow a thin searchlight beam down again into the vigilant city and understand how very fragile it was: a woman and a man holding hands, on streets made nameless by snow.

'I love you,' she said.

'Do you?'

'Oh, let's not go to my parents'. It isn't far to your place.'

There was an urgency now in the heat of their hands as they clung to each other. This snow would thaw. These winds would blow the clouds away. The next night might see a bomber's sky.

# DECEMBER, 1940

Alistair sailed the boat while Simonson – one of two other captains attached to 200 Battery, 10 Heavy Anti-Aircraft Regiment, Royal Artillery – fished for tunny with a trawling line. In a fourteen-foot sailing dinghy, half a mile off the east coast of Malta, with a breeze blowing in off the immaculate Mediterranean and with two bottles of the local beer in a string bag trailing in their wake to cool, the war seemed improbable and excessive.

'No, I'm afraid you will have to run it past me again,' said Alistair, nudging the tiller with his toe. 'There's a man called . . .?'

'Something Hitler,' said Simonson. 'Axel? Albrecht? German chap.'

'And he wants . . .?'

'To take over the running of the world.'

'What, all of it?'

'So it is rumoured.'

Alistair frowned. 'With all its tedious responsibilities along with the evident perks?'

'One imagines the fellow has weighed it up and decided to press on regardless.'

'Has he considered how vexatious it would be to find oneself in charge of us? Or how independent-minded the Americans are? I should think it would be frowned upon to turn up in Manhattan and start directing the traffic. As a European, I mean.'

'My dear boy, these are questions we Brits have thrashed out over centuries. One cannot expect a Hun to have quite the same level of insight.'

Alistair got his pipe alight while steering with one foot, trimming the jib with the hand he held the match in. He puffed white smoke that the wind scooped away prettily over the russet cloth of the mainsail.

He said, 'This German fellow sounds like a card.'

Simonson gave the trawling line an experimental tug. 'He has only one testicle, you know.'

Alistair raised an eyebrow.

'Oh yes,' said Simonson. 'It is well known.'

One thousand miles to the west lay Gibraltar; one thousand miles to the east, Alexandria. Though it was nearly Christmas and the water too chilly for swimming, it was pleasant in the sun and the two men were comfortable in white shirts and civilian slacks. Simonson pulled in the trawling line to check that the spinner wasn't tangled.

'Two hours and not a single bite. Fish are Nazis.'

'Maybe you're using the wrong lure.'

Simonson shook his head. 'The fish are mocking me. They know I'm famished and they're swimming six inches behind the spinner, in their silvery lederhosen.'

'They are goose-swimming,' said Alistair, using a hand to approximate the motion.

'Well of course,' said Simonson. 'They are the master plaice.'

While they both looked back at their wake, a floating mine bobbed in it. Just the topmost part, black and lethal with protuberances, broke surface in the troughs of the waves. They could only have missed it by inches.

'Ah,' said Alistair, 'the upwind mark. I must ask the Commodore to paint them a little brighter.'

They tacked the boat and had another look as they went back past.

'Would it have gone off if we'd hit it, do you suppose? With our wooden hull? Or do they only trigger by magnetism?'

'How curious are you to find out?'

'Absolutely not at all.'

'Let's try to miss it all over again then, shall we?' said Alistair. 'I suppose we ought to be getting home, in any case.'

'Oh god, is it wartime already?'

'Look on the bright side: it'll be dinner when we get back.'

Simonson groaned. Dinner that night would be with the regiment in Valletta, in Fort St Elmo at the mouth of Grand Harbour. Having shaved and dressed, they would go down into the bowels of the fortress that had survived Malta's great siege in the sixteenth century. In the officers' mess room they would sit at folding aluminium tables to eat the pitiful rations of the present blockade: a small lump of bully beef let down with flour and potato, and on every third day the tinned Maconochie's stew that was so foul it was almost a blessing to have it in ever-smaller quantities as the convoys became harder to fight through to the island.

Alistair grinned at his friend's displeasure. He pulled in the beer net while Simonson let out the trawling line.

'Do me a favour?' said Simonson.

'Ask away,' said Alistair, prising the tops off the beers.

'If we don't catch a fish, butcher me and tell the cook I'm pork.'

'Don't flatter yourself it hadn't already occurred to me. I'm a sentimental fool for letting you have a beer first.'

They headed for the land, pointing in to St Paul's Bay where the apostle had been shipwrecked. Alistair had checked every particular of the account in Acts against the relevant Admiralty chart and found nothing wanting. He had been on Malta three months now and he liked the way the island lived in the full embrace of time. In London, bedded in its clay, one viewed history as a reworkable legend, a great entertainment of doubtful veracity and liable in any case to revision whenever the next mudlark waded into the Thames at low tide and pulled out some iconoclastic sherd.

London was a crowd-pleaser, a protestant, a voluntary amnesiac, living to disinter stories only to arrange their bones in a sly new order. But Malta was permanent rock, with barely a scattering of topsoil. Time, having nowhere to hide, had colonised the surface instead and lay there with its full duration exposed. In niches in the limestone studded with fossil shells, Alistair had seen eight-thousand-year-old statuary hung with paper garlands on the feast days of the saints. In a tiny, dark, incense-smelling chapel into which he had strayed to have a moment away from the war, Alistair had found what he thought might be a Caravaggio. The priest had neither known nor minded – had simply replied that the painting was by a local artist.

Alistair finished his beer while it was still cold, and flipped the empty brown bottle over his shoulder into the depths. Their white wake hissed through the sea.

'What are you smiling about?' said Simonson.

'I had a love letter in this morning's post.'

Simonson yawned. 'I get three a week.'

'But my family is not disgustingly wealthy, so I can actually take it as proof of my looks.'

'Go to hell,' said Simonson, 'and tell them I sent you.'

'I suppose you own the place.'

'Fifty-one per cent, old boy. One maintains a controlling interest.'

'I'll be sure to keep it warm for you. She is called Hilda, by the way.'

'I didn't ask.'

'No, but you were curious.'

'My curiosity about you, Heath, is the curiosity Freud had for hysterics, or Mendel for peas. You help to confirm my theories.'

'She is called Hilda and she has fabulous eyes, like . . . well, I don't know. Like themselves. They're unique.'

Simonson looked thoughtful. 'O Hilda, your eyes like a simile, you wrote to a commoner in the military.'

Alistair ignored him. 'She declares her love in the first paragraph.'

'How impossibly vulgar. Oh, what now? What are you smirking about, vile man?'

'I'm flattered to have elicited such an unscientific response from you.'

'It is only that one cannot condone wilfulness, in women or in horses.'

'I'll be sure to let Hilda know. If you'll loan me a sugar lump, I shall pop it in the envelope.'

'Surely you don't plan to dignify her with a response?'

'I can't say I've given it much thought.'

Simonson ruffled Alistair's hair. 'That's more like it.'

Alistair had, though. How honest and uncomplicated Hilda had been, snuggled up beside him at the Lyceum. It would have been convenient if he could have fallen in love with her, and not Mary. They could have gone on weekends away, the four of them, and laughed with pristine teeth like those chummy couples in the ads for Blackpool Beach.

He turned the nose of the dinghy further into the bay.

'Damn it,' said Simonson. 'Must we really go back?'

'Anyone would think you didn't enjoy the war.'

'It's this island I can't stand.'

'You don't find it exotic?'

'Heath, I detest Malta. Anywhere grain will not grow is no place for a man. My greatest hope is that one of the bombs will hole this island below the waterline and it will sink, and then we can all go home with the Navy.'

'But you like the people, at least?'

'I loathe the people. They are feckless and swarthy and nauseatingly loyal. They are hardly better than niggers.'

'They've been hospitable to us.'

'They've been hospitable to the Phoenicians, the Carthaginians, the Romans, the Vandals, the Byzantines, the Arabs, the Christians and the French. If Mussolini had got here five minutes before us, the locals would be whistling Puccini.'

'Wouldn't we be innkeepers too, if we happened to live on the crossroads?'

Simonson drew himself up. 'If England has 28-ton breech-loading Mark Ten coastal artillery pieces, it is so that we need not be innkeepers.'

Alistair laughed. 'Haven't you caught a fish yet?'

Simonson tugged on the line disconsolately. 'It's the Kriegsmarine, isn't it? They radio our position to all the fish within a nautical mile.'

When they were still three hundred yards from shore, nearing the head of the bay, a fighter burst over the coastal bluff and dropped down almost to the sea. It headed straight at them. Alistair saw the pilot through the front panel of the aircraft's canopy, goggles up on his forehead, staring back with perfect surprise over the block of his radial engine. Alistair had time to think: *Oh, it's one of theirs*. Then the plane was overhead, howling, barely missing the mast. The propwash slammed into the sails, taking them aback and capsizing the dinghy.

Alistair gasped in the cold waves. The boat lay on its side with the sails flat on the water.

'Now we shall have to dry out our tobacco.'

'You told me you could sail these things,' said Simonson.

'It's just that the wind's a bit fluky at this end of the bay.'

They clung to the transom while Alistair released the sails and made ready to right the dinghy.

'We'll swim the boat around so it's across the wind, then we'll bear down on the centre plate until we come upright again. All right?'

Simonson glared at the receding fighter. 'He's an Italian, isn't he?'

'I think so. I'll bet he's calling us in as a probable kill.'

Simonson spat salt water. 'He's off home to have a sailboat stencilled on the side of his fuselage. His ground crew will administer fellatio.'

As they began to swim the dinghy around, they heard the note of the fighter's engine change. The pitch and the volume increased. Alistair saw the topside of the wings with their fasces roundels and realised that the aeroplane was banking round and coming back on them. It happened faster than the mind could usefully process, so that a part of him braced for emergency while another part enjoyed the tight curve the fighter was making, the dipped wing almost clipping the waves and a firm white contrail arcing over the glittering sea. The nose of the fighter lined up on them again. There was nothing at all to be done. Simonson, in a quiet voice, called the pilot a stone-cold bastard. Then the fighter roared overhead again and no shots had been fired.

'The devil is he doing?'

'He's getting lined up,' said Alistair. 'New to the job, I should think.'

The fighter banked around again and came back at them. Alistair turned his legs towards the onrushing plane and lay back in the water, angling his body to present the soles of his feet as the smallest possible target. As he let himself sink back, he saw the Italian slide open the cover of his canopy. An ungloved hand emerged and let go something white, and as the plane roared

205

overhead for the third time the scrap of white floated down to the sea. The fighter receded. The note of the engine faded into the chatter of the waves.

When it seemed that the plane was not coming back, Simonson swam for the thing the pilot had dropped. It was paper, balled up to float. Simonson smoothed it against the upturned hull. It was torn from the corner of an aviation map. In green navigation pencil the pilot had scribbled: '*Mi dispiace*'.

'He's sorry,' said Simonson. 'For capsizing us, I suppose.'

Clinging to the dinghy, they stared at the point on the horizon where the Italian had become indistinguishable from the sky.

'You never mentioned you knew Italian,' said Alistair.

'Mother has a place on Lake Como.'

Alistair laughed.

'What?' said Simonson.

'How gloomy for you, that one can no longer travel there.'

'Oh, I don't know. Italy always seemed an awfully long way to go for fascism and olives.'

'I rather like olives.'

'Mother rather liked fascism. We had to burn all the photographs when war was declared.'

They worked the boat upright, and shivered while they bailed with their shoes. When all was seaworthy they went back for the trawling line. The wooden spool floated on the water. Simonson retrieved it and began reeling in, but the spinner had sunk to the seabed and snagged something. The line took an age to come. While Simonson worked, Alistair lay back and let the sun warm him. The water lapped the hull and the idle sails flapped. Storm petrels crackled and purred as they quartered the waves for prey.

Simonson could say what he liked, but Alistair liked Malta. This blameless blue sea softened the memories of the retreat through France. Even the enemy's blockade had done him good. After a few sleepless nights with the terrors, the scarcity of alcohol had probably saved him. Now a rare beer made him cheerful – he no longer had to follow it into oblivion. He saw things clearly again: Hilda's smile, the endearing effort she had made to keep her makeup fresh. He decided he would write to her. She might enjoy hearing about the warmth, the cheerful press of locals, the little island out on its own.

'Why don't you take a turn?' said Simonson. 'I've had it.'

He flopped down in the bottom of the boat and closed his eyes while Alistair took over the job of reeling in the trawl line. It was sluggish and painful work, a foot at a time, with the cord digging into his hands as he heaved it in. The white line angled into deepening blue, with golden coils of sunlight following it down into darkness. After a few minutes Alistair saw a grey-green looming, thirty or forty feet below.

'Lump of seaweed,' he said.

Simonson yawned. 'I've been called worse, and by better-looking men.'

As Alistair worked, the shape came closer to the surface and resolved itself into a thing that ought to be recognised, but for the reluctance of the mind. When it was only twenty feet down, Alistair could see it distinctly. The dead man looked back at him with an expression as quiet and clear as the water, and Alistair shivered and took out his pocket knife and cut the line. He put away the knife and watched as the uniformed body rolled onto its front and began the long journey down, trailing blond hair and the long white filament of fishing line that Alistair watched until it blent with the coiling sunlight and was lost to sight.

'Damn it,' he said.

'Hmm?' said Simonson, half opening an eye.

'Line snapped,' said Alistair. 'I must have pulled too hard.'

'I paid three shillings for that gear.'

'I'll buy you another set.'

'Oh, that's quite all right,' said Simonson. 'You are miserably poor, and there's nothing down there in any case.'

They sailed the dinghy back to the beach and dragged it up through the narrow channel of sand that had been left between the barbed wire entanglements. They lowered the sails, stowed the rudder and left the boat in its spot for the next officers who got the half-day leave.

Their driver had waited for them. As the boat came in he had harnessed his bony horse between the shafts again, and now they climbed into the open calash for the bumpy ride back to Fort St Elmo.

The sun was sinking over the spine of the island. Alistair shivered as the heat went out of the day. The shadows spread across the yellow rock outcrops and the yellow rock walls. On either side of the road, women in black scratched at the thin earth of fields no bigger than tennis courts. The blades of their hoes rang as they struck the rock beneath the soil. Alistair watched Simonson, his fine black hair still wet, looking out over the scene. He was twenty-two but looked younger. He was muscled from swimming and sports, and he moved with an athlete's competence. When he walked, he seemed to need the ground only for balance. Now, at rest, his eyes glowed amber in the last of the light. His face was wonderfully kind in a way that Alistair was certain would infuriate Simonson if he knew. The face had the habit of subverting, with bashful smiles, the harshest of his talk.

Simonson wrapped himself in the horse's blanket and scowled at the bucolic scene.

Alistair grinned. 'Do you also disapprove of agriculture?'

'I think of the parties we're missing. Every letter I get stinks of champagne and orchestras.'

'From what I hear, London is catching hell.'

'It is a matter of perspective. With proper planning one can watch while hell is caught, from the safety of Claridge's roof. My dear elder brother hasn't been sober since this war started.'

'Doesn't it bother him, to stay behind?'

'Good god, why would it? Randolph has nothing to prove beyond being the firstborn son, to the actuality of which attests a certificate that he keeps in a safe.'

'Now I know you're not serious,' said Alistair.

'Jealous, is what I am. Randy will just be waking up now, in silk sheets, with a nice pink lover on either side. While we cling to this bilious rock.'

'Your brother will be called up eventually, I suppose.'

Simonson shook his head in simple pity. 'You really don't know how it works, do you?'

'I know how it has worked until now. But this war will change things.'

Simonson raised a horrified eyebrow. 'Not unless we lose. And even then, I daresay Mother will have squirrelled away a few choice photographs. Any family worth its arms has learned to hedge a few bets.'

Alistair's clothes were still sharp with brine – he sucked his shirt cuffs and shivered at the wonder of it. They had foundered in the bay where St Paul had almost drowned. They were taking the same coast road that Paul must have taken to Valletta. The horse's shoes rang out, and to left and right the people in their black clothes merged with the deepening shadows. Below the road, all around the points and crenulations of the bay, the waves bled black ink into the twilight.

He would reply to Hilda's letter, and he supposed it would be the start of things between them. Perhaps this was what love was like after all – not the lurch of going over a humpback bridge, and not the incandescence of fireworks, just the quiet under-standing that one should take a kind hand when it was offered, before all light was gone from the sky.

First, though, he would write to Tom. If he had been a prig to Hilda then he had been an inexcusable ass to his oldest friend. As soon as they got back to the fort he would write. He would apologise for the way he had been, and he wouldn't blame the war. He would ask Tom to forgive him, and when Tom did then he could reply to Hilda with an untroubled mind.

He felt better now, as the calash bounced along the rocky track and they wound through the stone walls older than Christ. He felt himself made new by the war, while the cool salt breeze blew in off the sea and the first star rose in the east.

# DECEMBER, 1940

**M**ary sat at the piano and smiled at Tom in the front row. All the children had managed to field at least one parent, which was good work at three in the afternoon on a working day reduced to six hours by the bombing. They all deserved 'A' for effort.

In the front row Zachary's father sat with Poppy's mother, and next to them were Kenneth's mother and both of Thomas's parents. In the back row Maud's mother was making a point, it seemed to Mary, of sitting as far from Zachary's father as she could – but at least she had come. There was something about the star, rising above the stable, that still pulled a crowd in from the fields.

She pressed out the last chords of the hymn, let her hands fall to her lap and nodded for the play to begin. Betty stepped forward into the improvised spotlight that George's father had made from an electric fitting and an empty baked-bean can.

Betty froze until Mary whispered: 'Long ago . . .'

'Long ago,' said Betty, 'in the city of Nazareth, an angel—'

'Behold!' yelled Kenneth. 'A! Virgin! Shall! Be! With! Child! And!—'

'Shh, not yet!' hissed Mary.

The boy clamped both hands over his mouth, eyes bulging.

Betty said, 'An angel came to Joseph and Mary. And the angel said . . .'

Mary willed Kenneth to say his line. 'Behold . . .' she whispered.

Nothing. In the front row the parents were agitated, and looking to her. Kenneth was staring up at the ceiling.

'Behold . . .' she said again, and still nothing happened.

Tom widened his eyes at her and pointed to his ear. Now she heard it, a low rumbling. The air-raid sirens began. Mary felt the familiar punch of fear, followed immediately by fury at the enemy. Today of all days, they had chosen to start the raid early.

She stood from the piano. 'We will go down into the basement. Children first please, calmly and quietly, holding hands in twos as we practised.'

She issued candles, one to each pair of children, as they went down the basement stair. Poppy went with George, Maud with Kenneth, Zachary with Betty, then Beryl on her own since she would not let anyone touch her, and finally Thomas in his father's arms, his wheelchair parked in the corridor.

Mary had Tom see everyone down the stairs while she went to the boiler room and shut off the electricity, the gas and the water. Back in the classroom she checked that no one remained. She tucked the Christ doll under her arm, closed the piano lid and walked down into the basement.

There was a confusion of places and a nervous laughter among the adults. The children squabbled for seats on the two long gymnasium benches that Mary had set up when she cleared the basement.

Mary clapped her hands twice. 'Right. Grown-ups, please move those benches as close to that back wall as you can, and sit on them. Leave this space in front clear – this will be our stage. It's less room than we've practised in, so shepherds, I need you to keep your flocks close, and angel – where are you, Kenneth? – angel, I need you to watch where you flap your wings. Betty and Maud, more candles please, in those jars, and put them on the floor along the walls. Yes, anywhere there is good. And now, children, places as you were please, and George, please can you bring that stool for Thomas to sit on? Very good. All right then, we shall go from "And the angel said . . ."'

'Behold!' said Kenneth. 'Behold!'

In the candlelight, the audience cheered. The children made no more mistakes and Mary sat to watch them, while the distant concussions of the raid sounded through the underground walls. The candle flames shone on the ancient shelves that lined the basement. The yellow light glinted on the dented globes. It glowed on the musty needlework. It made the laid-down maypoles into long bones, white in the darkness.

When it came time for the next hymn, Mary took a glockenspiel from its pine box, gripped the wooden beaters, and frowned at the instrument. It might be harder than she had allowed.

'Here,' said Zachary's father, 'let me have that. What's the song?'

'"No Room in the Inn".'

He began straight away, giving two bars and nodding the children in. He played evenly, not making any more fuss of the tune than it needed. Mary closed her eyes while the children sang.

Later, when Mary and Joseph had lain the doll in the glockenspiel case that took the place of the manger, and after the last hymn, the play was over but the bombing raid was not. The explosions came through the ground, no nearer but no fewer. The children clustered on the benches in the arms of their parents and waited for the all-clear. People spoke in whispers, as if the war were listening. Since there was nothing else to watch, they all looked at the doll in the manger with the candles ringed round it in jars.

Mary sat beside Tom on the end of a bench. 'Feeling Christmassy?'

'As an elf in rum butter.'

She put her head on his shoulder. 'Like it down here?'

He gave the basement a critical eye. 'It could use a woman's touch.'

She dug him in the ribs. 'I hate you.'

'This school is yours now, you know. I mean, after the war, everyone will come home and I daresay you'll have to hand the place back, but you and I will know who held the line when it mattered.'

'Oh, I'll be glad to give the key back. It'll be a relief not to be in charge.'

'I don't see you, somehow, taking orders from Miss Vine. Not after this.'

'No?'

'I don't see any of it being as it was. Just look at us, down here in the dark. Coloureds and cripples and cranks – but we're the ones holding on. When the rest get back they'll have to respect what happened here.'

Mary yawned, and stretched out her legs alongside his. 'I just want to get through. I must say I don't frightfully care who feels good once this is over, so long as it isn't the Germans.'

He grinned. 'I don't care about anyone at all, apart from you. If there is one person who—'

Three huge detonations came, knocking the breath from their lungs and blowing out the candles. Children and parents screamed. Mary found herself stunned, lying on top of Tom, both of them struggling to get up. She fumbled in her pockets until she found her lighter.

Zachary was staring back at her, eyes wide with terror.

'It's all right,' she mumbled, her tongue pasted with brick dust. She was slow from the concussion. 'It is quite all right. Quite safe down here.'

Another explosion came, huge and even closer, knocking the lighter from her hand. When she felt for it and flicked it back on, Zachary was gone. His footsteps banged up the wooden stairs that led up from the basement.

'No! Wait!'

She made to go after him but Tom pulled her back. 'I'll get him.'

He went, leaving her to bring order to the tangle of parents and children. She got the candles alight in their jars, then checked on the injuries. Zachary's father was badly concussed, swinging his head in confusion. Thomas's father had dislocated a shoulder and sat on the floor with his back against the wall, green-faced. The children had got away with bruises.

Once she had them all calm, she took stock. Her ears rang – she must have struck her head harder than she had thought – but at least the bombing seemed distant, for now. She didn't know how long Zachary and Tom had been gone – five minutes, perhaps. She went up into the corridor, stumbling on uneven legs – it seemed she had lost a shoe – and decided to take a quick look outside. She swung open the heavy front door and was amazed to find that it was still daylight. The street was deserted, with rubble strewn across it. A house was down in the middle of the row.

She looked up and saw no bombers. She took a few steps into the street, thought better of it, and hurried back into the shelter of the porch. It was ridiculous, of course – it was bombs that threatened, not rain – and yet in the corner of the porch a wooden box held the parents' furled umbrellas, and a sensible part of her mind realised that she ought to take one, since it must be better than nothing. Her hand was even reaching for one when she saw, through the open door, the child at the end of the street. He was Zachary's build, but white, in a white sweater and shorts, and she yelled at him to come into cover. The child stared at her, backed away two paces, and fled.

It was five streets before she caught him, with bombs beginning to fall again close by. When she finally got hold of Zachary, his eyes were blank with fright. She dragged him into an angle behind a wall, and gasped to get her breath. He cowered, arms raised as if she might strike him, and she wondered how it had come to be that he was white, and she also wondered why he was afraid of her. He was crying tears of a brown liquid, and she would not understand until later that they were ordinary tears, cutting through the white dust.

'Why?' she managed to say. 'Why is it always you who runs off?'

He howled, chest heaving. 'I'm sorry . . . I'm so sorry . . .'

She shook her head. 'You have to come back. We can't stay out here.'

'I'm not going back in the basement.'

'Oh yes you jolly well are.'

She half dragged, half led him back through the air raid, which was all around them now, and in the mouth of a side street she saw that Tom was lying on the pavement, asleep in the snow with the winter sun slanting over him. It was a stress reaction she had read about – the mind shutting down when it all got too much. She would have to go back for him as soon as she had delivered Zachary to the shelter. (How extraordinary that she was the one who was calm in this situation; who could take in everything clearly and without panic.) She hauled Zachary back to Hawley Street, with the bombing seeming distant again, and here there was an interesting phenomenon. (How glad her father would be to know that his daughter could be cool in a crisis.) This was how it sounded in her mind, as she held Zachary by his thin wrist and felt the pulse in it while the drone note of the bombers faded away into the east: *I am witnessing a phenomenon related to the bombing.*

The thing was that Hawley Street was there but the school was gone. She walked up and down the length of the street, twice, calmly but briskly, pulling Zachary by the wrist and looking for the school. Because of course the phenomenon would have a simple explanation: perhaps that someone unfamiliar with the area had taken the building and put it back in slightly the wrong place. She started laughing because it was silly that one couldn't find something so big and stolidly Victorian as Hawley Street School. All she could find was an enormous pile of red bricks, dotted with decorative London yellows. What a ridiculous place to leave bricks. And this was when her stomach fell and she understood that the problem was a perceptual one: that her concussion was worse than she had supposed, that she was hallucinating. It was frightening but at least it all made sense now: Zachary turned white, Tom fast asleep, the school absent without leave. How funny the mind could be. She sat in the thick white dust and laughed.

Afterwards they told her it was normal, with shock. Someone came and took Zachary away from her. They had to prise her fingers off his wrist. And then for hours all she could think was what a waste it was: a new carton of chalk had been delivered that morning and now it must be ruined, all twenty sticks of it. She explained to a nurse that they would simply have to make do, and write on the blackboard with the stubs of old chalk.

They took her to a rest centre and wrapped her tight in blankets. They told her that it helped to be swaddled like a baby. Days passed, which she experienced as the daylight flickering on and off. As if there were a bad connection. They told her that no bodies had been recovered from inside the school, only fragments. The only body was Tom's, recovered from the street, and they unwrapped her from the blankets long enough for her to be taken to identify him.

The morgue was an improvised facility, in a church hall. Someone had marked Tom's forehead with an X, in red grease pencil. It meant that there was an internal injury. They told her Tom had been killed by the pressure wave of a bomb, which was why there wasn't a mark on his body except for that X. Mary hardly heard them. It was evident to her that the bomb had done nothing to him – that the cause of death must somehow be connected to that terrible letter on his forehead: the unknown in all algebras, the singularity.

She explained this to the woman who was seeing to her in between signing for the deliveries of the remains that were still arriving at the morgue, in sixteen-inch rectangular cardboard containers requisitioned from a grocer, as and when the heavy rescue men brought them out.

Her mother flashed on and off. She told Mary that the heavy rescue crews had dug into the rubble for four days and nights, bringing out what remains they could, and then they had put lime down.

People asked questions of her. Mary answered that she was quite all right, thank you. No, she did not need more tea. Yes, she was able to supply a list of the pupils and parents who had been present at the nativity play. No, she and Tom had not been engaged; she had been waiting for the poor man to pluck up courage. No, she did not think that if God had seen fit to spare only one child then it was a pity it had to be the picaninny. No, she did not think that the darkies had the devil's own luck. No, she imagined that the poor child had run out into the air raid simply because he was unusually resistant to sitting where he was told. Well, and if they must put it like that, then yes, she was rather fond of the nigger.

There were no further questions after that, and Mary did not have the heart to trouble people with her own. Goodness knew, everyone at the rest centre was exhausted. Everyone had anguish of their own by now – what was every bomb that fell, if not endings under unbelievable compression? Grief was contagious, and Mary would no more speak of her own than she would cough, in a crowded train carriage, without putting her hand to her mouth.

And so she sat and watched the walls, in the grubby rest centre with its pinboard still announcing church business and cake raffles. She read the small advertisements for odd jobsmen and cat breeders.

She reminded herself to thank Tom, the next time she saw him, for going out into the raid after Zachary. A moment later she understood that this would not be possible, but the understanding did not prevent her from writing it down on a scrap of paper and tucking it into her sleeve: *Remember to thank Tom.* He had left the shelter to go into the thick of a bombing raid. That he was dead and that she must thank him the next time she saw him: for weeks it was possible to believe both these things at once.

Quite early on, even before the days slowed their flickering and began to come and go with their usual shopkeeper's frequency, Mary decided that she would never speak of how she felt. One could only trudge away from the place to which one had hurried in such hope at the start. One could only begin again, a year older, and resolve to carry oneself in such a way that the pressure wave of the tragedy was contained within one's own body, and could not spread one inch further.

# DECEMBER, 1940

On Christmas Day the regiment hosted the companies of all the convoy escort ships tucked into Grand Harbour. In sunshine, more than a thousand officers and men assembled in the courtyard of Fort St Elmo for a service of nine lessons and carols and a tot of Nelson's blood, supplied by the visiting Navy. Five hundred years of tradition having established the order of service, the rum was administered before the singing.

Though the enemy's blockade was biting and supplies on the island were scarce, Alistair supposed the War Office had established a vast cache of polishes. Two thousand black boots glowed as if with an inner light. Twelve trumpets, eight trombones, four tubas and a euphonium blazed like the armour of Achilles. It was the genius of motivated men that even when rendered impotent by conditions of total encirclement, they could make themselves preternaturally shiny. As the last chorus of 'O Come, All Ye Faithful' reached its triumph, Alistair was nearly blinded.

After the service he sent the men of his battery for a second trip to the rum urn, with instructions to make only a mild nuisance of themselves. He went up to his little cell high in the walls of the fort. When their battery's batman, Briggs, dropped by with an air mail fresh from the airfield, Alistair could have kissed the envelope. Warm from the Navy's liquor he really did feel a glow of goodwill towards all men, even those of the enemy persuasion. It was big of the Italian aviators to let a mail plane through the blockade on Christmas Day. One hoped that one's own side was reciprocating, in some other theatre where Britain was in the ascendant. One struggled to think where that might be – but at Christmas one could think of sleigh bells instead.

The aerogramme bore Tom's parents' address in the 'Sender' box. Alistair tore it open. How perfect that Tom's reply should reach him on Christmas Day. Assuming of course that Tom was writing to forgive him for the awkwardness at the Lyceum, then how apt.

The letter was from Tom's father. The handwriting was almost like Tom's, but slightly slumped. He was sorry to have to let Alistair know that Tom had been killed, on the nineteenth of December, in an air raid. Since Tom had thought of him as a brother, Alistair was to think of the Shaws as family and to write if there was ever anything they could do.

Alistair put down the letter and stood at the arrow loop window. He watched the forenoon glittering over the sea. In the distant haze he could just make out the flashing signal mirrors of the Italian blockade ships. If one forgot for a moment that the messages wished one evil, they were beautiful.

He washed off the parade grime by sponging himself from his metal basin. He put on a fresh shirt, and since there was still half an hour before Christmas lunch was to be served, he visited the men in their mess room. Post would have come for them too, and one couldn't second-guess the mood of the men. Air mail had the particular violence of recency – it might leave them upbeat, or homesick, or a queer mix of the two – and so it was prudent for their officer to drop by and project a soothing equanimity. Sweethearts might blow cold or hot after all, and mothers might ail or improve, but the 3.7-inch heavy anti-aircraft gun would always provide a stable firing platform, providing that the levelling jacks on each corner of its carriage were competently deployed. This was the sentiment an officer should diffuse.

He spent a brisk twenty minutes with the men, made a joke of their minor gripes and a note of their major ones, and reached the officers' mess in time for grace. Army and Navy together, they were sixty seated at two long tables with Lieutenant Colonel Hamilton presiding. Alistair was last to arrive and he hurried to his place, nodding his apology. Hamilton returned an affable nod, then bowed his head in prayer.

'Lord,' he said, 'on this holiest of days, we thank you for food and ammunition. May our ships get through and the enemy's get lost.'

They all said 'Amen' and then the orderlies brought in something that the cook had made out of breadcrumbs and canned malevolence.

Alistair lifted the corner of his with a fork. 'I don't know whether to put mustard on it, or marmalade.'

'Or whether to eat it or give it a Christian burial,' said Simonson. 'Did Santa bring you any post?'

'Not this time.'

'Maybe you weren't nice. Cheery bastard keeps a list, you know.'

'Whereas you . . .?'

Simonson twirled his knife like a swagger stick. 'I had four letters from three girls. They all think they're the only one, of course.'

'I'm sure you're the only millionaire they write to.'

'You don't know the right sort of girl, is your problem. When we go on leave, I'll introduce you around town.'

'I fear that your sort of girls would cut my poor body to ribbons, simply by using their accents.'

Simonson ignored him. 'Of course if I can just make major before we go back, then my damned brother shan't have the last laugh after all. When one is a major – dear god, the women one can have! I shall bag a gorgeous débutante and parade her in silks before Randolph's hag of a wife.'

'I suppose it's lucky the Germans started all this for you.'

Simonson frowned. 'Is everything quite all right? You seem out of sorts.'

'I'm weary from all the excitement.'

'Damn it, Alistair, if you get all out of shape over a brass band, wait until you see some real action.'

'Do remind me to tell you about my trip to France, one day.'

'Exchange visit, was it?'

'We exchanged withering fire, if that counts.'

'And do you still keep in touch?'

'Oh yes. You see, I'm hoping to go back one day.'

'But in all seriousness, what's wrong?'

For a moment Alistair considered telling him. But of course, it wasn't the right thing. The war, after all, was a legal riot and a bright pageant and a marvel of near misses. It was a perfect adventure until proved otherwise, and so it would hardly be a kindness, on Christmas Day, to produce evidence. One pulled crackers for the snap of their mild detonation.

Simonson patted him on the back and told him to buck up, and they ate with the chatter of their brother officers around them. For dessert the cook had turned up tinned apricots. They had them in the smallest bowls, but the fruit still looked lost. Each officer had exactly two and a half little apricot halves in a quarter-inch of clear syrup. They drank water from the fort's well, which tasted of its own yellow limestone sides and whatever Turks and Moors had been thrown down there over the centuries.

Hamilton stood and tapped his glass for silence. 'The King.'

They all rose. 'The King.'

They drank his health in well water and left in ones and twos, hungry.

Alone, Alistair set Tom's jar of blackberry jam in the arrow loop window and stared at it until a thin moon rose over the sea.

# JANUARY, 1941

In the place they had made for him in the chorus at the Lyceum, with twelve singers to his left and eleven to his right, Zachary stood in the red glow of lights that cast fire over a great painted backdrop of London. Its monuments were shattered, its walls breached.

In front of him, at centre stage, the new Interlocutor spoke to the audience in a deep voice modelled upon Zachary's father's. Staring at the man's back, seeing him silhouetted in the red light, Zachary believed that it really could be his father. He tried to make it true by force of will. He did not want to imagine it was impossible. His father had vanished and left no body behind, like an illusionist or a saint.

But every time the new Interlocutor spoke, Zachary knew his father was gone. 'And so, ladies and gentlemen, for this our final number tonight, we remember all those who have perished in this beloved city of ours, the city of mankind. And we remember that there is another city, both identical to ours and superordinate to it, where death has no dominion.'

The chorus began the hymn, and Zachary joined in as best he could. As they sang, the floodlights brightened, and in their soft glow a new backdrop was revealed: London, rebuilt and restored – but more than that. Every spire was taller, every bridge broader, each old familiar landmark improved. As the red floods brightened they were no longer flames but the glow of the sunrise.

Yellow and white lights joined the red, until eternal London shone in the full light of day. As the singers threw back their heads to raise the final chorus, the audience rose to its feet. Zachary felt nothing, except perhaps a dull surprise that they bought it.

When the curtain came down, the manager took him aside. They stood in the wings while from the auditorium came the muttering, shuffling sound of the audience departing.

'You winning, big man?' said the manager.

Zachary smiled. 'Sure.'

'Because from where I stood, I had twenty-three souls in my chorus, and then I had you.'

'I'm sorry. I'll try harder.'

'You do that. Happy negroes, that's what we serve here. One sad coon in my chorus, it's a hole in my bucket. All the magic leaks away, you know?'

Zachary shrugged. 'Maybe I can take a break.'

'And do what? So long as you're for sleeping in my basement, I'm for getting some work in return.'

'I could play piano in the interval.'

'With that long face? I'd sooner give the gig to a German.'

'I could bus the tables, then.'

The manager gave a weary look. 'I've got forty kids queuing up for that chorus. I'd just as soon take you off it, but all my players would say, "Give the boy a slot, you owe it to his father." And before I know it I've traded one sad face for nine. So come on, why won't you sing?'

Zachary shrugged again and said nothing.

'You shy? Because you've got a nice voice. I wouldn't march you down to Parlophone to cut a disc, but I wouldn't pour lead in my ears either.'

'It isn't that.'

'What, then? This is your break. You'd rather the street?'

Zachary hung his head. 'I'd rather something.'

The manager laughed. 'Think if you hold out long enough I'll open up my other box of jobs for negroes who can't write their name? What is it you're holding out for? Pope, or prime minister?'

Zachary said nothing, and finally the manager sighed. 'All right, bus my tables then. Collect the tips and good luck to you, but the job doesn't pay. Sleep in my basement, but if you want a wage then you'll damn well sing in my show. Got that?'

Zachary nodded.

Afterwards, when the players were gone, Zachary lit a candle and went down alone to the basement. He sat with a metal basin between his knees and a mirror propped against the wall at the end of the bench. With a cloth and cold water he scrubbed off the white greasepaint lips and the white rings around his eyes.

He clasped his hands. 'Sorry, Dad.'

There was no answer, though he listened for one in the silence.

'I'm sorry,' he said again.

Nothing. The darkness in the basement was frightening. It scuttled and knocked. A month had not cured him of the fear of it. He curled up under drapes in the corner, but sleep would not come.

'Are you there?' he said in the lowest voice he could.

He waited. His candle seemed to flicker, and perhaps this meant that his father was there.

'I don't know what to do.'

In the silence, in the endless underground night, the candle flame seemed to be steadier. Perhaps his father meant that he ought to be steady too. Zachary squeezed his eyes shut and pulled the drapes tight against the dark.

# JANUARY, 1941

**M**ary sat with Hilda on the train back from Tom's funeral. His had been the only body available to be buried – to each of the other families she had made do with sending flowers. Even this had been made difficult by the war, the Dutch blooms being no longer considered essential cargo and the English hothouses having been given over to food production. She had turned up a few early snowdrops, some forced hyacinths. She had hesitated to send them, uncertain if they would be a comfort.

In their compartment Hilda smoked, and jabbed at *The Times* crossword with a self-propelling pencil. She was likely, Mary felt, to infuriate the puzzle rather than to solve it.

'It was kind of you to come,' said Mary.

'I could hardly let you go with Palmer.'

Mary managed a smile. 'Palmer might have brought brandy.'

'Palmer might have exchanged places with the deceased. Is that not among his duties?'

The train shrieked steam into the plunging clouds. It didn't lighten them.

It had been an impossible way to meet Tom's parents for the first time. In the church, Mary hadn't known her place. It had seemed presumptuous to sit with the family and so she and Hilda had gone to the back. Tom's mother had fetched them and brought them wordlessly to the first pew. All through the service

Mary had looked straight ahead, at Tom's coffin beneath its lilies, wondering where they were from.

'They are lovely flowers,' Mary had said at the end.

'I went over to Cheltenham for them,' said Tom's mother.

Tom was dead, and lilies were available, and to Mary these things were equally incomprehensible.

They had walked out into flurries of snow. Four men, too old or infirm for the war, had lowered Tom's coffin into the ground on short ropes reserved for the purpose. The vicar had said, 'Death, where is thy sting?' There was a consensus that one couldn't feel a thing.

Three hours later, in the train, her body was still taut with the cold and the unreleased emotion. Yawing on warped rails, their train approached London Bridge. On either side of the line a thousand buildings were blown out.

'What do you suppose you'll do?' said Hilda.

'I must find Zachary, first of all.'

'And then what? Take him home to your mother? She'd be thrilled.'

'I've a responsibility to him.'

'You've nothing of the sort!'

'He was in my class and—'

'And nothing. You were ordered to teach that class grammar, not to adopt any survivors.'

'Now you're just being horrid.'

'Only because you're being ridiculous. Where would it end, if you went after him? You're not his family, or even his species. You can't give him a home – that's his people's job. And you shan't tell me he doesn't have people, because there were dozens and dozens at that theatre, conveniently colour-coded.'

'The negroes aren't all related, you know.'

Hilda paused, the idea seeming to strike her for the first time. 'Oh, they might be different tribes, but I daresay they put down the spears in times like these.'

'At least I should check that someone is taking him in.'

'Then make your enquiries if you must. But swear you won't promise that boy something you could never make good on. I know what a mule you can be when you get a notion in your head. You'd make the boy an exile from his people, and you a pariah among yours. It would be miserable for both of you.'

'You're right, of course. And yet—'

'And yet nothing. You must think only of yourself, and what you want to do. If you don't get on with your own life, you'll be no use to others at all.'

'I think I'd like to teach again.'

Hilda gave an exasperated groan.

'It would make Tom glad,' said Mary.

'You shan't live your life to make Tom glad.'

Mary lit a cigarette and watched the devastation roll by. These had been the city: these clubs and churches, these ordered landmarks. London had fitted her so perfectly that she had mistaken its shape for her own. Now each bomb was a breach in the carapace, laying bare the living nerve.

She said, 'It's easy to say.'

'Because it's true,' said Hilda. 'You must live on your terms.'

The loosened rails rattled as the train crept above the Embankment. Steam billowed over the grey river. On both banks, façades were down and buildings gaped. Mary had always supposed that she could endure if London could, but here the great old nautilus lay gasping and cracked at the throat of the Thames, at the place where sweet water met salt.

'Let's go for lunch at Claridge's,' said Hilda. 'You need a good feed.'

'I'm not hungry.'

'But you really must eat. You're thin as a harlot's excuse.'

'I think I shall go for a walk.'

'Then at least take me along. You're in no state to be on your own.'

Mary took her hand. 'You've done more than enough. You've always been good to me, and I know I don't make it easy.'

Hilda nodded. 'You're like a bad gundog. One can either put it down or make it the family pet.'

'I'm only pleased you've found a use for me.'

'Just don't pee on my rugs. And promise you'll consult me before you even think about teaching again.'

As the train came in to the platform they took their bags from the rack and disembarked. They embraced, and Hilda dissolved into steam. Once she was gone, Mary leaned into a corner for a while. No one interrupted her. Half the city wept into walls now.

Afterwards, she stood for a while on the empty platform. She pulled her gloves on and herself together, and walked out into the streets.

Everywhere there was rubble. Bathtubs lay exposed, their yellow ducks icebound. Beds in which women had been conceived and born and then conceived in and laboured in themselves – those brass theatres of involuntary dialogue – now lay silent and bent, see-sawing on bisected floors, weeping duck down into the street. The feathers swirled with the snow. It was too much for her – how easily she was discouraged now! – and she fled into a café and drank straw-coloured tea. She wrote to the manager at the Lyceum, asking if Zachary's whereabouts were known. When it was done and folded, the flat taste of the envelope gum lingered.

In the maps in the newspaper they brought her, the enemy's swastikas were pressed up against the neighbouring coasts – so close that one could look up from the page and almost smell the diesel and the sweat. In the Atlantic the U-boats completed the encirclement. On the inside pages of the paper were endless notices. London's districts had been divided and subdivided as the lines of communication shrank. There were ten new rules if one lived here;

twelve if one lived there. This was the place she had grown up in, whose singular law had recently applied from Bombay to Belize. Her great extrovertive city was besieged. Slowly the feeling returned that had come over her when she first took charge of her school. What one felt towards the enemy, finally, was fury.

She pushed the cold tea away and walked through the snow to Tom's old office at the Education Authority. In the lobby she knocked the snow off her boots and told the receptionist that she wouldn't leave until she was seen.

They let her up to see the new man, who was called Cooper. As he rose to greet her, he seemed to become blocked between his chair and the desk. He straightened ineffectually.

'Please,' said Mary. 'No need to get up.'

He sank back down, apologising with a vague gesture for what Mary took to be a bad back, or limited physical grace, or apathy.

Cooper was older than Tom – she put him in his mid-thirties. He was fair and slightly overweight. He had a moustache growing in. Behind him on the wall of the office was a small watercolour of Hampstead Heath that she had given to Tom in the summer. She had laughed until she gasped for breath as she watched Tom hang it there, one evening when his colleagues had all gone home. He had needed three nails and seven profanities. Afterwards they had been quite indiscreet, and a great deal of paperwork had fallen from the desk to the floor. Tom had always kept his desk in such a mess.

Cooper saw her looking at the picture. 'It's Hampstead Heath.'

'Is it?' Mary caught herself saying, quite automatically.

How soon one became diminished. The man made a gesture that was imprecisely dismissive – whether of her or the heath or the watercolour, she couldn't judge. 'Dreadful, I'm afraid,' he said.

Mary felt a sadness as weary as his manner. Of course the poor man dismissed the painting. Such was the past, after all: it left the present cluttered with objects the survivors were immune to. She sat, folded her gloves in her lap, and lit a cigarette. He clasped his hands on the immaculate desk and looked down at his cuffs, as though she might have asked his permission. There was an ashtray – Tom's, the heavy blue glass with the ambiguous inclusion in the heart of it that Mary had always rather hoped was an eyeball. Since Cooper made a point of not sliding the ashtray across the desk towards her, she made a point of using the carpet.

She said, 'I should like to be assigned a new school. My preference is for primary, but if the only vacancies are at secondary then I can teach French, Latin and composition, as it says in my file. I am available immediately.'

'Do you not think,' said Cooper after a moment, 'that under the circumstances it might be better to wait a while before you go back to work?'

'Wait for what? For children to forget their times tables? For aitches to be dropped in great mounds?'

He humoured her with a smile. 'I'm sure you know what I mean.'

'But I am quite all right. I am unharmed and able to return to duty.'

There was a long silence. 'Must I spell out the sensitivities?'

'I'd rather you gave me a job.'

Cooper wouldn't return her smile. He stood – apparently it was not so hard after all – and walked across the office. With his back to her and his hands clasped behind it, he looked out at the snow.

'My predecessor was very young, and decided to reopen some schools. I'm afraid the excitement of promotion got the better of his judgement.'

Mary shook her head. 'His duty was to provide school places.'

Cooper gave her the tone reserved for a child who had got the answer jolly nearly correct. 'Our duty, since you use the word, is to send the message that London under the circumstances is not the right place for the young.'

'And yet there are children the countryside won't take.'

'But I don't make the policy, and the policy is one of full evacuation.'

'Then what are we to do with the crooked and the coloured and the slow? Are we to let them rot, simply because it is not policy for them to exist?'

'If you must split hairs, it is policy that such children exist but it is not politic for them to be schooled here.'

'Does it not seem that what you say is monstrous?'

Cooper turned from the window. 'What is monstrous is that seven children and their parents are dead because my predecessor saw fit to let you play the pretty schoolmarm while the grown-ups were using the city for war.'

Mary blinked once, twice, then recovered herself. She fixed the man with a slight arch of the eyebrow as she lit a new cigarette.

He returned her gaze unsteadily. 'I suppose we both wish we could undo it.'

Her hands shook. 'We were hardly doing ballet on the roof. We were underground, in the shelter. People are killed in shelters every day.'

'Well it won't happen in any school of mine.'

'Apparently not, if neither will any teaching.'

He patted her on the shoulder. 'You're emotional because you were so caught up. You are charming and young, and I don't hold what happened against you. The one who should have known better is my predecessor.'

'Tom was my lover. It is well known. Won't you stop speaking as if we weren't both aware?'

'I am trying to protect your feelings, and the name of your family.'

'You might best serve both by letting me teach. There are hundreds of children in this district, you know full well. One sees them in every street, poking around in the rubble.'

'I'm afraid there's no position for you.'

'I apologise for becoming emotional. Please let me teach again.'

'Take a break,' he said gently. 'God knows, I would if I could. Get out of town for a few weeks, blow away the cobwebs.'

She turned her back on him. In the little watercolour she had given Tom, the light was yellow and frisky. If you went at that light with an egg whisk, you could work up a froth to stand a spoon in. London stretched away beyond the heath. The landmarks stood. They had been so firmly attached back then that the artist had had to paint the sky around them.

She went to the window. 'What can I do to change your mind?'

He said nothing. She moved closer, letting her arm brush against his as she smoked. 'We needn't put this city back the way we found it, you know.'

He gave an amused look that turned into something more serious.

'Look,' he said. 'It's overdue lunch. Why don't you and I go for a bite and discuss it?'

She tilted her head up to his, giving him the full benefit of her eyes. For a moment she let him drown himself.

'No, thank you,' she said brightly. 'I'm not at all hungry.'

He stared at her, colouring slowly. He seemed inclined to strike her, then turned abruptly and left her alone at the window. She heard him banging drawers in the desk, collecting his coat and hat from the peg, slamming the door behind him.

She turned from the window and went to stub out her cigarette. The small painting of Hampstead Heath hung in the grey light, in its golden frame. She let her hand linger, for a moment, on the cold blue glass of Tom's ashtray. She turned it on its axis – twice, three times – then left it where it was.

'I miss you,' she said to the empty office.

# JANUARY, 1941

They called the new club the Joint. As if it weren't a thing in itself but only a hinge between night and day. The bombers raised their tempo and the syncopated city matched the rhythm. When a raid interrupted the minstrel show now, the players rushed underground with the audience to join the big band that was already down there. They had cleared out the Lyceum's great basement to make the club. There was a stage at one end, a bar at the other and alcoves in between where soldiers pushed their luck.

Zachary fetched drinks from the bar in exchange for coins and cigarettes. It was weeks since he'd last seen the sky. It suited him. If you couldn't see the sky, it couldn't see you. People patted him on the head when he fetched their drinks. They called him Baby Grand. Everyone was christened again now, sometimes two or three times, as if by this expedient every person might stay ahead of the war's ability to call them by name.

No one cared if he drank, so he did. He slept under the bar and smoked like Bette Davis. He ate cocktail nuts, the glacé cherries from the bottoms of glasses – whatever he could get. Everyone was hungry. The new pianist discovered that if he waited a quaver after the beat and then hit down hard to give some heavy swing, then factory girls and airmen on leave could be made to dance even if they were weak from the rations.

Laying down drinks on the tables, Zachary picked up the gossip. Apparently so many souls were being lost every night that in the great mortuaries of Clerkenwell and Cheapside a dozen families would now claim any unrecognisable corpse as their cousin or mother or aunt. So now the morgue staff stripped the remains, tagged clothing and flesh with the same number, and had families identify the effects instead of the bodies. Zachary hadn't been asked to identify a thing. Not a tie clip or a ring. He wondered if his father was in some grave, being mourned under a new name. He prayed for him under the old one.

They said that above ground now, when only human fragments were recovered, the city assessed by weight how many bodies should be assembled. And if a few of the reincorporated dead had more than one left leg, then at least none of the coffins felt light. The drinkers caught him eavesdropping and they laughed and said, 'What do you think of that, Baby Grand?' He said, 'It sounds fair.' But he thought of his father, who had so carefully washed off his whiteface at the end of every performance, hashed together with white bodies.

Zachary drank what was left in the glasses and the big band played for forty-five minutes in each hour, all night, and whereas in peacetime the horns and the piano always used to play around each other in fast eddies, it was now discovered that if they all united instead in big block chords then at 3 a.m. and 4 a.m., with the air raid hot and heavy overhead and the dance floor jumping on its joists and dust pouring from the vaulted roof of the basement, then the slim negro band leader with his shirt soaked in sweat could lean in to his streamlined microphone as if into a great headwind and call at the crowded white dancers: 'Check down at your feet, good ladies and gentlemen, for so long as you are still dancing you cannot yet be dead!' And Zachary bussed tables and the orchestrated city tapped its great stock of shrouds and cardboard caskets, releasing a precise number each night in expectation of casualties predicted from cloud cover and bomber concentrations. And according to the gossip, if a piece of a Londoner could be collected with dustpan and brush then it would be sent downstream on the barges with the rest of the city's refuse to the great municipal middens at Durham Wharf, while all larger bodily phrases were composed into persons nameable and taken for classical burial. And the cavernous basement boomed. You were safe if dancing or dead. London remembered its oldest rhythm of putting the saints beneath it, and in the public cemeteries of Highgate and Nunhead and Kensal Green the old graves were dug up and the crotchety bones scattered to make room for new. The enemy enlarged its bombs from five hundred kilograms to one thousand and two thousand, and down in the basement the band leaders put together two bands, and three bands, so that six coloured men, and now nine coloured men, all swung in line in the horn section, and two negro drummers, and now three negro drummers, sweated at their kits on the big raised dais at the back of the stage, and Zachary remembered how his father had used his heavy left hand to stamp out the colossal chords – boom, boom, boom – and the limitless suburban cemeteries opened up fresh ground and the commuter trains in the middle of the day took the coffins out into Metro-land and returned with a toot on the whistle and the conductor's call of 'Empties!' And all the murderous night the big band drummers smashed out time while the stonemasons in their massed choir with their steel chisels in perfect orchestration tapped out the assumed names of the dead, in letters Zachary couldn't read. How unbearable it was that his father's name was lost. How thin his own limbs seemed. He heard the music and he heard the news from above, and it seemed to him now that the world above and the world below were playing the exact same tune.

Every morning when the club kicked out and the band put their horns back into velvet, he swept and put the stools up. The dawn left him deaf from the silence. No one had talk in them. Under the electric bulbs he ate with the band and the barmen, and then all of them went where they would, and Zachary curled up in his place under the bar where no one minded him.

If he woke before the crowd came back – if the stools were still up and the bombers far away – then he went to the piano. He played the quiet pieces the way his father had shown him: eyes closed, softly. He did what he could. His father hadn't wanted him to be in the show, and he wasn't, and yet there was this agony. He played the slow tunes and sometimes he almost had his father with him for an hour, and then the crowd flooded back and he smiled and fetched drinks for them.

When he played his father's music, he was almost back home. But a tune had no fixed place in time. It was a city before the eternal. It was only ever a joint.

# JANUARY, 1941

**M**ary sat with her mother and they read the morning's post while they waited for lunch. The manager at the Lyceum had replied: Zachary was in good health and being provided for, and Mary wasn't to concern herself. She frowned and folded the letter back into its envelope.

'What is it?' said her mother.

'Just Hilda,' said Mary. 'The men she favours, the shops she doesn't.'

'How dreary.'

'But it's Hilda so she makes it fun, of course.'

'Then why the long face?'

'I worry for her. I wish she could meet someone nice.'

'Well, click your heels together three times when you wish.'

Mary wondered if the manager had meant it kindly when he wrote that she wasn't to concern herself. There would be a natural wariness, she supposed, of whites. Perhaps she hadn't made it clear in her own letter that she was one of the helpful kind.

Palmer's footsteps were so delicate as to be barely audible when he brought lunch in at one. Cook had set a mixed shoal of shrimp and whitebait into clear aspic, using a mould in the form of a wave. The wave was encircled on its salver by a salad of *fruits de mer*, the whole resting on a bed of toasted golden seeds that made convincing sand.

Mary's mother put on her spectacles to examine the production, then had Palmer hold it up to the window so that daylight shone through the wave.

'And the beauty is that none of it is on the ration. People make such a fuss about the hardships, but one need only be inventive. What do you think, dear?'

'I'm astonished the poor haven't thought of it,' said Mary.

Her mother ignored her. 'Of course it's only a practice for the real thing.'

For a moment, before she understood that the dish was a prototype for the fully operational version of itself, Mary couldn't think what her mother meant. She stared at the tiny creatures as they flashed in the afternoon light, and wondered what could be the real-life experience for which this was preparation. (Drowning, perhaps? Quite close to the beach? In a well-stocked corner of the ocean?) She had stopped paying attention to the tireless campaign of dinners and cocktails through which her mother hoped to fight Father into Cabinet.

'Are you quite with us?' said her mother.

'Sorry,' said Mary. 'I hardly slept.'

'Oh, who does? But you might at least have an opinion.'

Mary squinted into the wave. 'The shrimp are rather sweet. Look at their little faces.'

'But darling, don't you notice something?'

Mary noticed that Palmer was trembling with the strain of holding up the salver to the light. The vibration caused a pulsation in the wave, as if it might crest at any moment and break into streaks of mannered foam.

'I think Cook has dyed the aspic, hasn't she? It's a very subtle green.'

Her mother made an exasperated sound. 'Yes, but the shrimp – don't you see? Half of them are swimming upside-down. And they would hardly be scattered throughout the wave like that, willy-nilly. Shrimp would be down near the seabed, feeding.'

'It's almost as if Cook has forgotten her marine biology.'

'Well, you mock me, but this is why we have a practice run. Oh Palmer, you may put the damned thing down now, and let's see how it slices.'

While Palmer set to with a serving knife, Mary's mother briefed her on the next evening's table plan.

'Father will be here on the left, giving the Minister the head of the table. Anderson will sit here with you on his right to make him laugh, which you are awfully good at. And you must try to show off your figure a little. You have worn nothing but sackcloth since . . . well, since you-know-when.'

'I am not entirely clear on my role. Am I to seduce Anderson, or to render him well disposed towards Father?'

'Would a little of both be beyond you? Anyway, you mustn't look at me like that. I have invited Henry Hunter-Hall just for you, and he will be sitting here, directly opposite. You may bother each other with your toes, or whatever it is that young people do since the art of conversation was lost.'

'It is too soon. I was in love with Tom – I think you know that I was.'

'Dear, you are twenty years old. We all have our practice runs.'

'You're relieved that Tom died.'

'Oh, not at all. I am dreadfully sorry when anyone is killed, doubly so if it is someone you were fond of.'

Mary smiled.

'What?' said her mother.

'Well you make him sound like a pony, or a Labrador.'

'It's only that he was never someone I thought of as a grown-up match for you.'

'He was killed trying to save one of my pupils. I thought it grown-up.'

'It is heart-breaking, I know, but one advances through such trials.'

'And hence Henry, to be seated opposite me, and in whom with your blessing I am to find consolation. Tell me, should I write out the place cards in Tom's blood, or would you prefer me to use my own?'

'Must you be like that? I am only anxious that you should get straight back on with life. Henry is a likeable boy, from a very good family, and you shan't tell me he isn't handsome.'

There was a sadness in her mother's eyes. Mary wondered whether it had always been there, becoming visible only now that she was attuned to sorrow's frequency.

'Mother,' she said, 'were you ever in love with Father?'

Her mother looked towards the salver where Palmer – before dematerialising – had carved the pristine wave into slices.

'We were very lucky to find each other,' she said.

'Yes, but were you?'

'Yes, we were very lucky.'

'Sometimes, Mother, I don't know whether you'd be glad if I went along with you, and attended your functions and married some outrageously suitable Henry, or whether you wouldn't secretly be much happier if I just said "hang it all", and flew as close to the sun as I jolly well dared.'

'Yes, you are quite right, you don't know that.'

A grey wind blew snowflakes past the windows. When the silence got too much, Mary said, 'Hilda thinks we should volunteer for the ambulances.'

'Hilda is jolly public-spirited.'

'You know as well as I do that she only covets the uniform.'

'I'm glad it's you who said it.'

'So, do you think we should?'

'Should what?'

'Join the ambulances.'

Her mother fetched the cigarette case from its place on the mantel. She took a cigarette and slid the case over to Mary. Palmer appeared and disappeared, in such a way that he left behind him two lit cigarettes, an onyx ashtray and no lingering image on the back of the eye.

It was the first time Mary had smoked with her mother. They said nothing. They tended their cigarettes while the sliced aspic, untouched, melted slowly in the heat of the dining-room fire, releasing fish and shrimp by ones and twos into an uncertain future.

# JANUARY, 1941

Alistair guessed that the arithmetic might not be encouraging if worked through to its conclusion. Malta was eight miles wide by eighteen long – as large as London, only with less to do in the evening. From this unpromising rock – their best remaining possession in the Mediterranean – the starving garrison had orders to hold out against the combined forces of Germany and Italy. Alistair tried to count the enemy's available armies, but he ran out of fingers.

'Heath?' said Lieutenant Colonel Hamilton.

'My apologies, sir – I was miles away.'

'I'll bet you wish you were.'

Alistair grinned. 'Sir.'

'Brief the men, will you? A pep talk would be nice. Otherwise any kind of talk they will listen to. Soliloquy, philippic . . .' He waved his hand as if it was all too wearisome. Alistair saluted and left the old man to his paperwork.

10 Regiment, Royal Artillery was mustered at easy readiness among the ramparts of Fort St Elmo. The men relaxed in the twilight and lounged against the stone walls, while below them Grand Harbour shone under a fulvous moon. The men had the news already: the carrier *Illustrious* had been badly smashed up and was on its way in to port. Now the whole spite of the enemy would be directed against the island, to finish the great ship off. It was up to Alistair to tell the men, officially, that they were in for it.

He swallowed his nerves, blew his tin whistle, and stood firm while two hundred men came to their feet with the grudging compliance they might have afforded to a football referee who could just as usefully have let play continue. The men got themselves into their three batteries, each battery subdivided into two troops of four guns apiece, each gun accounting for a sergeant and seven gunners.

They lined up facing Alistair while the senior officers assembled at his side – his five fellow captains and the three majors. As captain, Alistair commanded a four-gun troop. Even when one added his two subalterns and his warrant officer, only thirty-five of the men arranged before him were his own. It was nerve-wracking, which was why Hamilton did it – made his juniors take turns to address the whole of 10 Regiment.

The men fell quiet, waiting for Alistair to be a genius. They watched him with the world-class loyalty and affection that only the British Army could disguise as open sarcasm.

At his side, Simonson whispered, 'Your flies are undone, old man.'

With effort, Alistair stopped himself from checking.

Simonson whispered, 'Oh, and your mother telephoned.'

Alistair ignored him.

'I'm to let you know that your father's cock tastes of your dog's arse.'

To stop himself laughing Alistair had to bite his cheek.

He took a step forward. 'Well, men, as you all know, our loved ones are taking a beating back home and they are holding up superbly, and now it is our turn. The Admiralty tells us that one of their tubs, *Illustrious*, has undergone some unplanned modifications at sea. She's on her way in now, and we can be certain that the enemy will spare no effort to sink her in port.'

'Or brandy,' whispered Simonson.

'Perhaps we cannot do much against high-altitude bombing, but as you know we have a very effective anti-aircraft weapon in the 3.7-inch gun, and we intend by coordinated firing to establish a box within which the enemy's dive bombers cannot operate.'

'A lunch box,' whispered Simonson. 'A cricket box.'

'Gunners, your sergeants will be issued with the angular sectors and elevations for each gun. There will be a coordinated firing sequence in order to achieve the maximum coverage of shell splinters for the minimum expenditure of ordnance. The details will be—'

As Alistair spoke, he had noticed a growing agitation among the men. Now they were looking past him, over the ramparts. Alistair stopped talking and turned to see what they were watching.

Looming huge over the breakwaters, *Illustrious* was limping into Grand Harbour under cover of dark. Alistair had never seen a carrier and he was awed at the size of her. She wore no lights and the harbour was blacked out, but they could see her silhouette against the moonlight. She darkened half the sky. Her huge turbines throbbed as she ghosted in. The sea breeze brought the awful smell of her: scorched metal and flesh, burned aviation spirit, leaking oil. No one spoke. A dozen officers and two hundred men watched for two full minutes in silence. When the smell got too much, Alistair turned back to the men.

'All right,' he told them, abandoning the speech he had planned. 'As you can see she will be hard to miss, even for the Italians. We had better all get to our guns.'

Back with his own troop, Alistair felt all right. He busied himself with making each man as comfortable as he could. Since it would be a cold night he had blankets and bedding brought up from below, and thermoses filled with cocoa. He sent Briggs to the medical officer to secure a stock of eye drops and Benzedrine for the men, knowing from his experience in

France that it would be two or three more days at full alert before the stuff was needed, but that by the time it was, it would be gone. He split each gun crew into two watches of two hours, and he spent the long night walking the quarter-mile beat of his guns.

No attacks came.

Finally, with the hum of fatigue in his ears as the day dawned in grey cloud, he took himself down to the rocks below the fort. He looked at the sea and thought about Tom. The waves broke themselves on the rocks, each retreating with its wounded hiss to succumb to the surge of the next. They came from the horizon to do it. Alistair watched the incoming queue of them. Not one wave jumped its order or renounced its destination. Death, finally, was British; life chaotic and foreign.

The cloud clung to the island all morning, and at noon the lieutenant colonel had them stand the gun crews down. A long lull began. The cloud stayed so low that nothing could fly, and with so much of the Royal Navy still in the approaches, the enemy would risk nothing from the sea. All eyes peered upwards. At any perceived darkening of the grey, the men would remark that it was turning out nice again. Any slight break in the cloud brought anxious silence. In short order the men became authorities on grey, able to distinguish between the nuances of ash, dusk and silver; granite, slate and mouse. Their upturned faces took on the lifesaving pallor.

Leave was cancelled, officers and men confined to the fort. There were no more afternoons sailing or swimming. On the first day fresh barrels were fitted to the guns. Shells were brought out and inventoried and restocked into the underground magazines. When there was nothing more that could usefully be made ready, the men were given a hundred things to polish. The rubble-painted gun carriages, the brass oil lines, the optics of the predictor gear. When all the artillery pieces gleamed, the men moved on to cutlery, flagpoles, boots. By the end of the second day of the lull, the fort and all its contents were burnished to a furious sheen.

When there was nothing left to shine, there were walls of sandbags to be moved. It was discovered by the officers of the regiment, with their three batteries in eight-hour rotation, that if the men of the first battery moved a sandbag wall from A to B, the second from B to A and the third from A to B again, then the first battery would come back on duty satisfied that their work was still as they had left it.

By the third day of the lull even the most imaginative officers could no longer busy their men. Now the grey of the sky began to bleed into the soldiers' unguarded hearts. Men stared at the featureless clouds and saw enemy planes where there were none. There were false alarms and loud panics. Memory was blinded, and none could remember a time when they had not stood guard on the timeless ramparts. On their mean rations an ancient hunger slowed their minds. The ghosts in the old stone haunted them. Officers brooded and traced their fingers over the scratched graffiti of past garrisons. Men off duty woke screaming in the night, babbling that the Turks had breached the walls. A bloodied axe was found on the ground in the central courtyard, with tufts of blond hair still clinging to the blade. Some supposed the hair to be human, others thought it was goat. When a roll call was taken, one of each was found to be missing.

On the fourth day, all was quiet. The missing man was found in a village inland, injured only by drink.

Alistair tried to remember Tom's face. Already he could hardly remember it differently from Duggan's. He couldn't catch a glimpse of their old life together through the low grey ceiling of memory. Instead he saw Mary – her copper hair, her insubordinate grin – and he was sick at himself.

He lay in his cot, staring at his grey metal table with its lit candle. Its small flame, through Tom's blackberry jam, cast a bloody glow across the writing paper.

At dawn on the fifth day he went up to take the report of the off-going watch. He smoked his pipe while he looked out over the sea. The breeze was fresh on his face. He watched the red sun edge up into a vast pink sky, but it was a long time before he understood that the cloud was gone. He creased his eyes against the light. Already the horizon was starting to blue. It was a perfect bomber's sky. He tapped out his pipe on the stone, ran his fingers through his hair, and felt the familiar battle lurch in his stomach.

It was six, and the fresh watch was coming up from the fort. He hurried to get them installed but they were not even halfway ready before the fort's electric bells started up. A minute later, as men rushed to their stations and the fort erupted into action, the sirens began to wail across Valletta and all around the harbour.

The Germans attacked, so much harder than the Italians. The Germans were inflexible in their fury, deploying it in a pre-arranged configuration. For the next week there was not one hour when an attack did not come from their dive bombers or their high-altitude rigs. When it finally ended, on the eighth night, the men who had not been pierced by shrapnel or mutilated by their own guns' recoil were so deafened by a million bangs that their ears bled through the yellow dust that clogged them. They were so washed through with amphetamines and smoke that they saw visions as they collapsed – officers and men alike – into piles around their guns. Like children kept awake beyond endurance they slept where they fell, mouths agape, faces as still as death. All night the fine yellow dust, which had risen a mile high in the bombing, drifted down on the men in a shroud.

\*  \*  \*

When Alistair woke, the only sound was the keening of seagulls. He rubbed dust out of his eyes until he could see. Under a sky that was finally grey again, the harbour was black with oil and foul with sewage. Every pipe in the port must have cracked. The air could have stripped paint from the inside of a man's chest.

He stumbled up the stone stairs to the signals room, but when he picked up the field telephone the line was dead. After eight days and nights of dive bombing, nothing was connected to anything any more. The garrison was a join-the-dots puzzle, and Alistair was not sure he wanted to know what it looked like when it was completed.

He was the only soul awake. He roused Briggs – if he had had to shake him any harder, Alistair would have been doing the enemy's work. He held the man by his shoulders, gave him a stern look and said, 'Coffee.'

Briggs looked back at him from a distance measured in miles.

'Coffee,' said Alistair again. 'Koh. Fee.'

'Yes. Please.'

'No, Briggs. You make coffee. For officers.'

Briggs gave a clumsy salute and stumbled off to bang pots. Alistair went along the guns until he found Simonson. He shook him awake.

'What is it, you contemptible man?'

'I came to see if you were alive.'

'Well I'm not, so clear off.'

Alistair said, 'I thought you might want to know that the war is over.'

Simonson sat up in the dust and blinked twice. 'God. Jesus. Really?'

'Yes,' said Alistair. 'Telegram just in from London. Immediate cessation of hostilities. Troopships home for us within the week.'

Simonson closed his eyes and gave an ecstatic sigh. 'Oh, thank Christ.'

Alistair gave him twenty seconds and then said, 'No, not really.'

Simonson opened one bloodshot eye. 'You vile, vile bastard.'

'Returning the favour for your help with my speech last week. Coffee?'

'I hope it poisons you.'

'My man Briggs is brewing some. Come over to my room. And then we must rouse the men and get ourselves operational again.'

Simonson eyed the clouds. 'The Germans won't come today.'

'They won't need to, if we let this rot set in. Everyone's still snoring.'

Simonson pulled his jacket over his head. 'It worked for the French.'

Alistair laughed. 'I thought you wanted to make major.'

'Yes, so oiks like you can do the drudgery.'

'Did I mention,' said Alistair, 'that our friendship means the world to me?'

Simonson only groaned.

'But it does, you know. I'm mildly glad every time you're not killed.'

Simonson opened half an eye and leered at him. 'At last. Meet me in the showers at midnight, and for god's sake not a word to Matron.'

For the rest of the day the two captains saw to the men of their battery. There were the injured to be evacuated to the hospitals further inland, the badly battle-frayed to be rotated out for R&R, and the battery's eight guns to be consolidated down to six fully manned units. Everything needed repairing, cleaning and oiling. Each of the 3.7s needed re-levelling on its jacks, every sight wanted recalibrating, and every signal line had to be taken up, checked for breaks and re-laid.

Inside, in the labyrinthine fort, everything had been shaken from its shelf, or taken to the wrong place in the chaos, or stolen or eaten or sublimated. It was a mercy that every unit of the British Army came so fully documented that it could be reassembled from its constituent parts by men who had hardly slept. Alistair and Simonson worked their battery back up to readiness using the technical manuals and the quartermaster's equipment list. If they had happened to pick up the wrong instructions at the beginning of the day, it seemed to Alistair that they might just as easily have ended up with a bus company, or a small dairy farm.

At nightfall there was still so much fuel oil in the sea that Alistair half expected the setting sun to ignite it. He was too tired to think straight. He stumbled up the stone staircase to his room and sat down on his cot. Air mail had come during the day – a Wellington had slipped in through the lull in the enemy's air cover – and a letter was waiting for him on his desk. He slit the envelope open, not recognising the hand.

*Alistair,*

*I hope you shan't mind if I write. You must feel as rotten as I do without Tom. I was going through his things when I found a letter you wrote to him, asking forgiveness for the night you and I met. I do not know whether he managed to reply.*

*I thought it might do you good to know that Tom often spoke of you. He looked up to you. He was never reconciled to staying in London while you put your neck on the line. So if Tom seemed distant in his letters towards the end, you mustn't think that he meant to be. Some days he could seem a thousand miles from me, even though we would be sitting at the same table.*

*Everyone is tired here, after so many months of bombing. There is a distance between all of us now. I do not mean to be maudlin, only to tell you how it is in London.*

After the war of course it will be like the start of spring, which is always so brilliantly sudden. The leaves will burst back onto the trees and close the gaps between the branches and we shall be startled – shan't we? – as we are startled at the end of every winter. We shall think: oh, I had quite forgotten there were three liveable seasons.

Tom wouldn't want us to be sad. I took crocuses to his grave this morning. I arranged them as best I could, and then I came home. On the way home the train was crowded. I was hungry. There was a man in my compartment with an irritating laugh. One does not rise above the everyday simply because one ought to. In the end I suppose we lay flowers on a grave because we cannot lay ourselves on it.

Hilda and I have applied to work on the ambulances. It might be exciting to drive an ambulance – although to listen to my father, my driving would be certain to cause further casualties. In any case, they will not let me teach. It is too bad, but perhaps they are right. It is my constant regret that my class would still be alive if I had not insisted on carrying on once the air raids began. We live, you see, and even a mule like me must learn. I was brought up to believe that everyone brave is forgiven, but in wartime courage is cheap and clemency out of season.

Unless you tell me otherwise, I shall keep up the rent on the garret. I thought you might like it to be there when you got back. In your wardrobe you have three viable ties, four shirts of which two are almost serviceable, and a lounge suit in a style that I can only describe as conventional. Forgive me if you feel that 'dull' is a better word. I have applied mothballs, though I was tempted to use

*something more flammable. You must let me know what*
*you want to do about arrangements.*
    *Sincerely,*
    *Mary North*

Alistair put down the letter and stood up. For a few minutes he looked out over the devastated port and the black harbour sickly with oil. Then he sat back at his metal table and took up a stub of pencil and an aerogramme sheet.

*Dear Mary,*
    *Thank you for your kind letter. You must surrender the*
*garret and let me know what you have paid in rent so I*
*can reimburse you. As for my poor old clothes, surely*
*there is some yokel in your father's constituency who can*
*hang them on a scarecrow. Furthermore*

He hesitated. What had she meant by 'You must let me know what you want to do about arrangements'? He read her letter through again, finding it impenetrable. If it was a simple request for instructions, perhaps there were too many crocuses in it. If it was something more, then perhaps there were not enough roses. He screwed up his page and began again.

*Mary,*
    *If you really do not mind, I hope you will keep the*
*garret on, at least until I have a chance to come and say*
*goodbye to the old dump. I would like a place to remem-*
*ber Tom by. Of course it is your place now, yours and his,*
*so you must do what you feel is*

He crumpled that page up too. Was she asking him to talk about Tom, or allowing him not to? She missed Tom, he missed

255

Tom – but the living must live with the living, this was understood in her letter. Therefore, how boorish of him to bang on about Tom.

He rubbed his eyes. It was impossible. In the history of the world there was not one example of a man ever having written a satisfactory letter to a woman who mattered to him. How could he even attempt it, after eight days and nights of bombing? And yet this is when he must write: now, in the lull between attacks, when his letter would go straight out on the next available aeroplane. War made one do everything when one wasn't at all ready. Dying, yes, but also living.

*Mary,*
   *Damn the garret and damn my old clothes, I wish I*
*were there with you.*

He stopped. Perhaps he was entirely misreading it. Now that he read her letter again, he was ashamed. She loved Tom, and Tom was dead, and her letter was a game attempt to buck herself up. She was a child talking herself into courage and she wanted a brotherly word from him, nothing more. She needed him to tell her that it was all right, that he felt hollow about Tom too – that this was simply how it was with the dead, and it did not mean that one had not loved them enough. And yet at the same time, her letter seemed to say, 'I love you – can anything be done?' after only the mildest decryption.

He put his head in his hands and groaned. She had had this effect on Tom too, of course – had driven his poor friend around the twist wondering if it could possibly be true that she liked him. If Alistair could believe that he felt Tom laughing at him from beyond the grave, it might make everything easier. But the truth, of course, was just as Mary had put it. One felt nothing at all from the dead. They died, and then they were gone, and one's heart ached from the sudden absence of feeling more than from any surfeit.

He held Mary's letter and breathed in the smell of it: soap and cigarette smoke. Here it was, in his hands, this hour of her life in London that he supposed had not been straightforward.

He picked up his pencil and began again.

*Mary,*

*I do not mind what you do with the garret. I mind if you are happy. Do not keep the garret on my account. Keep it if you feel better there. Please consider not taking the ambulance driver position. You know that it is danger- ous work in a raid, and you have lost quite enough already. What I find with my men is that they will rush into harm's way after they have lost a friend. Partly it is the desire to avenge, but it is more than that. I tell them that the war is not their fault. I give my men permission to feel guilty if they die themselves, and not before.*

*Do not let them tell you that you cannot teach any more. If you are good at it, then teach. Find a way – I do not think you are one to follow orders. We are all of us orphaned by this war – the world that bore us is gone and now we must be useful where we can.*

*Yours,*
*Alistair*

He folded the aerogramme, addressed it, gave it to Briggs and collapsed back onto the cot.

His letter flew off the island on the same Wellington that had brought Mary's. The aeroplane also carried a burned RAF man, bound for home via Gibraltar. The casualty lay on a carpet of mail bags in the narrow tunnel of the tail section that ended in the rear gunner's turret. The pilot kept the Wellington at sixty feet until they were out of range of Axis fighters operating from Sicily, and then he climbed and began to thread a high line between Sardinia and the Barbary Coast.

Sixty miles north of Tunis, the burned airman died of his wounds. It happened quietly in the drone of engine noise, and in the last minutes the numbing cold of high altitude was a comfort to the man. There in the sweet sacking smell of the mail bags he understood that he was dying, and it pleased him that he was going in the company of so many soft words home. He looked down through the Perspex side panel of the Wellington and watched the endless blue Mediterranean wash the blood away from all shores.

The crew of the Wellington experienced no mechanical problems and encountered no enemy aircraft. Leaving Algiers to port, the pilot turned across open water to Gibraltar. There was cloud in the western Mediterranean, and as they closed on the Spanish coast it came lower. By the time the pilot made radio contact with the tower at Gibraltar, he had been forced down below one thousand feet and a southerly wind was buffeting the Wellington from side to side. The tower had the pilot make a west-to-east landing from the Atlantic side.

As they came in behind the rock, the crosswind kicked up a sudden gust and yawed the plane just as its landing gear touched down. The Wellington lifted one wing, dug the other wingtip into the deck, and spun sideways off the end of the runway into the sea. In the cold water off Gibraltar, Alistair's letter sank to three hundred feet along with eleven hundred other letters, the burned airman and the six-man aircrew, and none of them ever made it home.

# FEBRUARY, 1941

A month went by with no reply from Alistair. When a letter came accepting her for a post as an ambulance driver, Mary smoothed it out on the writing table of her bedroom at her parents' house. She frowned at it, holding her cigarette any old way, not caring if it stained her fingers. Smoke had gone over to the enemy's side in any case. It had once been the same stuff that curled from a genie's lamp. Now it only reminded one.

What ought she to do? Perhaps she should give in and let her mother marry her off. Or she could join the ambulances, and see what good she might do there. The war might punish either choice with equal probability.

The longer she thought about it, listening to the maid dusting on the landing, the more daunting any choice seemed. To begin life the first time had been a breeze. Being so newly fledged, one had only to step off the bough and be astonished by the sudden rush of air. Now, at twenty, it was hard to begin again. One had to take off from the ground. Every wing beat had to be forced against an unsympathetic gravity.

In the half-light from the courtyard, in the silence that lay on the white crocheted bedspread, she felt herself dissolving. Her father was away at his constituency. Her mother was spread thin with her coffees and committees, achieving a busy translucence. Some days Mary lay on the bed for hours.

At first, with the funeral, and boxing up Tom's things, and writing to Alistair, she had crackled with a desperate energy. She had been certain that Alistair would reply. It had seemed to her that she would be fine again with just the slightest word to get her started in some direction. Now she cringed when she thought how foolish she had been, to imagine that he might mind about her. And it wasn't only Alistair. Since receiving the manager's letter she had written to Zachary directly at the Lyceum, and received nothing in reply. Perhaps this was what it was to grow up: this realisation that the world was already staffed with people and that one was not particularly needed.

She lay on the bed and stared at the ceiling. The covings depicted an endless rope. At each corner the rope described an inward whorl before embarking on the next cornice line. One could follow the rope all day.

The telephone rang downstairs, and presently Palmer came up to call her to it. Nothing had changed in his tone. That he continued to treat her as if she was not greatly diminished – as if she required no particular sympathy – struck her as a colossal kindness. She followed him down the central stairway as a girl might follow a grown-up, in her bare feet on the soft runner, still wearing her nightgown at noon. The telephone was off the hook on the console table in the hallway. White narcissi overhung it, vased in crystal grey.

It was Hilda. 'So, did you get yours? Your letter?'

'Yes,' said Mary.

'And you're accepted, too?'

'Yes.'

A squeal came down the line, as if a kitten had inhaled a kazoo. 'Oh, we'll have an adventure!'

Mary leaned her head against the wood panelling. 'I'm not sure.'

'You haven't been thinking, have you? There's really no need. You see, there will be a peaked cap, with a badge.'

'You know I'm not a uniform girl.'

'But it's hardly for your benefit, is it? It will work on men like catnip.'

'I'm not in the market.'

'Nonsense, darling. I telephoned the speaking clock. The time for mourning is over.'

'But you are outrageous!'

'Now look here,' said Hilda. 'If you were mourning then I'd leave you to it. But now you are just moping. You're almost certainly the reason Hitler is still bombing us. You know the Nazis cannot stand a funk.'

'I just—'

'Stop it. Say you'll take the ambulance job. I've never worked a day in my life and I'm hardly going to start without you.'

Mary stared at the flowers. Their trumpets screaming with pollen. The grey light surprised into colours by the vase. 'I'm just not sure if . . .'

'Oh, do come along now,' said Hilda in a plaintive voice. 'Won't you put down the handset, whoever you are, and fetch my friend Mary to the telephone?'

'I don't feel as if I'm *for anything* any more, that's the trouble. I used to know straight away what was the right thing to do.'

'Yes but never mind, because that was infuriating.'

'I'm sorry. I don't deserve you.'

'The only thing you don't deserve is what's happened to you. Of course you feel low. But the longer you hide in your room the worse it'll be.'

'I just don't know if an ambulance job will help. It might only remind me.'

'But don't you already think about it now?'

'Constantly.'

'It will be the same, then, only with uniforms and badges. Why wander through your thoughts when you could drive through them quite recklessly, with sirens? The worst that could happen is that we might help someone.'

Mary smiled despite herself. 'Us. Imagine.'

'I know! Don't tell me you can't picture it. Screeching to the rescue – "Oh, where did I put those bandages? I'm sure they were in this box but it seems to be full of glamour . . .".'

Mary hesitated. 'I suppose we could try it for a while, and see.'

'That's the spirit. Or at least, it's something to put your spirit in when we find it again.'

Mary closed her eyes. 'Thank you.' And when no reply came, 'Hilda?'

'It's just that you've never thanked me for anything before.'

'See?' said Mary. 'You should try being nice more often.'

# MARCH, 1941

At sunset Mary reported to the Air Raid Precautions station at St Helen's Church in Bishopsgate. The church was undamaged, with only the windows boarded up. The area all around was laid waste, but Mary made a point of not looking. If one kept the great yellow mounds of smashed brick in the corner of one's eye, then the mind understood them as the contours of nature and forgot its trick of making one unhappy.

A man wrapped in a grey blanket was sitting outside at a trestle table.

'I've come on church business,' said Mary. 'I'm the new vicar.'

The man raised his eyes with what Mary felt was impressive weariness.

'Mary North,' she said. 'I'm to be the new driver for the Joint War Organisation stretcher party.'

He looked her up and down. He was fiftyish and gaunt, with red eyes and a silver two-day beard. He wore knee-high Wellingtons and his jacket bloomed with water stains. His breath was vapour in the thin light of the sunset. 'You can drive?'

'Was it in the job description?'

At last, the man smiled. 'I'm Huw. I'm one end of the stretcher. Clive is the other. He'll be here once he runs out of beer money.'

'Glad to know you,' said Mary.

'You won't be. Have you done this work before?'

'It's my first time.'

He angled a thumb over his shoulder. 'Well the van's around the back if you want to familiarise yourself. There's no bells or whistles. It'll be just like a normal Sunday drive, only with bombing. The new nurse is already there – keen little thing she is, says she's been here since two.'

'That's my friend Hilda. Hates to miss a party. We signed up together.'

'You wait years, then two come along at once.'

The ambulance was a black Hillman saloon with red crosses on the door panels and four stretchers in a rack on the roof. Hilda was done up in a uniform coat two sizes too big for her. She was organising the medical bag, and when she looked up her cap fell down over her eyes.

'Should we hug or salute?' she said.

'Shall we do both, to be safe?'

Hilda's Red Cross brassard slipped to her elbow on the backswing.

'Idiot,' said Mary. 'Let me fix that for you.'

'Thanks. You'd think I might put it on properly, wouldn't you? I can bandage an arm recurrent, figure-of-eight or spiral reverse, and I have a brand-new certificate to prove it.'

'It's always harder on oneself,' said Mary, re-pinning the band.

'I hope they'll send us out with a proper nurse, just to start with.'

'But you are a proper nurse. Look at you, with your hat and armband. All you're missing is a fob watch.'

'I've had two weeks' training! I took longer than that to learn to use a gas oven.'

'Well, if we do pick up a casualty, I shall just have to drive us to the hospital quickly.'

'Do you know if we actually have to wear the tin hats, by the way? Only mine makes me look like a mushroom. It's all right for you tall girls, you can carry it off.'

'You know they become fashionable during the raids.'

Hilda tugged at her lower lip with her teeth. 'I suppose . . . but goodness, it's hard to make anything of this uniform. I've tried it like this with the skirt and stockings and I've tried it with the trousers, which are just *urgh*. I've been up since five, you know.'

Mary said, 'You look fine.'

She had simply put on the skirt with which they had issued her, cinched the belt around the jacket, and jammed a pack of Craven "A"s into each pocket. She lit one now.

'Oh,' said Hilda, 'are you cold? Let's sit in the van, shall we?'

Mary's hands were trembling. It was something they had done since the disaster – a bore, really – and it was sweet of Hilda to pretend it was only the cold. It was pleasant in any case to get into the Hillman. Mary settled in the driver's seat and cracked the window an inch to let the smoke out. The interior smelled nicely of laundry, which must have been the cargo until the van was requisitioned.

In the passenger seat Hilda checked her makeup in the mirror. She reapplied her lipstick, clicked the top back on, and said, 'Alistair still hasn't replied to me.'

'I'm sorry,' said Mary.

'It was a long shot, but I thought he might at least write back.'

Mary found that she couldn't hold Hilda's eye.

Hilda stared. 'You aren't writing to him as well, are you?'

'No,' said Mary, electing to interpret Hilda's tense as the present simple.

'I suppose he's just a cad, then,' said Hilda.

'I thought you liked him?'

'Only if he likes me more. Those are the rules.'

Mary nodded. 'Sometimes you are almost Christ-like.'

'You can say you were my first disciple.'

'I'll say I did your hair.'

Hilda looked at her watch. 'I'm terrified, aren't you? We wouldn't be doing this if it was really dangerous, would we?'

'You know what you should really worry about? It's that so many girls have volunteered, it won't seem exotic any more.'

'You suppose men won't care?'

'Goodness, no. Ambulance girls are two-a-penny.'

'You ruin everything.'

'Well you can't have it both ways, can you? It's either a dangerous duty, and dashing, or a breathtaking bore, and banal.'

'I liked it better when I was petrified.'

'Then hush and let me work this van out. It's fine for you, Miss La-Di-Dah with your two weeks' training. All they gave me was my bus fare here.'

Mary worked the pedals and moved the lever through the three gears in the box, plus reverse. The whole set-up was far looser than her father's Austin Windsor. It would need to be sworn at quite robustly, but she felt it could just about be driven. Now that it was finally happening – now that the war had put her in uniform and issued her with a steering wheel and clutch – she felt more resignation than excitement. She supposed that there would be chaos now, and fire and furious noise, and yet it seemed much less of an adventure than her class had been. How her nerves had buzzed with it, back then. Perhaps one died in slices, like a loaf.

'Do you suppose they'll give us tea?' said Hilda.

'They've told me nothing. You're the one who always knows things.'

'Oh, that's just gossip,' said Hilda. 'No one tells me facts.'

'Maybe they're worried you'd repeat them.'

'Well I wouldn't mind knowing *something*, even if I am only here to dish out aspirin and sticking plasters. The matron wouldn't trust me with anything, you know. She had me on bedpans half the time I was supposed to be training, so of course I never caught sight of a healthy man.'

'Well that is rather the point of nursing, isn't it?'

'But I wanted to go on the ward rounds with the junior doctors.

The way the nurses get themselves up, the poor men don't stand a chance. They're married with two children and a Labrador before their pulse gets back below a hundred. I wonder if we're meant to write down any supplies we use or whether someone comes and checks it at the end of the shift? I wonder if—'

Mary put her hand on Hilda's arm. 'You'll be fine, you know.'

Hilda froze. 'Does it show so badly?'

'They wouldn't have passed you for duty if you weren't ready.'

'I just can't stop thinking: what if I make a mistake? What if some poor so-and-so is hurt and I can't save them?'

'I thought you only cared about the uniform.'

'Yes, but one is not entirely against human life. Oh, did I mention there's a party tomorrow morning at the hospital? All the girls on nights at St Bart's, and as many of the doctors as can be dragged in, even if the nurses have to sedate and rope them. Apparently there's a boy from obs and gyn who makes a very realistic martini using ethanol. He gets up a whole vat of the stuff and they bring buckets of ice from the morgue, and someone turns up with a gramophone. You will come, won't you? And you won't bag the nicest man there, just because you can?'

'Not unless you see him first.'

They laughed with the careful muting Londoners used now, knowing that the war homed in on the sound.

The raid began just before five thirty and they went down into the crypt of the church, where the area post was set up. The stretcher man, Huw, was already down there. The Air Raid Precautions chief and his messenger were taking damage reports. Two busy telephones and three full ashtrays stood on a carved communion table. On the wall was a pinboard map of four square miles. The bombs, when they got going, got closer.

'Jerry's on the money tonight,' said Huw.

The ARP chief sniffed. 'I assume we are all aware that Jerry suckles from the breast until he is six years old?'

'The men shave their armpit hair,' said Hilda. 'The women plait theirs.'

Everyone winced as a bomb struck close by, resonating in the crypt.

'This is what comes of it, of course,' said the ARP man. 'They are up there now, at twenty thousand feet, with fishnets under their flying suits.'

Mary couldn't bring herself to join in. For her part, she found it hard to imagine that a race with so many peccadilloes could be annihilating her city quite so thoroughly. When the ARP chief sent them out into the night at half past six, it was a relief. Every moment underground made Mary want to run.

Outside, the noise was fearful. There was an ack-ack gun right outside the church, a Bofors letting go dozens of rounds a minute. Red tracer streaked up into a smoky sky impaled on the blue-white lances of the searchlights. Clive, the other stretcher-bearer, was snoring in the back seat of the ambulance. Huw cursed him awake and pushed in beside him, while Hilda took the passenger seat and opened the A–Z.

It was only a quarter of a mile away but the direct routes were blocked. Mary gunned the Hillman's little engine and made what speed she dared in the dark streets and the sudden drifts of smoke. Hilda braced herself against the glove box and used her cigarette lighter to read the map.

In Gravel Lane a house was down in the middle of the terrace. The front was blown out and the upstairs floor had swung down on the pivot of the back wall. Another stretcher party was already leaving, with two casualties they had brought out of the mess. Huw and Clive joined a rescue squad to clear the weight of the tiles and the roof joists, after which they would set up their A-frames to lift the collapsed floor. They waved Mary and Hilda away. All the two of them could do was wait.

Mary put on her tin hat, lit a cigarette and sat on the running board of the Hillman with her elbows on her knees and one hand on the back of her neck, trying to smooth out the jitters. A stick of bombs came down a few streets away, the flashes arriving before the bangs. The air was already sour with burning wood and spent explosive. Hilda took the medical bag from the boot.

'Find shelter,' said Mary. 'I'll fetch you if they bring anyone out.'

'What about you?'

'I'll be fine.'

'Then I'll be fine too, won't I?'

They sat together with their backs up against the van for whatever protection it gave. Without being asked, their bodies made themselves small.

Hilda said, 'It feels wrong, being outside in a raid.'

Mary offered her a sardonic look.

'I mean it feels sort of naughty,' said Hilda. 'As if we're out of bounds.'

They waited.

'Look at those searchlights,' said Hilda. 'I hope they'll keep them, after the war. Just think, ordinary people don't get to see this. I wonder if . . .'

Mary looked to the sky. Perhaps it was true that the searchlights were beautiful. With the night chill, and the endless deadening concussions of the ack-ack, she felt flat. Hilda babbled on, her observations neither irritating nor illuminating. This was how Tom had talked, in that awful raid. She wished now that she had known how to comfort him. How miserable Tom must have been, close to the end. She had tried with a willing heart to love him – to smile as brightly as she ever had. But of course he had known that it was ending. He had been so thoroughly good about it, so careful not to make a scene. This was how a kind heart broke, after all: inwards, making no shrapnel. Dear Tom. Without the war they might have finished as friends.

Now the rescue crew had their A-frames assembled to lift the collapsed upper floor. When they had made enough of a gap, a man crawled under. After a minute he shouted out. Huw and Clive ran to the van and lifted a stretcher off the roof.

'There's a man in there. They're going to bring him out.'

Mary and Hilda ran across the road, Hilda carrying the medical bag.

Hilda called out, 'Tell them not to move his head!'

'Well they're hardly going to leave it in there,' said Clive.

They waited. The drone of bombers continued and the blasts still came, seeming further away for the moment: the constant nasty crack of the 250-kilo bombs and the occasional punch of a 1000-kilo brute that shook the earth.

The man was brought out after a few minutes, on his back on a pine door that four men carried between them. They set him down in the road. One of the rescue men held up a battery lamp with a blackout shade, casting a slim cone of light. The casualty's eyes were open.

Hilda knelt. 'Was anyone in there with you?'

He shook his head. Hilda felt along his arms and legs, and the man groaned. She cut a trouser leg away.

'You've a badly broken ankle, I'm afraid. Does anything else hurt?'

He shook his head again.

'I'll splint your ankle, then we'll get you to a doctor. You'll be fine.'

She administered a syrette of morphia, and in a minute the man's face relaxed. She worked fast, and soon had him ready to move. She marked a baggage tag with the letters T and M and tied it to the man's wrist. Huw and Clive strapped the man into the stretcher, secured him on the roof of the Hillman and jumped into the back. In the passenger seat Hilda called out the turns while Mary drove to St Bart's Hospital. They delivered the patient and Mary drove the four of them back to St Helen's Church.

Down in the crypt, in the dim orange light from the bulbs, Huw made them all tea. Hilda shook so badly that she couldn't hold hers.

'The state of me!' she said.

'You did a marvellous job.'

'Was I all right? I hardly remember a thing.'

'I had no idea a splint could be put on so thoroughly. In another minute you'd have bandaged him up to the eyes, like Tutankhamen.'

Hilda smiled. 'I didn't think we should hang around, with the bombs.'

'What were the T and the M for?'

'Oh, the tag is for the triage nurse. "T" is "trauma". "X" is "internal injury", "M" is "morphia given". In training we practised on the porters. They feigned injury and we tagged them. We invented codes too. We had "D" for "dishy", "P" for "possibly", and "N" for "not if I was fat and this was the last man on earth".'

Mary told the others she had to check something on the van. She sat in the cold with her knees drawn up and her back against the wall of the church. The raid droned on, the explosions sometimes close, and she hardly flinched any more. She thought about the X they had drawn on Tom. When she pictured his face, the X wouldn't leave it. It was even there in her memory of their walk on Hampstead Heath, when she had tried to get them lost in the mist. It was as if he had always been marked – as if he had known the ending.

When she went back down into the crypt, someone had opened rum. From who-knew-where, one of the ARP girls had turned up some sugar. It was after eleven now, and cloud had rolled in from the estuary to blind the bombers to their targets. The crypt was filling up and becoming more convivial as the raid died away and the stretcher crews returned.

'To the Nazis!' said Clive. 'May their Reich indeed come third.'

'May their gentlemen's nylons never ladder.'

'The Nazis!' they all shouted, but Mary wouldn't join the toast.

When their mugs were empty Clive filled them again. A dash of tea was added for the sake of decorum, in case the King should walk in.

By three in the morning the raid was as good as over. There was no more ack-ack fire, no more detonations, and just an occasional thin droning overhead as a last, lost bomber sought its way home. In the crypt the conversation had fallen to a murmur. People slept rolled up in their coats.

The all-clear sounded at four thirty, and Hilda shivered with relief.

'Thank god. It wasn't as bad as I thought it might be.'

'Are we still going to the party?' said Mary.

Hilda nodded, and checked her makeup. 'Bloody Hitler. It's one thing to keep a girl up all night, but it's quite another to leave her looking it.'

'Look on the bright side. You didn't kill a soul, and I didn't put a scratch on the van.'

Clive was snoring in a corner so they left him to it and went upstairs with Huw. As they stood making their goodbyes, a flash lit the whole sky. The glare lingered in their eyes and the sound of an explosion came, huge and heavy, followed by a crashing of falling debris that lasted for half a minute.

'Wonderful,' said Huw, in the silence.

'What was it?' said Mary.

'Delayed-action bomb. Big one.'

Hilda put her helmet back on. 'Mary, bring the van up front. I'll go downstairs and get the address when it comes in. Huw, would you wake up Clive?'

Mary drove. The searchlights had all been extinguished and there was only a dull orange glow on the underside of the clouds, reflecting the fires in the east. The narrow slits of the headlights were not enough. Twice Mary almost crashed, pulling up hard a few feet from a wall, then reversing to make the turn she had missed. She felt disconnected from the reality of it. The war, the fires, the driving – one saw it all through slits.

At Billiter Street they understood straight away that it would be nothing like the first call-out. A crowd was pressing, in various states of dress from pyjamas to coats, with a policeman struggling to keep them to one side of the street. With the raid over, people had been making their way home from the public shelters. And now this. Mary used the horn and nosed the ambulance through the crowd.

When they got to the centre of the damage there were a dozen houses down in one terrace. The ones where the bomb had hit were simply gone, while those at the blast's extremity gaped open. The scene was ten minutes old, and no one knew which houses had been occupied. People milled in the dark and yelled for their families. More police arrived and tried to push people back. An ARP patrol searched by torchlight in the shattered houses.

A woman was struggling with the police, demanding to look for her son. She was hysterical, hitting out.

Mary took her arm. 'We can look for him. Tell me where he is.'

The woman pointed at a house. The front was gone, and inside Mary could see ARP men playing their torch beams over the interior walls. It was not a wallpaper she would have chosen.

The missing boy's mother said that they had just got back from the shelter at the corner of the street, and that she had left her boy inside while she went to fetch a candle from a neighbour.

'Wait for us here,' said Mary.

She went into the house with Hilda. They climbed over the pile of brick that had been the front wall. They found the ARP men picking through the front room and the kitchen at the back.

'Anyone?' said Mary.

The men shook their heads.

'Upstairs then,' she said to Hilda.

They went up together. The banister was gone, fallen into the hallway below, and the stairs hung from the party wall they were keyed in to. The staircase swayed, but it held. There was a stair runner up the middle of the treads, patterned with a broad stripe up the centre. At the head of the stairs was a bathroom, and by the flame of Mary's lighter they could see there was no one in it. The ceiling was down, the contents of the attic poking through the joists in a muddle of albums and suitcases.

On the landing that ran back parallel with the stairs, there was a faecal smell in the air – a soil pipe must have cracked. The landing gave onto two bedrooms. Hilda took the first and Mary the second. They trod as softly as they could since the floor was unsupported at the street end and the whole thing was bouncing nastily. She flicked on her lighter, looked for a moment, then snapped it off and knelt in the dark, forcing breath in and out of her body. In the snap of light she had seen a boy lying still, his face grey, his body covered in shreds of blue flannel pyjamas and some foul-smelling mess that must have come from the broken waste pipe.

'Hilda,' she said. 'Could you come as quick as you can?'

Outside, the mother was still shouting, the fear in her voice more awful now the crowd was quietening down. Mary made sure that the place she was kneeling couldn't be seen from the street. She flicked her lighter back on, and set it on an upended toy box.

'Oh,' said Hilda when she came in.

They knelt beside the boy's body. Hilda put her ear to his mouth.

'Anything?' said Mary.

Hilda shook her head. The mess was not from a broken pipe. The boy's insides were out.

'Oughtn't we to pump his chest?' said Mary.

'How should I know?' said Hilda in a small voice. 'It might make it worse.'

'Worse how?'

Hilda knelt very still with her back straight.

'Come on, Hilda, what shall we do?'

'I think it might be hopeless,' said Hilda.

'But there must be something we can do. There must have been something in the training?'

'I'm sorry,' said Hilda, covering her face with her hands.

The boy was brown-haired, slight, eight or nine years old. His eyes were open and his grey face was fixed in an agony that was hard to look at. In his bedroom there were postcards on the wall: silhouettes of every aircraft type. On a chest of drawers was a trophy collection of the kind boys had: fallen iron splinters, a brass shell case from a Bofors gun, a scrap of tortured aluminium that looked as if it might once have flown. The metal on its ridges had been polished to a shine by the boy's fingers. Outside, the mother in a raw voice was shouting, 'Mouse! Mouse!'

Mary stood, took her lighter and left the room. Outside on the warped landing, she fought back nausea. The stripe along the centre of the carpet was not a pattern after all. Even now the stain was widening as the sisal took it up. Mary lit a cigarette. The boy had been downstairs when the bomb hit and he had dragged himself up to his room, and died.

'Hilda?' she said.

Hilda came, and Mary passed her the lit cigarette. Hilda couldn't hold it, so Mary held it to her lips while she drew on it, then exhaled.

'What are we doing?' said Mary. 'What are the two of us doing?'

Hilda hugged herself tight around the stomach. 'Don't.'

'Remember after that first raid? When we took a cab to see the mess?'

'But everyone was doing it, it wasn't just—'

Mary cut her off. 'Do you think we've seen enough now?'

'But it's different now. We're helping.'

'Are we?' said Mary. 'How many rooms are there in your flat?'

'Oh I know what you're trying to do, but—'

'Isn't it awful? I've honestly never counted. Two dozen rooms in my house, I should think, and six in your flat, and hardly a bomb has touched Pimlico. If we truly wanted to help, we could have hosted this whole street in your place and mine, instead of digging through their rubble.'

'We do what we can.'

'We visit by night and we fly west at dawn. We are ghouls, I'm afraid. We are monsters.'

Hilda closed her eyes and let her head fall back against the wall. 'So what would you have us do?'

'I don't know. We've never done anything, have we? We've no talent but conversation.'

'Then go and talk to the policeman who's with the mother. Have her taken somewhere. Then bring Huw and Clive. Quickly, while I can still cope.'

Mary stared for a moment, until understanding passed between them.

'Oh,' she said.

When Mary came back with Huw and Clive, Hilda had rolled the dead boy in the rug that he had bled on in his bedroom. They took up the runner on the stairs and the landing, and made a second roll from that. They carried both rolls out on stretchers, each covered with the standard grey blanket, and secured them on the roof of the Hillman.

At dawn, the sun rising through smoke, they delivered the boy to Moorgate. In fine cursive Hilda wrote in the mortuary logbook that the child had died instantly and with no suffering, in a tidy and well-kept home. This was what the mother would read when she came for her son's body.

They went to the party and got nastily drunk at opposite ends of the room. Hilda left with a flight lieutenant. Mary left with a spinning head and a certainty that she was not up to encountering her mother. She walked to a taxi rank and gave the address of the garret.

She sat in the cab with her cheek pressed against the window. She watched London, with its gapped teeth and blinded eyes. It got to her all at once, for the first time since the disaster. All the emptiness in the world drew her in, and she rolled her forehead on the glass. There was no sense to it – this was the unendurable thing. The war was ten million severed and jangling nerves. It was all loose ends.

Before, life had been a tradition, a tendency to forgiveness, a regression to the mean. The city she loved had been one of plane trees that had grown for three centuries, of bridges improved as horse gave way to steam, of great coordinated endeavours in which every convergent component could be relied upon: of symphonies. But now any light could be snuffed without warning. When she had seen the dead boy, she had thought of Zachary. A child was lost as easily as a shilling. And once one had understood that, though one's heart continued to beat, one lived arm-in-arm with the lamented. She knew, now, why her father had not spoken of the last war, nor Alistair of this. It was hardly fair on the living.

On reaching her destination she was pale and the taxi driver asked her, 'Are you all right, my love?' and she smiled brightly and said, 'Yes, thank you.'

When she let herself in to the garret it still smelled faintly of

Tom. She switched on the electric heater, took off her shoes and lay down on his bed. When she opened her eyes again, Tom had made her tea in one of his stock of jam jars that resisted all her attempts at improvement. She sat up to kiss him, since she did try hard to show him that everything was all right, and as she kissed him she woke up and it was noon.

She washed her face in the corner basin, with cold water and a small grey fossil of soap. Everything remaining in the garret was Alistair's. She had boxed Tom's possessions weeks ago, and sent them to his mother. When everything he had owned was packed and labelled, with Caesar in the last box and the tip of his tail just sticking out, Tom's things had filled six cardboard boxes, each eighteen inches square by nine inches deep. A man left ten cubic feet.

Mary went to Alistair's room, opened the wardrobe door, and stood looking at his empty clothes. She pressed his shirts to her face. She noticed a cuff that was beginning to fray, found a needle and thread and sat down to mend it. She was not at all good at needlework. At home the rule was that the maid did anything fiddlier than dealing cards, while Palmer lifted anything heavier than a gramophone arm.

She forced herself to be patient; to keep her stitches small and neat. It was something to do. If she could bring little to the war, nor bear to side with her mother in avoiding the whole thing entirely, then at least she could fix these frayed edges.

When the shirt was mended, Mary hung it back in Alistair's cupboard. And then, because she needed to live for the new hour at least, and because a pen and paper were available, she sat down at Alistair's rickety table and wrote to him again.

# MARCH, 1941

For a whole month the northwest wind blew cold and imperious. The siege drew taut around the island. The enemy's capital ships, black-hearted and lupine, circled just below the horizon where the coastal artillery could not reach them. Their warplanes wound white ropes of vapour around the blue dome of the sky, weaving the island a net to starve in.

Alistair, alone, was happy.

*Alistair,*

*I mended a shirt of yours, even though it is an awful shirt that ought properly to be torn into strips, plaited into rope and used to hang your tailor. I have not mended a shirt for anyone before, so you must count yourself lucky.*

*In any case, whether or not you wish me to proceed to the rest of your wardrobe (and perhaps you had better let me know), your dreadful blue shirt is mended.*

*Affectionately,*
*Mary*

Since Mary's letter had got through the blockade, Alistair had not minded at all about the millions of tons of material that hadn't. The island was without fuel oil, electric bulbs, aspirin and margarine. His regiment was without new barrels for the artillery pieces. The magazines were down to five days' worth of shells at the present rate of usage. Islanders and soldiers alike were beginning to eat dogs, starting with the kind without collars.

Alistair cared little. He roared with laughter when Simonson read out his own letters from his duplicitous girlfriends. The two captains aped the Knightsbridge voices together. The stews grew leaner, the meat giving way to bones that were used and reused until the marrow was gone and they leached more good than they gave.

Alistair didn't mind. The bread became one eighth sawdust and then three sixteenths and then one fifth. He took it with a shrug. He felt a solidarity with the wood-boring insects, and cheered his men by performing impressions of the bugs. Soon they were all eating insects in any case. Alistair organised beetle hunts and commissioned an engraved trophy – the Cup of Plenty – for the man who collected the most bugs each day. Fruit could not be found at all. Men's teeth worked loose. The local children in their black church trousers with their knees yellow from dust began to have the restless eyes of card sharpers or poets. Alistair sneaked them crackers in his pockets.

*Mary,*

*I do not know what you have against my shirt. It will be fashionable again, one must simply take the long view.*

*It is inconvenient that I cannot rush home to London to thank you in person, but the oddest thing has happened. The Axis, who disapprove of sentimentality, have encircled Malta with the greatest concentration of warplanes and shipping ever seen, in order to prevent me from coming to see you. I expect they are doing the same sort of thing at your end? I suppose we must be flattered.*

*Please do your worst with my wardrobe. In return I*
*shall make good such treasures as you may condemn to*
*my care. As a conservator I am trained to repair all kinds*
*of damage invisibly. Expect me at around five past the end*
*of the war. My shirt will have come into its own by then, I*
*assure you.*
*Warmly,*
*Alistair*

Alistair could not lose his smile, though the bombers were wicked and rapacious. Sometimes there was only an hour in each day for the civilians to swarm up from the shelters, to throw out the night soil, to queue for kerosene, and to take in the new ridges of rubble where the ageless streets had stood. Then the bombers came again and everyone fled back underground. The surface became foreign, the underworld familiar.

Sometimes Alistair was caught in a raid and had to go to ground with the islanders. In the neolithic burial chambers where the old bones had been pushed to one side, in the Roman catacombs reconsecrated with miniatures of the Virgin, in the cold and dripping new tunnels gouged deep in the yellow rock, the fathers of the crammed-together families met his eyes while the walls shook. The children whimpered and the mothers rocked them, and Alistair joined them to pray: Heart of Jesus, heart of Mary, make the bombs fall in the sea or in the fields.

*Alistair,*
*I cannot imagine what you are moaning about – a*
*blockade by the enemy is nothing. Think of what I go*
*through in Pimlico, entirely encircled by the inferior types*
*of Chelsea and Belgravia. It is hell.*
*There is opportunity here for your restorative talents, if*
*you have the heart for it. You should report to me at your*

Whenever the air mail made it through, Alistair forgot the hunger. At all other times he was obsessed with it. One early morning he put the jar of Tom's blackberry jam into the bright slit of light from the arrow loop in his room. The aperture commanded a field of fire across the harbour approaches. Conversely, it drew in the full brightness of the rising sun and fired it through the jam jar. The colour rose with the sun, from venous to arterial. Every tiny pip, suspended in its matrix, cast a black light of shadow.

Sharpness flooded his mouth. How far had he carried this jar? How many different tents and barracks and forts had he shared with it? Once he had hoped to eat it with Tom at war's end; now he hoped to take it to Tom's grave. Surely he wouldn't crack now. And yet his mind, unsolicited, came up with endless helpful reasons why it would be sensible to open the jar.

These mornings were the hardest, just after waking, when one splashed the well water on one's face and drank a bitter yellow glass of it to fill the stomach. The water tasted of Malta itself, ancient and recessive, steeped in cordite and blood. The stone was porous, the hunger insatiable. Alistair put his hands to the jar and began to twist the lid. He stopped himself, and picked up a pencil instead.

*would carry off better than I) and a cap with a polished*
*leather peak. If it were not for the legitimising effect of*
*guns, enemy, etc, then the outfit would suggest nothing*
*more nor less than the presence, within the psyche of the*
*wearer, of perversion of the most florid stripe. Your hand-*
*writing conveys the same to me, by the way.*

   *Astutely,*
   *Alistair*


Today the battery was to rotate to Fort Bingemma, away from
the city, on an escarpment high on the Victoria Lines in the
northwest of the island. It was time. Alistair's men were broken
and somnambulant. Three of his thirty-five were dead, and seven
in Simonson's troop. The enemy's bombing had not let up for
eighty-six days and nights. Up in the hills the regiment could
regroup and re-equip. Perhaps, in the countryside, there would
be a little more to eat.

Alistair looked out to sea one last time. The northwesterly
screamed through the signalling masts of the ships in Grand
Harbour. The waves came in and in, as they always had. To the
horizon clung a haze from the smoke stacks of the encircling
warships, corralling the island in time.


*To: Cpt Alistair Heath, RA*
*From: Mairie & Northe, Solicitors at Law*
*Re: Slander*

*Sir,*
   *We are commanded by our client, Miss Mary Anne*
*Elizabeth North of London, SW1, to convey her intention*
*to pursue you in law in the eventuality that you do not*
*immediately and in full retract in writing your vile*
*calumny, viz, that our client is delusional. Your comments*

*apposite to her handwriting our client will allow to stand,*
*but wishes us to communicate to you a fact of which your*
*own various letters constitute proof abundant, viz, that*
*our client's written submissions are qualitatively superior*
*not only in calligraphy, but also in composition, to your*
*own.*
   *Legally,*
   *Mairie & Northe*


When Alistair looked up, he was surprised to find the war. She had done it again, her trick of making it all disappear. He laced up his duffel bag, shouldered it, and put on his uniform cap as he stepped into the bleaching light of the fort's central quadrangle.

'Heath! There you are, you tardy bastard!'

'Simonson,' said Alistair, saluting with as much precision as it merited.

'Get in the truck, won't you? Anyone would think you didn't want to go on holiday.'

Alistair climbed up into the passenger seat of the Bedford. Simonson started the big petrol engine and put it into gear straight away, so as not to waste an iota of fuel. The men had gone ahead in a fleet of requisitioned charabancs and wagons, most of them horse-drawn, dispatched along the road at irregular intervals so as not to draw the enemy fighter aircraft that were now almost unopposed. Alistair and Simonson drove out over the main drawbridge. The quartermaster had issued them with a full load of artillery shells to take to the fort, and enough petrol – measured with a metal pipette to the nearest fluid ounce – to get them exactly to their destination providing that they coasted down hills.

Simonson piloted them through the ruins of Valletta. Alistair dropped the side window and enjoyed the warmth of the early morning. It was the right time of day to be making the trip out of the city. The sun wasn't too hot yet. The aces of the Luftwaffe were still on the ground in Sicily, signing photographs of themselves or doing whatever they did between bombing trips to a defenceless island.

The two captains rolled through the winding canyons that had been cleared through the vast acres of rubble. Every building seemed to have been reduced to the infinite repetition of the same yellow stone block, two feet long by one across by one deep. It was the atom of civilisation, the largest component that two men could lift between them.

Simonson scowled through the dusty windshield.

'Looks like my alphabet blocks, after Randy found the castles I made.'

'Heard from your dear brother lately?'

'Oh, he won't write. I'd be astonished if the bastard can even read.'

'Hasn't he had his call-up yet?'

Simonson fixed Alistair with a look of delighted condescension. 'Dear boy. They have to keep a few good men back. Otherwise we chaps might all get home from this jolly and demand the keys to the kingdom.'

'Would that be so frightful?'

'You are a sluggish learner. Perhaps you are slightly retarded.'

'I'm sure you used to be funny.'

'Too many casualties of late, Alistair, that's all.'

Alistair looked at him, and Simonson looked ahead at the road. It was the first time Simonson had used his first name.

Alistair said, 'I never thought you minded much, about the men.'

Simonson cut the engine and coasted to a halt. He pulled the handbrake on and searched for his cigarettes in the pockets of his tunic.

'I didn't mind at first. When Dryden was killed, I thought, well, that's his lookout. And then Norris got it – such a terrible bloody aimer – and I was just glad it wasn't someone useful, like Carter.'

Alistair nodded. 'I'm sure Norris is a better shot now he's dead.'

'Well, exactly. And in any case I have never been fond of the men the way you are. I hardly understand them and I always supposed I had no more feeling for them than I do for cats. But then the next week Carter was killed after all, and I remember looking down at his body. We knew it was him by his wristwatch. His face wasn't where he left it, you see, and it made me furious. I don't know why that should be. It's not as if he was a handsome man in life. And yet I remember thinking: I would bury you myself. You know how hard it is to dig a grave on this island. Three inches of soil and then solid rock. But I would have done it, if the men had let me. And then Vickers was killed, and Cullen, and Casey, and Urquhart – all in that one dreadful week, do you remember? – and I have been desperately angry ever since. I actually loathe being an officer.'

He exhaled smoke and pressed his thumbs to his eyes.

Alistair patted his shoulder. 'It could be worse – you could make major.'

Simonson took Alistair's arm and held it. 'All of this will stick to us, you'll see.'

'After the war, you mean?'

'The men will loathe us. If any of the poor bastards are left.'

'The men don't hate officers.'

'It is the men's function to hate us. The fact that you don't understand it only shows your lack of breeding.'

Alistair grinned. Simonson turned the ignition. 'My brother won't be called up, and England won't change. It was built with its blocks, the same as this damned island. When they reuse the rubble you will see that it can only fit back together one way.'

'I will bet you five pounds that England is different, after the war.'

'Oh, spare us.'

'Don't you think we shall all be kinder to one another? I hope one's class will matter less and one's convictions more. I hope we might be more inclined to pardon one another for our errors with both.'

'I bet you five pounds we shan't see war's end.'

'That's not a bet I could ever collect on.'

'See how it works?' said Simonson.

He let out the clutch and steered the truck down the rubble-strewn road. They lurched on, through the interlocking turrets and ramparts that marked the limit of the city. They were terrific fortifications and would prove their worth the next time the Ottoman Turks invaded. In the meantime they would be useless against the German air assault.

Perhaps Simonson was right that the regiment would not survive the siege. They were all turning to stone from hunger. They took cover behind stone walls. They painted their trucks and their helmets and their guns to resemble stone blocks, as if by sympathetic magic some hardness might accrue. They saw rubble walls when they closed their eyes at night. Sometimes, when one was particularly hungry, the omnipresent yellow lime-stone had the exact hue of cheddar, and when the enemy's para-troopers finally came it would afford about as much protection.

Alistair rested a notepad on the dash and dug out a stub of pencil.

To: Mary North, c/o Mairie & Northe
From: Allis, Terre & Heythe, Solicitors at Law
Re: A guided tour of the island of Malta

Madam,
    Our client, Alistair Heath (Cpt, RA) commands us to convey to you

'Oh for Christ's sake,' said Simonson. 'You are like love-struck schoolchildren passing notes.'

Alistair looked back at him mildly. 'So?'

'So, teacher says there's a war on.'

'It's just a bit of fun.'

'Well it is sickening to be around. So you're in love – bully for you. You're not obliged to rub it in everyone's face.'

'Oh come on, Simonson, you know I only have eyes for you.'

He looked over, but Simonson only stared ahead at the road. Alistair put the pad back in his pocket.

At the city's edge the fortifications gave way to a treeless plain of small fields no larger than suburban gardens, enclosed as far as the horizon by a tracery of drystone walls. It was arid land, with dry yellow grasses in tufts. Poor crops of oranges and artichokes struggled in the thin yellow soil. Dusty stands of barbary fig rose along the lines of the walls, and in the ditches teasels and reedy bamboo were footed in unseen damp. There were small rock escarpments, indistinguishable in hue from the walls, so that the eye lost the distinction between the man-made and the natural. One scarcely cared in any case. It was wretched country, the kind no man would bother to wall in if any other land were available.

'Damn it,' said Simonson. 'I'm sorry.'

'No, you are quite right.'

'You must write as and when you please. Don't mind my sour grapes.'

'I wouldn't mind grapes of any kind. Who's fussy these days?'

Simonson smiled in a way that did not entirely release the tension. Four 109s barrelled overhead in an asymmetric V, uncontested and exultant in the blue. Simonson swung the van off the road and they jumped from the cab and threw themselves into the ditch. They lay with their hands over their heads for a minute while the aircraft noise diminished. The Germans had either not noticed them or not considered them worth the ammunition, and flown on into the west.

Simonson and Alistair climbed out of the ditch and sat in the shade of a yellow stone wall, dusting themselves off. Black bees droned in the thyme beside the road. Dogs barked from farm to farm. Birds gave monosyllabic cries, harsh and unlovely, as if describing the landscape. The wind worried up twists of dust from the road. Fat-tailed lizards ploughed the dirt, and from far away came the boom of the coastal batteries.

Simonson looked out over the ruined country. 'You know who'd miss me if those planes had shot us up? No one.'

Alistair shrugged. 'I might miss you.'

Simonson seemed not to hear him. 'It would keep one going, to have someone who gave a damn.'

'What about your three nice girlfriends?'

'If I died they might wear the grief like a brooch for a while.'

'I thought you were fond of those girls.'

'The clue is in the plural, isn't it?'

'Then perhaps you ought to pick one.'

'But there's nothing to choose between them, don't you see? They spend their mornings in bed and their afternoons at Claridge's. They are indistinguishable among thousands. They are fireflies.'

'Whereas you want the actual fire.'

'Must you mock me? You know me less well than you imagine.'

'I wasn't mocking. Well, only a little.'

'It is too easy for you.'

Alistair held up his hands. 'I'm sorry.'

They remounted in silence and drove on, while Alistair drafted the letter to Mary in his head.

*. . . commands us to convey to you his fulsome apolo-*
*gies for his libellous comments, which arose merely from*
*our client's state of happy distraction, brought about by*
*the many utopian delights afforded by his present*
*location.*

Cresting a rise they saw a pillar of smoke a mile ahead, thickening as they approached. Slow from the hunger, Alistair hardly
noticed it.

*The food and the drink on this island are enough to*
*render a man dizzy with delight. The foie gras has only*
*one fault, which is its superabundance. The caviar is so*
*consistently good that one gets a little weary of it.*

The smoke was half a mile high now, directly ahead on their
route.

*There is a host of charming local rituals, many of them*
*involving fire.*

'I think we had better pull over here,' said Simonson.
'Mm?'
'It's just that we are carrying three thousand pounds of artillery shells and it seems prudent not to drive them through
flames.'
Simonson stopped the Bedford a safe distance from the fire,
and upwind of it. They got out to see what was going on. In a
village of two or three hundred houses, the church was ablaze.
The wreckage of a bomber and the bodies of its crew were strewn
around. Flames blew across the road and the air stank of burning aviation spirit. People ran in and out of the church, bringing
out artefacts to save.

*Next there are the art treasures, which the locals are*
*quick to display.*

It seemed the fire was burning itself out. The buildings were all of stone, of course – there was little wood to catch light – and now that the aviation fuel was burning off, there was only an angry soot being lifted in the shimmering, superheated air. In the little stone square before the church, a crowd was gathering. Alistair and Simonson pushed through it.

*It is an al fresco culture and one is never bored as there*
*is always something going on in the town square.*

A German airman was on the ground and the villagers had encircled him, kicking and spitting. A blade of bone protruded through one trouser leg. The side of his mouth was torn, the wall of the cheek hanging in a flap and revealing a row of bloodied molars. He was pleading with his tormentors in good English, accented only by his wounds.

'Damn it,' said Simonson.

*The locals are hospitable to the British, though less well*
*disposed to other foreign tourists.*

Alistair shook his head savagely, forcing himself to concentrate on the present moment. His mind changed focus so sluggishly now, after the months of starvation. The enemy airman looked up at him, beseeching. Alistair felt a tightness in his throat. It was a scene he had come across during the long retreat through France. If an aviator had to bail out, it might be better to shoot himself on the way down than to parachute into the hands of people he had been bombing.

'Leave that man alone!' Alistair's voice was lost in the din. 'Leave him!'

The people looked through him. Some grinned. It was a bad sign that there were no women or infants in the crowd. Evil made warning ripples.

A boy of eleven or twelve in a clean white shirt, black trousers and a black cloth cap, laughing, kicked the German in the crotch. The airman drew into a foetal tuck, which caused his smashed leg bone to dig in the dirt. He screamed, and as he did so another man kicked him.

'Please! I did not want to fight you! God save the King!'

A man took a handful of dirt and tilted the airman's head back and packed the bloodied and protesting mouth. The man gave a choking moan. A purple mud of dust and blood escaped in clots through the rent in his cheek. There was laughter in the crowd, since the joke was now on the enemy. How pleasing it was that the whole great logistic of armies and states, of countless millions of fighting men and their associated materiel, could deliver a punchline to any grid coordinates at any time.

The fire from the downed aircraft had spent all its fuel now. The haze caught at the back of the throat. More villagers closed in on the broken man.

'I am a British Army officer!' Alistair shouted. 'Leave that man alone!'

He put himself between the German and the people, but they got the better of him. He took an elbow to the neck and another to the solar plexus and he found himself winded, at the back of the crowd. He could no longer see the German.

Simonson took his arm. 'Come on. One mustn't expect more.'

'You aren't serious?'

'They've been bombed for months. What would you have us do?'

'I'd like you to help me,' said Alistair, taking his .38 from its holster and turning the cylinder to check the load.

'For pity's sake! We have a ton and a half of H.E. in the truck, and the enemy is already airborne. You know how many men died to convey that ammunition, and you want us to leave it sitting in the open while you play white man's justice? The man is dying in any case – you saw him.'

'Yes, but I will shoot these people before I let them torment him.'

'Then I will leave you to it, Alistair, because I am not going to lose a truck full of shells for the sake of your pristine conscience.'

The two officers stared at each other for a moment.

'Fine,' said Alistair.

He stepped around Simonson and cocked the hammer of his revolver. He fired five rounds into the air and the jeering stopped. The locals spun around, startled at first, then with faces turning sullen.

'It's quite all right,' said Alistair. 'I might do the same in your shoes. But you may go to your homes now. I haven't seen your faces and I shan't be taking names.'

He stood with the Enfield pointed at the ground. He looked at his shoes. The wind piled dust up against his toes and scooped out hollows to the leeward. As he watched he became aware of a slow movement in his periphery, a receding and a lightening. When he looked up, the square was empty except for the squirming body of the airman.

He holstered the revolver, buttoned it down and knelt beside the man. The poor devil was face down and heaving as he tried to breathe through his smashed and bloody nose. As Alistair turned the head and began to scoop the dirt out of the mouth, he saw that the man's eyes had been put out. They didn't bleed – the sockets had been packed with yellow dust like the mouth. A bloody foam hissed in and out of the man's nostrils as he fought for air. Alistair removed dirt until finally the man could breathe, in coughing gasps that sprayed blood.

'I'm so sorry,' Alistair said.

He cradled the man's head. The black hair was sticky with blood and the yellow dust had caked onto it. He was older than Alistair – in his late thirties, perhaps. An hour ago he had been flying, his tie neatly knotted.

'Look what they've done to you. I am godawfully sorry.'

The man's jaws snapped tight around the side of Alistair's right hand, opposite the thumb. The splintered teeth, horribly sharp, sliced all the way through to the bone. Alistair yelled. He smashed his free hand against the man's jaw, but the teeth only bit down harder. Alistair twisted to change the angle, but agony gave the other man an awful strength. He dragged Alistair down to the ground.

'Stop it!' yelled Alistair. 'Please! I am helping you!'

But the man no longer knew what was happening to him. He took Alistair's throat, the thumbs pushing into the wind-pipe. With his free arm Alistair tried to push him away. Sparks began to slide across the blue sky, which faded to indigo, and to black.

A shot came, and the thumbs released his throat. Alistair drew a long, rattling breath. The teeth loosened on his hand and released it. Alistair rolled away through the dust. As his breath came back he managed to kneel. Simonson, who had shot the German through the side of the head, was still aiming the revolver. He wore an expression of distaste, and his lips moved silently for a while.

'Get up,' Simonson said at last.

After a long moment it occurred to Alistair that Simonson meant him. He stood unsteadily. A near-semicircle of flesh was missing from the side of his hand. Blood ran into the dust. Between him and Simonson, the German lay on his back with his arms laid neatly at his sides.

'Excuse me?' said the German.

Simonson and Alistair stared. Blood and yellow fluid drained through a hole in the man's temple and another hole in the opposite cheek.

'Excuse me?' the man said again.

Simonson shot him a second time, in the chest. Alistair supposed that some invariant politeness had caused him to wait until he was sure what the man had said. The German's body bucked twice, arching and relaxing. Then he drew a long, hissing breath and said, 'Sorry, I think you are speaking English?'

Simonson lowered his pistol and looked furiously at Alistair.

'I am confused,' said the airman. 'I have had maybe an accident. Excuse me . . . for my English.'

'Your English is fine,' said Alistair.

'You are . . . too kind.'

Alistair knelt beside the dying man. 'I'm sorry.'

'Please let me go. Do not make me prisoner. I have fear for . . . my son. He is . . . not a forceful boy and I worry . . . that he might . . . excuse me . . .'

The man fought for breath. Bloody foam leaked from his mouth.

'It's all right,' said Alistair. 'It's quite all right.'

'If I am . . . prisoner . . . he might . . . at school be bullied . . . and . . .'

Simonson pushed Alistair out of the way and shot the German again, the bullet striking in the chest. The man's ruined mouth worked as he tried for another breath. Simonson shot him three times more in quick succession, the bullets destroying the abdomen. Blood and fluids welled through the dark flying jacket.

'And . . .' said the man, 'and . . .'

'I've no more rounds,' said Simonson.

'And the . . . child is . . . so . . . so . . .'

Alistair took his revolver, aimed it quickly and fired with his eyes almost closed. It was not a good shot, the bullet striking to the side of the man's forehead, lifting away a part of the scalp and exposing the skull but not penetrating it. The force of it had knocked the head to one side. It was Alistair's last round too. The man took another breath, and another.

Alistair dropped to his knees and did the only possible thing, taking two handfuls of the yellow dust and pressing them into the man's mouth. He still felt the hot breath hiss from the man's nostrils, so he pinched the nose closed and held the body down until it ceased to struggle.

When it was over, Alistair stood. He and Simonson watched the man in silence, not at all sure he was dead. If the war had proved anything it was that life had unexpected resistance to the instruments with which men had been issued.

Simonson lit a cigarette. 'I shan't forgive you for this.'

'No,' said Alistair. 'I don't suppose I would.'

'We have to go. When we get to Bingemma we'll send a burial detail.'

'I'd sooner stay and bury him now.'

Simonson shook his head. 'It wouldn't make either of you feel better.'

The Maltese, who had watched the whole thing from their doorways, emerged into the street to give the two officers a slow, ironic handclap. The sound rang in the square while Simonson and Alistair walked to the truck.

Between the yellow stone buildings, in front of the soot-blackened church, the cold northwesterly began its work of covering the dead man in dust.

# MARCH, 1941

**M**ary arrived at St Helen's Church at ten to four, in premature twilight under smoke. The city smelled of brick dust and charcoal. The hush was already on it – people had gone down to the shelters early.

'Sleep well?' said Huw.

'Dreaming of you.'

'Go on with you. The little one's out the back already.'

Mary joined Hilda in the cab of the Hillman. In the yard behind the church the wall was down, revealing the acres that used to be Bishopsgate. In drizzle, boys in shorts picked through the ruins for shrapnel and brass.

'Look at it all,' said Hilda. 'They say we shall win, but how?'

'Father says the city will have to move underground if this goes on.'

'I should hate that, shouldn't you?'

'I suppose there will be ventilation shafts and skylights.'

'Well there's something to look forward to. And are there to be murals down there, of woodland glades and seascapes?'

'Look on the bright side,' said Mary. 'There might be—'

'There isn't a bright side underground. It's just dark.'

'We must simply do our best then, with Tilley lamps and "Kumbaya".'

'Lovely,' said Hilda, 'but I might take my chances on the surface.'

'They won't let you. Even after we win, Father says prepared-
ness will be the thing. Society will be organised, and people will
live where they're told, and do the jobs they're given, and be
permanently ready to fight. Father says that was our mistake,
after the last war. We let people live willy-nilly.'

'Yes, it was lovely.'

'Father says it lasts about twenty years. After that, anyone half
organised will do this sort of thing to us.'

Mary cranked the wipers to clear drizzle from the windscreen,
the better to indicate the rubble.

Hilda said, 'If that is really the future, then what is the point
in living?'

'We could have hobbies.'

'One of my hobbies is tea. Shall we go to the crypt and drink
some?'

'Don't you care about the future of civilisation?'

'No,' said Hilda, 'I care that Alistair still hasn't replied to my
letter.'

'Oh,' said Mary.

'I can't stop thinking of him. Aren't you the slightest bit
sympathetic?'

Mary's heart caught. 'I'm sorry.'

'Oh, it isn't your fault. Come on, let's go for that tea.'

Soon the sirens howled up to their huge C-sharp and swooped
down again to start their cycle. The first bombs fell and the night
was begun, and they were sent out to the first casualties.

Clive was drunk before they even began. Huw was white with
fatigue. They picked up two deceased and were halfway through
their first run to the mortuary when Mary took a corner and
both the bodies on the roof flew into the street. Clive and Huw
had forgotten to strap the stretchers down. The men worked
together to recover the first body, making a count of one, two,
three, *lift*, but they discovered – after two attempts and a long

interval of confusion in the slits of the ambulance's headlights – that Clive had been lifting the arms of one corpse and Huw the legs of the other. Mary watched them curse and begin again.

As softly as she could, she said, 'I've been writing to Alistair.'

Hilda looked straight ahead and said nothing.

'I'm sorry,' said Mary. 'If that counts for anything.'

'You're sorry . . .'

'I waited for what I thought was a decent time. I wouldn't have written if I thought that you and he were hitting it off.'

Hilda still looked straight ahead. 'Who wrote first? You, or him?'

Mary rested her forehead on the wheel. 'I don't blame you for being angry.'

'Angry isn't the word. You've done this since we were children.'

'I know. I'm sorry, Hilda.'

In the useless headlights the men got one body back onto its stretcher. They lifted it unevenly and the corpse rolled off again.

'At every party you left with the nicest man. And whatever second-choice boy I kissed was closing his eyes and thinking of you.'

'Well it won't happen again, I promise.'

'Oh, so Alistair is the last one you'll take from me?'

'I didn't want it to happen.'

'When did you know?'

'When I took his bag to the station.'

'So you did kiss him.'

'No.'

'Did you hold hands?'

'No. I was with Tom, remember? You don't know what it was like.'

'Why? Do you suppose I've never been in love? I feel these things, Mary. Hopeless as I am, I feel them. But you are always there – aren't you? – to rescue me from love.'

Mary closed her eyes. 'I'm sorry.'

Hilda said nothing. A swing tune played at the edge of Mary's awareness, somewhere in the white noise: a phantom melody. Nobody slept.

When the corpses were loaded again, Mary drove to the morgue. Now it took an age to get everything off the roof, since the men had made doubly sure with the strapping. Their cold hands struggled with the knots. With an effort Mary kept her head from drifting down to the wheel again.

'It's getting harder,' said Hilda.

'What is?'

'To believe that this is endurable.'

Mary supposed she either meant their friendship, or the bombing. Tens of thousands were dead now, and everyone left was sickened. This was something about war they did not warn one of: that death was an illness of the living, a cumulative poison.

When Clive and Huw had got the empty stretchers on the roof at last, Mary drove back to the church. They were all too weary to go down into the shelter. They listened to Tom's wind-up gramophone, which Mary kept in the ambulance now. Clive passed a bottle around. They worked at getting drunk enough to be able to do the job, without being so drunk that they couldn't. Through the windscreen, in the orange glow of fires, the rubble stretched to the limit of sight.

'It's all right for you,' said Hilda. 'But I don't have anyone.'

'You will. You'll see.'

'Listen to yourself,' said Hilda.

The sadness calcified.

The ARP controller tapped on the ambulance window with a fresh address. Mary parked the gramophone's needle and drove. Hilda rested her head against the passenger window and watched the ack-ack gliding up.

The incident was in Farringdon, past their usual patch, and when they got there the scene was already busy with ambulances and fire crews. An office building had come down on top of the shelter beneath it, and the wreckage was ablaze. The crews had worked an access route down into the shelter, and Clive and Huw joined them to bring out the wounded. The firemen played hoses on the steaming rubble around the access tunnel, and the stretcher parties were coming out drenched.

Hilda took her medical bag and went down without a word. After a minute Mary couldn't bear it and went down after her. The tunnel began under a bowed steel lintel and tended steeply down a stairway that had been filled by rubble when the building collapsed. It had been excavated sufficiently to permit passage if one doubled over. Freezing water poured from the roof of the tunnel.

The dim light from the flames outside surrendered to a darkness broken by battery lamps every few yards. Mary's knees scraped on the sharp rubble and her tin hat slammed against a beam, so hard that she was stunned for a moment. Shouts were coming up from the darkness. She forced herself to continue.

The tunnel opened out into what Mary took to be a large water tank, in which for some reason the men of the rescue crews were wading thigh deep by the bewildering light of torches.

'Where's the shelter?' she asked a rescuer.

'This is it.'

She must have looked blank, because he said: 'It's water from the fire hoses. Flooding.'

The survivors seemed all to have been brought out – the people down here were rescuers – and Mary saw them going down into the black water, plunging in and staying under for long moments before surfacing with gasps.

Hilda came over to her. 'They're only looking for bodies, I'm afraid. Let's go back up.'

Mary took a step forward and a heavy weight came down on the back of her legs, pushing her down. She knelt, chest deep. Hilda took her arm to help her up. Mary tried to stand but found that she couldn't. In the cold water her breath came in gasps.

Hilda held her under both arms. 'Oh do get up, won't you? We're all exhausted, you know.'

Mary felt down her legs with her hands. A heavy beam – it felt like metal – was pressing into the angle of her knees. Her knee-caps were pinioned to the uneven rubble of the floor. She strained against the metal. It wouldn't move at all. There was no effect except to grind her knees into the rubble, which hurt. She reached down and felt along the beam, left and right, but it stretched away further than the span of her arms.

A rescuer splashed up and shone his torch on Mary. 'All right here?'

'I'm very sorry,' she said. 'I seem to be stuck.'

She smiled, which was all one could do when embarrassed. The rescuer had Hilda hold the torch while he knelt beside Mary and tugged along the length of the beam. 'It's good and stuck, isn't it? Are you in pain?'

'Only when I try to move. Which is silly, isn't it?'

'Well you just stay calm, darling, while we get this sorted out.'

'Thank you very much,' said Mary. Until the man had told her to stay calm, it hadn't occurred to her that there might be reasons not to.

Hilda held her hands. More rescuers came and began to duck under, bringing up a brick here and a piece of bar there, but whatever was trapping her was too heavy to shift. Mary gathered that the beam was set in concrete at both ends, and the concrete lodged under obstructions. She took in the men's nervous voices and the efforts they made not to alarm her.

They became more methodical, searching underwater obstructions with their fingertips, trying to understand how to dislodge the beam. The sound of pouring water was loud in the sudden calm. Hilda undid her hair clips and fixed Mary's hair back to stop it going in her mouth.

'Be a dear and do my lipstick next,' said Mary, her teeth chattering.

Hilda said, 'You're doing very well.'

The water was rising in the basement – now Mary understood this – at about an inch a minute. While she had been kneeling the water, which had been up to her sternum, had risen to the base of her throat. It poured down from the ceiling, faster now that the rubble above was saturated. Some of the rescuers left and Mary stared after them, wild-eyed, until someone told her they had gone to rig pumps.

'What can we do?' Mary said.

Hilda looked at her strangely. 'This.'

Now Mary began to struggle. She heaved against the beam as hard as she could, not minding the pain as the metal cut into her calves. She thrashed and bucked, and when the rescuers held her arms to keep her still she began to fight against them. Water gushed from the ceiling in torrents.

When the level reached her mouth, Mary tilted her head back to keep her face clear of it. The water rose to her ear lobes.

Hilda squeezed her hands until she was calm again. In the wavering light of the torches, Mary saw the look in Hilda's eyes. Now she understood that the most awful thing was going to happen to her. Grief came. Its level rose. The water was over her eardrums now, muting the splashing of the rescuers as they made their last, frantic attempts.

Mary felt unbearable misery that Kenneth Cox was gone. His voice was still alive – this was the terrible thing. The boy never would be told to hush and now he yelled away, still, somewhere in the impossible music that was flooding her. Grief poured down from fire hoses.

'It's all just a dream,' said Hilda. 'Shh now, just a dream.'

'SHHUSSSSSHH!' shouted Kenneth. 'It! Is! Just! A! Dream!'

It was agony that he was gone, agony that pretty Beryl Waldorf had died mute and unconsoled, agony that Betty Oates still smiled, even now, when Mary shut her eyes. She arched her body back and forth. She wrenched against the beam that pinned her, and it was more than she could bear, it was really far too much, and it was so clear now that one had not believed in death at all – neither how quickly it came up on one, nor how fathomless its sadness was – until this moment when it was suddenly here.

She groaned in the darkness, and then she felt the sharp scratch as Hilda punctured her arm, through the fabric of her jacket and blouse, with the needle of a morphia syrette.

Hilda was looking down at her calmly. 'Shhh now. Just . . . a . . . dream.'

After a minute Mary's breathing came under control and the chill of the black water was gone. A glow spread through her belly and up her spine. It was unfamiliar and yet perfectly native and good. She felt Hilda's hands on her face, holding her up. 'There now.'

Mary was still aware of what was about to happen to her, but only in the same way that one was aware of the crossword. It was something difficult that one might pick up, or might not. The relief of the morphia was upon her and she understood that the drug was a simple and a merciful thing, no less appropriate than a bandage for a cut.

'Better?' said Hilda.

Mary supposed there was an answer. The water was almost up to her lips. How pretty Hilda was, how luminous and constant in the fickle light of the torches. Mary watched her friend, this débutante who had learned the habit of going out among bombs, with no more protection than a tin hat and an armband, to bring home the bodies of strangers.

It seemed to Mary that Hilda had asked a perfectly simple question. Certainly she should respond. The water, when the first trickle entered her mouth, tasted rather strange. How cold it was, and how sharp with soot and brick dust. How odd that London wanted to trickle into her. She smiled, but the water poured in and she supposed that she ought to close her mouth and breathe through her nose while she could.

How lovely was each breath. How peculiar that one had never noticed.

She felt certain that Hilda had asked her a question.

Morphia was the discovery – and it seemed obvious now – that every breath was perfect. The knowledge had been there all along, unnoticed and perfectly straightforward. How strange that one had never seen it. Was it an incapacity, a specific blindness of the mind? Or was it a mannered oversight? It would hardly be polite to go around noticing that every breath was lovely. She giggled, and water flooded in until she closed her mouth again.

The agony of her children's deaths still sounded in an undiminished cacophony – yes, she was perfectly aware of it – but the anguish was no longer particular to her. It simply was: one could hear it clearly, and listen to it calmly, picking out its individual timbres and notes, distinguishing its great themes and minor phrases. She grieved for every quiet sigh Beryl Waldorf had made. Her heart broke for each timid inflection in Thomas Essom's voice. She heard every harmonic in the screech of the chalk on the blackboard when she had written Tom's surname after her own. Of course: nobody ever really died. Life lingered. Every breath would persist forever, written in the clay of the city. And given that this was so perfectly obvious, it suddenly seemed imponderable that the enemy would make the effort to pack high explosive into a metal casing, fight it through the defending fire, and drop it from twenty thousand feet over a city of immortals.

Hilda was watching with her eyebrows raised in a question, and Mary realised that this had been the case for some time, and possibly forever. 'Better?' said Hilda again, or perhaps it was still the first time she had asked: the word dissolved into the ground water of the city, the word without end.

Mary strained to place her mouth into air. 'Yes, thank you. Much.'

Hilda seemed ready to cry.

Mary said, 'I'm sorry I wasn't kinder to you.'

'Oh, don't be sorry, it's . . .' Hilda looked up at blackness. 'It's . . .'

Mary watched the incomplete phrase float up into the night and come to rest there, glittering in bright points at the furthest extremity of the sky. This was how the stars had been made, after all: each the end of an unfinished thought, each an answer that one had known all along. She realised, of course, that this was not the sky and the stars, only the torches of the rescuers and the black roof of the basement, but she also understood that it was the same thing.

And now she realised – as the black water rose above her nose and eyes, as the light of the stars became blurred through the water – that this breath inside her was her last. She smiled, exhaled, and sank.

Hilda squeezed her hands. The two of them had always known each other, of course. They were one person – she, and Hilda, and Alistair, and Tom. They had gone too far into the unendurable dark and now they glittered there, too far apart to be a comfort to one another any more, but not so scattered that a godlike eye could never make of them a constellation.

The night lasted a moment, then forever.

In the dark, silhouetted against the stars of the rescuers' torches, she watched Hilda's face come down through the water towards her. Hilda's black hair floated in strands against the

306

light. *Now she will have to have her hair re-set*, thought Mary. *Why is she sinking down with me?*

And then Hilda's lips pressed against hers, and Hilda's fingers pinched her nostrils closed, and Mary felt Hilda's breath, sharp with tobacco and unutterably perfect, flooding into her. The breath hung suspended inside her, glowing and lovely. Mary held the breath until the life was gone from it, then sent it up to the surface. Against the torchlight she watched the silver bubbles rise. After a moment, Hilda's mouth came down and breathed into her again.

Again and again Hilda breathed, and Mary learned the habit of breathing only when Hilda's lips pressed against hers. How long it went on, and how silently. When finally the water level fell, and words came back into the world, and she heard Hilda saying she must breathe on her own now, Mary had become so dependent on Hilda's lips that at first she did not dare to breathe without them. She clung to Hilda, and pressed her face to hers, and it took a long time of Hilda gently pushing her away before she understood that her mouth was above water again.

The level fell. The rescuers had managed to run the intake pipes from the fire engines down into the basement, and soon it was pumped dry. They brought a hydraulic jack and lifted the beam that had pinned her. They laid her on a stretcher, wrapped her in blankets and took her to the surface. Hilda took a grease pen and painted a letter M on her forehead.

People were saying how much blood she had lost. Through the slow warp of the morphia Mary tried to listen, although it was becoming harder to make out words. It seemed that the beam, pinning her left leg, had cut into something that bled. Everyone moved faster now, and she watched them all rush around. How funny they were. It was because they did not understand that the air was all one needed. Now this perfect breath; now this one; now this. Hilda tightened a tourniquet around her thigh. How silly she was. They wrapped her in more blankets, and then Clive and Huw lifted her stretcher onto the rack on the roof of the Hillman. Somebody drove, impossibly fast. The Hillman screeched and slewed. Mary thought, *I hope they have remembered to strap the world onto me*.

Here was the indigo sky, noisy with stars. Mary stared up at them, all the unslaked billions. How gamely they faded. Without fuss, and faster now, the stars were losing their brightness. And as the stars dimmed, by kind degrees and quietly, the stars and the night became one. It was softer than one imagined, at the end. The final thing was the sound – lovely, in its way – of the last, lost bombers of the enemy droning home through the air that had been there all along. The air, then, quietening now, which would be there after they were gone. The ageless air, barely perturbed by their slipstream.

# APRIL, 1941

A sirocco blew dust in from Africa. The sun, even at noon, cast red light over the island. The wind blew for six days, so dry that exposed skin cracked like fired earth, so hard that the emaciated children could not walk against it and instead careened from alley to alcove in the ruins. The windblown grit scourged their legs until they bled.

The sea was ripped and dyed by the dust. Under the darkened sky the waves, breaking on the southwest coast, bloomed crimson at the foaming crests and purple in the troughs. The islanders hauled their fishing boats up the beaches through the last remaining channels between the mines and the barbed wire entanglements. In the red light they furled their sails, folded their ragged nets and weighed them down with rocks.

In Fort Bingemma, the wind dragged the sky across the unglazed rifle port of Alistair's room. He shuttered his mind against the howl. He removed the dressing from his right hand where the airman had bitten it. It came away without pain, drawing with it soft strands of yellowish glutinous matter. It didn't smell right – but then, Alistair told himself, nothing did. After a year of the siege everything on the island was foul, including the water to wash it in.

The whole edge of his hand was gone now, the fort's surgeon having excised a little more each time. The infection didn't want to be cut out. His little finger no longer moved, while the ring finger twitched a slow rhythm of which Alistair was not the conductor. In the deepest part of the wound a tendon shone dully. It was a mercy the light was no better.

With his left hand Alistair knocked a tin of sulpha powder to break up the lumps. He scattered a pinch into the wound. His head festered. The headache was sickening, extending down his spine to his liver. He shook with fever. The body could barely fight back. Not when the bread was one quarter sawdust, and the water was down to the mud at the bottom of the well.

When he stood to put the tin back on the shelf, he saw stars. There was less of him now. There was less of them all. Officers and men dragged themselves around in uniforms three sizes too big, new holes punched into every belt, every collar hanging loose. They were a garrison of skinny boys performing a play about soldiers. It would not have been surprising to discover that their stubble and scars were drawn on with greasepaint.

Fingernails bled. Everyone coughed. For weeks the men had lined the ramparts, looking down on the terraces that covered the escarpment. There, under strict supervision, the crops were harvested for the island's collective ration. It was maddening for starving men to watch the almonds and apricots ripening sixty feet below. The garrison had pet names for each farmer, each terrace, each tree. Using artillery spotters' binoculars aligned with clinometers on sandbagged and stabilised tripods, the battery's trained observers monitored the ripening of each individual fig, gave it a number in the military system, and ran a book on the day it would be picked.

Lately the men had begun to give ranks to the fruit: this fat-arsed pear a major, this smug plum a brigadier. When food was collected they stood at attention and saluted the trucks leaving for the warehouse. When a farmer ate a tomato behind a wall, the men knew it. They lined the ramparts and beat out their indignation on pan lids. And still Tom's jar of blackberry jam stood unopened in the alcove of the rifle port in Alistair's room. If he opened it, the dust would get into everything he minded about.

'I should think you will lose the hand, don't you?'

Simonson had appeared at the door. He eyed Alistair's wound. Alistair took a clean dressing and began to wrap it.

'If I do lose it, you can come and gawk at the stump.'

'I think you should call me "Major".'

Alistair lifted one weary eyebrow. 'Really? They made you major?'

'In their wisdom. As soon as two little brass crowns can be fought through on a convoy, you will see them on these shoulders.'

'What about Anderton?'

'I never thought he was major material, did you? Plus, he was killed last night. Car went in the sea near Valletta – wind took it clean off the road.'

'I used to enjoy your sense of humour.'

'I couldn't make it up. After all this – killed by the wind. Imagine writing that to the poor man's wife.'

'I expect they'll say "killed in action", don't you?'

'And that he was a credit, etcetera.'

'Well,' said Alistair, saluting with his bandaged hand. 'Major.'

Simonson returned the salute. 'Heath.'

'So, the command of the battery?'

'Mine, all mine, old soldier. Logan will take over my troop. You can keep yours, if you like. Or hurry up and lose that hand, and I can have you shipped home on the next available empty. With luck you'll be torpedoed.'

Alistair worked to remove any expression from his face.

'If only that Hun had brushed his teeth,' said Simonson.

Alistair wished he would leave. Simonson poked around the room, picking up books to peer at their titles. He nudged at a rack in which Alistair kept his bottles of turpentine and thinners. 'What are these?'

'I use them to clean my wound.'

Simonson took the bung from a bottle of acetone, sniffed, and recoiled.

'Goddamn it! If you put this on your wound it would bloody well catch fire. What do you really use it for?'

'I fuel a squadron of tiny enemy bombers upon which my men practise firing with tiny anti-aircraft pieces. Afterwards we make tea for our dolls.'

'Oh come on, though. Really.'

'I'm restoring a painting, sir. As I did before the war, sir.'

'That was another life. Is the Tate still there, do you suppose?'

'I couldn't say.'

'Who can? London might be ashes by now and none of us would be the wiser. There'd be a Ministry of Letters, forging notes from all our girlfriends.'

Alistair tried not to think about it. He hadn't heard from Mary in a month. For a while she'd written every day and then, abruptly, nothing. Everyone else had got post. Every now and then a mail plane was shot down, but it didn't seem likely that nothing at all from Mary had got through.

Simonson peered at the thinners. 'So what are you restoring?'

'Nothing important,' said Alistair. 'Local artist.'

'Go on, I'd like to see it.'

'Sorry, but it's private.'

Simonson closed his eyes for a moment. 'Alistair, it's been weeks. So we had a ding-dong. So bloody what.'

'I put you in an unbearable position.'

'No, you did the decent thing. I'm sorry I didn't come to help sooner.'

The two men shook hands – Alistair had to use his left – while the red sand hissed in through the rifle port. Simonson held

Alistair's hand for half a minute before he let go. 'I used to be less of an ass, you know.'

'It gets to us all. I used to be Ginger Rogers.'

'Explains why the men are so sweet on you.'

'The painting is under the bed. If you actually care.'

'Get it.'

'Get it yourself, you lazy sod.'

Simonson crouched by the cot and pulled the painting out. He unwrapped it and set it on the mattress. It was a Madonna and child in the Caravaggist style – the woman in a carmine dress, the child with amber skin, the contrast of the strict chiaroscuro diminished by a layering of soot. Four feet by three, the gilt frame blistered and charred on the left, which was also the side from which light entered the painting. The impression was of a pacific moment caught in time and lit by the residual heat of catastrophe.

'Where did you turn this up?' said Simonson.

'It was rescued from that church the plane crashed into.'

'You went back there?'

'The priest gave it to me to restore.'

'As your penance?'

'Something like that.'

Simonson went to the rifle port and looked out, hands in pockets. 'You know we're allowed to kill the enemy? That it's encouraged?'

Alistair said nothing. His head throbbed and fever crept down his back. He only knew that it soothed him to make the painting good again. He liked the Madonna's slightly vexed smile, as if something inconsequential had just been knocked over and would need to be swept up. As if she might have just sworn under her breath. He liked the honey tones of the child's skin, the paint not scoured by wind or crazed by concussion. He liked the clean smell of the thinners cutting the forlorn odour of soot.

313

'It is a fine painting,' said Simonson.

'Isn't it?'

The two of them stood together, looking.

'One forgets,' said Simonson.

'Forgets what?'

He waved a hand in irritation. 'I don't know. Women. Light. Oh, carry on.'

He turned and made to leave. The wind bellowed, shaking the tower.

Alistair said, 'I haven't heard from Mary.'

Simonson took a step back into the room. 'There will be a sound explanation. Perhaps she has realised how ugly you are.'

'Heard from any of yours?'

'Oh, Alistair, they write without pause or reason. There is nothing I don't know about the menu at Blacks' or the fashion at McIntie's. I am fully apprised of the current *mot du jour*, which is "swell", and of the words now considered déclassé – including "war", apparently, which we must now refer to as "this trouble". I know everything, you see, apart from how to reply. I can hardly write that we are down to skin and rivets. That the enemy could knock us into the sea with a well-timed look.'

'Perhaps you should tell them how it is. It might winnow them down.'

'Having three women suits me fine. It takes a royal fool to pick one. I can't imagine why you're so good at it.'

Later, under the violent sky, Alistair took his troop gardening in the moat. The Victorians had taken the ditch as they found it, simply building its walls higher to make the fort, which defended the western segment of the Victoria Lines, which in turn defended Grand Harbour – the Mediterranean base of the Victorian Royal Navy – against a land invasion from the north. In short, as Alistair's men delighted in pointing out, the moat was the perfect thing to protect something that no longer existed against something that would never happen again. 'Well then, you clever bastards,' Alistair told them, 'you might as well plant potatoes in it.'

He split his troop into its four guns as he had each day for a fortnight, putting each seven-man team of gunners to dig and plant a strip across the moat. He reckoned to cultivate around thirty yards in a two-hour shift from 4 to 6 p.m. Two hours of labour was all the food ration allowed. Even then, Alistair sometimes looked at the men's gaunt faces and their sharp, shirtless ribs as they worked, and discovered that his watch must be running slow. He usually declared 6 p.m. at a quarter to.

Today was the worst it had been. In the bloodied light the men sweated and swore as the dust storm screamed above the moat. The parched earth would not submit to shovels and required to be loosened with picks before the lumps could be put into sacks and smashed against the stone walls of the fort. Only then did the stuff resemble soil. And when the precious seed potatoes were planted in their shallow drills and irrigated with the foul water from the kitchens and with the men's own urine, the moisture was baked out instantly. It was difficult to believe that a crop would sprout from terracotta.

With his rotten hand Alistair could offer no help. He made himself as useful as he could, bringing water from man to man and finding errands on which to send the weaker ones to give them some reprieve. A little before five, the men unearthed something. When Alistair saw a deep opening he called them off straight away and sent them back sixty feet.

The picks had broken through into a cavity, and the danger was the possibility of unexploded ordnance. The opening was around three feet square, and Alistair tiptoed to the edge. Lying flat, he looked over the lip of the hole and waited for his eyes to adapt. He could smell his hand, even with the wind.

The base of the hole became visible, and it wasn't deep. He lowered himself in. His feet touched bottom while his head and shoulders were still above ground level. He motioned for the men to wait where they were, then ducked down out of the wind. He waited for the bile to sink back in his throat. His head pounded. Out of sight of the men, he allowed himself to close his eyes and recover for a moment.

He lit a match. Bones shone. The pit was small, five feet long by four broad. The bones were human, three skeletons aligned east–west with their feet towards sunset. They had neither skulls nor hands. Alistair was crouching on ribs that cracked under his shoes.

It was the fourth such pit they had found in the moat. There were no artefacts this time, nothing by which a layman might date the bones. In any case the story didn't change. The island had been contested so many times, and the ground was so impenetrably rocky, that one did not have to dig for long in any patch of workable earth to learn what had happened to all the garrisons before one's own.

He closed his eyes again. How nice it would be to lie down in these bones, and quietly die.

He struck another match. These men had got off rather lightly. With any luck they had lost their heads before their hands. In another pit, a week earlier, they had found a skeleton with every long bone broken and the rusty flakes of nails driven through the spine. Anyone might have done it – Malta was eight thousand years of nails. It was nothing one wanted the men to think about while they waited for the enemy's paratroopers to arrive.

Alistair put his head and shoulders back out into the wind, gathered the last of his strength, and hoisted himself up on his good arm. He went over to the men and stood them down. He watched them disperse into dust, bent against the wind. Every bump of their spines was visible.

He kept Briggs back. The two of them said a few words over the remains, ran bayonets across some of the moat's retaining sandbags, and filled up the burial pit with sand. When they were done it was gone six and Alistair was exhausted. His eyes wouldn't focus. He hauled his headache up to his room and took the bandage off his hand. It oozed yellow poison. He boiled water on his Primus, salted it, let it cool, and cleaned the wound.

Through the rifle port the sun was setting. The scream of the wind fell slightly. He lit a lamp, reducing the wick so that it burned as little kerosene as possible. He propped the painting against the wall. Its gilt frame shone in the close glow of the lantern. The figures were best in such confidential light. He was so tired that he fell asleep sitting up. When he woke he found himself reaching out to the painting with his wounded hand, in the fragile light as the kerosene exhausted itself. He stared at the dying hand before him, and for a moment he wondered which poor chap's it was.

# APRIL, 1941

Palmer brought morphia in a brown glass bottle with a pipette built into the stopper. Mary thought it ingenious. Everything about the tincture delighted her – that its smell was soberly medical, that a few drops on the tongue were a remedy for feelings, and that Palmer seemed able to procure it without fuss. On her return from hospital he had taken to appearing at three-hourly intervals with the pewter tray – not the silver, since her father was still away at the constituency. From the tray he would set down the brown bottle and a glass of iced water, on pewter coasters backed with green felt, together with fruits in a porcelain bowl.

Palmer would then dematerialise, leaving Mary to dispense the morphia at her convenience. This was proper since it placed the stuff in the category of remedies, which were taken in private, and not of tonics, cocktails, or pick-me-ups, which were mixed to order and then taken while the butler hovered in case the blend was found to want celery salt, or bitters. The little bowl of fruit was appropriate too, since fruit was something – just like morphia – that one could easily take or leave.

Mary thought Palmer so painstakingly humane that she felt unable to disturb his sleep by ringing for him at three in the morning when she awoke in a sweat from nightmares that wouldn't release her. Instead she sat up in bed with the covers pulled tight, wide-eyed while hallucinations of her dead children scratched away at the inside of the wardrobe doors. Kenneth Cox whispered behind the fire screen, behind the cheval mirror, behind her head so that she had to keep looking around.

It was a horribly long time until Palmer came in at seven with the tray, and then it was difficult to wait while he opened the curtains and laid out the newspaper and unfolded the newly issued day. Only when he vanished could she fall on the morphia and squeeze the red rubber bulb to draw up the seven trembling drops that the doctor had prescribed, and the further ten drops by which the doctor had underestimated things.

Mary lay back on the bed and dissolved into the immaculate morning.

At nine, finding her fingers still too relaxed for fine work, she needed her mother's help to dress.

'You will want to quit that stuff as soon as you can,' said her mother, buttoning Mary's blouse. 'I don't know what you plan to do with the day, but I cannot see it involving successful interactions with objects or persons.'

'You know the morphia is only till my wound is healed.'

Her mother picked up the brush and began on Mary's hair. 'It has been a whole month, darling. If you had cut something actually off, one might not begrudge you the paregoric. But you are a North, Mary. We don't go south over flesh wounds.'

'The doctor says I shall have a limp.'

'Then live the rest of your life seated, if you must, but please do it sober.'

Mary stared out of the window, bracing her head against the tug of the hairbrush. She watched the freshly laundered clouds dissipate and resolve. The eye was an extraordinary instrument. How mysterious that it could be brought to bear on that tiny, distant pigeon – there – and then refocused in an instant on an object that existed only in memory. She watched herself at the same window, aged five, sucking on an orange boiled sweet, popping it out of her mouth from time to time to check how much remained and to peer at the slowly resolving city through the translucent glass of the candy.

'Mary!' Her mother set down the hairbrush with a bang. 'I won't have you go to pieces like this. Tell me your plan for the day, and I shall expect an update over supper. Why don't you write to that man of yours?'

'To Alistair? Oh no. I haven't written to him since I was hurt.'

'Why ever not? The poor thing must be frantic.'

'I no longer enjoy any happiness I have taken from Hilda. I hope Alistair will understand.'

'But you were so serious about him!'

Mary tried to bring her mother's face into focus. 'You have always insisted that I am not a serious person.'

'Then won't you go for a walk, at least? Take an umbrella for the showers, and call on Hilda.'

'Hilda will be sleeping. We work nights, as you know.'

'Enough of this "we". You are not to go back to the ambulances. If you'd only listened to me . . .'

'Then I'd be Mrs Henry Hunter-Hall by now, in Gloucestershire, berating the keeper for displaying poachers' heads on the railings.'

Her mother set to with the hairbrush again. 'But would that be so awful, darling? To be the prettiest thing in Brimscombe-and-Thrupp?'

'I should rather die.'

'You nearly did.'

'Yes, but I tend to blame the Germans.'

'Well I blame you for getting in their way. There are a dozen ways of serving, for a young woman of your abilities, that are safer and more beneficial to the cause. Do you think less of your father, for example, that he serves in the House rather than in the street?'

'Of course not. But I let the War Office decide how I was to serve, and they made me a schoolteacher. Everything else has followed from that.'

Her mother looked away. 'All the other mothers wrote letters to Whitehall, of course. But at your father's level one must be so careful about the exercise of influence. I feel awful about it now. I never imagined the War Office would be so obtuse as to assign you to the ordinary lottery.'

Mary kissed her cheek. 'I really don't mind in the least.'

'Because you are intoxicated, darling. But I mind, very much. What is the good of influence if one can only use it on strangers?'

'But I am happy. Isn't that what matters?'

'You aren't ready to make your own choices. Look where it's got you.'

'Where has it got me? Here I sit, in the very same room as you.'

'And yet you are miles away. It kills me to see you so dissolute.'

'You kill me, Mother. You hate my choices but make none of your own. We tiptoe on our carpets, deferring some imagined joy to a hoped-for day when Father will do some good for people. And in the meantime we do not live among people at all. We swim in aspic.'

The quick April clouds sent white and grey shades through the room.

'Your father was my choice. You were my delight. You may despise my life for its smallness – it may seem as nothing to you – but please do not think it is nothing to me. And the smaller it becomes, the more frightening I find it, because all that is left is so dear.'

Her mother had tears in her eyes, but Mary could not feel a thing.

# APRIL, 1941

**M**ary walked to the Lyceum, limping on her left leg. The craters in the Strand were a bore, but the wags had put up signs beside the deepest: GRAND CANYON, and JOURNEY TO THE CENTRE OF THE EARTH, 2/6. London slipped by with no trouble, parting its late-morning crowds around her. It smelled of all the smokes promiscuously: cigarette, pipe, locomotive, house coal, and roof joist. At the theatre the huge portico was pocked by shrapnel but otherwise unharmed. The manager told her that Zachary was out, but Mary went down to the basement anyway, since she supposed he could not stop her. He would hardly lay hands on her.

Underground, the empty dance floor was sticky with sweat and beer. The electric bulbs – their array much degraded – interfered with the fraying light of the morphia. She had a small jolt of feeling, but it didn't have to last. She picked her way between the unmatched tables and chairs. The basement was deserted but there were children's voices coming from the bar on the far side. She made her way over.

The bar was of rough wood and everywhere reinforced, a certain amount of dancing upon it being inevitable. In their racks the glasses were of the indestructible variety. She missed the lightness of things – the jeu d'esprit in which the stuff of the world had once been made as finely as possible, in anticipation of forces falling within a mannered range. She put down her bag and dug out a bottle of morphia. She took a dozen drops and lit a cigarette, listening to the children's voices. She peered over the bar top.

'Can't a person get any service around here?'

Zachary's head emerged over the counter.

He gave her a cautious look. 'Are you angry?'

'Not at all. Did you get my letter?'

He shook his head. 'I thought you hated me.'

'Should I? You probably saved my life.'

A coloured girl's head appeared over the bar. She was seven if Mary had to guess, with gapped teeth and a minor squint. 'I'm Molly.'

'I know,' said Mary.

'How?'

'Because you just told me.'

Molly grinned. 'Do you want to wobble my tooth?'

'Thank you, I should love to.'

It was a premolar in the lower jaw and it did have a good wobble to it. It was immensely satisfying to nudge it to and fro. *Sound the air-raid warning*, thought Mary. *We are losing our milk city*. Molly chattered away. Mary gathered that she had lost her parents, and that the minstrels were supporting her and Zachary. Both children seemed to accept this as natural.

'How many ration books do you have between you?' said Mary. 'Really? None at all?'

'We eat down here,' said Zachary.

'What, exactly? You're both awfully thin.'

'Biscuits. Bread. Whatever they're selling.'

'Really? People come in here and take money from children for food?'

'And milk and sweets.'

'When was the last time you ate eggs, meat, or fruit?'

Molly's lip began to tremble. 'Are we in trouble?'

'Only from scurvy.' She grabbed each of them by an arm and marched them up to the alleyway. The children blinked and screwed up their eyes against the light. Zachary had on a stained white shirt and a black bow tie. He needed seven kinds of haircut.

'You mustn't tell Molly I can't read and write,' he whispered.

Mary looked over at her. The girl wore a purple dress with white bows. She was staring at the sky as if it might be ordered away.

'Would she mind?' said Mary.

'I told her I was clever. You know – so she'd stay.'

Mary smiled. 'It doesn't work like that.'

'How does it work?'

'People stay if they can.'

He squinted up at her. 'Are you all right?'

'Fine, thank you.'

The dark look boys gave to a pale answer. Years went by. Feelings almost came. The war ended, and saplings grew through the rubble.

Mary blinked. It was the morphia that sent time in these meandering rivers, orphaning a loop without warning and leaving it isolated, a little oxbow of memory with no clue of how it had got there. She was seeing the look with which Zachary had dismissed her, on the day of the evacuation. In his face as he flicked away his imaginary cigarette had been this same hint of a sadness evolved beyond consolation. As if misery, winged and pelagic, had left behind the doughy shore and its brood of flightless comforts.

She had the children wait in the alleyway while she flagged down a cab on the Strand. When the driver stopped she held the door and the children piled in. In his rear-view mirror the driver's face was a picture.

He said, 'Where are we taking the piccaninnies?'

'To Piccadilly. Where else? The Ritz.'

'It's your neck,' said the driver.

Molly put her head on Zachary's shoulder and fell asleep. He looked out at the city. The driver watched them in the rear-view mirror with an expression of perfect disgust. When it became tedious, Mary gave the man a bright smile and said, 'They are from Timbuktu, you know. I got them for six strings of coloured beads and a daguerreotype of the King. Didn't I do well?'

The driver reddened. 'I would of kept the beads.'

'I would *have* kept the beads,' said Mary, and now the man made them get out and walk the last half-mile.

'I thought I was the stupid one,' said Zachary.

Mary gave him a wounded look. 'Yes, but it is absolutely your fault for being as black as pitch, don't you see?'

He smiled, for the first time that day. 'Why did you come?'

She nodded in the direction of Molly, who was skipping ahead. 'I was jealous of the attention you were getting.'

'But really?'

'I thought you might be lonely.'

'I've got Molly to look after.'

*Fine*, she thought, *but would you mind awfully if I stuck around anyway?*

At the Ritz her father's name was good enough for a table, despite the unconcealed anguish of the staff from the head waiter down. Mary and the children were seated for lunch as far from the other guests as the great dining room permitted, but even so a couple objected and required to be moved to a more distant table. Mary gave them a wave.

'They're mine,' she explained loudly. 'From different fathers, I think – one loses track.'

'Madam,' said the waiter, 'I must ask you to consider our guests.'

'Waiter,' said Mary, 'I must ask you to bring us Tamworth ham, cheeses of the mild sort, bread rolls, diced avocado pears with lemon so they don't go brown, Cumberland sausages, scones with and without currants, fruit jams but please not peach, cocoa but not too hot, two large oranges, and some hard-boiled eggs thinly sliced.'

'Hen or duck, for the eggs?' asked the waiter, recovering.

'Whichever's still laying. Oh, and coffee. Oh, and an ashtray.'

'Very good. Will there be anything else?'

'That will depend,' said Mary, 'on whether anyone is sick.'

'Very good, madam.'

The children watched with wide eyes as the waiter receded.

'Are we even allowed in here?' said Zachary.

'It's this place that shouldn't be allowed. Your only crime is hunger.'

Mary drank coffee, geeing up her third cup with a dozen drops of morphia. She managed half a scone. Her stomach was tight from sleeplessness, and the drug queered her appetite anyway. Across the dining room, a pianist was playing the 'Blue Danube'. Mary watched the children eat everything on the table, beginning with what was nearest to them and finishing – when there was no more bread to spread it on – by licking the last of the butter from its dish. They passed it between them, without ceremony but with no imperfection of manners that Mary could detect. Zachary left a little extra for Molly, who was very small and frail. The girl laid her head on the perfect white tablecloth and fell asleep again, with her mouth open and her arms hanging vertically.

From their tables the other guests watched, over the tops of ironed newspapers. It would be minutes rather than hours, Mary realised, until the scene was relayed to Pimlico. With the morphia it was possible to know that this was unfair on her mother, and also not to mind.

Zachary wiped his face on the tablecloth. 'May I have a cigarette?'

'Not until you are thirteen. Tell me, do you like looking after Molly?'

'It's all right.'

'You're good with her.'

'I'm no good at anything.'

'Nonsense. You're a fine musician and a champion paste eater.'

'Everyone should be able to read and write. You said it yourself.'

'I was wrong,' she said. 'I have buried a man who could read, you see, killed by people who can write.'

She tried to light a cigarette, but the flame and the end of the cigarette wouldn't converge. Zachary had to guide her wrist.

'Thank you,' he said.

'What for?'

'For coming to find me.'

She supposed she must have. And here she was, apparently, in the Ritz, with negro orphans. Diners stared back at her, stiff with condemnation. And here she was – oh, here she still was, yes – even now, with no clear idea, just for the moment, of how one might have got here.

# MAY, 1941

The wind pushed a raft of cloud over the island, and the bomb-ing stopped for six days. Alistair rotated with the battery, back from the highlands to Fort St Elmo. It was cooler by the sea, and the officers found a sharpness in themselves again. When the wind blew some Sicilian fishermen into Grand Harbour – their engine had thrown a piston – Alistair hatched a plan that Simonson liked enough to take to the lieutenant colonel.

The Sicilians were hauled up on the dock and invited in exchange for their lives to spit on a photograph of Mussolini. This done, they were treated to a feast. They had roast meats and fancy breads, a gramophone and brandy. The officers of the Royal Naval Dockyard, dressed in their parade best uniforms and whistling airs from Gilbert and Sullivan, repaired the fisher-men's engine, not neglecting to fasten a portrait of the King to their cabin's central bulkhead using star-headed brass screws that could not be undone except with a particular issue of Royal Navy screwdriver.

The work being finished and the wind falling calm, the combined brass bands of the various regiments defending Grand Harbour were assembled on the quayside in tropical dress, with folded blankets secreted beneath their tunics where their bellies ought to have been. They shouldered their tubas and played an extended medley of Vaughan Williams and Elgar while the fish-ermen were escorted back out through the harbour's mine cordon by the polished mahogany launch of the Admiral of His Majesty's Mediterranean Fleet Andrew Browne Cunningham, the First Viscount Cunningham of Hyndhope, flying the white ensign. Thus the enemy's fishermen carried home the intelligence that the island was doing very much better than the enemy had imagined, and ought not to be invaded just yet.

When the signals officer on the ramparts of Fort St Elmo put down his binoculars and reported that the fishing boat had gone out of visual range, the brass bands were stood down. Officers and men folded their parade uniforms and put on the frayed and malodorous battle dress that they had lived in these many months. The admiral's launch was returned to its mooring and covered with the stained tarpaulin that made it look, from the air, like any of the harbour's little boats. Its tank was drained of diesel oil, which was needed for the electric generators in the forts. The admiral himself, who was on the same rations as the men, found that he could barely lift his arm to return the salute when his subordinate came to report that the operation had been a success.

The scraps of food that the fishermen had left were collected into a basket, covered with a cloth, and taken to the central stores to be allocated to one of the batches of soup that would be distributed to the starving garrisons.

'Well,' said Simonson, his feet up on Alistair's metal desk, 'you are not a handsome man, but I will admit that your plan went off well.'

'The men were magnificent, weren't they?'

'I daresay they needed it. Nice to be the ones dishing it out for once.'

Alistair lurched, sat down on his cot and closed his eyes.

'All right?' said Simonson.

'Give me a moment. I'll be fine.'

Simonson lit a cigarette, rocked back on his chair, and exhaled. 'I don't think you will be fine, Alistair.'

'No, I don't suppose I will.'

'Do you think we might get that arm taken off for you now?'

'The surgeon still feels I can keep it.'

'We wouldn't be keeping the surgeon if we had any choice. He is a sawbones and I'll bet he learned medicine at the Army Veterinary College.'

'Then be glad he hasn't put me down.'

'But he is killing you, isn't he, in his way? Letting your arm fester like this? Look at you – it's up to your shoulder.'

Alistair tried to think, through the nausea. 'We haven't had much luck, have we, with the men who've gone into his theatre?'

'We'd get you a Navy surgeon. They'd pipe you aboard, whip the arm off, and send you away with rum. We'd just have to watch they didn't issue you with a hook hand and a parrot – you know the Navy.'

Alistair cradled the arm. 'I'm not sure.'

'Think of that girl of yours. She'd put you straight.'

'She still doesn't write.'

'But I shall still have to write to her, if you die from this infection. You know how I hate writing those letters.'

'Drop it, won't you? It makes me nervous when you're tedious.'

'It makes me tedious when you're dying. Be a good chap, won't you, and get the arm taken off? Then I can have you evacuated. There's an orderly queue of cripples and grotesques. As soon as your number comes to the top of it, they fly you home on the mail plane.'

'I'd rather stay and help.'

'You're no help dead.'

The sirens sounded. Simonson stood wearily.

'Enjoy every moment,' said Alistair.

'Will you think about what I said, and let me have your answer?'

Alistair turned away, then nodded.

'Good man.' Simonson put on his cap and left, and the garrison crept back into its shell to take another beating.

Alistair looked out over the harbour. He heard the aircraft before he saw them. They came in as they always did, from the north, and he steadied his field glasses to watch them. They were Heinkels, lined up along the horizon with their fighter escort larking above. The RAF had nothing to put up against them and so there was nothing for the German fighters to do. Alistair imagined they practised aerobatics and scored the others' manoeuvres for aesthetics and technical difficulty, while far beneath them the grubby Heinkels laid their turds of high explosive.

Through the glasses one could sometimes catch a glimpse of a bomber pilot through the frontal glass of his aircraft. They still wore jackets and ties to the fight. Alistair tried to make out the pilots' faces, but they were too distant. He would have liked to know how the enemy looked as he approached the Maltese coast.

Alistair tracked the bombers until they were almost overhead and the stonework blocked his view. The fort's Bofors guns and 3.7s opened up. It was not the ceaseless barrage it had been a year ago. Now, having little ammunition, the gunners did their best. The bombs began to fall. Alistair was too weak to go down to the shelters and he sat on an empty ammunition box, took up the brushes with his left hand and worked at the restoration. The explosions made dust. Grit got into the thinners.

He had cleaned every part of the painting now, making good around twenty square inches a day. The Madonna, now that she was freed from her soot, was a catch. She made Alistair forget the hunger and the nausea of his infection. He had long ceased to make any distinction between his own Mary and the one who was restored, inch by inch, as he worked. Bombs hammered down, falling all around the fort, cratering its great courtyard. Alistair ignored them. He hardly worked, simply looked back at Mary. The poison from his arm slowed his mind.

He had started with the hem of her dress, working up the lines of the obscurest folds, perfecting the mix of the thinners and learning the minimum pressure required to shift the grime and soot. Next he had moved on to the dress's salients, revealing profane shifts of red. Her hair came next, imperfect, tangled here and there, swept back from the face but otherwise scarcely tamed. After two months he had trusted his technique sufficiently to expose her hands, and finally her face.

He looked from Mary to the Christ child, for whom he had developed a fraternal affection. The painter clearly hadn't liked the boy – Alistair supposed no artist had ever much cared for the child whose presence was only an excuse to frequent the model. So here was Christ the awkward, Christ the inconvenient, Christ the pint-sized chaperone. Sooty, pug-faced Jesus, wanting a feed. Alistair had worked on the painting for days before he noticed that while Mary had been provided with a halo, the child had only the benefit of a pot on a table in the background, its rim catching the incidental light. The table was in such deep shade and the pot so very nearly matched to its background that one would have to be the painter, or the painting's restorer, to see the trick. Alistair's heart went out to the boy. Maybe that was the point.

The bombing tailed off and Alistair dragged himself back to watch the enemy bombers departing. He was glad when they got away now. He raised his glasses and watched them fleeing above the waves, the tail-enders yawing desperately and trailing long streaks of soot. Well, it had been a long war, and everyone was trailing smoke. He was surprised at how easy it was to excuse the enemy. They had never promised fraternity, only bombs. What Alistair had done to Tom was worse. Mary must have come to feel the same for her part in it. He supposed it was why she didn't write.

Now that the raid was over the men mustered in the courtyard. Alistair watched them harvest the seedy grasses that grew in the cracks between the flagstones. They chewed, slow jawed. Gun drills had been abandoned weeks ago, physical training prohibited. When not specifically told to do something, the men had orders to do nothing.

Alistair watched through the glasses while the local children emerged from the rubble beyond the fort's walls. They kindled tiny fires with splintered furniture, and roasted snails on sticks. In the alleys, men stood between the poles to drag their traps and carts. Their horses were long gone for stewing. Dogs were extinct. This was the worst thing now: the silence in the aftermath of a raid. There had always been the raucous indignation of dogs, but the island no longer barked.

His head throbbed. He retched, but nothing came up.

Later, Simonson brought Alistair's ration. There was a two-ounce block of a thing they were calling bread, and a half-tin of paste. He watched with indifference as Simonson put the food down, pushing aside the bottles of thinners to make a place. Simonson sat heavily, threw off his cap and rubbed dust from the inside of his collar.

'Aren't you going to eat the food?'

'You have it,' said Alistair.

'Don't tempt me.'

'I'll have it later, then.'

'Suit yourself. Good view of the raid from up here?'

'It was lovely.'

Alistair took the jar of blackberry jam from its safe place on the floor and placed it back in the arrow loop. Simonson swallowed. Alistair enjoyed the effort it cost his friend to take his eyes off the jar.

'Why won't you eat that stuff?'

'I prefer strawberry. How did the raid go?'

'We lost two local gunners. Zammit and Sillato. Another breech explosion. Zammit's children came to the main gate and howled. Two boys and a little girl the wind could lift like thistledown.'

'Those guns aren't safe to use.'

'But the poor men make such elementary mistakes. Apparently Zammit had the breech half closed and Sillato called it ready to fire.'

'Have trigger guards made and run chains to them from the breech door, on the far side from the hinge. Make them just the right length and the trigger won't clear until the gun is properly closed up.'

Simonson frowned. 'You think?'

'We did it in France when we had to use French gunners.'

Simonson looked over at the picture. 'Aren't you going to fix the frame?'

'I like it with the marks of the fire on it. It carries its own story.'

'Suit yourself. It will end up hanging in Berlin, in any case.'

'You don't mean that.'

Simonson sighed. 'The men never made these mistakes under you.'

'They weren't so hungry, back then.'

'You flatter me.'

'But it's true. You're not absolutely the worst major in the Army.'

Simonson snorted. 'Now I know you're dying.'

Alistair screwed the tops back on the bottles of thinners. It was hard to get the tops on with one hand. Simonson, who could have helped, only looked at him doing it.

'Don't make me beg. Will you let them take the arm off?'

'Why do you insist?'

'Because I want you evacuated before the enemy parachutes in. You know very well we'll be killed, and I would feel less awful if you were companionable enough to let me die alone.'

'Self-centred of you.'

'Isn't it? Still, I would consider it a favour.'

'When we first met, you considered me too common to live.'

'Perhaps I have come to see some low merit in the lower orders.'

'This helpful war. It makes us better people and then it tries to kill us.'

Simonson grinned.

'What?' said Alistair.

'Well you make it sound just like Harrow.'

'Do you miss it?'

'Badly. Not the food, though. God, yes, even the food.'

'I'll look the place up for you when I get home, then.'

Simonson glanced up sharply. 'So you will let us take off the arm?'

'Just make sure they leave the good one attached, will you?'

'Oh, there's every chance. Fifty-fifty, at least. I shall alert the Navy immediately and have them sober up their best surgeon.'

# MAY, 1941

When her mother ordered Palmer not to give her any more morphia, Mary moved into the garret and took the last two brown glass bottles with her. She would give her mother a little space in which to become reasonable.

East of Pimlico, London was broken beyond hope in a way that was perfectly obvious, but which caused Mary no distress whatsoever. The impossible realism of the opiate shunned the impossible reality of the war. The two were oil and water. Even when something happened to shake one up, the day and the drug only separated into a million busy droplets, flowing around each other to rejoin their own kind. And then there one was again, on top of things, buoyant on the hour.

At the Lyceum, Bones was at the baby grand rehearsing 'Hitler Has Only Got One Ball', reducing the piano part to the crudest single-piston pump and whining the vocals through his nose. After the first verse the lights snapped up on the stage and revealed a full big band and twenty-four minstrels who went straight into a colossal reprise of the song, with close harmonies and outrageous swing. The effect was magnificent, and Mary laughed with delight as she made her way down to the basement.

At the sound of her footsteps, three heads appeared over the counter of the bar. There was Zachary, Molly and a new boy of perhaps nine years, with puffy eyes and a green felt fedora.

'The hell are you?' said the new boy.

'Do you mind?' said Mary. 'It is *Who* the hell are you? Or more elegantly, *Who in hell's name* are you? I'm Mary. Glad to meet you.'

The heavenward glance he gave, as if she were too much. He exhaled a smoke ring. Mary realised that he had held his hand out for her cigarette as if it were the most natural thing in the world, and that she had passed it to him in an absence of mind while he had her so flustered.

'Give that back this second, you menace!'

He gave a superior look and exhaled through his nose. 'I'm Charles.'

She snatched the cigarette back.

'You're strung out, aren't you?'

Mary smiled. 'Don't be silly.'

He widened his eyes. 'You think I don't see people high? We get big bands here. We get players.'

She started to protest, then gave it up and leaned on the bar top. 'I was injured. It's only until my wound is healed.'

'What is it, opium?'

'Morphia.'

'What even is that? Stronger or weaker?'

'Goodness, Charles, how would I know? My family favours sherry.'

'You can hardly see straight.'

'You also believe I should stop, I suppose.'

Charles shook his head. 'I think you should *share*.'

'Certainly not.'

'Come on, just let me try a little.'

'Don't be ridiculous.'

'Then don't you be ludicrous.'

'Then don't be preposterous.'

He steepled his fingers. 'Then don't be . . . unreasonable.'

337

'Vocabulary: B-plus,' said Mary. 'But your hat: D-minus.'

The perfect grin boys gave when victory was absolute.

'Sorry about Charles,' said Zachary.

'He doesn't know better,' said Molly. 'He never had parents.'

Charles shoved her. 'You got none neither.'

Mary opened her mouth and closed it again. The children were laughing now as they pushed each other around. Here they were, driven underground and yet – so far as Mary could tell – still uncured of joy.

She taught them reading and composition until they began to tire, and then she said to Zachary, 'How long since you saw daylight?'

He wasn't sure, so they left the two younger children and walked up into an improving day. The smoke was lifting after the night's conflagrations but the air was still blunt with haze. The sun was a flat white disc. Zachary and Mary walked with arms linked while the people they passed looked knives at them. Mary made sure to smile back brightly. It was simply a peculiarity of the British that they could be stoical about two hundred and fifty nights of bombing, while the sight of her with a negro child offended their sensibilities unbearably.

'You're better,' said Zachary, looking up at her.

'I'm happy to see you doing so well. You've your hands full, I suppose, with Charles and Molly.'

'Charles isn't so bad. He just talks. Molly's the worst.'

'What, little Molly?'

'She steals.'

'No! And here was me about to check her shoulders for wings.'

'She steals my tips to buy buns.'

'And does she share?'

'Does she hell.'

'How come you're so cheerful, then? Do you qualify for some kind of prize if London is finally destroyed?'

'I don't know. I'm just happy.'

She put her arm around his shoulders. 'Idiot.'

He leaned his head against her. 'Fool.'

'Work on your vocabulary. You wouldn't want Charles to get ahead.'

'No I wouldn't, you bonehead.'

'Stop it!' she said, pinching his arm.

Both of them laughed, and then a woman passing in the opposite direction lifted a blue-gloved hand and slapped Mary full in the face. The shock put her on the ground, with bright points of light flashing.

Zachary was kneeling over her, one hand under her head to keep it off the flagstones, the other hand smoothing her hair away from her face.

'I'm quite all right,' she said. 'I'm fine.'

His shock was too much. She collected herself and managed to sit upright. He looked as if he might cry.

'Don't,' she said. 'It's not your fault.'

She looked around for the woman who had hit her, but it seemed she hadn't stopped. There was only the city, in irreconcilable fragments.

'Help me up,' she said. 'It's nothing, you know.' She smiled, to show that it really was. 'Let's go to the river, shall we, and regroup?'

Down at the Thames, the water flowed as it always had and the soft breeze smelled of the sea. The tanned longshoremen worked their lines while the brown tide swelled beneath them. Mary thought that everything might be fine after all. But as they sat on the wall – now that her back was to the city – she began to sob. She couldn't stop.

'It's all right,' said Zachary. 'It's all right.'

'It is not all right.'

Her voice shocked her – shrill, brittle. The attack had knocked the last of the morphia out of her. Her face was hot where the woman had slapped it, but her body crawled with ice. Her bones froze and cracked. Her hands shook so hard that she had to ask Zachary to take the bottle of morphia from her bag. He held her head and managed to get a dozen drops into her mouth. She was beyond shame, not caring that Zachary knew what she had become.

After a few minutes the pain was chased from her bones by a warm and forgiving kindness.

Zachary's eyes were on her.

'You're right,' she said in a hoarse voice. 'I'll give it up.'

'Sorry,' said Zachary, and threw the brown bottle into the Thames.

'Oh,' said Mary. It didn't matter yet. Morphia dulled any feelings of despair at its disappearance. The worst imaginable eventuality – that of the morphia being gone – was the event for which it was the only cure.

What a perfect trap it was. And all her own work, too. Even Hilda could not have sprung it better. Now the air-raid sirens began. They soared up, and she was amazed at the thrill in her chest as they started their downward swoop.

Back at the theatre Mary taught the children all afternoon. She invented a game for Zachary: the letters on a page were enemy soldiers he'd captured, and he had to interrogate them individually. If he never gave the letters a chance to compare stories, they couldn't conspire to swirl and change and confound him. She had him use his thumbs to isolate each letter and sound it out. In this way he made quick progress at reading the commoner words, and she saw again his expression of mild disappointment when there turned out to be less sorcery in reading than he had imagined. They enjoyed themselves so much that she lost track of time in the windowless basement, and when the air raid began she was stuck underground with the children.

It was the worst night of bombing so far. The earth lurched and liquefied. London seemed to bleed. Mary watched, astonished, as red fluid streamed down the walls of the Lyceum's basement and puddled on the dance floor. It seemed impossible that anyone would survive, and when the all-clear sounded it was the most unlikely flourish. It was as if a conjurer had flipped a coin one thousand feet into the air and made it land on its edge.

She left the children to sleep, and went to see if the garret was still there. It was, though its windows were blown in. She didn't mind. What was important was that when she fished in the dustbin for the last discarded bottle of morphia, there were still a few drops in it. She took them, then ran water into the bottle, rinsed it around, and drank it. When she began to feel more domestic, she swept up. The window glass sounded lovely as it surrendered itself to the dustpan. This was what the best composers would write from now on: orchestral scores for broken glass and brooms. She threw the morphia bottle in with the shards. She smiled because this was so ingenious. By tossing it in with all the other spent glass, without ceremony, one would move on from the whole episode.

Withdrawal from morphia would be perfectly manageable. She placed it in that category of hardships over which the faint-hearted made a terrific fuss but which could actually be borne quite readily by a person who had been brought up to put on a sweater, rather than complain of the cold. The withdrawal would be more of a melancholy than a suffering – like taking the train home after a holiday in Devon.

The May morning blew in unimpeded. Even if there was smoke, it was a tonic after the stale air in the Lyceum basement. Mary couldn't find the makings of tea. She looked out over London but the city didn't seem likely to furnish her with tea either. It stood in stunned silence, with white ash upon it in a shroud. Flames crackled here and there in the ruins. The morning cast a directionless shade through the smoke.

She hoped she might find a café open somewhere. She put on an overcoat of Alistair's, rolling up the sleeves. In the Strand the ancient sundial of St Clement's made no shadow. Nothing was open. She wandered to the river. The waves were anxious and pale. *Tea*, she thought, half remembering why she had come. The word sounded in her head without finding meaning – *tea, eee* – unrequited, like the bleating of herds in thick fog.

Mary sat on the wall of the Embankment, her back to the disheartening river. In the silence of the morning no traffic moved in the streets. Women with ash faces and charcoal eyes swept neat piles of glass and mortar, neat heaps of splinters and flint, neat barrows for all that was lost. Now Mary began to feel uneasy. The music no longer seemed delightful. The hissing of the brooms carried a whisper: that life was cracked and gone. That any life left behind was not the good kind, which stubbornly built on rubble.

Aside from the brooms there was silence. London was a stopped gramophone with no hand to wind it. It smelled of cracked sewers and escaping town gas and charred wood, wet from fire hoses.

How hadn't she noticed this? The ageless mechanism of the city's renewal had faltered. Women only waited now, and swept. Rope cordons ringed unexploded ordnance. Chalk crosses marked the doors that the rescue crews had not yet opened. Mary thought of the mortuaries with their unclaimed dead lying in senseless paragraphs, line after line with an X against each body in the ledger. The point to which she had hurried at the start of the war was gone now, along with all fixed points. Now X marked only the unexploded, the unexamined, the unconsoled. One waited – with the shuffling rhythm of brooms – for some inexplicit resurrection.

It overwhelmed her. Every sense was scoured raw by the retreating grit of the morphia. The Thames was the issue of all the world's wounded hearts, the billions. The pale brown flow was unending. *Oh* – she half remembered – *I came out to find tea*. The Thames was before her, infinite and inexplicable. How brown it was. *Oh*, she thought, *I came to find tea*. The Thames was . . . *oh*.

Hilda answered the door in her nightdress. The left side of her face was bandaged and pinned, the eye covered. Blood showed through.

'What happened?' said Mary.

After a pause, Hilda said, 'I think it's my cheek.'

343

'Goodness, Hilda . . .'

'Oh Mary, your face! Do I look dreadful?'

Mary made herself smile. 'It always looks worse than it is.'

'Well come in, won't you?'

Hilda moved with care, her neck painfully straight. Mary followed her through to the little kitchen. She ran water into the kettle and put it on the stove. The pressure was feeble and the gas made a minuscule flame.

Mary said, 'I hope you like your tea slow.'

Hilda slumped at the kitchen table. Mary hugged her. 'What happened?'

'New driver. Stupid little thing. We dodged bombs all night and then she put us straight through a UXB cordon. The crash set the horrid thing off.'

Mary's stomach turned. 'Oh Hilda, I'm so sorry.'

'How bad do you suppose my face is? They wouldn't let me look.'

'Does it hurt?'

'Awfully. Like it's still being cut.'

'Do you have morphia?'

Hilda gave her a look. 'Are you asking for me, or for you?'

Mary closed her eyes for a moment. 'Both.'

'I'm trying not to use morphia, unless it gets desperate.'

'You're shaking enough to bring down the building.'

'But they need it for the soldiers. We really have been so thoughtless.'

Mary took her hand. 'But how else can one live through this?'

'As ordinary people do. We must learn to live, with no help, on our own.'

Mary said nothing. After a while Hilda said, 'Sorry.'

Mary shook her head. 'Do you have bandages, at least? You're bleeding through. Let me change them.'

Hilda swallowed. 'In the cupboard over the sink.'

Mary fetched bandages and antiseptic. She had Hilda sit back in her chair while she undid the pins.

'Does this hurt?'

'Only horribly.'

'I'll be as gentle as I can.'

The bandage came off, dragging clotted blood and saffron-coloured serum. Hilda yelped. 'Sorry,' said Mary. 'I'm so sorry.'

Hilda was shaking so hard that Mary couldn't hold her. 'Try to keep your hands off your face. Please, you mustn't touch it.'

Mary clasped Hilda's hands together and held them. Dabbing a clean bandage in the antiseptic, she cleaned the wounds. It was hard to do it properly – she was shaking almost as much as Hilda. When she was finished, she took a careful look at Hilda's face.

'Now you must tell me where the morphia is.'

Hilda whimpered. 'Is it as bad as that?'

'Tell me where it is, darling, and then I will bring the mirror.'

Hilda hesitated. The left side of her face was gore, the right was fear.

'Be brave,' said Mary.

Hilda closed her eyes and said, 'Handbag.'

'Good girl.' Mary took two syrettes and they used one each.

Hilda took a deep, shuddering breath. 'You were quite right, of course.'

'Cigarette?' said Mary, offering.

'Rather.'

Mary tuned the wireless. The Kentucky Minstrels played 'Love's Old Sweet Song'. The sharp midday light softened into afternoon.

'Fix your hair?' said Mary after a while.

No answer. Hilda's cigarette, forgotten, drooped a sadness of ash.

Mary fetched Hilda's hair brushes and got to work. Hilda was sleepy and loose, and she would keep coming towards the brush so that Mary had to nudge her head upright again. With the wireless they sat in warm silence while Mary worked until Hilda's pompadour was restored. There was no need now for sugar water to set it. No one's hair was clean.

'How is it looking?' said Hilda.

'Fine. I'll fetch the mirror, shall I?'

'Oh yes, do.'

When Mary brought the mirror, and set it on its stand on the little Formica-topped table, they held hands and looked together. There were three cuts, all beginning on the left cheekbone. The deepest ran back, towards the ear. The longest curved downwards, almost to the point of the jaw. The cruellest ran towards the eye, missing the eye itself but resuming on the other side of the socket to cut through the eyebrow and end in a nasty bifurcation on the forehead. The cuts had been stitched, but not very well. Mary imagined the scene at the hospital: the worst night of the bombing, the floors streaked with blood.

'You've done a much better job than last time,' said Hilda.

'Oh, thanks.'

'The trick is really to get a good tight curl from the start, isn't it? And then the rest looks after itself. Oh by the way, did I tell you that poor Huw was killed?'

'Oh dear,' said Mary, the morphia making it no more serious than a bun that had rolled off downhill.

'And Clive, at the same time.'

'What a shame,' said Mary, wondering if Hilda was dead too and then realising that of course she couldn't be, since here she was now. It was hard to keep up with who was and who wasn't.

Hilda watched herself in the mirror. Softly at first and then rising to a piercing scream, the kettle finally boiled.

'Oh,' said Mary, who had forgotten.

Outside the kitchen window, the city tended to evening. Mary looked out and remembered there was a war. She made tea in the brown glazed pot, with leaves that had been used before. *That's right*, thought Mary. *I came out for tea.*

Something had changed in the set of Hilda's shoulders. The stiffness had come back to her neck again. There was a brittle edge – in Hilda, and also in how Mary understood Hilda's mood. Mary found it hard to explain to herself. The morphia had levels, visible from below but not from above.

Without taking her eyes from the mirror, Hilda said, 'I expect I shall hate you, once this wears off.' Her own thought seemed to surprise her, and she followed it by saying, 'Oh.'

Mary poured them each a cup, in which neither of them had the slightest interest, and set to work to redo Hilda's bandages.

Hilda said, 'This wouldn't have happened if you'd been driving.'

'You know the ambulance was too much for me. I had to stop.'

'I only carried on because I thought you'd come back. You've taken it all from me now. Every man I ever liked, and now my looks.'

Mary fastened the bandage with a pin, though it spoiled the hairdo a bit. 'I've tried to make it up to you for Alistair. You know I've stopped writing to him.'

'Well now you might as well. He won't want me now. No one will.'

'You mustn't say that.'

'But you must see it.'

'Please,' said Mary, not really knowing what she asked for.

Hilda said nothing. The wireless crackled and jived.

Mary finished off the bandage and pinned it. 'It will heal, you know.'

'As if anything does.'

They snagged eyes in the mirror then, and Mary caught something bleaker than she could bear in Hilda's face. The whole world was shattered, the pieces falling away from each other. The morphia was hardening as it cooled. Soon it would shatter too.

Outside, it was looking like dusk. 'I should go,' said Mary. 'The raids . . .'

Hilda emptied her handbag on the table. Lipstick and keys clattered out. Ration book, hat pins, a dozen syrettes of morphia.

'What are you doing?'

'If you care about me at all,' said Hilda, 'take all these doses away.'

'Why?'

'Because you have to live with yourself.'

Mary tried to take Hilda's hand, but Hilda wouldn't let her. 'Please . . .'

'Just go. Before this one wears off completely and I tell you what I think of you.'

Mary cast down her eyes. 'I suppose you rather have.'

'Please go,' said Hilda. 'I don't think I can stand you any more.'

Mary looked at the syrettes on the table, knowing she must leave them where they were but also that it was impossible. She picked up six of the doses, turned, and left the flat without speaking. The last she saw of Hilda was her slim back and the armoured black curve of her hair.

# PART III

*RESTORATION*

# JULY, 1941

Alistair had Briggs wrap the painting in blankets and take it to the fort's central courtyard. He followed Briggs down. A month on, Alistair still found it hard to balance without his arm. One had never realised how quietly an arm just got on with the business of equilibrium – counterbalancing here, giving a little nudge there. One hadn't suspected that life was a circus trick, requiring exquisite balance and grace.

'All right, sir?'

'Quite, thank you, Briggs.'

'You're not though, are you, sir?'

'No,' said Alistair. 'Go and find the quartermaster, will you, and have him issue me with a new right arm, salutes for the execution of.'

'Gives you much pain, does it?'

'Think how much pain it will save me. I can never hit my thumb with a hammer again. It's you chaps I feel sorry for.'

'Thank you, sir. Help you with anything else, can I?'

'Left pocket of my jacket. Pill box. Take two out, would you, and find me a drink of water?'

The man fished out the pills and brought Alistair a canteen. The truth was that the pain was a bore, worse than it had been before the amputation. The phenacetin helped only a little, and in the meantime his evacuation number was taking forever to come up. He was still only eightieth in the queue, with a single mail flight leaving the island every day if enemy action permitted. Often one's number rose up the queue only to fall down again when some brass hat pulled strings for a favourite of theirs. And the mail plane carried only two casualties home at a time, sometimes one. It depended whether the island's garrison had found much to write home about.

'Anything else?' said Briggs.

The man was skin and bone, painful to look at. Alistair supposed he might not look any prettier himself. He nodded at the painting.

'I need us to take this back to a church near the Bingemma Gap. I want you to persuade the quartermaster, using all the arts at your disposal, to issue us with a truck and a ration of petrol. Note that I have spent three months restoring this painting. It is the best work I have ever done, and it means everything to me to get it back. I don't suppose you can help the QM not to be a bore about it?'

Briggs thought for a moment. 'I shall tell him it's maps for the anti-invasion plans, sir. If that doesn't work, I'll tell him I know what he does with His Majesty's Vaseline.'

'Thank you Briggs, you are wicked in a way that is thoroughly expeditious. Bring me the QM's chit and I'll sign it. Don't speak a word of this. In return, I shall issue orders for all bombs and shrapnel to miss you by at least two hundred feet from now until the day of our victory.'

'Thank you, sir. Very handy indeed.'

When Briggs brought the Bedford up and loaded the painting into the truck bed, Alistair got the cab door open and struggled into the passenger seat. Briggs drove them across the drawbridge, the fort's gates swung closed behind them, and they were out in the blue morning.

Alistair closed his eyes, too weary for chat. At least the nausea of the infection was gone. In its place he felt a sort of grief. He must have loved the arm, in a way. He didn't know what had become of it – whether it had been incinerated or buried. There had been no words to mark its demise. There was no ritual when one fell apart, society preferring to wait until one was lost entirely.

The surgeon had given Alistair a briefing that lacked no medical detail. *Disarticulation of the elbow with amputation through the joint, pronator and dermal flaps to be folded over, stitches to effect closure, the whole to be done under anaesthesia induced by intravenous barbiturate. Sound about right to you, old man? Any questions?*

None, Alistair had said, since the obvious one – how will I possibly bear it? – seemed unwelcome. The operation would have seemed less daunting if the surgeon had been able to acknowledge, even tangentially, that it was an awful thing to happen to a person. Perhaps there were simply certain procedures, such as wielding a scalpel or firing a 3.7-inch anti-aircraft piece, that were always going to affect the subject more than the operator.

The truck lurched and swayed on the ruined roads. Briggs whistled. In the intervals between the deepest potholes the motion was soothing.

'Isn't it something, sir?'

Alistair opened his eyes. Briggs was indicating a sweep of countryside beyond the walls of Valletta.

'Oh, you like it?' said Alistair. 'Me too.'

'The people can't do enough for you. It's like Liverpool, only with beaches.'

'Think you'll come back on holiday?'

'After the war I'll bring my wife here and we'll open a pub.'

'Good show. Germanic or traditional, do you think?'

'I think the English style might be more of a hit with the locals, sir – at least for the next thousand years or so.'

353

'You have it all worked out.'

'Don't you, sir?'

'Oh, I don't know what I'll do after the war. But that's officers for you, isn't it? Each pip on these epaulettes represents a point we're missing.'

'I'm glad you said it, sir. I couldn't possibly.'

They drove a little way further and then a 20-millimetre shell from an enemy 109 shattered the windshield, punched through Briggs' chest at the level of the sternum and continued through the driver's seat. Four more shells followed, two piercing the cab and two coming through the canvas canopy. On impact with the truck bed the shells disgorged hot phosphorus into the wood. Fragments pierced the fuel tanks and lit them up. Alistair was out of the cab immediately, the battle instinct delivering him to the roadside ditch. He watched the truck roll slowly off the road and take fire. Briggs made no sound as he burned. The truck went up with an orange roar and clouds of back diesel soot.

Alistair scanned the sky but saw no sign of the fighter. He scrambled from the ditch and went as close as he could, holding his left hand before his face to shield against the heat. The truck's canvas back was burned away, the metal hoops arching over a bed of embers. He went up to the cab, looked at Briggs, and wished he hadn't. Up and down the road for thirty yards he searched both ditches, hoping that by luck the painting might have been thrown clear.

The road snaked away in both directions over low hills, its yellow gravel losing its distinctness in the yellow grass of the verges and the yellow stones of the walls. He couldn't get his pipe lit.

After an hour a local man came by in a donkey cart. They said prayers for Briggs, and Alistair rode back on the tailgate of the cart. At the fort he reported the incident and stayed on his feet as far as the stone staircase, where he sank to his knees before he found the resources to climb up to his room. He only wanted to close his eyes for a few minutes – to collect himself – but the fort's bells began almost immediately.

The fresh attack came in, the bombers dragging their shadows across the cerulean sea. Alistair took the jar of Tom's jam from the arrow loop and put it safely on the floor. He sat on his cot and got out the phenacetin. He almost called for Briggs to make coffee.

After the raid, Simonson came up with an aerogramme. He flipped it onto Alistair's desk, took off his cap and threw that at Alistair.

'Damned if I know why anyone would write to you. I got two letters, by the way, in case you were wondering which of us was the more popular.'

Alistair stretched for the letter. Simonson slouched in Alistair's chair.

'You know what worries me about the enemy? It's the violence. It is almost as if he thinks he can solve every problem this way. I sometimes feel we shall have trouble rubbing along.'

'Please don't joke,' said Alistair. 'Briggs was killed this morning.'

Simonson said nothing.

'It was my fault,' said Alistair. 'I had him drive me, and we got lit up. I was taking my painting to the church to give it back.'

'No other cargo?'

'None.'

'No other purpose for the journey?'

'I'm afraid not. I falsified the requisition – said we were taking invasion maps to the outer forts.'

Simonson closed his eyes.

'Lost a Bedford, too. Burned. They'll bring you my report.'

'What about you?' said Simonson. 'Are you all right?'

Alistair stood, balancing with an effort. 'Briggs had a wife.'

'Children?'

'No.'

'Well, that's something.'

'I shall have to write to her,' said Alistair.

'Do so, and then move on and don't brood. You must be kind, of course. Write that he was killed by enemy action during a liaison operation.'

'Yes. But I'm telling you the truth, Douglas. As my senior officer.'

'And what would you have me do? Court-martial you?'

'You'll probably have to, won't you? When the lieutenant colonel sees my report, I shouldn't think you'll have much leeway.'

Simonson stood and paced. 'You're a first-class officer and in any other circumstance you would have been back in London long ago, invalided out. You are exhausted and you showed poor judgement, that's all.'

'It isn't as if I've stolen a tin of margarine. I've killed Briggs.'

'The enemy killed him, and you must live with it as you can. If I were you I might weigh it against all the ones I had saved.'

'Oh, but who keeps count?'

'God almighty keeps count, you fool, and when He loses count He checks with me, as your commanding officer.'

Alistair had been flipping the aerogramme over and over in his good hand, absent-mindedly, and now he noticed that it was from Hilda. The ghost of his hand moved by instinct to the flap of the envelope and pushed a thumb under it before it realised – with a feeling of absolute surprise that Alistair shared – that it did not exist. He overbalanced, his left arm having compensated for the movement of the phantom right. He fell sideways onto his cot. The aerogramme fluttered to the floor. While Alistair struggled to a sitting position, Simonson retrieved it. 'Here,' he said, 'let me.'

'Please don't,' said Alistair. 'I'm not in the mood to read it.'

Simonson ignored him and opened it.

'Do you mind?' said Alistair.

'Don't be so precious! We could use some diversion, don't you think?'

*Dear Alistair, I am sorry to write to you under difficult circumstances.*

*Oh,* thought Alistair: *Mary has been killed.* His blood began to stop.

*I find it my duty to tell you that Mary has been acting outrageously.*

Alistair went light with relief.

'Mary is your girl, yes?'

'I'm not sure.'

'No one is ever sure. And who is this Hilda?'

'Her friend. Here – give that back, won't you?'

Simonson held the letter beyond his reach. 'Your Mary seems to have got this Hilda's back up.'

*I will come to the point because it is something you have a right to understand, since I know that Mary has been writing to you.*

'But she hasn't, has she?'

'Not for months.'

'Or so you claim,' said Simonson.

'Just read, will you? Or give me the letter.'

Simonson snatched it away.

*I am sorry to say that she has given up her duty on the ambulances and become a slave to morphia. Out of*

*loyalty I would have said this was her business, but now
our friendship is finished and I feel a duty to you that I no
longer owe to Mary. Please know that I admired you from
the moment we held hands.*

'You dog!'
'But it isn't like that,' said Alistair.
'Says you. I think we must let Hilda tell us what it is like.'

*The worst of it is that Mary is consorting with negroes.
She spends days at the Lyceum and carries on as if it is the
most natural thing. I suppose the morphia is her only
counsel in the matter. Of course it is too awful for her
parents. Their name suffers – I need not tell you how
people talk.*

Simonson whistled. 'That really is the limit.'
'I'm sure it's nothing.'
'Of course it's not nothing. Damn it, man – you look as if the
devil has you by the scrote.'

*I wish you to know that I do not hope to reopen
anything between us. My circumstances have changed and
I would not be an attractive proposition to you in any
case. Rather, please know that I choose to close things
between us by discharging the duty of honesty that I owe
you for the kindness you once showed me.*

'How does she sign it?' said Alistair.
'*Sincerely.*'
'I see.'
'And of course you are thinking "bitterly", but you will see
that she is right, I'm afraid. If half of what she says is true then

you are best off without Mary, and this Hilda has done well to warn you.'

'I should like to know Mary's side of the story.'

'I shouldn't be curious. Niggers are niggers, there's no consortable kind. And morphia – my god. It's filthy stuff. It's for doctors and whores.'

Alistair flushed. 'Mary taught children who were killed. And there was a friend of mine she was practically engaged to, and he was killed too. One makes allowances.'

'One makes allowances, Alistair, for fatigue and pain and misjudgement. But morphia and blacks? The woman is utterly fallen.'

'Women fall differently, that's all. We die by the stopping of our hearts, they by the insistence of theirs.'

'Oh do give it up, Alistair. She's lost.'

'I don't believe that. Everything can be restored. If one won't believe that, how does one endure all this?'

'One doesn't have a choice, which makes the decision easier.'

Alistair sighed. 'Anyway, I like her. A medic once told me to find a nice girl and forget the war – and so long as I think of Mary, I can.'

'So you won't give her up?'

'Not even if I wanted to. Doctor's orders, you see.'

'Well, poor Hilda's letter seems to have backfired, wouldn't you say?'

'Oh, Hilda's not a bad egg, you know. She is funny, and rather pretty and . . . oh, in another life, a girl like that . . .'

'Yes, but it is rather a desperate letter.'

'It is rather a desperate war.'

Simonson put his arm around Alistair's shoulders and they looked out at the sea.

'What shall we do about you?' said Simonson.

'There's nothing to do. I'll accept what punishment the lieutenant colonel thinks fitting. In the meantime I'll arrange a burial detail for Briggs.'

'Briggs won't mind if you don't, you know. That's what's so admirable in the dead – they never ask one to do anything they wouldn't do themselves.'

'Still, I should feel bad if I didn't organise the service.'

'How would you like to fly to Gibraltar instead, and then take a boat on to England?'

'My number won't come up for weeks.'

'But there is an evacuation order and then there is a social order. I was at school with half of Med Command. I could have them bump you onto the next flight out.'

'I'm not wild about taking another man's place.'

'Then you'll be here forever, because other men are cheerfully taking yours. Come on, we can have you away before the lieutenant colonel gets to your report. You'd be doing us both a favour – he wouldn't enjoy disciplining you any more than I would.'

'It would only catch up with me in London instead.'

'It might not, you know. If this war has taught me anything, it's that no crack is too small for our procedures to fall through.'

'Listen to us. Can you imagine us thinking such a thing, a year ago?'

'Survival hadn't been invented, then. One can hardly blame us for not using something that didn't exist.'

Alistair smiled. 'How long this war has been.'

'I'll say. One hardly remembers how we lived before. Lightly – not worrying much.'

'Do you suppose we shall ever live that way again?'

'Oh, who knows? Given sufficient champagne and ether.'

'Maybe if we stay drunk to the end of our days, we shan't remember.'

'That will take systematic drinking. We'll need to stay drunk in cities, towns and villages. And in the hills and in the fields – how does it go . . .?'

'. . . and on the beaches and on the landing grounds.'

'Yes, exactly. We'll have to stay drunk in some inaccessible spots.'

'And with growing confidence and growing strength in the air, don't forget that.'

They leaned shoulders companionably and looked out to sea. Perhaps it was true, thought Alistair, that Septembers would come again. People would love the crisp cool of the mornings, and it would not remind them of the week war was declared. Perhaps there would be such a generation. Blackberries would ripen, carefree hands would pick them, and jam would be poured into pots to cool. And the jam would only taste of jam. People would not save jars of it like holy relics. They would eat it on toast, thinking nothing of it, hardly bothering to look at the label.

Alistair let the idea grow: that when the war's heat was spent, the last remaining pilots would ditch their last bombs into the sea and land their planes on cratered airfields that would slowly give way to brambles. That pilots would take off their jackets and ties, and pick fruit.

He understood that he was finished with the war. He could not stop seeing the enemy airman, choking on yellow dust. He could not stop smelling Briggs, burning. It was too much. He had given everything that had been asked of him: fighting when fighting could be done, retreating when retreat was wise, and holding fast when it was all that remained. He had not favoured himself, or measured his effort, or taken more than his share. He had done his best to help the men, and now all he wanted was to go home and see if he could help Mary. When set against the great corruption of the war, one's own small rot seemed, if not excusable, then at least unexceptional.

'You know that I joined up voluntarily?' said Alistair.

'Bully for you. So?'

'So, will you think less of me if I leave the same way?'

'I'd be furious if you didn't.'

Alistair hesitated. 'Then I believe I will take up your kind offer.'

'Very sensible. The food on this island really isn't as advertised.'

Alistair made to shake Simonson's hand. His right arm surprised him again by not being there, and the lurch almost toppled him. Simonson held him steady.

'I shall pick you up at midnight,' he said. 'Do try not to fall off the floor in the meantime.'


They left the fort on foot, under extravagant stars. A raid came in after they went, and they made their way southwest while the flashes sent their shadows flickering before them on the road. It was five miles to the airstrip at Luqa, and they said nothing on the way. Though they walked together they were distant. Alistair supposed this was the only possible end for a war: when men and women, who had thronged together to join it, made their way home alone.

On the airstrip the Wellington was already running its engines. An orderly hurried across the field to meet them. Alistair felt sick.

'Well,' said Simonson, 'goodbye.'

They shook hands, with the left.

'Goodbye,' said Alistair. 'I can't even begin to—'

'Then don't. Don't begin.'

'I shall miss you, Douglas.'

Simonson wiped his eyes. 'Yes, well, let's just hope the enemy does.'

They embraced. The orderly helped Alistair up the steps and into the belly of the aircraft. They put him in the companionway, forward of the rear gunner, on top of the mound of mail bags. They lent him a sheepskin coat and told him not to go anywhere the aeroplane wasn't going. The engine noise swelled, the airframe shuddered over the uneven runway, and Malta dropped away into the night.

Alistair lay back on the sacks. As soon as the aircraft door closed, the war was over. The hot, thyme-scented air of Malta was sealed outside. In here in the cold, with the smell of sacking and oil, London was already close. They would land at Gibraltar, and decant him into a convoy for England. There would be children and women and food, and clothes that weren't all brown. Alistair slept until fifty miles from Gibraltar, when the pilot put the aeroplanc down on the sea.

Alistair came awake in a frenzy of shouting and spray. The incredible deceleration shunted him and all the mail bags up to the navigator's position. Water rose through the rips in the canvas skin of the fuselage. They all got out through the astro hatch.

· The five of them who had survived the ditching clung to two small rubber rafts. On a warm and glassy sea, they watched as the engine fire that had downed them extinguished itself with a prolonged hissing. A plume of steam rose in the moonlight, and the aircraft sank by the nose. After that it was quiet.

It was a long, chilly pre-dawn, drifting on a flat silver sea beneath a flat silver sky, the weld between the two watertight and seamless. For hours nothing happened and there was nothing to be done. Then, as the sun rose huge and bloody, a breeze got up from the west. The wind blackened the wide red band that the rising sun made on the water.

There was not enough room for them all on the little yellow rafts so they took turns, two men at a time, to have fifteen minutes out of the water. Alistair was given half an hour, his missing arm making it more tiring to tread water.

He got his shoes off and let them sink. It occurred to him that this might be the furthest point offshore at which a British Army officer had ever lost a pair of the standard-issue brogues. They could add it to the crimes on his charge sheet.

By nine the sun began to contribute a little warmth, but the wind was increasing. For the men on the rafts the motion was sickening, and for the men in the water it was hard to hold on. For Alistair, with only one hand, it was a struggle. From time to time he choked on salt water when he couldn't keep his mouth high enough. The others helped him where they could, but they were tiring too.

In his next turn on one of the rafts, a gust came and he toppled into the water. This time he went several feet under, and if he managed to kick back up it was only because the navigator swam down to help. On the surface he gasped, and only just managed to cling on.

He tried not to imagine the odds now. As his strength failed, little things began to amuse him. He thought of the great chain of consequence that had brought him to here, at the end, bobbing in a vast empty sea with four strangers. After everything, a simple engine fire had brought them down. It had happened with no enemy help. Perhaps there was a tiny victory, in wartime, in not being killed by the war. He laughed, and could not understand why the others looked at him so soberly.

At noon the wind died down and the wave tops sparkled. They all took their clothes off and let them sink. Alistair drifted in and out of sleep. He would come to, again and again, with his arm hooked through the encircling rope of the raft. Each time he wondered where he was. When the sun set, he didn't notice. He woke up as usual, shivering violently, but this time it was dark. Lightning blazed above. Around him the men spoke in soft voices.

'When we get to Brighton Pier I think we should just tie up and have fish and chips, don't you?'

'A pint of beer with mine.'

'Tom?' said Alistair. 'Is that you?'

No one replied. The lightning gave them the coldest eyes, he thought.

Between the peals of thunder he heard voices shouting. He strained to hear. Men were calling his name, but he could not tell what they wanted. He called back but they didn't hear. Their voices resolved into individual shouts that he recognised. He thought it might be his men, needing orders.

'Hold on!' he shouted. 'Just hold on!'

They called louder, and he felt the terror in their voices. He shouted to the men to hold on to the rubber raft with him, if they could, and to pull themselves up out of the sea. He couldn't see them but he heard their voices, and he comforted them and begged them to pull themselves aboard.

There was no moon and there were no stars. He yelled out that he was sorry, and after shouting for a long time he noticed that Duggan was clinging to the raft beside him. Alistair was glad, since Duggan would help him now. Duggan would help his men too, and Alistair closed his eyes tight and drifted off.

In his sleep a deeper roar sounded beneath the surging of the waves. The roar increased in volume and broke into his dreams until he came awake with Duggan shaking his shoulder.

'Come on Huh . . . Heath, look luh . . . luh . . . lively!'

Alistair looked, through eyes blinded by salt. Searchlights were coming, over the sea. They came from the same place as the roaring. The lights turned the black sea silver. Spray gleamed, visible whenever the little rafts climbed to the top of a wave, then disappearing from sight in the troughs. The roaring sound grew enormous.

His men began calling to him again, and he watched their grey backs plunging all around, and he called out to them as they changed from men to dolphins and back to men again in the shifting beam of the searchlights. Nothing stayed still. The sea heaved, voices yelled all around him, and Alistair felt an unfathomable grief for his men, to be lost in such a lonely place, so far from the kindness of sight. He murmured the words he had used at so many burial details. *Comfort us again now after the time that thou hast plagued us: and for the years wherein we have suffered adversity.* Spray filled his mouth and he choked. He lost his grip on the raft and he was alone in the sea, naked and sinking.

Under the waves there were still the lights, cold and holy, cutting the surface above. Simonson was sinking with him. They watched the lights together. Mary was there too, and Tom, and the enemy airman, and Briggs, and all the men Alistair had lost. Everyone was restored. As the lights and the roaring noise faded, they all sank together through the warm and ageless sea.

Duggan took his hand. 'Come on Huh . . . Heath. Let's get you huh . . . home.'

# SEPTEMBER, 1941

It was six weeks since Mary had finally written to Alistair again, and a month since she had received a reply from his commanding officer, a Major Simonson. Alistair was missing in action over the sea, presumed killed. The major conveyed his regrets and wished her to know that Captain Heath had been a courageous officer who had spoken of her in the gladdest terms.

Morphia helped. It threw sorrow over the wall, into London where everyone's tragedies multiplied. One could leave it out there for the time being, in the city of stopped clocks, pending the day when.

Mary took to walking. Her leg was improving, though the limp returned if she went too far. She liked to rest on the steps of the National Gallery and look down on Trafalgar Square. It had been months now since the last serious air raid. The square was full of courting couples. How they laughed! As if the blackened world were new already. Every sight was agreeable to them, every diversion gay. Mary had not remembered that there was so much entertainment in watching pigeons squabble in the fountains.

She still thought that Alistair might have survived. The authorities might presume a man killed, but that was the authorities for you. To presume was always vulgar, while life was sometimes gracious. In the meantime she watched the lovers in Trafalgar Square, so as not to forget how it was done. In the bright square the couples clung, continually adjusting their grip.

Now their fingers entwined, now their arms encircled the other's waist – as if life was not at all on their side, as if it might place the tip of its lever into any distance they allowed to open up between them. Watching them, Mary supposed the odds were against her. It was lovers who trusted luck least.

She marvelled at the ease with which the young women moved. She watched them laugh and flush. They were all hope and helium, lovely to watch. Two years ago it had been her.

When it got too much, she walked down to the Embankment and sat on the granite wall. She ran her fingers over the iron dolphins that swam around the lamp posts. Beneath her the brown water churned with all that was lost, and today she had no more morphia. It had been harder and harder to come by, and now it was gone. As the last of it wore off, she realised that she had no idea how to get more.

One often saw bodies at low tide, on the mud spits by the pontoons of the half-finished Waterloo Bridge. Whether they were long dead and only now surrendered by the mud, or whether they were the newly despairing, Mary couldn't tell. Bodies didn't lie cleanly on the ground, the way they did in the cinema. In real life they appeared not to have been strewn, but sown. The dead were filthy, half buried, sometimes barely distinguishable from the mud or the rubble they lay in. One didn't understand, until one had seen a great many bodies, the unconscious effort that one must be making every minute simply to keep one's hands and face and clothes clean. The world's surfaces were so filthy that the living touched them only with the tips of their fingers and the soles of their shoes. How grubby it was to die, to give up making that effort.

Above the mud spits, the lovers never looked down at the dead. Mary watched them clinging tight, their gaze on the horizon. It was a rule that lovers looked east towards the sea. She made herself look that way too.

A boat was unloading onto the Embankment steps – for Parliament, the longshoremen were saying. A case broke open and there were oranges, the first she had seen in months. They rolled across the grey granite and bounced down the mud-brown steps. They splashed into the brown river and sank from sight and bobbed up again, so vivid that she gasped. Tears came to her eyes because she understood how drab the world had become, how grey-brown, how close to fading entirely. She put her hands to her mouth and watched the oranges floating upstream on the tide. They were so . . . so . . . *orange*.

A confusion crept up on her. The waves rose and fell. The oranges were lost from sight. Was Alistair dead, while life continued? It was too startling. She could not remember whether she had received the letter from Major Simonson, or whether she had dreamt it. One dreamt so many things. Morphia was utterly convincing, that was the trouble – while life carried on blithely as if it had no competition in the business of conviction, and in consequence seemed less real. And meanwhile here were all these lovers, legions of them, daring themselves across the scaffold of Waterloo Bridge for the thrill of it. Was it possible that she was not numbered among them? The confusion grew worse until it was terror. Mary covered her eyes.

A golden retriever put its paws on the wall where she sat, and licked her face. Mary looked up to find it nose to nose with her. The dog was hopelessly tight on life, as if it had taken forty-five times the recommended dose. It inclined its head, blinked at her, and trembled with unguarded joy.

'Hello you,' said Mary.

A man appeared – tall, uniformed, RAF. 'I'm so sorry.'

'Why, what have you done?' said Mary, producing by instinct a small grin.

The man laughed. 'The dog, silly. Oh look here, are you all right?'

'It's nothing. Please don't worry. I'll be fine in just a moment.'

'But you're upset. Can I do anything? Can I stand you a cup of tea?'

Mary stared up at the man. Of course he was ablaze with consolations. But when she opened her mouth to say something in her usual vein, Mary simply couldn't. His looks made her ache, his kindness left her miserable. She felt his negative image, the absence a man left.

'I'm sorry,' she said. 'Please, just go.'

'But you're upset,' he said again, his head inclined to the same angle the dog had adopted, as if all degrees of upset might very simply be cured – perhaps by throwing a stick.

How nice it would be to link arms with him – to go to a café. *If only I weren't dead*, she thought.

'I'm sorry,' she said again, and fled.

Her limp was worse, and pains shot through her body. Several times she became confused once more and had to stop. It had started raining without her noticing, and now the blacked-out night crept up on her too. Music rose from the dancing cellars. The swing beat boomed and a hot steam of exhaled smoke and body vapours rose through the air vents and grilles, as if the city were formed from the magma of such rhythms, cooled to a provisional solidity by the sober English rain.

She felt alternately distraught and euphoric. Sometimes she stumbled, and at other moments it seemed to her that she moved with no effort, gliding left and right to let the umbrellas pass, one-two-three, waltzing on the pavement while the cellars swung beneath her. London had always had this trick of living in two time signatures at once – the urgent and the always – each in earshot of the other.

She realised, with a cold sweat, that she probably ought not to go back to the garret alone and without the benefit of morphia. It was the same feeling she'd had by the river: not that she might do away with herself, but that she might not know the difference if she did.

It was queer the way things crept: the night, and these feelings. One was brought up to scorn the tendency to despair. But it seemed that the darkness knew this, and found a way to reach one nevertheless. It was patient and subtle, gauging the heart's output of light. Her confusion grew, the heart lucent and the mind lucifugous, the great clash of music in an endlessly accelerating rush: on and on and on.

She came to, the steam from the nightclubs rising around her, surprised to find her cigarette only half smoked. She felt a fear that was close to panic, and hurried off again. She didn't stop until she reached the Lyceum. The minstrel show was going on in the auditorium and she went in through the stage door from the alleyway.

In the basement it was quiet except for the laughter and applause from above. The children were sitting on the low raised stage where the band had played during the worst months of the bombing. The nightclub had gone back above ground now. Zachary was at an upright piano while Molly and Charles argued and Ruth, a new arrival, moped in a corner.

When Zachary saw her, he stopped playing. 'What happened?'

'I'm quite all right,' she said, giving the children a bright smile. 'I think I might just sit down for a moment.'

She woke hours later, wrapped in blankets. Her body was wet with sweat and wracked with unsparing pain. Molly was holding her hand. Zachary was kneeling beside her, laying a cloth on her forehead.

'You fainted,' Molly said.

She sat and looked around. Her joints were packed with hot glass.

'Oh . . .' she said. 'Oh . . .'

Zachary turned to Molly. 'Go off and play.'

Mary collected herself. 'Zachary,' she said in her teaching voice. 'Would you find whoever handles these things among the players, and fetch me just one dose of morphia?' Then she added, with perfect cunning: 'Say it isn't for me.'

But his face! As though she had asked him to murder someone. It was too bad that she had taught him geometry but no sense of proportion.

'Do go, won't you? There must be some around here.'

'I can't.'

'But it is perfectly simple. Just put your shoes on, and go!'

He wouldn't meet her eyes. 'Have a cigarette instead.'

He took them from her bag and lit one for each of them. She didn't try to forbid him and so, without fuss, he passed from her power. She almost laughed. He watched the glowing end as if it contained lost summers, then stubbed out the cigarette half smoked – not crushing it but rolling the point until it was extinguished, to keep for later. Mary smoked hers till it blistered her lip.

'Please?' she said.

He lifted a strand of hair from her eyes and tucked it behind her ear. His *no*, the louder for going unspoken. Her mood – which had cooled to a pale despair – now boiling over again into furious irritation.

'After everything I have done for you! You act the man but you are an ungrateful child. I might have known your sort would never come right.'

He shrugged.

'But you are incorrigible!' she said, unable to stop a miserable grin curling at the corners of her mouth. 'You are a lazy, unappreciative nigger who will not lift a finger to help.'

He said nothing.

She raised a warning hand. 'Don't look at me like that. I'm from a good family and if it weren't for you I'd be with them now. I wish I'd never come looking for you. I wish I'd never come to this nasty jiggaboo club.'

Zachary didn't change his expression at all. The light seemed to be dimming and she did not know if they had any candles. She did not know if candles were still available. She was not convinced that light was still manufactured.

Her anger was gone. She did not remember ever being angry. There was only a feeling of dread: of the darkness finding its way. And here was the boy. She shivered in her blankets as his eyes became Alistair's. She moaned and turned away.

Now, finally, the full gaze of the war came upon her. Her mind was fragments, each loud with its voices. She fought to keep one image of herself alive at the centre. She was rushing across town with a willing heart, to a point marked with an X. She was wearing her alpine sweater. Yes, that was it. But war had been declared, and it was thrilling and then it was terrible. The heaviest thing about life was that it began with a lightness of heart.

'You mustn't have any more morphia,' said Zachary.

Her eyes snapped open and she stared at him, wondering how it was possible that he was still here, unchanged, when she had gripped the blankets and shut her eyes tight through the terror of eternity.

'What?' she whispered.

'No more.'

'Just a little, don't you see? Just to take the edge off.'

'No.'

'Please . . .'

'No.'

'You're cruel because you don't yet understand,' she said, and closed her eyes.

She slept, and when she woke her mind was clear. Alistair had arrived. She sat up, her heart soaring. He was just as she had last seen him, on the platform at Waterloo. He cupped her face in his hands and she let herself be kissed. Orange sparks floated on the night. The cold air of the basement made her shiver, and she held him for his warmth. Oh, the slow dances they used to play, back when needles could still be found for the gramophones. His eyes were electric bulbs, and as she stared back into them she realised that she was awake, and sitting alone.

'Oh . . .' she whispered, disintegrating again.

When she awoke she was in her blankets, shaking monotonously in the dim light of the bulbs. Zachary was at her side.

'Thank you for coming back. I'm so very sorry for what I said.'

Zachary produced something from his pocket. 'I didn't have the money. The manager says you can owe him.'

Just looking at the syrette of morphia flooded her with relief. She had forgotten how to be alive, that was all, and now she remembered the trick of it. She stretched out her hand. 'Thank you.'

Zachary held out the syrette, balled in his fist. She watched his hand with rapt attention, the smooth brown skin and pink quicks. 'Please . . .'

'Remember how you always said no, when I asked for a cigarette?'

'Don't be like that. It wouldn't have been appropriate.'

'This isn't appropriate for you.'

She made herself smile. 'No, darling. It's only medicine. Like aspirin.'

'Aspirin didn't call me a nigger.'

She looked from his hand to his face. 'Please . . .'

'You can have it if you want. But if you do, then don't come back here. It's not like we can't live without you.'

'It's not *as if*.'

'It's not as if we can't live without you telling us it's *as if*.'

374

He held his hand out, his grip seeming to loosen. She gasped. She needed the syrette more than she had ever needed anything.

'Do you want it?' said Zachary.

'No, thank you,' said Mary, and tried to smile, and burst into tears.

All through that day and night Zachary watched as she lay between wakefulness and sleep. Once she sat up and told Poppy Brown not to eat the blackboard chalk. She shouted at Kenneth Cox for never sitting still. Around noon she spoke in French, then fell asleep. Later there was a long, muttered conversation. She whispered that she was sorry, over and over. Zachary left her bedside and went over to see what was the matter with the other children. Ruth was tearful, and Charles and Molly weren't helping. Zachary got her to come and sit with Mary. He warmed water on a Primus stove and had Ruth wash Mary's face and hands while she lay, half conscious. Ruth still wept.

'What's wrong?' said Zachary. 'Is it because the others pick on you?'

She shook her head, her plaits flailing.

'Are you hungry?'

She shook her head again. He took her hand but she pushed him away. A roar of laughter came from the theatre overhead. It must be the matinée already. He squeezed his temples to push away the exhaustion. He lit a cigarette and wished he knew what to say. He wished an older child would come to the Lyceum, so he wouldn't have to be in charge. He wished someone would come who didn't need looking after.

'You like sweets?' he said. 'I could get you some.'

Ruth shrugged and said nothing.

'What about that doll you had? You want me to fetch your dolly?'

Ruth only crumpled again. Zachary supposed he ought to know what to say, but he could find no comfort in himself to transmit to her. It was just as the players said: it was a war, and they were negroes, and even their side wasn't on their side. All they had was themselves: nineteen minstrels, nine musicians and four stray children, besieged in a city besieged. If he'd still had his father he might have felt strong about it – proud, even. The players were kind to him, but however close they drew, he felt that he didn't belong.

His father had wanted more for him than minstrelsy, and now that his father was gone he felt no ties to it. Life held him in this place, that was all, like a scream trapped in a jar. There wasn't even a grave he could visit, a fixed place to start his own life from. While his father was lost, he was lost with him. All he could do was hug Ruth and tell her everything would be all right. It was the same thing the government posters were claiming.

When he went back to Mary, she was awake.

'Zachary . . . can you get me something?'

His chest went tight. He knew she was going to want morphia.

'Sorry,' she whispered. 'I'm so hungry.'

He brought her coffee, bread and margarine. He played piano for her. In the evening the fever came again and she talked for hours to a man named Alistair. She argued with her mother, sometimes angrily, sometimes tearful and pleading. When her fever finally broke, she slept. He brought the other children over, and they took turns to watch her through the night.

When morning came and Mary still slept peacefully, Zachary smoothed her hair on the pillow. He stood and stretched away the night's cramps. Then he ate all the biscuits he could find, played some piano, injected the syrette of morphia into his shoulder out of pure curiosity, and went up from the basement into the Strand. He laughed out loud while the great rebuildable city glowed in the sunrise, and the old London stones in the rubble piles breathed in and out with a slow rhythm that seemed, without question, to swing.

# DECEMBER, 1941

At dawn rain beat on the garret roof and leaked here and there in drips. Mary reached out a hand and tasted it. Now that the morphia was long gone from her system, the clarity of sensation was extraordinary. Things no longer shifted and warped. Until now she had never understood how much one could love this dignified stillness of still things.

There had been no major raids since May. It might all start again, of course – Mary found that she knew less of the war the longer it went on. Certainly it was still growing, drawing countries in, and when it reached sufficient size perhaps it would come back for London. The newspapers had stopped printing situation maps, which suggested that the picture was dispiriting. She kept her anxieties to those she could do something about. Zachary had still to learn his times tables beyond six. Charles must be encouraged not to use the geometry compass as a weapon. The war expanded and the world shrank.

Memory retreated to its old boundaries and renounced its incursions into sight. Emotions submitted to the authority she had learned in childhood to exercise over them. Pleasant sensations she allowed their effervescence, dark thoughts she quarantined. Rain drove against the skylights and streamed down the panes in sheets. It was a steady and confident rain from a vast and sombre sky that seemed installed for the duration.

A knock came in the early morning: the landlady, with the post. Mary thanked her and went back to bed to slit the envelopes open. The first was a begging letter from her old finishing school, inviting her to help a fresh batch of girls to – well, to finish, she supposed. The second was an aerogramme from Major Simonson.

*Dear Miss North,*

*I am sorry to write again. I assume the Army has told you that Alistair is safe but I imagine it has exercised discretion in communicating the details.*

Mary put the letter down on the blanket and stared at it. It was too early in the morning to cry, the day having not yet delivered enough venom to be expelled. She leaned back on the headboard and closed her eyes tight. Her fingers scratched at the sheets. It was as if her body wanted to burrow.

When it was finished, she sat for a while in a daze.

*I do not know how things stand between you and I do not wish to pry, but I am informed that Alistair is forbidden from sending or receiving letters. I do not know if you have been made aware of this and I write to apprise you.*

*Following the loss of his arm, Alistair was to be invalided home but there were perhaps irregularities in the repatriation list. These came to light after Alistair reached Gibraltar, where he was taken by the Navy, having been recovered when his aircraft ditched.*

*The upshot is that Alistair has been sentenced to twelve months' imprisonment for absence without leave. He is to serve this time in Gibraltar. I have tried to get the sentence set aside, emphasising Alistair's selfless record and his*

*wound. My efforts have been unsuccessful, and I pray you*
*will both forgive me. Though Alistair was under my*
*command, it is as his friend that I write.*

Mary read it through again. Her hands clasped and unclasped. The world increased. It had been so long since she had numbered herself among the fortunate that she had lost all immunity to the shock of it. Joy, at first, was foreign and unsettling.

After the first hour she began to wonder what one might do. It wasn't possible to travel to Gibraltar as a civilian. Nor, apparently, could she write to Alistair there. She thought it through, but nothing came. In the end, reluctantly – but it hardly dragged at her at all, she was so elated – she supposed she ought to talk to her mother.

She put on her mac and limped through the sleet to untouched Pimlico. At her parents' house on Warwick Square the white stucco façade, the classical portico and the first-floor balcony with its sculpted box bushes all spoke of exemption from the things she had lived through. She climbed the six steps to the black door with its leonine knocker but as she lifted her hand, the door swung open. One couldn't know what mechanism of housemaids and semaphore detected one's approach.

'Good morning, Miss Mary.'

She stepped inside as if it were nothing. 'Hello, Palmer. Are you well?'

Palmer afforded the minutest inflection of an eyebrow, sufficient to relegate his wellbeing to the category of things without import. Mary found that her raincoat was already across his arm.

'We expect Madam home at eleven. Shall you wait for her by the fire in the morning room?'

'Oh yes, very good. Thank you.'

The slightest nod. Palmer was so invariant that Mary herself was suddenly unsure whether she had been away for seven months or seven hours. In the morning room she sat on the green settee. On the pewter tray Palmer brought cocoa with golden amaretti and a hint of apology.

'Unless Miss might prefer sherry?'

'Even for a monster like me, it's a little early.'

His face didn't change. 'I shall make a note.'

Her mother came home, spilling over with cut flowers and instructions for their display. Her greying hair was dragged back in a bun. When Mary showed herself in the hallway, a single strand escaped to lift in the winter draught.

'Hello,' said Mary.

'Darling,' said her mother, the production of the word being necessary according to Newton's third law.

'I hope it isn't a bad time,' said Mary.

Her mother let her coat be taken. 'You do understand that you cannot make a scene. Your father is *this close* to being called up to Cabinet – he may return at any time, and perhaps with a visitor. We are being careful not to display the wrong sort of periodicals, let alone . . . well, there is no need to elaborate. Oh, you've been crying.'

'No, but . . .' she said in a small voice, and then tears welled up and her mother's arms were around her. 'I am so tired, Mummy.'

'Darling, of course you are . . . oh, how we have missed you.'

Behind her mother the front door closed with a tidy click of the latch. The war was muted. One felt the relief of the heart as it fell in with the old, shuffling rhythms of the maids. Everything would be well again. She would have Alistair – it still seemed only half real. And so what if he had lost an arm? It was easily done in these times. The brooms swished as they swept the quiet chambers of the house. The dusters banged between balusters.

In the hall a Christmas tree, decked with Venetian glass, stood in its great brass bowl.

Mary followed her mother through to the drawing room, where Palmer brought tea in blue china. He served Mary's according to her most recent preference: without milk but with three sugars, the way she had taken it when the morphia had sweetened her tooth.

'Thank you, Palmer, but if it isn't too much trouble I should like my tea the old way.' She spoke deliberately, making sure her mother understood.

'Very good,' said Palmer, in the neutral tone he used whether one needed him to arrange a taxi cab or a resurrection. He produced for her a tea without sugar, and withdrew to his own measured bounds.

'Mummy,' said Mary, 'I am so sorry for everything.'

'Oh, shh. No one could expect perfection from you, after so much loss. You'll find your room just as you left it.'

'Thank you – but I'm not moving back.'

'No?' said her mother with the mildest incredulity, as if Mary had declined a macaroon. 'But it would be so nice to have you home for Christmas.'

'The thing is, I need to ask you for something.'

'I see. You are yourself again, at least.'

'I haven't touched morphia in months.'

'I'm glad. It wasn't you at all. Shall we just forget it? You haven't done irreparable damage to your father, provided you and I now embark on a comprehensive tour of the salons. When they see you like this again, the rumours will seem far-fetched. You'll find that I have rather talked up your wound sustained in the line of duty – I hope you don't mind – since it clothed your more naked indiscretions.'

'I'm sorry for the scene at the Ritz.'

'So am I. The Ritz, with a brace of niggers? If you had to send me a message, it might have hurt less to tie it to a stick and beat me with it.'

'Must you call them "niggers"? They've done nothing to you.'

'Except to hook my daughter on morphia.'

'The reverse, Mummy. One of them got me off the stuff.'

Her mother blinked. 'But then why? Of all the people a girl might consort with.'

'I am not consorting. I'm teaching.'

'Well it kills me that you are doing so on my shilling. At least their parents ought to pay you a wage. Or do they even have parents? One hears that the fathers in particular have no more domestic feeling than do fishes.'

'I don't feel I give the children any more than they give me, but I will stop drawing the allowance if it pleases you.'

'So what do you want from me, if it is neither money, nor sane opinion, nor my simple invitation to make your poor father happy?'

Mary took her mother's hand. 'The man I told you I was keen on. Alistair. I love him.'

Her mother stared for a moment. 'I suppose you'll tell me his people are fascists, or some such thing? You don't ever make it easy.'

'Oh, he's from a good family. Before the war he was a conservator at the Tate.'

Mary felt her mother's hand relax. 'When you say a good family . . .?'

'We don't know them, if that's what you mean. But you must imagine there are families, unknown in our circle, that nevertheless orbit the same sun and do so without eclipse or indiscretion.'

'I suppose they are socialists, then.'

'Do you? One day you must teach me how you can tell.'

Her mother took her hand back. 'So why do I sense a caveat?'

'Alistair lost an arm in Malta, and—'

'Oh for heaven's sake, so what? He can always grow a new one.'

Mary smiled. 'I do love you, Mother. That's just what I thought.'

'You are a dear girl. If you weren't impossible I shouldn't love you half so much. You're what I might have been if I'd ever had the courage to tell my mother to mind her own business.'

'And you're what I might hope to be, if I could put family before myself. I know I've been selfish. I shan't make any more scenes at the Ritz, but neither can I be Mrs Henry Hunter-Hall, however much it would help.'

Her mother sighed. 'I am sure some middle ground can be found. And I know you will give me your indulgent smile when I say this, but you will find that it is different in any case, once you are married. Our own passions become muted – well, perhaps that isn't the best word – our passions become lighter, and seem to weigh on us with less urgency. Do you imagine that I was not idealistic at your age? I was for women's votes, you know. I chained myself to things.'

'Why did you stop?'

'I suppose you will say I chained myself to your father.'

'You are happy though, aren't you?'

'Happy? Oh goodness, is that even a word in wartime?'

'But the war hardly touches you.'

'I expect you think nothing does.'

Her mother took a cigarette from Mary's pack and lit it with hands that shook a little.

'Mother . . .'

'I am not to be pitied. I still believe it our duty to leave the world improved. Do you suppose you will marry this Alistair of yours?'

'I don't know. He is far away and we haven't spoken of it. But yes, I hope so.'

'You must choose a husband carefully, you see, because his ideals must stand in for yours. Ideals will become ambitions, and ambitions need allies, and allies require soirées and galas and seating plans.'

'You don't think it will be different between men and women, after this war? You don't feel we are on the cusp of something?'

'We should make a tapestry of the cusps we've been on.'

Mary smiled. 'I'm glad you're all right.'

'You are trying to distract me, I know. What did you come to ask for?'

'It's Alistair, Mummy. He's being detained, in Gibraltar.'

'Well there is a war on.'

'Detained by the authories, I mean. In a . . . well, you know. In a building.'

'But why?'

Mary kept her voice even. 'They say he went absent without leave. He is sentenced to twelve months.'

Her mother put her teacup down with a click. 'Palmer? Would you bring us a little brandy?'

Back the pewter tray came, with glasses and decanters. Palmer set it down on the occasional table and let a measure of syrup into each of two glasses. He scalped an orange and placed a shaving of peel in each glass. These he compressed with a pestle sufficiently to release their oils but not to macerate them. He added a dash of bitters and a measure of brandy to each glass, finishing with ice.

Mary sipped her drink. Her mother drained her own glass and put it down. 'You are quite determined not to make this life agreeable for any of us.'

'I'm sorry. I truly am. However it looks, I hope you know that

I do not go out into the world hunting for disgrace to bring home to you.'

'A deserter, though? I might have preferred a nigger after all.'

Mary gathered herself. 'Absence is hardly desertion. Father isn't here from one moon to the next, and yet we keep his books dusted.'

'Don't.'

'Sorry,' said Mary.

Her mother was silent for a moment. 'So what is the situation?'

'I think France shook him up. It was just before we met. He had saved goodness knows how many of his men's lives, but he was awfully rattled by it all. I know he did his best in Malta. And I can't imagine losing an arm, can you?'

Her mother said nothing.

Mary flushed. 'But how they can judge a man for the one time he comes up short?'

'What would you have me say? When Abel's blood cried out to the lord, one supposes it was to complain of being spilled. Rather than to recall the glad years of fraternity.'

'But Alistair hasn't murdered anyone. I think perhaps all he did was to leave a little soon.'

'It is a war, not a mixer. One cannot quit if it gets dreary.'

'I know, Mummy, but—'

'Your father did not *leave a little soon* at Ypres or Pozières. If he had, I should never have married him.'

'But surely he would understand Alistair's case better than anyone?'

'Your father's understanding of absence without leave might not extend beyond the range at which the absentee ought to be shot.'

'But we have moved on since those days. Do we still have no mechanism for forgiveness?'

'What would you have me say?'

'Won't you ask Father to use his influence? A letter to the War Office would carry tremendous weight. He need only state Alistair's character.'

'This was why you came to see me? To get your man off the hook?'

Mary made herself small and said nothing.

'Do you understand what it would cost me, from my own capital of influence with your father? I have my own causes, which you might have noticed if you were the noticing type. And those in addition to the drain it makes on my stock each time I have to defend you. Do you even guess at how loyally I have pleaded your corner before him? And now you would drive me deeper into his debt, and subordinate my own hopes to yours.'

'I'm sorry. I wouldn't ask if I didn't have to.'

'If I do this for you, the other nonsense must end. Not one drop of morphia, ever again.'

'Of course. I promise.'

'And you will go to the War Office and ask for another assignment. If they send you back to the ambulances, you will go gladly. If they send you to the factories, you will don the overalls without a whimper. I will have this family's name speak of duty again.'

'All right.'

'And you will come back to live with us, until you are married. You will join me with good grace at the lectures and the coffee mornings. I shall not make unreasonable demands on your time, but I will expect you to make peace with society. At least make peace to the extent that your wedding, when it does come, will feature on the 'society' page and not on the 'gossip'.'

Mary hung her head. 'Fine.'

'And you must stop carrying on with the negroes. I shall do you the favour of calling them negroes, and you will reciprocate by cutting ties. You will neither frequent their entertainments, nor school their numberless brood.'

'But Mother—'

'Because it is not even a kindness that you do for them, pretending they can be helped. They have their world and we have ours, and there can be no more traffic between the two than there is between heaven and earth.'

'And so we prescribe the countryside for our children and the bombing for theirs? How can you ask me to make peace with a society that makes this kind of war?'

Mary's mother sat down beside her. 'Please. I was the same at your age.'

'Honest, you mean to say?'

'I shan't rise to that. The young see the world that they wish for. The old see the world as it is. You must tell me which you think the more honest.'

'Fine,' said Mary, 'I will do everything else you ask, since the cost is to me alone. But I won't stop teaching those children.'

'But why, dear?'

'Because everyone insists that I must stop.'

'And it doesn't occur to you that perhaps everyone is right?'

'They are blind to what's wrong. I see the wealthy untouched by this war and the poor bombed out by it, and yet rich and poor alike make not a murmur. I see negro children cowering in basements while white children sojourn in the country, and yet both camps beg me not to rock the boat. Look at us, won't you? We are a nation of glorious cowards, ready to battle any evil but our own.'

Her mother took her hand. 'Enough. If we must negotiate then please remember I have played this game longer than you. You ask me to try for Alistair's release, and I have set out my conditions. Attach your own if you must, but please don't pretend you would choose a principle over a husband. What about

Alistair's happiness, festering there in prison? Is that yours to weigh against your ideals?'

'You might sentence him to a year in his own company, Mother. I shan't sentence him to fifty with a hypocrite.'

'Please don't punish us like this. Whatever else it is that we have done to you, do be brave enough to spit it out. But please don't pretend you would choose niggers over family.'

'They are only children, Mummy, and they have helped me without attaching conditions.'

They watched each other for a moment.

'Must we fight the whole thing out again?' said her mother. 'Perhaps we can leave any decision for a while, until we have both had a chance to settle down. Only do come home for Christmas, darling. Do let us be a family again.'

Mary used her mother's own trick of smiling when there was nothing else to be done.

Her mother stood. 'Well, you must consider it. I shall go out, I think, and collect myself a little. I shall return for supper at six, and you must let Palmer know if we should expect you. If you are here when I get home, then I shall assume my conditions are acceptable. If you are gone, then it's best we don't see each other for a while.'

'Mother . . .' said Mary.

'Six o'clock. Please don't be late – I don't think I could bear it.'

'I am so sorry, Mummy.'

Mary watched her mother make herself smile. And so now they both smiled, and kissed on both cheeks with precision, *here*, and *here* – since after all the heart was not the foundation of manners and must not by its collapse undermine them.

After her mother left, Mary sat with her elbows on the table. She lit a cigarette, blew the smoke through her nose, and the old house exhaled with her. Now that her mother was gone, the maids could sing as they made the beds upstairs. From the kitchen, pans clattered and Cook found laughter in something.

After a while Mary felt a presence in the room, an inflection of the light. 'Palmer?'

'Miss Mary?'

'Might you bring me another small brandy? On its own, no fuss?'

'Very good.'

'And would you have a cab pick me up? And let my mother know, when she's back, that I'm afraid I can't make it for supper.'

There was an unaccustomed pause.

'My apologies, Miss Mary, but I should like to make sure that I have the message correct. I'm to tell Madam that you won't be joining her?'

'Thank you, Palmer, for always getting the message.'

A pause. A breath. And then, with no expression, 'Very good.'

When Palmer returned with brandy, he carried it on the heavy silver tray. Mary glanced up. 'Oh, is my father back from the House?'

'Not until this evening, madam.'

'Then . . .?'

His impartial eyes. 'Forgive me, Miss North.'

'Oh, Palmer . . .'

'Will there be anything else?'

'No, thank you. That will be all.'

'Very good.'

Half an hour later, when the door clicked shut behind her, Mary found Hilda in the back of the taxi that waited on the kerb.

'What are you doing here?'

Hilda's scars were puckered and raw, her confusion twisting them still further. 'I thought you had asked for me?'

'I did nothing of the sort.'

'Oh . . . but on the telephone Palmer said I was needed very urgently.'

Mary softened. 'And you came for my sake?'

'I have missed you dreadfully.'

Mary hesitated only for a moment. 'You had better get out then, hadn't you? We can hardly go for a stroll with you sitting in there.'

Mary paid off the taxi driver, linked arms with Hilda and they walked through the rain. They spoke of small things at first, since it was best, when reattaching threads, to begin with the easiest knots.

Later, Mary said, 'Alistair's alive.'

Hilda put her hands to her mouth.

'I love him,' said Mary. 'Do you hate me?'

'No. I'm glad for you.'

'I've missed you too, you know.'

Hilda took her hands. 'Come and stay at the flat for the weekend, won't you? There's a sofa bed, the wireless, and as much tap water as you can drink. Unless you need to be at the Lyceum?'

'Maybe my taking a weekend off would do everyone good. You and I have met people on fire who made less fuss than children being forced to learn reading.'

'You're a dreadful teacher anyway.'

'Thanks. And you're a useless nurse.'

'So, you'll come to stay?'

'Thanks, I should love to.'

They walked east and north towards Hilda's flat, the undamaged streets giving way to the general destruction. The sleet came harder now. As they approached Regent's Canal only a thin path had been cleared between the mounds of rubble.

'Don't mind the mess,' said Mary. 'I shall build cottages along here for you – little thatched things such as one sees in Lowestoft

– and I shall arrange for a handsome and unattached man to be installed in every one.'

'Tall?'

'You'll need a ladder to kiss them. One of those two-step efforts you get in libraries.'

'Dark?'

'I shall organise them by street for you. Dark, blond, funny, rich. If you want more than one quality, you just knock near an intersection.'

'Uniform?'

'Any you like. Soldier, sailor, engine driver. Every house will have a dressing-up box.'

'I believe I will like your new London very much.'

'Then you shall be mayor of it,' said Mary, sweeping an arm in a magnanimous arc.

'I suppose it should be me. You'll be too busy with Alistair.'

Mary saw the twitch in her friend's smile. 'I'm sorry, Hilda.'

'Don't be. You'll be married, I suppose?'

'He's in prison, in Gibraltar.'

Hilda stopped. 'What for?'

'He left Malta before he should have.'

Hilda looked miserable. 'I sent him a letter, you know. I told him you were gone to the dogs.'

Mary considered it. 'I can't say you were wrong.'

'Yes, but it wasn't right. It's no wonder I'm alone.'

'Stop it. You'll meet someone soon.'

'But how? There aren't any parties any more. Either that or there are parties everywhere, and no one tells me.'

'Yes, I should think it's that. You've always struck me as a charmless and unpopular girl.'

'But it's these scars,' said Hilda. 'They're the only known anti-dote to me.'

'Then we'll find you a man with scars that match.'

Hilda smiled.

'See?' said Mary. 'You're pretty when you do that.'

'I don't suppose I have done it much, since we fought.'

'Me neither. From now on let's remember the trick of not fighting, shall we? Why do you suppose we ever forgot?'

Hilda sniffed, turned her face up to the grey sky, and caught sleet with her tongue as it fell.

'Hard to tell,' she said. 'Perhaps it's something they put in the bombs.'

# DECEMBER, 1941

**M**ary put on her mackintosh and sou'wester hat, stubbed her cigarette and went out into the morning. The cold weather had brought her limp back and she nursed it through Regent's Park, skirting the deserted zoo. By the lake, its surface quick with rain, the rowing boats were drawn up under canvas. The park wardens waited under the bandstand for the weather to pass. They smoked pipes, their clothes rolled and pinned where limbs were missing. The bare oaks with their ageless trunks held up the woebegone sky.

She carried on through Marylebone and Fitzrovia, which had never seen the worst of the bombing. Only a few gaps spoiled the Georgian terraces, and the rubble had been carted away. Where there were craters the rain had flooded them, so that the spaces between the houses mirrored the sky and made from each loss if not beauty, then at least a quiet neighbour.

Mary walked down to the Embankment and looked out over the broad sweep of the river from Parliament to Blackfriars. She no longer lingered here but it was not possible to lose the lover's habit of looking downstream, to the sea. She tightened her mackintosh at the throat and hurried on to the Lyceum.

This was the best part of the day, looking forward to teaching her class. There were nine coloured children living in the basement now. It had taken the war to reveal London's heart, centrifugal for white children and gravitational for negroes. When it was all over, she supposed, Miss Vine would bring her school back, and all her teachers would carry on quite deliberately as if nothing had happened. They would even make a virtue of it, in makeshift classrooms, thinking themselves the stoics. They would have no idea at all that life had soldiered on without them.

In the auditorium the minstrels were taking a break from rehearsal. They sprawled around the stage on boxes and folded drapes, smoking.

'Good morning, Miss North,' Bones called out.

Mary stopped at the foot of the stage. 'Good morning, Mr Bones. How goes the minstrelsy trade?'

'In its usual way – thank you for asking – which is to say, proportionate with your people's kind purchase of tickets. How goes teaching?'

'In its customary manner, thank you, with two steps forward and one point five back, or half a step forward when expressed in net terms.'

He came to the front of the stage. 'A minute of your time, Miss North? Which I believe is one sixtieth of an hour when expressed as a fraction?'

They climbed up to a high row in the auditorium and sat on the fold-down seats, leaving an empty one between them.

'This thing you're doing for our children,' he said. 'So kind. Though there's been some talk that it might be better if you didn't come every day.'

She smiled. 'Children will say that, won't they? But the truth is, letters and arithmetic come best through daily practice. I try to make it fun, but there's no substitute for the weekday grind.'

Bones looked at his hands. 'The talk that you might come less often. It isn't from the children.'

'Oh. I see.'

'It isn't that we're not grateful. What you've done for them is terrific. I see kids who couldn't read who are writing now. I see kids who wouldn't talk, and suddenly they won't quit nagging me for money.'

'Well, then . . .'

'It's just that these things don't always end well. See what I'm saying?'

'I'm not sure I do. Surely it doesn't harm them to learn? Quite the reverse: when their peers come back from the countryside, they'll need to hold their own.'

'We're not saying they shouldn't be learning. We're maybe asking, respectfully, if you're the best one to teach them.'

Down on the stage the minstrels were rehearsing a slapstick piece, with a long plank and all its attendant physics. Mary had never realised how many men must be hit in the face before such a thing became funny.

'The fact is,' said Bones, 'we've got our thing going on here, and people leave us alone. We have our trade, and this theatre to work in, and a home of sorts for the children who've lost their people. While it's just us, no one pays us mind. But if people thought we were mixing, they'd pay us more attention. Which for us is like daylight for vampires, you see what I'm saying? There's an understanding between life and the coloured entertainer. Your people give us a corner of the night, and we don't darken your day.'

'But I hardly come and go with a fanfare. I use the stage door and I teach in the basement.'

'You may come discreetly into our place, Miss North, but I wonder how carefully you leave yours.'

'I don't brag about what I'm doing, if that's what you mean.'

'Do your friends know? Do your mother and father?'

'Yes, but—'

'And do they wholeheartedly approve?'

'No, but that hardly—'

'And so they talk to people, and people talk. Are we licensed for the number of shows we do? Are we allowed to sell drink? Did any of those orphaned children come with adoption papers and ration cards? And yet we are afforded the comfort of our small community because it would take wearisome paperwork to scatter us. We are forgiven our skins, you see, so long as no one – officially – notices.'

Mary hung her head. 'You want me to stop coming.'

'It's not anything I want, Miss North. We're all partial to you. But you mustn't think the children won't get their schooling. I may not have your facility, but I can give them the language. And the manager – he isn't going to be teaching them any mathematical theorems – but he has been known to balance the books.'

'What if I started coming less often?'

He pursed his lips and looked down on the stage. 'Fine. What if you started today?'

And so here she was, leaving before she'd even had time to take off her raincoat. She wondered if perhaps the months of morphia had weakened her tendency to resist. Or else it was the solitude, in which the self hardened but also grew brittle.

It was always a lurch, coming out of the Lyceum into the crowd of white faces in the Strand. There was a period of acclimatisation, until one stopped finding white skin strange. Until then it seemed unnatural and rather horrid, as if something medical or blanchingly industrial had happened to everyone. There was a moment before one understood that one belonged with them – a moment outside time, as if one had stood up too suddenly.

# JANUARY, 1942

The four local men who brought Captain Braxton's body back up the cliff to Fort St Elmo had done the best they could to make it decent, straightening the limbs and wrapping a shirt around the ruined head. Simonson thanked them with a promissory note for kerosene, then had the surgeon decant the dead man into a coffin and nail it shut. The nails had to be extracted from the door posts of the fort, and straightened on an anvil.

Simonson stubbed out something they were still calling a cigarette. He pawed at his tongue for the bitter tobacco fragments that had stuck there. His head pounded.

The battery under his command stood at seventy-seven men, with Braxton freshly subtracted. There were rations enough for thirty. It was a feature of the tactical situation that the more men he lost, the more the rest could eat. When a raid came, one didn't know whether to send the men down to the shelters in their tin hats or up to the ramparts in their PT shorts. Occasionally an officer dealt with this and all other uncertainties forever, by taking a stroll at dawn and not stopping when he came to the sea cliffs.

Simonson supposed one should feel pity at a suicide, but he rather hated the dead man for it. Absent Alistair's good humour, the island had become lethal to his spirit. It was as if an invisible bile seeped from the bomb craters. He loathed every yellow rock. Since there was nothing to eat, he smoked in an uninterrupted chain, until smoke seeped into the gaps between every cell of his body. Until it was only force of habit that caused the smoke, and not his person, to disperse.

All morning his subordinates plagued him. Captains Appleby and Fisk had fallen out over which of their guns ought to receive a new barrel that had been fought through. Simonson flipped a threepenny bit along the corridor and had them chase after it to decide. Lieutenant Spencer reported, assuming he would be Captain now that Braxton had left the situation vacant. Five minutes later, Lieutenant Cooper dropped by to confirm – just as a nudge, between Old Harrovians – that he, and not the overweening Spencer, was in line for the same promotion.

All afternoon it went on, while the enemy attacked. Down poured the rain of blood and sulphur, and up slunk these privateers from the underground parts of the fort. Here was Major Huntley-Chamberlain, hoping that it would be his favourite, Ives, who took the vacant captaincy. Here was Major Hall, lobbying for Williams.

At dusk, at last, Lieutenant Colonel Hamilton summoned him to his office. For the first time in weeks, Simonson felt something akin to gratitude. Having noticed how overstretched he was, Hamilton must finally be disposed to take some of the heat off. Simonson put on his cleanest shirt, blew the dust off his cap and hurried down to the ops room.

Hamilton glanced up from his papers when Simonson knocked.

'Too bad about Braxton.'

'Dreadful, sir.'

'Married?'

'No. Just parents.'

'Well, that's something. "Killed in action", I suppose?'

'I'll get the letter off tonight.'

'Fine. Do sit.'

Simonson did. He crossed his legs and put his cap on his knee. He supposed he was to be loaned to HQ for a spell. It didn't do to think of it as a holiday – one ought to relish the added responsibility – but just now he felt only relief at the prospect of release from daily command.

Hamilton returned to his papers. He paged through the quartermaster's weekly provisions report, and it seemed he intended to read the thing in its entirety. Simonson felt a snap of unease. The longer one was made to wait, the harder it was to like what one waited for. He kept his eyes on the wall map of the island, as if the siege might be lifted by further study.

Hamilton finished the report, took a red pencil and made careful annotations in the margins of several pages. This gross of biscuits to be issued; that ounce of aspirin to be allocated to sick bay. Finally he took off his reading glasses, lit a cigarette, and slid a typed sheet across the desk.

'Have you any explanation for this?'

He rocked back in his chair and watched Simonson read the document. It was a signed statement from a junior officer at Luqa, admitting to having moved Heath up the evacuation order under instructions from Royal Artillery.

Simonson looked up. 'The poor man has completely misunderstood, of course. I brought no special pressure to bear, and I certainly issued no order.'

'He must be exaggeratedly stupid, then.'

Simonson gave a thin smile.

'Amused, Simonson?'

'I hoped you'd called me in for good news.'

Hamilton stood and went to the narrow, barred window. With his back to Simonson he looked out over the darkening courtyard where four hundred men, following orders, were lying on the ground to save strength.

'I know you were friendly with Heath. You sunbathed. You sailed.'

'I try to be agreeable with all my fellow officers.'

'Don't soft-soap it. You two were thick as thieves.'

'Not really, sir. Heath meant no more to me than the others.'

Saying it made him feel as close to ashamed as starvation permitted. How good it had been, back then, to chat with Alistair of this and that while the sun tanned them and the local beer softened their responsibilities. They had lain sprawled together like puppies, laughing till their sides ached. They had shared a grace that even the enemy sensed. Fighter pilots had stayed their hands on the firing switch. Mines had missed them by inches, by the gap between auguring stars.

'The word is important,' said Hamilton. 'Are you quite sure the two of you weren't friends?'

'If you must know, I thought Heath rather inferior. If I made an effort with him from time to time, it was because I felt sorry for him.'

'To be clear, you thought him socially inferior?'

'It's hardly a man's fault, but yes. I'm afraid it comes down to that. Anyway, he wouldn't be the first who'd queered things to get off the island.'

'No, but he'd be the first from an honourable regiment. I hope you still appreciate the distinction.'

'I do, sir.'

'So you say Heath pulled strings, and you had nothing to do with it?'

'Goddamn it, yes.'

'And if I were to ask Heath the same question, no doubt he would say that it was you who pulled the strings, and that he had no hand in the affair?'

'If he has any sense at all, I hope that's exactly what he'll say.'

They watched each other while the old war turned through another minute of arc.

'I see,' said Hamilton at last.

'I'm very sorry.'

'Do you know what my days consist of now? HQ gives me orders that are almost supernatural. This calorific requirement to be transcended, these mortal wounds to be healed, those laws of nature to be revoked. As if we weren't soldiers but saints.'

'I remember when we were human beings.'

'Yes. Well, I don't suppose you'd have let Heath take the swing on his own, back then.'

Simonson closed his eyes. A girlfriend had written the week before: Catherine, trusting he was having fun. He remembered her at Oxford. Her hair, smelling of strawberries. Their punt, adrift among the meadows of the Cherwell. His cheerful incompetence with the pole. The summer sun fixing the memory, immortalising her laughter even as it pealed.

Outside, another raid was starting up. The courtyard emptied as everyone hurried to the guns.

Simonson stood. 'I should go to my men . . .'

'Stay where you are. What good to them is a man like you?'

Simonson sat back down. The bombs came, shaking the earth, deepening his headache until he felt his skull must crack. Officers, bloody and dishevelled, began to bring their reports – communications with HQ were cut; number nine gun was a total loss; Grandfield and Barlow were killed.

Hamilton sat behind his desk and took the reports one by one.

'Do you see it yet?' he said in a lull. 'Do you see it from my point of view? Because I have all night, you know. We can do this as long as you like.'

More reports came.

'Oh, look,' said Hamilton, sliding a damage chit across the desk. 'That aimer on Nine Gun – you know, the Geordie – he's

401

had the front of his foot blown off. Shall we give him an evacuation number, do you think, or should we pull some strings?'

Simonson held his aching head while bombs blew it apart.

'Interesting,' said Hamilton, replacing the handset of the field telephone. 'There's a second casualty from that hit on Nine Gun. He—'

'All right,' said Simonson, 'you've made your point.'

The war would grind them down until all that remained was this bitter and sullen fury, pounding in the centre of his skull. The war would find the true hearts of them all as it found his own heart now: incensed, incandescent, unconsoled.

The raid died away, the guns fell silent. In the hiatus before the all-clear there was the stuttering sound of the damaged tail-enders fleeing.

'I hope you also see it from my point of view,' said Simonson. 'For someone he cares about, a man must do what he can.'

'Regardless of the social order?'

'Regardless of the evacuation order.'

'I see. So, you cut a few corners for Heath. I won't say it's unnatural, only unbecoming. Of an officer, you understand.'

'I admit nothing,' said Simonson.

'Then we must do it by the book. One of you pulled strings, and if it wasn't you then logically it must have been him. So I will wire the CO at Gibraltar, and have him put that to Heath. And as you say, if Heath has an ounce of sense he will deny any knowledge and you'll both be off the hook. I expect that's what he'll say, don't you?'

Simonson turned his cap over and over.

Hamilton said, 'It's just that you would need to be certain – wouldn't you? – that Heath shared your cynical disposition. Otherwise there's no guarantee he won't simply do the honourable thing and own up, and serve out the whole of his twelve months in the loneliest gaol in the Empire. Might not even survive it, in his condition.'

'Please. I do understand.'

'Then I shall give you till dawn to think it over. Let me have your answer then. Dismiss.'

Simonson turned in the doorway. 'Sir, why must you do this?'

'I wouldn't, if we had any bread. All I've left to give the men is fairness.'

Back in his room Simonson sat on his cot. A damaged moon was easing itself up from the sea, and he wished it wouldn't. One would be released from all cares, at last, if the moon and sun didn't always pop up like hospital visitors. He wished the Germans would make an effort and sink them both for good.

The orderly had brought a new stack of paperwork and squared it away on his desk. Alistair had gifted Simonson his jar of blackberry jam, and he laid it on the stack now as a paperweight. He rubbed the fatigue from his eyes and sat to write the next day's manning order. Number One Gun would have a full crew, Number Two would be half manned, Number Three would be . . . oh, but it hardly mattered. The magazines were empty.

His eyes strayed to the jam, where the moonlight crept through the jar. The deep ruby colour connected directly with his hunger. He could hardly force himself to stop looking. Saliva flooded his mouth. He spat, and lit another bitter cigarette.

If Alistair was too stupid to deny everything, then surely that was Alistair's lookout. After the surprise and humiliation of his interview with Hamilton, Simonson shook. How could Alistair put him in this position? This was the disappointment with grammar school boys: they pounded on the door and then had no idea how to behave once admitted.

He found his eyes on the jar again. However irritating Alistair was, to eat the jam would be a betrayal – he was supposed to keep it, to share it with Alistair at war's end. But it wouldn't do any harm to take off the lid, surely, and smell it. It would not reduce by any fraction the quantity of jam that remained. And how many months had it been since he had smelled anything but smoke? Gunsmoke, smoke of cigarettes and pipes, smoke from conflagrations terrestrial and naval, smokescreens laid down for cover. He was curious to know if he could still smell anything else. He unscrewed the jar and breathed in. He tried again. Nothing.

The two possibilities arising – that the jam was odourless, or that he had lost the facility for scents less brutal than smoke – seemed equally bleak. He replaced the lid and picked up his pen again, but he was too hungry for paperwork.

Perhaps Alistair would deny all knowledge, and they'd both be in the clear. Simonson considered it with a quick kick of hope, then came up short. Of course Alistair would do nothing of the sort.

He eyed the jam again. If he had lost his sense of smell, what else had he lost? It was known that battle stress numbed the senses one by one. What he feared most was that his will was gone. It was said that the self surrendered by small degrees before it finally collapsed. Panic tightened in his chest. What if he could not taste?

He unscrewed the lid again, scooped jam onto the blunt end of his pen, and tried it.

All over the desiccated island the bomb craters filled with rainwater. They overflowed, voiding their poison, until the water that pooled in them was sweet. Soon the first green algae began to bloom in their waters. Little creatures, outlandish and fitfully ambulant, multiplied on the bounty. Their tiny bodies quivered with unheard laughter. They lived and died and their resonant forms drifted down to the depths and as the sediment grew richer, plants took root in it, and reached up for the light, and were salves and banes and lilies. Their leaves unfurled and their stamens shook with laughter. Finches came and rested on the stems – the leaves trembled, the birds swayed like gymnasts, the laughter shook the air. More rains came, and seasons, and early evenings with light so delicate and shimmering that the laughter made ripples in the light, and turned the light to its own form, and the light made itself into the undulant bodies of lovers. Catherine looked up at him, while the river looped around meadows.

Simonson cradled his head. It was the most beautiful thing he had ever tasted. How tired he had been, how lost.

He screwed the lid back on the jam and replaced it on top of the stack of paperwork. One found new uses for the equipment one had. He would tell Hamilton the truth and finish the war as a sergeant, yelling at buttons and shoes.

At dawn he shaved, combed his hair and went down to the ops room.

'Sir,' he said to Hamilton. 'Heath knew nothing. He'd recently lost his arm, he'd lost Briggs who was his friend, and he was in no state to make judgements. I ordered Heath to take the paint-ing back to the church, and the loss of Briggs and the truck was my responsibility. I ordered Heath onto the evacuation flight. He had no agency in any of it, and nor did Med Command. I told them it was orders from top brass.'

Hamilton came out from behind his desk to shake Simonson's hand.

'You understand, Douglas, that I really shall have to write this report? That the entire thing falls on you?'

'I understand, Fraser. And I'm sorry to ask you to do it.'

'You shall have a rest now, at least.'

Simonson tried for a smile. 'Well, that's something.'

Hamilton sighed, sat back down and nodded at the wall map of Malta. 'Now we can speak freely, what would you do, if you were in charge of the show? With the strength we have, and the provisions remaining, and the enemy able to parachute in to any location?'

Simonson studied the map. 'I think I might ask the men, sir.'

Hamilton blinked. 'I certainly never had you as a democrat.'

'I mean I might ask for volunteers. There are some who will surrender in any case when the chance comes, and it seems useless to require them to fight if they can bear a life in captivity. And there are others who will prefer to resist, even though the outcome is clear. I think we have all been here long enough to know our minds by now.'

'So you would split our force?'

'Into two camps, yes. One to yield, another to hold.'

'And in which of the two camps are you?'

Simonson smiled. 'Who knows which takes more courage – to die in battle, or to live in vain? It cuts all of us in two, I suppose.'

Hamilton frowned at the map. 'And yet, you see, we are only issued with one island.'

# MARCH, 1942

In the first big southwesterly of the year the Americans arrived in London. They came with the storm at their backs, up from Southampton in trucks. They ran a muscular breed of convoy, widening the roads where they had to, shrugging off the bombed-out houses with big-chested bulldozers they had shipped with them from Maine. When they reached the capital, though the officers were too good to mention it, they were amazed at how tiny it was. The landmarks were bigger in their photographs. The British themselves were quite small.

'Say that again in your accent,' said a lieutenant who had asked Mary for directions. She did, and it made both of them laugh. To discover that one had an accent was quite unexpected and wonderful.

Mary had seen the column rolling along the Strand, on her way to the Lyceum. The children had already been out watching it, and it was hopeless to imagine that she could teach them on a day like this. She had joined them instead as they stood in a neat line on the pavement, oldest to youngest, waving American flags they had made.

'What's with all the negroes, ma'am?' said the lieutenant.

'Oh,' said Mary, 'you'll find that almost everyone in Britain is coloured. Didn't they tell you in your briefing?'

The lieutenant looked at her in perfect bafflement. 'No ma'am.'

'Well, I'm surprised. As far as the Scotch border we are as dark as pitch. It's only north of there that the race is diluted.'

'And you, ma'am?'

'I'm an albino. Oh, don't look so worried. It's fine, really it is, once one gets used to the persecution.'

She had the class salute him as he climbed back into the cab of his truck, laughing and shaking his head.

Mary turned to Zachary. 'Did you think they'd be like this?'

'I thought they'd be like my father.'

His tender expression, his nonchalance briefly overwhelmed. Mary tried not to smile. Men were empty hats after all, from which rabbits popped only by a learned effort of conjuring.

'Did you think they'd come in white gloves, playing the baby grand?'

'I thought there'd be some black people.'

'Hitler will only fight them in separate units. He's a snob.'

'Look at all this. Look how many soldiers there are.'

'And all come to save us. I can tell you now how worried I was.'

'We'll win now, won't we?' said Zachary.

'All I know is that it's good not to stand alone any more. I don't suppose we could have held out much longer, on our own.'

'And what about you?'

'Oh, I'm hardly alone. I have my friends and my family.' She looked at him. 'And I have . . .'

He touched her arm. 'If you ever need me, I can come and help. Wherever I am, if you start at the theatre they can find me.'

She smiled, thinking how sweet it was at his age. 'Thank you,' she said, 'but I'll manage. I'm ever so . . .'

She tailed off, noticing how steadily he held her eye. The convoy rolled on. When the next gap in it came, the children would cross back to the theatre side of the street and she would stay on her own. She realised this was understood now. The convoy would continue and she would not. The true moments of one's life were sadder for the fact that they must always be synchronised with the ordinary: with rail timetables, with breaks in the traffic.

'Well,' she said. 'Thank you.'

It came after a few minutes: a let-up in the flow. One heard other people's conversations again, over the engine noise. One looked up and there was the opportunity. There was no time to fuss over it – the children crossed the street while they could. And now the soldiers came again, on and on in their two-ton trucks, blocking her view of her class. The Americans came in a ceaseless river to end the lease of evil on earth. What loads this would impose on the heart everyone was curious to discover, but it was said they carried fuel oil and provisions for two years. Their bulldozers bellowed, and red sparks roared from their stacks. The convoy came without end. The asphalt shrieked and the children cheered. London's long siege was broken.

The soldiers stood with their feet wide apart in the truck beds, saluting the children smartly. They raised eyebrows at the great mounds of rubble in the streets that the locals were too weary to arrange back into buildings. The Americans were tall men on full rations and it clearly made no sense to them that exhaustion should have the last word in the common language of English. *How come?* Mary heard them yelling to each other, over the noise of the engines. *How come they just left it broken like this?*

# APRIL, 1942

At the Public Record Office, on the fourth day of trying, Zachary had found his father's name. He hadn't asked for help and he hadn't wanted it.

Now the rain came in with the wind. There was an avenue of chestnut trees and he found the broadest for shelter. There was bright sun between the showers, and the light fell green through the leaves. Jackdaws pecked at the edges of the walkways. They hopped among the headstones, finding the worms the rain had brought up and helping them into the light.

Next to his father's name, which he had recognised from long familiarity, had been: EHZT NOLNOD CMETYRE. He had frowned at the words in the register: sometimes they could be made compliant. He had tried looking from the corner of his eye, then surprising them. EZTA NALDON MCFETRY.

The rain would soon blow through. On the graves the jackdaws fussed at the moss that grew through the gravel. Zachary lit a cigarette. He had waited for a rainy day, to be here alone.

EATS NNLDNN CEMTHGY. He had drawn his thumbs together, isolating each letter as Mary had shown him. He had made a one-letter prison between his thumbs and slid it across the first word: E . . . A . . . S . . . T. He had repeated the word to himself, then interrogated the whole sentence. EAST LONDON CEMETERY. Beside the location had been written a plot number for a mass grave.

The rain stopped. Water dripped from the chestnut leaves, the city inverted in each drop. Zachary came from under the tree and walked among the numbered plots at the margins of the graveyard. There was so much freshly dug earth. Weeds would take before grass.

His father's plot was marked with a two-inch metal plaque on a wooden stave. The plot was twenty feet by ten, its boundary made with stakes and green twine. One didn't know how many were buried there. Zachary stood for a while. Dandelions covered the plot. There was a smell of wet earth.

'I'm sorry it took me so long,' he said.

In the footlights his father had addressed the audience at the close of every show: *For those who couldn't be with us tonight.*

Zachary flicked away his cigarette. He could start now. He would try south, across the Thames. There was a rumour that his kind was trying there. Flat rubble waited for them on the far bank of the river. Rubble to build on caught no one's attention but theirs. It did not catch the light, having no promise but what they brought with them.

He tried not to be afraid. London was a lightening of the sky. It was the bloody last hour of a milk tooth. It was a city dying to begin.

# MAY, 1942

Hilda poured tea, propped an elbow on her kitchen table, and read Simonson's note again.

*It was brave of you to include your photograph in the last letter. What a terrible mess – you must be devastated. That pompadour will have to go. As for the scars, I do not see what you are fretting about – one hardly notices them. In any case, it is only your face – this is why we were all issued with two.*

She held the aerogramme to her cheek. It smelled of smoke and mail sacks. Through the open window, pigeons were cooing in that emollient, slightly medical way they had, as if it were a purgative for heartaches metropolitan.

Having no photograph to hand, Simonson had drawn her a self-portrait in blue ink. He had made himself scrawny and bearded, more castaway than soldier. In his cartoon he wore sergeant's stripes and bawled at men on parade. Hilda thought it adorable that he was so touchy about his demotion. She resolved to sew him various insignia, denoting ranks of her invention, which she would include in subsequent letters.

*You write that it was clever of Alistair to induce the two of us to correspond, but I do not think him bright. It will*

*have been no more than simple visual association on his*
*part, since you are rather pretty and I am strikingly hand-*
*some. I should also like to correct any lies with which he*
*might have supplied you. He may claim that I correspond*
*with several girls, while in fact I only have ink for you.*

Hilda smiled. Well, and so what if the man wrote around? She thought his letters reckless and sweet, as unworn as London in May.

Through the window the traffic rumbled. On the street, beneath the barrage balloons, couples finished each other's thoughts again. Strapped shoes had been brought out for the season, hems raised by an inch and a half. The capital had remembered itself. Hilda closed her eyes and breathed in the smell of the letter. How good it would be to fall in love – how perfectly, anciently new.

# JUNE, 1942

'Yes but I'm like a piano,' said Hilda. 'I need men to move me.'

'And Simonson?' said Mary.

'I like the convenience of mail-order.'

They were at the Ritz, at a table where they could be seen from the door. Mary spread her hands on the pristine tablecloth. 'But there's always some problem with the delivery, isn't there? Oh, why do I feel so anxious?'

'Insufficient drink,' said Hilda, snapping her fingers the instant her diagnosis was made. Two more gin fizzes appeared.

'Thank you for coming out,' said Mary. 'I know it's silly, but I couldn't wait for him on my own.'

She brushed away ash where it had missed the ashtray, and moved the flowers in their vase to catch the light from the chandelier at the centre of the room.

'Did he say when he would come?' said Hilda.

'Straight from Waterloo, off the nine o'clock.'

'Any minute, then. Do stop fussing, or I shall have the waiter etherise you.'

'I just want everything to be perfect when he gets here. After all this, I couldn't bear for him to be put off by a little thing.'

'He didn't mind when I told him you were a wreck. I shouldn't think he'll mind ash on the tablecloth.'

'You're quite right,' said Mary, thinking that Hilda was quite wrong. The heart was a bicameral thing, both stoical and skittish. Who was to say that it mightn't endure the years of separation and the abrupt reversals of fate, only to be repulsed by a misaligned vase, by a lipsticked tooth, by a hundredth of an ounce of ash?

'I've been meaning to ask,' said Hilda. 'Where did you get that hat?'

'White's, in Burlington Arcade. Do you like it?'

'I actually think I must eat it.'

'Thank you,' said Mary. 'The feathers are real phoenix, you know.'

'And your dress is just right. Any more décolletage and you'd look rather as if you might; any less and you'd look as if you might rather not.'

When Hilda was on form she was hard to resist – and in any case it was fun to be back at the Ritz, which seemed to have excused Mary sooner than her family had. Here they honoured one's name in that generous way the Ritz knew, which was to remember it only when one was sober. Seated at the grand, the pianist played some Schumann.

Mary began to believe that everything really might be all right. Since Alistair's exoneration they had exchanged letters almost weekly while he waited for a convoy home. Her letters were full of apology, his of understanding. She had confessed to passing up the chance to have her father write a letter that might have reduced his sentence. *But if you hadn't your ideals*, he'd written, *you'd be no different from the others, sipping champagne at Blacks'*. For his part Alistair found it hard to believe that she did not despise him for jumping the evacuation queue. But perhaps this was love, at the second time of asking: the understanding that each would not mind what had been necessary locally.

415

In the light of the chandelier, men in lounge suits converged on their table in oblique trajectories described by the pull of desire and the push of manners. They noticed Hilda's face when they were already too close, and swerved. Some had prepared opening gambits that they swallowed. Others made attempts of varying skill to demonstrate that they had only been on their way to the lavatory.

Hilda looked into a third gin. 'This will be my whole life, you know.'

'You mustn't think that.'

'It's hard to stay gay, though. Do they imagine I'm cut all the way through?'

Mary was drunk enough to touch Hilda's scars. 'What's this on them? Healing cream?'

'It's foundation, damn you.'

Mary drew her hand back. 'I'm sorry.'

'Not that it does any good. I could wear a carnival mask and the scars would still show through.'

'And so? Damn these spivs and idlers. A million better men will come home from the war, and they shan't want a girl who sat it out. When Simonson looks at your scars, he'll see someone.'

'I'm afraid he won't want to look. That he shan't want to be reminded.'

Mary leaned back, exhaled, and watched her smoke rise. 'What sort of a man do you want anyway?'

'Tall. Funny. Never came top of his class or pulled the wings off bees.'

'Yes, but I mean really? When all of this is over, and assuming we win—'

'Oh, I think we'll win, don't you? Now that the Americans are all-in?'

'Yes, but there'll be such a mess to sort out. Not just all the rebuilding. We'll have to put society back together, in some better configuration.'

Hilda snorted.

'What?' said Mary.

'Well, we want such different things from men. You earnestly want someone who will help you reform society.'

Mary smiled. 'Whereas you . . .?'

'. . . just want a tall man and a stiff drink. You could even swap the adjectives.'

Mary looked out over the tables, each white linen world orbiting the great central chandelier of the lounge, each world encircled in turn by its moons of women and men, laughing and drinking, occulting and eclipsing. How rudderless one was, in truth. How governed by unmastered forces.

Hilda touched her hand. 'I haven't upset you, have I?'

'Not at all,' said Mary.

But now her own heart faltered. For these long months she had held on to the idea of love so fiercely that she had not considered a daunting possibility: that she didn't love Alistair after all – that his great merit was in having known her only before she fell apart, while her great cowardice was not to have admitted to him that she was diminished. She wasn't the girl who had once walked in bombs as if they were drizzle. She had lost her exemption from the ordinary, and as soon as he realised it he wouldn't love her either.

She twisted her hands in her lap. How well did they know each other, after all? She and Alistair had never had the civilian progression into love by small and reversible steps, by increments of dancing and dinner in which joy was imperceptibly solemnised. All they had had was an air raid, and a moment at Waterloo Station, and two pounds by weight of aerogrammes that might one day be discovered, in a suitcase, in some attic being converted to a flat, and flung into a waste cart with old books and cups.

'But you look so glum,' said Hilda.

'Don't be silly.'

'You're getting cold feet, aren't you?'

'It's just . . . I mean what if – oh Hilda, I can barely remember his face.'

'You're panicking, you silly fruit.'

'Do you think?'

'He's a little late, that's all it is, and you have altar nerves. I'll bet Alistair's just the same – he'll be in a pub round the corner, getting up some Dutch courage. Breathe – that's it! Take a really good deep breath.'

Mary felt a little better. Drinks came, magnifying the effect.

'Now listen,' said Hilda, licking gin from the end of her cocktail straw and jabbing it in Mary's direction. 'What you need is to take out his photo.'

Mary laughed. 'I shan't sit here mooning over him.'

'You know the trouble?' said Hilda, rummaging in Mary's bag for her. 'Your mother bred all the sense out of you. Now look,' she said, slapping the brownish vignette of Alistair down among the ash and the coasters. 'Look at that and tell me you're not in love.'

How many times Mary had stared at Alistair's photograph. Once it had provoked a simple gladness.

'Oh, I don't know,' said Mary. 'What would you have me say?'

'That he is beautiful. That you love him. Only that.'

'But it's been so long, and I'm such a mess. I hardly remember—'

'Then think: what was the spark? The hour you looked into those eyes and thought: *I want no one else*? God knows, I can remember.'

Mary stared at Alistair's portrait. It didn't seem kind to tell Hilda that it hadn't been his eyes at all, but his back. She'd known with certainty that she needed him only when he had turned away from her on the platform at Waterloo. How her heart had dropped – as if there were no end to falling. When the hour had come for the war to take him away, that had been the first and last moment she had known without doubt that she loved him.

One knew how one felt only when things ended. And yet here was the world of white tables, insisting on beginnings. And here was Alistair now, with a footman throwing open the door of the lounge. Here was Alistair, tall and gaunt, the chandelier showering him with light. Here he was in his uniform, smiling and unsteady, his right sleeve empty and pinned. Here was Alistair, meeting her eye.

Mary stood, knocking over her drink. Gin sluiced over the tablecloth and deepened the red plush of the carpet.

'Alistair,' she said, so overcome that she forgot to embrace him and instead offered her hand to shake. It was ridiculous – and even worse since she offered her right, which he had to take with his left.

'Hello, Mary.'

They disengaged. He raised and then dropped his good arm, helplessly. 'Sorry I'm late. There were Germans.'

Mary managed a laugh; Alistair too.

'Hello, Alistair,' said Hilda. 'Gin all right with you?'

'Gin? Fine. Hello, Hilda, how are you?'

'Back in a jiffy,' said Hilda, giving them the table.

'Her poor face . . .' said Alistair as Hilda curved to the lavatory.

'Shrapnel,' said Mary.

Gin came, and Alistair took a sip. He grimaced and widened his eyes.

'Nice?' said Mary.

'I'd almost forgotten what we were fighting for. And you only look more beautiful.'

'You're very kind. But it's the war, I'm afraid. I'm so much older.'

Alistair gave her a look so tender that she thought she might dissolve. The two of them might be all right, she realised. She must make more effort to take it slowly this time, that was all. Life took longer to reassemble than it did to blow apart, but that didn't mean it wouldn't be lovely, providing that one remembered to go for country walks, and to tune the wireless to music.

'You haven't missed the weather,' she said. 'It's mostly rained since you left.'

Alistair took in the Ritz's lounge – the laughter, the crystals of light that flattered the crowd. He said, 'I thought I wouldn't make it back to all this. I was sinking by the time the Navy pulled us out. I was going down and there was this great roaring noise, which was the sound of the rescue launch's engines, but I thought it was the end. They had to pump my chest.'

The words struggled to connect, and Mary found herself already saying, 'And of course it snowed a lot in January.'

Hilda appeared back at the table, all purpose and powder. 'Well,' she said, 'I shall leave you lovebirds to it.'

Mary took her arm. 'You mustn't go.'

Mistaking her terror, Hilda kissed her on both cheeks. 'Don't be silly, I'll be fine. I shall call at the garret tomorrow to catch up on all the news.' She gave Mary a look of tipsy significance. 'But I shan't arrive before noon.'

'Oh Hilda, you really don't need to—'

'Nonsense. Now be good, you two, and if you can't be good, be a warning to others.'

She was gone with a wave of the fingers, weaving between the tables. A waiter dimmed the chandelier. The pianist took a break.

'In Malta it was mostly sunny,' said Alistair. 'But there could be a terrible wind.'

'I was so desperate when I heard you were missing,' said Mary at the same time.

420

Their hands, a foot apart on the tablecloth, could not seem to make the junction.

The pianist sat back down and played 'La Campanella'. More drinks came. Alistair packed his pipe – not making too bad a fist of it with one hand, Mary thought. A waiter arrived to light it from a cut-glass lamp. The staff at the Ritz had the quality of apologising with a murmur for each of their perfect actions. They smelled of nothing and had faces that made no demands on the eye or on the heart. They melted into shade, not allowing themselves to be silhouetted against the chandelier. They eluded cognition entirely, like sorcerers, or fathers. At the tables all around them the guests chattered away as if life were not on the meter, while the waiters took away ash.

'I think I should warn you—' said Mary.

'I ought to let you know—' said Alistair.

'You go,' said Mary.

'Please, you first.'

Someone dimmed the chandelier further, until it seemed to cast a light that was darker than its absence. The high notes scattered from the piano. They glittered in that thin register where one heard the strings and hammers.

'What were you going to say?' said Alistair.

'Oh, it was nothing. You?'

'Only that . . . oh, it can wait.'

Drinks came. The pianist played some nocturnes of Chopin. Black-coated waiters appeared out of the black background to light Mary's cigarettes. One had only to think of fire and fire came, as if the incendiary thought scorched the air. One had only to need a drink, and the pull of the need itself caused the drink to arrive on a heavy tray in a glass that had been handled with white cotton. It might carry on all night, Mary supposed: this matching of an equal and opposite solution to every resolvable human need – done with this exquisite precision that extended to the fullest extremity of the possible and therefore only made one ache all the more despairingly with doubts that could never be soothed by lackeys. It was the perfect antithesis of the war, this torment of solicitude. How strange, that the struggle and its absence should leave one equally afraid.

'Mary, are you quite all right?' Alistair had his hand on her arm.

'Thank you, darling, I am fine.'

And she would be fine, of course: she would make conversation when the air seemed the right shape for it, and she would laugh when laughter seemed a better fit. It was nice that the drinks kept coming, since the glow they gave was terrific.

He took his hand away. 'What would you like us to do now?'

'Well, they do a nice dinner here – although it's getting rather late – or we could go to one of the cafés on Haymarket, or if you're not hungry we might even still make the cinema.'

'Yes,' he said. 'But I suppose what I meant was, what would you like now, for us?'

Mary gripped the table. The room revolved around the chandelier. Their white planet spun through the plush black smoky space.

'I'm sorry,' said Alistair. 'I'm ahead of myself. Ignore me – this is what I was like after France. That's what I was trying to warn you about, earlier on.'

'It's all right. I've so looked forward to seeing you again. I thought I would know just what to do when you came. I'm sorry.'

He nodded and looked away, to the other tables where guests glowed in firmer orbits.

'On Malta, with the blockade, one doesn't imagine that people live like this at home. It is hard to imagine how hungry everyone is on the island.'

'I can imagine it,' she said, feeling even as she said it what a foolish thing it was to blurt out.

He smiled kindly enough, but now she saw herself as he must. In the bright light of the chandelier, before he arrived, London's circle had seemed quite equal to the earth's equator. Now she saw the smallness of it. How vain she had been in her nest, feathering it with mirrors. She was a teacher nobody needed, a daughter whose parents despaired. And now here was Alistair, this man who had stood up to the enemy while she had been so proud of standing up to her mother. Did she really sit at this table, even now in her new feathered hat, wondering if she loved him?

'I'm sorry,' she said.

His face was pale with concern. 'Whatever for?'

'Forgive me,' she said, standing abruptly so that the chair fell to the carpet. 'Please, darling, forgive me . . .'

She fled into the blacked-out night, into the ruined city beyond the consolation of chandeliers.

For a moment Alistair thought to go after her, but he was afraid that he could not have understood the situation. There must be something monstrous about him that had made her run. He was even more ruined than he had thought.

He sat in his uniform at the empty table while a waiter righted the overturned chair without irritation or comment. The pianist played without interruption. Mary's place was cleared: the glass and its coaster removed on an electroplate tray, the tablecloth swept of ash until there was no sign she had ever been there. How abruptly people were taken. His body grieved, while his thoughts struggled to recall how he had got there. He had carried her body all the way back to barracks, and collapsed unconscious in the guard house. No, that wasn't it. He had not opened the jar she had given him, carrying it instead to war's end.

No, that wasn't it at all. He had loved her.

It had been the tiniest chance that he would still be sitting there, and when Mary saw him she cut corners between the other tables, not minding the diners' indignation. When she appeared by Alistair, out of breath, it seemed to startle him. He looked up from a drink that couldn't still have been his first.

'Mary?'

'This place,' she said. 'It isn't me. Think what you like of me, but I wanted to tell you that.'

He stood, needing the table for balance. 'What place is more you?'

'I don't have a place any more.'

'Is there somewhere you might feel better, at least?'

'I like the river,' she said. 'I went there, sometimes, when you were missing.'

'Should we go there now?'

'I don't know. It's late.'

He checked his watch. 'What time do they switch the Thames off?'

'Are you furious at me?'

'No. I thought you were disappointed.'

A waiter had been hovering, uncertain whether to bring cognac or coats.

'What would you like to do?' Mary asked Alistair.

'I'll walk, if you'd like to. We don't have to go anywhere in particular.'

'I'm slow on my leg, I should warn you.'

'I'll do the sprinting, then, if you'll do the handstands.'

Outside, an unused moon was rising. It shone along the axis of Piccadilly and sent their shadows west. As they walked down to the Embankment, Mary's mood – which had lifted for a moment – began to sink again. Alistair could take her arm only with his left, and since her left side was the one needing support, they tended to separate. The awkwardness leached into the silence between them. The Thames, when they reached it, was no help. With its silvered crests in the soft night air it should have seemed dear, but she saw the slick blackness of the troughs, and felt on her skin the sobering drop in temperature.

They walked south along the river. Parliament seemed indigo in the light. The plane trees of Millbank had limbs splintered here and there by the bombing. They spoke of these small things, grateful when they presented themselves.

When they reached the Tate they saw that the bombing had blown its roofs off. Alistair was shaken and wanted to look. Inside, the mosaic floors were wrecked and the rain had washed their tiles out. Ten thousand coloured marble chips, blued by the moonlight, lay in a mound at the foot of the stairs.

Alistair went ahead into the galleries and Mary hung back, poking at the mess with her toe. It seemed redundant to follow him, now that he had seen her as she was. She had only ever been an imprint in the London clay, of inherited money and looks. How pleased she had been with the impression she made, thinking it her own. But there were thousands of her stamp, and thousands more would come, each imagining they escaped the pattern. There would be countless small rebellions, numberless mothers defied. After the war these tiles would all be picked up and stuck back where they'd fallen.

She stood beneath the shattered central dome of the gallery. Above, between the bare iron hoops, a halo had formed round the moon. She lit a cigarette. The sound of the lighter rang in the empty space and sent pigeons clacking up through the dome.

What good was she to him? And yet days still came, and had to be faced. Perhaps she should go back home. As soon as an occasion presented, her mother would invite the Hunter-Halls. Mary would seat herself as instructed, which she supposed would decide everything else. Society was not complicated, after all. One had only to follow one's first name from table plan to wedding banns and all the way through to the headstone.

She stubbed out her cigarette and edged through the gloom in the direction Alistair had gone. In the galleries a damp line had risen from the floor, a pale fungus in numberless dots marking the creeping edge of it. On the ashen walls a thousand lighter rectangles showed where each painting had hung, and to where it would be restored. How foolish she was, still to hope that Alistair could love her. And yet she followed him, into the dark, even though she knew that each step took her no further from who she was. When the war was over the evacuees would return. The zoo animals would be put back on trucks and returned to their old labelled cages. The world could not wake from its pattern.

The tarnished brass title plaques were still screwed into the gallery walls. In the moonlight they glowed dully. Precisely here and here had been the Constables and the Turners. Here had been *Ophelia*, and here she would be again, chanting snatches of old tunes.

Footsteps came, and she turned.

'Why did you run out?' said Alistair.

'I couldn't bear myself. You, with everything you've been through. And then me, and my small miseries, and the Ritz.' She put her face in her hands. 'The Ritz.'

He looked around. 'This place doesn't feel like me either. I don't think I'm anxious to fix it.'

'Do you think, if you can stand it . . . we might try to find a place for us?'

His face hardened a little and he said nothing.

'Alistair?' she said, her heart racing.

'I don't know. Do you think you'd even be happy?'

'My mother thinks that isn't even a word, in wartime.'

'I don't mind what your mother thinks.'

'I would try to be happy. I can be fun, you know. I hope we can be that way again.'

'I might let you down,' he said. 'I don't sleep. My mind isn't right.'

'But we do let each other down – don't we? – and it isn't the end.'

'I don't know. You might have been right when you ran out.'

She dropped her hands to her sides. 'But you might have come after me! I only needed one kind word, you know. I don't know how to begin, now that we finally might.'

'I'm sorry. I wish I hadn't let you go.'

'And I wish I hadn't run. But this is us from the start, don't you think? We get so close each time. Darling, we get so close.'

'Were we wrong from the start?' said Alistair. 'To pretend we weren't in love?'

'I was wrong. I was a coward not to tell Tom. Do you despise me for it?'

He shook his head. 'I should have said I loved you. Would that have been the difference?'

'It's the difference now. Do you think you might tell me if you still do or if you don't? It's all right either way, you know. I'm sure now that it's braver to say it.'

He got his pipe lit and leaned back against the wall of the gallery. She leaned beside him, an arm's width away, and they looked at the pattern of the absent paintings.

'I don't know how to answer you,' he said. 'I don't have feelings as I used to. These pictures used to move me.'

'I used to move you.'

He took her hand. 'I went so far down before they pulled me out. I'm sorry.'

She looked at her hand in his. 'You still care, at least.'

'I care that your leg must be aching. I care that I must be making you sad. I care for a thousand things I would like to make better for you.'

'Then might you still try, Alistair? Could you love me again, with time?'

'I'm so afraid in case I won't.'

'And I'm so afraid in case I always will.'

She kissed him and they stood for a time without speaking. Mary felt the weight of their silence but there was no sadness in it because the silence had not yet found its moment to slip from the heart and lodge itself in the ordinary. Perhaps, if the two of them were careful, then it never would. Perhaps the real work of lovers was to hold themselves apart from theatres and train stations, from jam jars and picture frames, from all the bellicose everyday things that sought to beat one with time. Even to hope for love was a trap, Mary supposed, if when one said love one only meant armistice. Maybe it was foolish to imagine any more definite thing – since the heart, after all, did not declare victory. The heart declared only forgiveness, for which there was no grand precedent and no instrument of surrender.

Her leg was giving out, and she sank to the floor. Alistair joined her. In the empty gallery they sat a little distance apart – not so far that life could easily get between them, but not so close that it couldn't if it tried. They stared into the pattern of lighter grey shapes where paintings ought to be. Through the holes in the roof and the cracks in the walls the city grew lighter around them – their ancient city with its ordered tides reverting to the sea.

And now from the river in the east rose a vivid red sun, surprising Mary. She hadn't meant to sleep. The day had got in through the broken dome and flooded the gallery wall. It blinded her and she blinked until the world was restored. Beside her in the ruins Alistair lay with his eyes closed, without a mark on him. The quick bright shock of the light between the cloud and the eastern horizon: an unimaginable thing, thought Mary, a life. It was an unscrewing of tarnished brass plaques. It was one tile lost to the pattern. It was an air one might still breathe, if everyone forgiven was brave.

# AUTHOR'S NOTE

One day during the harrowing siege of Malta my maternal grandfather, Captain Hill of the Royal Artillery, was assigned to mind Randolph Churchill, the brilliant but dissipated son of the British Prime Minister. *'Look after him, David,'* said the Major General who conferred this extraordinary duty, *'and if at all possible keep him out of trouble.'*

The novel began with me wondering what that instruction meant, exactly. The Axis had maintained a two-year stranglehold on the island of Malta, reducing garrison and islanders alike to a state of advanced starvation. Into this theatre poor Randolph was parachuted, groggy and overweight. It was hot and he wanted to go swimming, so my grandfather took him to the beach the officers used, where a thin strip had been left between the mines and the barbed wire entanglements.

Randolph was known to be fantastically brave, prone to strolling through gunfire to deliver orders. On Malta he might cheerfully get himself killed or – much worse – captured. In the pivotal phase of World War II, the Prime Minister's son would have made a hostage of some significance. My grandfather had been issued with a Webley Mk IV revolver and a delightfully ambiguous order.

This novel, then, started out as a sort of stage play exploring the power dynamic between the two men. Yet in the end I was more interested in my grandfather. Something of Randolph found its way into the character of Simonson, but I leave the man himself – a great man in his way – to his excellent biographers.

Instead I went to Malta and spent some time trying to understand my grandfather's experience. Elderly islanders were kind and answered my questions patiently and in detail – I belong to the last generation of writers who can still talk to people who lived through the Second World War. I switched off my mobile phone, and slept only in places where my grandfather had been billeted.

Both my grandfathers served in artillery. Wherever they were stationed one still finds the great concrete emplacements on which the guns were levelled, and the walls and crenulations that defended them. And so it was possible, when my grandfather told me that he was stationed in a certain spot on Malta, to go and find that exact place.

I spent time in the military cemeteries, too. In a memoir my grandfather had recorded the names of some of the dead who were known to him. Here were those familiar names carved into stone: I traced them with my hands. The sadness of the war came over me in a way that I have heard other people speak of in relation to such places. Still, it was surprising and overwhelming.

I noticed that the cemeteries in Malta are different from Allied war graves elsewhere, in that four, five or even six men lie under each stone. I asked about it and was told with a grin to try digging a hole anywhere I liked on the island. I discovered that there is seldom more than six inches of topsoil above Malta's yellow rock. Men on starvation rations had simply done the best they could, breaking up the limestone with blunt picks. This was how I came to feel about writing the book. It would inevitably fall short of doing justice to its subject. But perhaps that is the work of a novelist after all – to dig one small hole that must host a great number of men.

My grandfather died while I was writing the novel – but, as he might have remarked, it wasn't necessarily my fault. I regret that he never saw the book. I had finished the third draft of what turned out to be five, but I had decided to wait until the novel was perfect before I gave it to him to read. What a fool I am. If you will forgive the one piece of advice a writer is qualified to give: never be afraid of showing someone you love a working draft of yourself.

David Hill really did sail a fourteen-foot dinghy between floating mines, for fun, in the sparkling seas off Malta. He really did verify St Paul's account of his shipwreck in Acts 27 by reference to the relevant Admiralty chart. He volunteered on the day war was declared, and for reasons that remain mysterious he really did once go absent without leave for five weeks – and upon his return (for reasons equally obscure) his colonel greeted him by glancing at his watch and asking "*Why are you late?*".

Apart from the above-related facts, the character of Alistair in the novel has little in common with my grandfather, and certainly the book's plot is an invention. The novel is inspired by my grandfather and it would not exist without him, but it is not at all based on his true story.

Mary North became the novel's central character for the same reason Randolph Churchill did not: I felt that I should draw on my family's history rather than presume to know the world's. Mary is inspired by my paternal grandmother, Margaret Slater, who drove ambulances in Birmingham during the Blitz, and by my maternal grandmother, Mary West, a teacher who ran her own school and kindergarten.

Neither of my grandmothers could ever be persuaded to talk about the war, or if they did then it was simply to fend off our questions with a smile and a wave of the hand. Talking with them as children we got the impression that the war had been brief, uncomfortable and not worth wasting breath on. One would not guess that Margaret, an artist, had driven an ambulance through bombs. Or that Mary's first fiancé had been killed at her side in a cinema in an air raid on East London, which nearly killed her too and of which she always bore the scars.

When the real-life Mary became engaged again, to my grandfather David in the blackout of 1941, her engagement ring had nine diamonds – one for every time they had met. Days later David boarded a troopship for Malta and they didn't meet again for over three years. Theirs was a generation whose choices were made quickly, through bravery and instinct, and whose hopes always hung by a thread. They had to have enormous faith in life and in one another. They wrote letters in ink, and these missives might take weeks or months to get through if they made it at all. Because a letter meant so much they poured themselves into each one – as if there might be no more paper, no more ink, no more animating hand.

We still have every letter that David sent to Mary. Of her replies to him we have none at all – the whole treasured bundle of them travelled from Malta on a different ship from David's, and halfway home they were sunk by a U-boat.

When I was beginning the project I might have said that by writing a small and personal story about the Second World War, I hoped to highlight the insincerity of the wars we fight now – to which the commitment of most of us is impersonal, and which finish not with victory or defeat but with a calendar draw-down date and a presumption that we shall never be reconciled with the enemy. I wanted the reader to come away wondering whether forgiveness is possible at a national level or whether it is only achievable between courageous individuals.

As I wrote, though, I realised I was digging an even smaller hole than that. Now I hope that readers will see the book simply as the honest expression of wonder of a little man descended from titans, gazing up at the heights from which he has fallen.

The first picture is of my grandfather David Hill (standing on the right) with the SAS in Algeria, 1944. The second, also from 1944, is of my grandparents David and Mary. The photo was taken by a Polish RAF officer who was sharing their honeymoon hotel.

# THANKS AND ACKNOWLEDGEMENTS

My friend Matt Rowley told me to drop the novel I was on and write this one instead. Thanks, Matt.

I had many enjoyable and fascinating discussions about the novel's structure with my friend and Australian publisher Matt Richell, of whom there is a great deal in this book – both in presence and sudden absence. Matt was killed in a surfing accident while I was writing. I miss him very much. He was funny, inspiring, unstinting and generous. As Hannah knows and I hope their children will understand, I am not the only writer he encouraged to go further than they thought they could. He was brave and his mark on life is beautiful and enduring.

Like a planet with twin suns I am daily saved from darkness by my agents Peter Straus and Jennifer Joel. Nor can I sufficiently thank Nikki Barrow, Amber Burlinson, Kristin Cochrane, Suzie Dooré, Jonathan Karp, Kiara Kent, Jessica Killingley, Zack Knoll, Drummond Moir, Marysue Rucci, Francine Toon and Carole Welch for their tireless engagement and countless contributions.

In particular I would like to thank Marysue Rucci for her honesty when I wasn't getting it right, and for her insistence that I could. And I'm grateful to Damian Barr for being an early enthusiast and for letting me read from the work-in-progress at his famous Literary Salon.

Thank you to Sarah Ager at the BBC for finding me hours and

hours of the BBC's *Kentucky Minstrels* radio show, deep in the forgotten archives. I would also like to acknowledge my debt to Michael Pickering of Loughborough University, whose *Blackface Minstrelsy in Britain* (Ashgate, 2008) was the gateway to all of my subsequent research into what was perhaps the most popular – and now is certainly the most conveniently forgotten – genre of light entertainment in the UK until as late as the 1970s.

Similarly *The Evacuees*, edited by B.S. Johnson (Gollancz, 1968), was my starting point for understanding the realities behind the received history of the evacuation. I also leaned heavily on *Evacuation Survey*, edited by R. Padley (Routledge & Sons, 1940), and *Out of Harm's Way* by Jessica Mann (Headline, 2005).

The novel's account of the crash landing of a Wellington bomber at Gibraltar draws on George Beurling's account in *Malta Spitfire* (Oxford University Press, 1943) of surviving a Liberator crash.

Thank you to the Commonwealth War Graves Commission for their help in locating graves on Malta, and also for maintaining the military cemeteries with a respect that goes further than duty demands.

A very heartfelt thank you to every reader who sent me kind words, or who wrote generously about my novels, while I was working. I was running on fumes for a while, so if you are someone who gave me a top-up then a line of the novel is yours. Please choose your favourite.

I would like to thank Clémence and our children for always helping me through. The same goes for my family and friends. Thank you.

Chris Cleave
London, September 2015

# READING GROUP QUESTIONS

**1.** Letters are very important in the novel. Do you still write them? If not, why not?

**2.** *'I was brought up to believe that everyone brave is forgiven, but in wartime courage is cheap and clemency out of season'.* Which character do you think shows most courage in the course of the novel?

**3.** *'Let us imagine, she thought, that this war will surprise us all.'* How did the novel's portrayal of war – both for soldiers and for those back home – differ from other fictional treatments of war, in both novels and films?

**4.** The author shows us a number of human relationships tested to extremes. Think about Mary and Hilda, then Tom and Alistair, and discuss the novel's portrayal of friendship.

**5.** We associate the allies' wartime efforts with heroism, but the novel reveals many prejudices and intolerances. Discuss society and behaviour.

**6.** *'How good it would be to fall in love – how perfectly, anciently new.'* Think about young love and romance during wartime – do you imagine it was easier to fall in love, or more difficult?

**7.** Discuss the role of humour in a novel about war.

**8.** If you have family members who remember the war or its aftermath, what do you think they would add to this story – and what would you ask them now?

**9.** What does it mean to be brave in our times?

# LETTERS IN WARTIME

*CHRIS CLEAVE, 2016*

I mentioned in the Author's Note that my family still has all the letters my grandfather, David, wrote to my grandmother, Mary, while he was besieged on Malta and she was teaching in and around London. Here they are:

For each letter sent or received, my grandmother recorded in an exercise book the date it had been posted and arrived (see next page). In a separate diary she summarised its contents and her feelings. Just to see the care with which Mary curated the cherished letters is to understand how different was that generation's relationship with pen and ink.

Communication today has no smell and no rustle, no caress but that of the keyboard. True, we don't have to wait for email to be delivered, but neither is it invariably worth waiting for. These days messaging is about constant, low-level reassurance – erring on the safe side, perhaps, since one wouldn't want one's deepest feelings to end up splurged all over the internet if the relationship ever went sour.

But in the long separation of World War II, letters arrived with low frequency and made up for it in intensity. One couldn't have the loved one but one could have the page their hands had held, bearing more between the lines than in them, and carrying perhaps a hint of their pipe smoke. Oh, and the letter was intimate, and private, and it arrived in an envelope just for you. And when you wrote a letter in those years, you wrote with no certainty that you'd be alive to write again tomorrow. Every word mattered, and so you exhausted your reservoir of emotion along with the ink.

*Everyone Brave is Forgiven* really began when I read the above letter, sent from David to Mary in 1941. He's just learned that his best friend, Geoffrey, has been killed in his Spitfire. 'My sweet and precious Darling,' he writes. 'I've just heard about Geoffrey and am rather stunned, especially as the news has come indirectly. Presumably the letter telling me about it is still in transit, so I don't know what happened and don't think I want to.'

(The really awful thing, which David doesn't know as he writes, is that Geoffrey wasn't killed in battle but instead when something went wrong while he was doing a low-level pass over his family home, for a rare chance to wave hello.)

'All I know,' writes David, 'is that I have lost something in my life which only you can hope to replace. Nobody ever had a friend like him – we did everything together and I believe at times even thought together. I was afraid that when I fell in love with you and we got engaged, he would feel slighted, but he didn't, and now there's only you. Once we are together again, we must never be parted like this.'

I was hooked and I read letter after letter – there are more than a thousand of them. Some are lighthearted and playful, like this next one where Mary draws a dress she's planning to make. (There are a very few letters from Mary, from the early part of the war before David was posted away.)

Often, for the sake of the censor or to spare Mary the worry, David's letters don't reveal the unpleasant details of his situation on Malta. Here is an upbeat telegram my grandfather sent after he had been extremely ill – he didn't let on how ill until after he came home.

I read through all their letters and discovered two young people falling more and more in love. It was beautiful and eerie. I have shown only a very little of their correspondence here, for the sake of their privacy, but I thought it important to show something in the hope that it might put you in mind to go and dig out your own family letters one day, if they're still around. If you do get the chance then you can hold them in your hands, as I did, and have the moment of realising: this is where I came from.

This is where we all came from, more or less. Because it was a world war, everyone you look at is the result of our recent ancestors somehow, against whatever odds, coming through WWII intact. If you are reading this then you are very likely the glad result of two lovers, issued with pen and ink, writing themselves an almost impossible love story through the chaos of a total war.

I wanted to make that love glow in the letters between my two separated fictional lovers, Mary and Alistair. I wanted those letters to be the bright centrepiece of the novel because it is so terribly brave, to dare to fall in love when the world is falling apart.

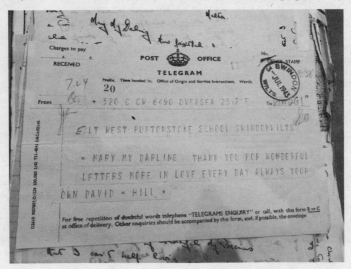

**Find out more about the story that inspired**

# EVERYONE BRAVE
## *is* FORGIVEN

Visit chriscleave.com

for photos, blog posts and news

Follow Chris on Twitter and Instagram:

**@ChrisCleave**

# Also by *CHRIS CLEAVE*

**Winner of
the Somerset
Maugham Award**

'**STUNNING**'

*New York Times*

**Shortlisted
for the Costa
Novel Award**

'**SUPERB...
shocking, exciting
and deeply
affecting**' *Independent*

**The
International
Bestseller**

'**INSPIRATIONAL**'

*The Times*

𝕊

# Join a literary community of like-minded readers who seek out the best in contemporary writing.

From the thousands of submissions Sceptre receives each year, our editors select the books we consider to be outstanding.

We look for distinctive voices, thought-provoking themes, original ideas, absorbing narratives and writing of prize-winning quality.

If you want to be the first to hear about our new discoveries, and would like the chance to receive advance reading copies of our books before they are published, visit **www.sceptre.co.uk**

SceptreBooks